Mister October

An Anthology in Memory of Rick Hautala
Volume 1

Edited By
Christopher Golden

JournalStone
San Francisco

JOURNALSTONE
YOUR LINK TO ARTISTIC TALENT

JournalStone books may be ordered through booksellers or by contacting:

JournalStone

www.journalstone.com
www.journal-store.com

The views expressed in this work are solely those of the authors and do not necessarily reflect the views of the publisher, and the publisher hereby disclaims any responsibility for them.

ISBN:	978-1-940161-05-1	(sc)
ISBN:	978-1-940161-06-8	(hc)
ISBN:	978-1-940161-19-8	(hc—limited edition)
ISBN:	978-1-940161-07-5	(ebook)

Library of Congress Control Number: 2013945701

Printed in the United States of America
JournalStone rev. date: November 8, 2013

Cover Design:	Denise Daniel
Cover Art:	Glenn Chadbourne
Interior Art:	Clive Barker, Glenn Chadbourne, Stephen R. Bissette, Morbideus W. Goodell
Edited by:	Christopher Golden

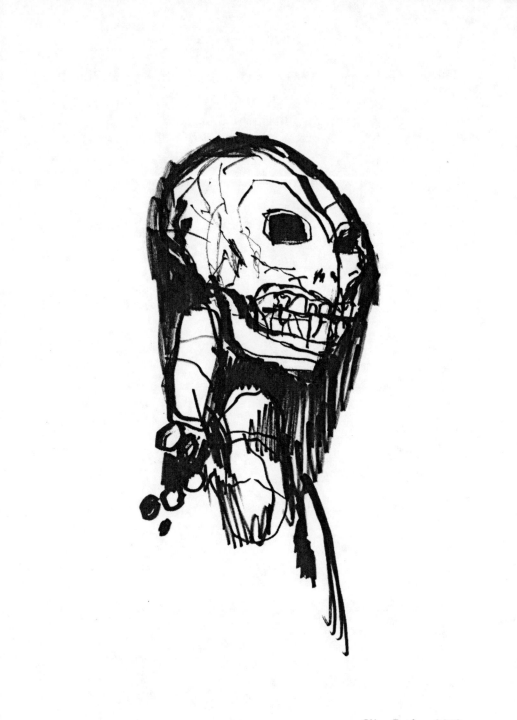

Clive Barker, 2013

Introducing Mister October

On March 21st, 2013, I received a phone call from Holly Newstein telling me that her husband, Rick Hautala, had suffered a massive heart attack. That piece of information shocked me into a surreal sort of panic, so much so that at first I could not make the leap to the next thing she said...that he had died. It seemed impossible. Rick had been such a good friend, such a consistent and stable force in my life, that the idea of him being so suddenly removed from this world...I just couldn't make sense of it.

This isn't the place for me to put my grief on display. Suffice it to say that Rick's passing hit me hard. Not a day goes by that I do not feel the pain of his absence.

Soon after his death, I remembered that he had told me—only weeks before—that his financial struggles had caused him to let his life insurance lapse. I thought it would be temporary, that in time he would get a new policy, but it was not to be. The timing of his death was the cruelest of ironies. Rick has left a fantastic legacy of wonderful novels and stories, but his wife and sons would have no financial help in dealing with the expenses related to his death and no insurance to help make the transition to life without him. Nothing could be done to alleviate their grief, but some financial assistance would help to ease the burden of that transition.

Within days of his passing, I shot off e-mails to dozens of writers and artists who I knew were either friends of Rick's or who had not known him but had admired his contributions to horror literature. I wanted to put together an anthology in Rick's memory, the proceeds of which would go entirely to benefit his widow and his sons. I also wanted to do it as quickly as possible, which meant it would have to be a reprint anthology—I didn't want to wait for people to find time in their schedules to write something brand new, and without pay.

In the midst of my mourning, I sent out dozens of emails. Dozens. And I never stopped to consider that nearly *everyone* would say yes. Thus, what had been intended as a single volume quickly became TWO volumes, featuring an astonishing array of talent. And when the stories came in, many of the reprints were true rarities, including Kevin J. Anderson's tale, which has only ever been published in ebook form. The real surprise, however, was that not all of the stories were reprints. I received unpublished stories from Mark Morris, Tom Piccirilli, JF Gonzalez, Stephen R. Bissette, and Matthew Costello. And Jeff Strand did something wonderful...he went off immediately and wrote "Hologram Skull Cover," an original story written specifically for this anthology, a story that revolves around a teenage boy discovering Rick Hautala's novels for the first time, and the evil that inhabits the boy's copy of *The Night Stone.*

And then, at the very end of my work on this book, I received the final story, also an original. Matti Hautala, Rick's youngest son, emailed to tell me that he'd written his first short story a while back and his dad had thought it wasn't half bad. Did I have any interest in looking at it for potential inclusion in the anthology? Of course I did. Matti's story, "Never Back Again," is a fine piece of work—a lot better than my first effort—and it gives me great satisfaction to be able to present it to you.

Rick would truly never have imagined that so many amazing people—wonderful writers and artists—would want to honor him like this. Those of us who loved him are not at all surprised.

Perhaps the most startling bit of kindness related to *Mister October*, however, came on the part of its publisher. Only weeks before his death, Rick announced that he'd made a deal with JournalStone to publish what would end up as his last two novels, *The Demon's Wife* and *Mockingbird Bay*. I'd been in touch with Christopher Payne from JournalStone about another project, and so when *Mister October* occurred to me, I emailed him to ask if he'd consider putting out the book...and donating all profits to Rick's heirs. Publishing, my friends, is a business. As kind as many people who work in the industry are, it is still a business. JournalStone seemed the right home for this project, but I didn't know Chris Payne other than through a handful of emails. When he agreed—

emphatically—to publish this project and take only the actual costs of the project, not a penny of profit for himself or his company, I knew Rick's final novels were in excellent hands.

I have no doubt that readers will treasure this two-volume set. It is my hope that as you read, you will ruminate a little bit about the man for whom we all have come together within these pages. And I hope you'll urge others to pick up their own copies of *Mister October* as well.

That's enough about the anthology.

I want to share a little bit with you about the man who inspired it.

In the aftermath of his death, I have written a great deal about him, but my thoughts on his passing and what it meant to him to be a writer are probably best expressed in the following piece, originally written for my (rarely updated) blog.

****

WRITERS AND PUNKS

I have written about Rick Hautala many times over the years—his bio when he was Guest of Honor at our beloved Necon; the introduction to the reissue of his wonderful first novel, *Moondeath*; and the announcement of his HWA Lifetime Achievement Award, among others—but I never thought that I would be writing this. I hope I might be forgiven, then, for plagiarizing myself in these dark days, when words don't come easily. The things I've written about him before are all still true—it's just that they mean more to me, now.

I've talked elsewhere about Rick as a friend and as a man—about his humor and his struggles and his love for his wife and sons. But in truth, if you'd asked him what he was, he wouldn't have said a friend or a man or a father or a husband…he'd have said he was a writer. He believed more firmly than anyone I'd ever met that writers were born, not made, that he had no choice in the matter. His career had some breathtaking highs, but even at the lowest points, when others might have urged him to cut his losses and find some other vocation, Rick felt helpless in the face of his nature. He didn't even truly understand the suggestion that there might be some alternative. He was a *writer*. How could he conceive of being anything else?

I loved him for that.

Rick liked unique and funny t-shirts and would always have a new one to show off at Necon every July. The best—the one that author Jack Ketchum and I recently agreed best represented the true Rick—was emblazoned with the following:

What are you, a writer *or a punk?*

That was Rick.

No one wrote horror with as heavy a heart, or with as deep a sense of foreboding and sorrow, as Rick Hautala. His characters are ordinary people, so full of worry about mundane, human things that when the extraordinary begins first to invade and then to tear apart their simple lives, we feel the tragedy on a visceral level that so many who came after Hautala never achieved.

Right from the beginning of his career, Rick achieved something that marked him out as a force to be reckoned with—he didn't write like anyone else. When you crack the pages of a Hautala novel (whether under his own name, or his AJ Matthews pseudonym), there's no mistaking that voice for anyone else. There's an anguish in his characters and a terrible claustrophobia to even the most open of settings that indelibly mark his novels.

With Rick Hautala and the modern ghost story, author and subject formed a perfect bond. The horror in Rick's work is the sorrow of isolation and the fear of the unknown future that lies ahead, often laced with echoes of past mistakes. He didn't go for the cheap scare, ever. Instead, he created a supernatural catalyst with which he deconstructed human frailties and the fragile ties that bind us.

These themes are found everywhere in Rick's work. Some of the best examples include the million-copy, international bestseller *Night Stone*, the milestone short story collection *Bed Bugs*, and the extraordinary novella *Miss Henry's Bottles*, which may be Rick's finest work. Fan favorites include the novels *Little Brothers* and *The Mountain King*. Hautala's in top form in *Winter Wake* and *Cold Whisper*, as well as the novels he wrote as AJ Matthews, in particular *Looking Glass* and *Follow*.

With *The Demon's Wife*—the last novel he completed—he had begun a new phase in his writing career, written something truly unique. We can only wonder where his ruminations would have taken him next.

The tragedy of Rick's life was that he never knew how many people loved him, how many held him in high regard—or if he knew, he never quite believed it. He never knew how good a writer he was. Oh, he wanted you to read his novels, and he wanted you to like them, but even the books of which he was most proud he dismissed with comments like, "I think that one worked out pretty well." That was the highest compliment he could give himself.

Rick Hautala was the horror writer's horror writer. He never looked down his nose at the genre but embraced it instead. Legendary for his kindness and his generous spirit, he influenced a great many young writers and exuded a sense of camaraderie that became infectious. In Rick's view, we were all in the trenches together. Self-effacing and approachable, he combined a blue collar work ethic with literary sensibilities shaped by his love of Shakespeare and Hawthorne. His passion for the horror genre was second only to his love for writing, and all of those elements conspired over decades to transform him into a determined mentor, offering critical feedback and quiet encouragement to many new authors as they began their own careers. Despite the mark he has made on the genre and his quiet mentorship of other writers, Rick was rarely recognized for his work until 2012, when he received the HWA's Lifetime Achievement Award. That honor meant the world to him.

I worry that Rick Hautala and other masters are in danger of having their legacy forgotten. That can't be allowed to happen. Go and pick up a copy of *Winter Wake* or *Little Brothers* or one of Rick's fantastic short story collections. Connecting with readers, making them feel…that was the only reward that ever really mattered to him. So go and read some Hautala, and spread the word.

Don't forget.

—Christopher Golden
Bradford, Massachusetts

Table of Contents

Glenn Chadbourne

FEEDERS AND EATERS

By Neil Gaiman

This is a true story, pretty much. As far as that goes, and whatever good it does anybody.

It was late one night, and I was cold, in a city where I had no right to be. Not at that time of night, anyway. I won't tell you which city. I'd missed my last train, and I wasn't sleepy, so I prowled the streets around the station until I found an all-night café. Somewhere warm to sit.

You know the kind of place; you've been there: café's name on a Pepsi sign above a dirty plate-glass window, dried egg residue between the tines of all their forks. I wasn't hungry, but I bought a slice of toast and a mug of greasy tea, so they'd leave me alone.

There were a couple of other people in there, sitting alone at their tables, derelicts and insomniacs huddled over their empty plates. Dirty coats and donkey jackets, buttoned up to the neck.

I was walking back from the counter with my tray when somebody said, "Hey." It was a man's voice. "You," the voice said, and I knew he was talking to me, not to the room. "I know you. Come here. Sit over here."

I ignored it. You don't want to get involved, not with anyone you'd run into in a place like that.

Then he said my name, and I turned and looked at him. When someone knows your name, you don't have any option.

"Don't you know me?" he asked. I shook my head. I didn't know anyone who looked like that. You don't forget something like that. "It's me," he said, his voice a pleading whisper. "Eddie Barrow. Come on, mate. You know me."

And when he said his name I did know him, more or less. I mean, I knew Eddie Barrow. We had worked on a building site together, ten years back, during my only real flirtation with manual work.

Eddie Barrow was tall and heavily muscled, with a movie star smile and lazy good looks. He was ex-police. Sometimes he'd tell me stories, true tales of fitting-up and doing over, of punishment and crime. He had left the force after some trouble between him and one of the top brass. He said it was the Chief Superintendent's wife forced him to leave. Eddie was always getting into trouble with women. They really liked him, women.

When we were working together on the building site they'd hunt him down, give him sandwiches, little presents, whatever. He never seemed to *do* anything to make them like him; they just liked him. I used to watch him to see how he did it, but it didn't seem to be anything he did. Eventually, I decided it was just the way he was: big, strong, not very bright, and terribly, terribly good-looking.

But that was ten years ago.

The man sitting at the Formica table wasn't good-looking. His eyes were dull and rimmed with red, and they stared down at the table-top, without hope. His skin was grey. He was too thin, obscenely thin. I could see his scalp through his filthy hair. I said, "What happened to you?"

"How d'you mean?"

"You look a bit rough," I said, although he looked worse than rough; he looked dead. Eddie Barrow had been a big guy. Now he'd collapsed in on himself. All bones and flaking skin.

"Yeah," he said. Or maybe "Yeah?" I couldn't tell. Then, resigned, flatly, "Happens to us all in the end."

He gestured with his left hand, pointed at the seat opposite him. His right arm hung stiffly at his side, his right hand safe in the pocket of his coat.

Eddie's table was by the window, where anyone could see you walking past. Not somewhere I'd sit by choice, not if it was up to me. But it was too late now. I sat down facing him and I sipped my tea. I didn't say anything, which could have been a mistake. Small talk might have kept his demons at a distance. But I cradled my mug and said nothing. So I suppose he must have thought that I wanted to know more, that I cared. I didn't care. I had enough problems of my own. I didn't want to know about his struggle with whatever it was that had brought him to this state—drink, or drugs, or disease— but he started to talk, in a grey voice, and I listened.

"I came here a few years back, when they were building the bypass. Stuck around after, the way you do. Got a room in an old place around the back of Prince Regent's Street. Room in the attic. It was a family house, really. They only rented out the top floor, so there were just the two boarders, me and Miss Corvier. We were both up in the attic, but in separate rooms, next door to each other. I'd hear her moving about. And there was a cat. It was the family cat, but it came upstairs to say hello, every now and again, which was more than the family ever did.

"I always had my meals with the family, but Miss Corvier she didn't ever come down for meals, so it was a week before I met her. She was coming out of the upstairs lavvy. She looked so old. Wrinkled face, like an old, old monkey. But long hair, down to her waist, like a young girl.

"It's funny, with old people, you don't think they feel things like we do. I mean, here's her, old enough to be my granny and...." He stopped. Licked his lips with a grey tongue. "Anyway... I came up to the room one night and there's a brown paper bag of mushrooms outside my door on the ground. It was a present, I knew that straight off. A present for me. Not normal mushrooms, though. So I knocked on her door.

"I says, are these for me?

"Picked them meself, Mister Barrow, she says.

"They aren't like toadstools or anything? I asked. Y'know, poisonous? Or funny mushrooms?

"She just laughs. Cackles even. They're for eating, she says. They're fine. Shaggy inkcaps, they are. Eat them soon now. They go off quick. They're best fried up with a little butter and garlic.

"I say, are you having some too?

"She says, no. She says, I used to be a proper one for mushrooms, but not anymore, not with my stomach. But they're lovely. Nothing better than a young shaggy inkcap mushroom. It's astonishing the things that people don't eat. All the things around them that people could eat, if only they knew it.

"I said thanks, and went back into my half of the attic. They'd done the conversion a few years before, nice job really. I put the mushrooms down by the sink. After a few days they dissolved into black stuff, like ink, and I had to put the whole mess into a plastic bag and throw it away.

"I'm on my way downstairs with the plastic bag, and I run into her on the stairs. She says, hullo Mister B.

"I say, hello Miss Corvier.

"Call me Effie, she says. How were the mushrooms?

"Very nice, Thank you, I said. They were lovely.

"She'd leave me other things after that, little presents, flowers in old milk-bottles, things like that, then nothing. I was a bit relieved when the presents suddenly stopped.

"So I'm down at dinner with the family, the lad at the poly, he was home for the holidays. It was August. Really hot. And someone says they hadn't seen her for about a week and could I look in on her. I said I didn't mind.

"So I did. The door wasn't locked. She was in bed. She had a thin sheet over her, but you could see she was naked under the sheet. Not that I was trying to see anything, it'd be like looking at your gran in the altogether. This old lady. But she looked so pleased to see me.

"Do you need a doctor? I says.

"She shakes her head. I'm not ill, she says. I'm hungry. That's all.

"Are you sure, I say, because I can call someone, It's not a bother. They'll come out for old people.

"She says, Edward? I don't want to be a burden on anyone, but I'm so hungry.

"Right. I'll get you something to eat, I said. Something easy on your tummy, I says. That's when she surprises me. She looks embarrassed. Then she says, very quietly, *meat*. It's got to be fresh meat, and raw. I won't let anyone else cook for me. Meat. Please, Edward.

"Not a problem I says, and I go downstairs. I thought for a moment about nicking it from the cat's bowl, but of course I didn't. It was like, I knew she wanted it, so I had to do it. I had no choice. I went down to Safeways, and I bought her a readipak of best ground sirloin.

"The cat smelled it. Followed me up the stairs. I said, you get down, puss. It's not for you, I said. It's for Miss Corvier, and she's not feeling well, and she's going to need it for her supper, and the thing mewed at me as if it hadn't been fed in a week, which I knew wasn't true because its bowl was still half-full. Stupid, that cat was.

"I knock on her door, she says come in. She's still in the bed, and I give her the pack of meat, and she says, thank you Edward, you've got a good heart. And she starts to tear off the plastic wrap, there in the bed. There's a puddle of brown blood under the plastic tray, and it drips onto her sheet, but she doesn't notice. Makes me shiver.

"I'm going out the door, and I can already hear her starting to eat with her fingers, cramming the raw mince into her mouth. And she hadn't got out of bed.

"But the next day she's up and about, and from there on she's in and out at all hours, in spite of her age, and I think, there you are. They say red meat's bad for you, but it did her the world of good. And raw, well, it's just steak tartare, isn't it? You ever eaten raw meat?"

The question came as a surprise. I said, "Me?"

Eddie looked at me with his dead eyes, and he said, "Nobody else at this table."

"Yes. A little. When I was a small boy—four, five years old— my grandmother would take me to the butcher's with her, and he'd give me slices of raw liver, and I'd just eat them, there in the shop, like that. And everyone would laugh."

I hadn't thought of that in twenty years. But it was true.

I still like my liver rare, and sometimes, if I'm cooking and if nobody else is around, I'll cut a thin slice of raw liver before I season it, and I'll eat it, relishing the texture and the naked, iron taste.

"Not me," he said. "I liked my meat properly cooked. So the next thing that happened was Thompson went missing."

"Thompson?"

"The cat. Somebody said there used to be two of them, and they called them Thompson and Thompson. I don't know why. Stupid, giving them both the same name. The first one was squashed by a lorry." He pushed at a small mound of sugar on the Formica top with a fingertip. His left hand, still. I was beginning to wonder whether he had a right arm. Maybe the sleeve was empty. Not that it was any of my business. Nobody gets through life without losing a few things on the way.

I was trying to think of some way of telling him I didn't have any money, just in case he was going to ask me for something when he got to the end of his story. I didn't have any money: just a train ticket and enough pennies for the bus ticket home.

"I was never much of a one for cats," he said suddenly. "Not really. I liked dogs. Big, faithful things. You knew where you were with a dog. Not cats. Go off for days on end, you don't see them. When I was a lad, we had a cat, it was called Ginger. There was a family down the street, they had a cat they called Marmalade. Turned out it was the same cat, getting fed by all of us. Well, I mean. Sneaky little buggers. You can't trust them.

"That was why I didn't think anything when Thompson went away. The family was worried. Not me. I knew it'd come back. They always do.

"Anyway, a few nights later, I heard it. I was trying to sleep, and I couldn't. It was the middle of the night, and I heard this mewing. Going on, and on, and on. It wasn't loud, but when you can't sleep these things just get on your nerves. I thought maybe it was stuck up in the rafters or out on the roof outside. Wherever it was, there wasn't any point in trying to sleep through it. I knew that. So I got up, and I got dressed, even put my boots on in case I was going to be climbing out onto the roof, and I went looking for the cat.

"I went out in the corridor. It was coming from Miss Corvier's room on the other side of the attic. I knocked on her door, but no one answered. Tried the door. It wasn't locked. So I went in. I thought maybe that the cat was stuck somewhere. Or hurt. I don't know. I just wanted to help, really.

"Miss Corvier wasn't there. I mean, you know sometimes if there's anyone in a room, and that room was empty. Except there's something on the floor in the corner going *mrie, mrie....* And I turned on the light to see what it was."

He stopped then for almost a minute, the fingers of his left hand picking at the black goo that had crusted around the neck of the ketchup bottle. It was shaped like a large tomato. Then he said, "What I didn't understand was how it could still be alive. I mean, it was. And from the chest up, it was alive, and breathing, and fur and everything. But its back legs, its rib cage. Like a chicken carcase. Just bones. And what are they called, sinews? And, it lifted its head, and it looked at me.

"It may have been a cat, but I knew what it wanted. It was in its eyes. I mean." He stopped. "Well, I just knew. I'd never seen eyes like that. You would have known what it wanted, all it wanted, if you'd seen those eyes. I did what it wanted. You'd have to be a monster, not to."

"What did you do?"

"I used my boots." Pause. "There wasn't much blood. Not really. I just stamped and stamped on its head, until there wasn't really anything much left that looked like anything. If you'd seen it looking at you like that, you would have done what I did."

I didn't say anything.

"And then I heard someone coming up the stairs to the attic, and I thought I ought to do something, I mean, it didn't look good, I don't know what it must have looked like really, but I just stood there, feeling stupid, with a stinking mess on my boots, and when the door opens, it's Miss Corvier.

"And she sees it all. She looks at me. And she says, you killed him. I can hear something funny in her voice, and for a moment I don't know what it is, and then she comes closer, and I realise that she's crying.

"That's something about old people, when they cry like children, you don't know where to look, do you? And she says, he was all I had to keep me going, and you killed him. After all I've done, she says, making it so the meat stays fresh, so the life stays on. After all I've done.

"I'm an old woman, she says. I need my meat.

"I didn't know what to say.

"She's wiping her eyes with her hand. I don't want to be a burden on anybody, she says. She's crying now. And she's looking at me. She says, I never wanted to be a burden. She says, that was my meat. Now, she says, who's going to feed me now?"

He stopped, rested his grey face in his left hand, as if he was tired. Tired of talking to me, tired of the story, tired of life. Then he shook his head, and looked at me, and said, "If you'd seen that cat, you would have done what I did. Anyone would have done."

He raised his head then, for the first time in his story, looked me in the eyes. I thought I saw an appeal for help in his eyes, something he was too proud to say aloud.

Here it comes, I thought. This is where he asks me for money.

Somebody outside tapped on the window of the café. It wasn't a loud tapping, but Eddie jumped. He said, "I have to go now. That means I have to go."

I just nodded. He got up from the table. He was still a tall man, which almost surprised me: he'd collapsed in on himself in so many other ways. He pushed the table away as he got up, and as he got up he took his right hand out of his coat-pocket. For balance, I suppose. I don't know.

Maybe he wanted me to see it. But if he wanted me to see it, why did he keep it in his pocket the whole time? No, I don't think he wanted me to see it. I think it was an accident.

He wasn't wearing a shirt or a jumper under his coat, so I could see his arm, and his wrist. Nothing wrong with either of them. He had a normal wrist. It was only when you looked below the wrist that you saw most of the flesh had been picked from the bones, chewed like chicken wings, leaving only dried morsels of meat, scraps and crumbs, and little else. He only had three fingers left, and most of a thumb. I suppose the other finger-bones must have just fallen right off, with no skin or flesh to hold them on.

That was what I saw. Only for a moment, then he put his hand back in his pocket, and pushed out of the door, into the chilly night.

I watched him then, through the dirty plate-glass of the café window.

It was funny. From everything he'd said, I'd imagined Miss Corvier to be an old woman. But the woman waiting for him, outside, on the pavement, couldn't have been much over thirty. She had long, long hair, though. The kind of hair you can sit on, as they say, although that always sounds faintly like a line from a dirty joke. She looked a bit like a hippy, I suppose. Sort of pretty, in a hungry kind of way.

She took his arm, and looked up into his eyes, and they walked away out of the café's light for all the world like a couple of teenagers who were just beginning to realise that they were in love.

I went back up to the counter and bought another cup of tea and a couple of packets of crisps to see me through until the morning, and I sat and thought about the expression on his face when he'd looked at me that last time.

On the milk-train back to the big city I sat opposite a woman carrying a baby. It was floating in formaldehyde, in a heavy glass container. She needed to sell it, rather urgently, and although I was extremely tired we talked about her reasons for selling it, and about other things, for the rest of the journey.

Glenn Chadbourne

UNDER THE PYLON

By Graham Joyce

After school or during the long summer holidays we used to meet down by the electricity pylon. Though we never went there when the weather was wet because obviously there was no cover. Apart from that the wet power lines would vibrate and hum and throb and it would be...well, I'm not saying I was scared but it would give you a bad feeling.

Wet or dry, we'd all been told not to play under the pylon. Our folks had lectured us time and again to keep away; and an Electricity Board disc fixed about nine feet up on the thing spelled out DANGER in red and white lettering. Two lightning shocks either side of the word set it in zigzag speech marks.

'Danger!'

I imagined the voice of the pylon would sound like a robot's speech-box from a science-fiction film, because that's what the pylon looked like, a colossal robot. Four skeletal steel legs straddled the ground, tapering up to a pointed head nudging the clouds. The struts bearing the massive power cables reached over like arms, adding a note of severity and anthropomorphism to the thing. Like someone standing with their hands on their hips. The power cables themselves drooped slightly until picked up by the next giant robot in the field beyond, and then to the next. Marching into the infinite distance, an army of obstinate robots.

But the pylon was situated on a large patch of waste ground between the houses, and when it came down to it, there was nowhere else for us kids to go. It was a green and overgrown little escape-hatch from suburbia. It smelled of wild grass and giant stalks of cow parsley, and of nettles and foxgloves and dumped house-bricks. You could bash down a section to make a lair hidden from everything but the butterflies. Anyway, it wasn't the danger of electricity giving rise to any nervousness under the pylon. It was something else. Old Mrs Nantwich called it a shadow.

Joy Astley was eleven, and already wearing lipstick and make-up you could have peeled off like a mask. Her parents had big mouths and were always bawling. 'The Nantwiches,' she said airily, 'could only afford to buy this house because it's under the pylon. No one wants a house under the pylon.'

'Why not?' said Clive Mann. It was all he ever said. Clive had a metal brace across his teeth. He was odd; he stared at things.

'Because you don't,' said Joy, 'that's why.'

Tania Brown was in my class at school (she used to pronounce her name "Tarnia' because of the sunshine jokes) and she agreed with Joy. Kev Duffy burped and said, 'Crap!' It was Kev's word for the month. He would use it repeatedly up until the end of August. Joy just looked at Kev and wiggled her head from side to side, as if that somehow dealt with his remark.

The Nantwiches Joy was being so snobbish about were retired barge people. Why anyone would want to rub two pennies together I've never understood, but they were always described as looking as though they couldn't accomplish this dubious feat; and then in the same breath people would always add 'yet they're the people who have got it'.

I doubted it somehow. They'd lived a hard life transporting coal on the barges, and it showed. Their faces had more channels and ruts than the waterways of the Grand Union.

'They're illiterate,' Joy always pointed out whenever they were mentioned. And then she'd add, 'Can't read or write.'

The Nantwiches' house did indeed stand under the shadow of the giant pylon. Mr Nantwich was one of those old guys with a red face and white hair, forever forking over the earth in his backyard. Their garden backed up to the pylon. A creosoted wooden fence closed off one side of the square defined by the structure's four legs.

One day when I was there alone old Mrs Nantwich had scared me by popping her head over the fence and saying, 'You don't wanna play there.'

Her face looked as old and green and lichen-ridden as a church gate. Fine bristles sprouted from her chin. Her hair was always drawn back under a headscarf, and she wore spectacles with plastic frames and lenses like magnifying glasses. They made her eyes huge, swimming.

She threw her bead back slowly and pointed her chin towards the top of the pylon. 'Then she looked at me and did it again. 'There's a shadow orf of it.'

I felt embarrassed as she stared. She was waiting for me to speak, so I said, 'What do you mean?'

Before she answered another head popped alongside her own. It was her daughter Olive. Olive looked as old as her mother. She had wild, iron-grey hair. Her teeth were terribly blackened and crooked. The thing about Olive was she never uttered a word. She hadn't spoken, according to my mother, since a man had 'jumped out at her from behind a bush'. I didn't see how that could make someone dumb for the rest of their life, but then I didn't understand what my mother meant by that deceptively careful phrase either.

'Wasn't me,' said Mrs Nantwich a little fiercely, 'as decided to come 'ere.' And then her head disappeared back behind the fence, leaving Olive to stare beadily at me as if I'd done something wrong. Then her head too popped out of sight.

I looked up at the wires, and they seemed to hum with spiteful merriment.

Another day I came across Clive Mann, crouched under the pylon and listening. At that time, the three sides of the pylon had been closed off. We'd found some rusty corrugated sheeting to lean against one end, and a few lengths of torn curtain to screen off another. The third side, running up to the Nantwiches' creosoted fence, was shielded by an impenetrable jungle of five-foot-high stinging nettles.

It had been raining, and the curtains sagged badly. I ducked through the gap between them to find Clive crouched and staring directly up into the tower of the pylon. He said nothing.

'What are you doing?'

'You can hear,' he said. 'You can hear what they're saying.'

I looked up and listened. The lines always made an eerie hissing after rain, but there was no other sound.

'Hear what?'

'No! The people. On the telephones. Mrs Astley is talking to the landlord of the Dog and Trumpet. He's knocking her off.'

I looked up again and listened. I knew he wasn't joking because Clive had no sense of humour. Like I said, he just stared at things. I was about to protest that the cables were power lines, not telephone wires, when the curtains parted and Joy Astley came in.

'What are you two doing?'

We didn't answer.

'My Dad says these curtains and things have got to come down,' said Joy.

'Why?'

'He says he doesn't like the idea.'

'What's it got to do with him?'

'He thinks,' Joy said, closing her eyes, 'things go on here.'

'You mean he's worried about what his angelic daughter gets up to,' I said.

Joy turned around, flicked up her skirt and wiggled her bottom at us. It was a gesture too familiar to be of any interest. At least that day she was wearing panties.

I had to pass by the Dog and Trumpet as I walked home later that afternoon. I noticed Mrs Astley going in by the back door, which was odd because the pub was closed in the afternoons. But I thought little of it at the time.

Just as we became accustomed to Joy flashing her bottom at us, we were well inured to the vague parental unease about us playing under the pylon. None of our parents ever defined the exact nature of their anxieties. They would mention things about electricity and generators, but these didn't add up to much more than old Mrs Nantwich's dark mutterings about a shadow. I got my physics and my science all mixed up as usual, and managed to infect the rest of the group with my store of misapprehensions.

'Radiation,' I announced. 'The reason they're scared is because if there was an accidental power surge feedback...' (I was improvising like mad) 'then we'd all get radiated.'

Radiated. It was a great word. *Radiated*. It got everyone going.

'There was a woman in the newspaper,' said Joy. 'Her microwave oven went wrong and she was radiated. Her bones all turned to jelly.'

Tania could cap that. 'There was one on television. A woman. She gave birth to a cow with two heads. After being radiated' The girls were always better at horror stories.

Kev Duffy said, 'Crap!' Then he looked up into the pyramid of the tower and said, 'What's the chances of it happening?'

'Eighteen hundred to one,' I said. With that talent for tossing out utterly bogus statistics I should have gone on to become a politician.

Then they were all looking up, and in the silence you could hear the abacus beads whizzing and clacking in their brains.

Joy's parents needn't have worried. Not much went on behind the pylon screens of which they could disapprove. Well, that's not entirely true, since one or two efforts were made seriously to misbehave, but they never amounted to much. Communal cigarettes were sucked down to their filters, bottles of cider were shared round. Clive and I once tried sniffing Airfix but it made us sick as dogs and we were never attracted to the idea again. We once persuaded Joy to take off her clothes for a dare, which she did; but then she immediately put them back on again, so it all seemed a bit pointless and no more erotic than the episode of solvent abuse.

It was the last summer holiday before we were due to be dispatched to what we all called the Big Schools. It all depended on which side of the waste ground you lived. Joy and Kev were to go to President Kennedy, where you didn't have to wear a school uniform; Clive and I were off to Cardinal Wiseman, where you did. It all seemed so unfair. Tania was being sent to some snooty private school where they wore straw hats in the summer. She hated the idea, but her father was what my old man called one of the nobs.

Once, Tania and I were on our own under the pylon. Tania had long blond hair and was pretty in a willowy sort of way. Her green eyes always seemed wide open with amazement at the things we'd talk about or at what we'd get up to. She spoke quietly in her rather posh accent, and she always seemed desperately grateful that we didn't exclude her from our activities.

Out of the blue she asked me if I'd ever kissed a girl.

'Loads,' I lied. 'Why?'

'I've never kissed anyone. And now I'm going to a girls' school I'll probably never get the chance.'

We sat on an old door elevated from the grass by a few housebricks. I looked away. The seconds thrummed by. I imagined I heard the wires overhead going chock chock chock.

'Would you like to?' she said softly.

'Like to what?'

'To kiss me?'

I shrugged. 'If you want.' My muscles went as stiff as the board on which we perched.

She moved closer, put her head at an angle, and closed her eyes. I looked at her thin lips, leaned over, and rested my mouth against hers. We stayed like that for some time, stock-still. The power lines overhead vibrated with noisy impatience. Eventually she opened her eyes and pulled back, blinking at me and licking her lips. I realised my hands were clenched to the side of the board as if it had been a magic carpet hurtling across the sky.

So Tania and I were 'going out'. Our kissing improved slightly, and we got a lot of ribbing from the others, but beyond that, nothing had changed. Because I was going out with Tania, Kev Duffy was considered to be 'going out' with Joy, at least nominally; though to be fair to him, he was elected to this position only because Clive was beyond the pale. Kev resented this status as something of an imposition, though he did go along with the occasional bout of simulated kissing. But when Joy appeared one day sporting livid, gash-crimson lipstick and calling him 'darling' at every turn, he got mad and smudged the stuff all round her face with the ball of his hand. The others pretended not to notice, but I could see she was hurt by it.

Another time I'd been reading something about hypnotism, and Joy decided she wanted to be hypnotised. I'd decided I had a talent for this, so I sat her on the grass inside the pylon while the other three watched. I did all that 'you're feeling very relaxed' stuff and she went under easily; too easily. Then I didn't know what to ask her to do. There was no point asking her to take off her clothes, since she hardly needed prompting to do that.

'Get 'er to run around like a 'eadless chicken,' was Kev's inspirational idea.

'Tell 'er to describe life on Jupiter,' Clive said obscurely.

'Ask her to go back to a past life,' said Tania.

That seemed the most intelligent suggestion, so I offered a few clichéd phrases and took her back, back into the mists of time. I was about to ask her what she could see when I felt a thrum of energy. It distracted me for a moment, and I looked up into the apex of the pylon. There was nothing to see, but I remembered I'd felt it before. Once, when I'd first kissed Tania.

When I looked back, there were tears streaming down Joy's face. She was trembling and sobbing in silence.

'Bring her out of it,' said Tania.

'Why?' Give protested.

'Yer,' said Kev. 'Better stop it now.'

I couldn't. I did all that finger clicking rubbish and barked various commands. But she just sat there shaking and sobbing. I was terrified. Tania took hold of her hands and, thankfully, after a while Joy just seemed to come out of it on her own. She was none the worse for the experience and laughed it off; but she wouldn't tell us what she saw.

They all had a go. Kev wouldn't take it seriously, however, and insisted on staggering around like a stage drunk. Clive claimed to have gone under but we all agreed we couldn't tell the difference.

Finally it was Tania's turn. She was afraid, but Joy dared her. Tania made me promise not to make her experience a past life. I'd read enough about hypnotism to know you can't make people do anything they don't already want to do, but convincing folk of that is another thing. Tania had been frightened by what happened to Joy, so I had to swear on my grandmother's soul and hope to be struck by lightning and so on before she'd let me do it.

Tania went under with equal ease, a feat I've never been able to accomplish since.

'What are you going to get her to do?' Joy wanted to know.

'Pretend to ride a bike?' I suggested lamely.

'Crap,' said Kev. 'Tell her she's the sexiest woman in the world and she wants to make mad passionate love to you.'

Naturally Joy thought this was a good idea, so I put it to Tania. She opened her eyes in a way that made me think she'd just been stringing us along. She smiled at me serenely and shook her head. Then there was a thrum of electrical activity from the wires overhead. I looked up and before I knew what was happening, Tania had jumped on me and locked her legs behind my back. I staggered and fell backwards onto the grass. Tania had her tongue halfway down my throat. I'd heard of French kissing, but it had never appealed. Joy and Kev were laughing, cheering her on.

Tania came up for air, and she was making a weird growling from the back of her throat. Then she power-kissed me again.

'This is great!' whooped Kev.

'Hey!' went Clive. 'Hey!'

'Tiger, tiger!' shouted Joy.

I was still pinned under Tania's knees when she sat up and stripped off her white T-shirt in one deft move.

'Bloody hell!' Kev couldn't believe it any more than I could. 'This is brilliant!'

'Gerrem off,' screamed Joy.

Tania stood up quickly and hooked her thumbs inside the waist of her denims and her panties, slipping them off. Before I'd had time to blink she was naked. She was breathing hard. Then she was fumbling at my jeans.

'Bloody fucking hell!' Joy shouted. 'Bloody fucking hell!'

The lines overhead thrummed again. Tania had twice my strength. I had this crazy idea she was drawing it from the pylon. She had my pants halfway down my legs.

Then everything was interrupted by a high-pitched screaming.

At first I thought it was Tania, but it was coming from behind her. The screaming brought Tania to her senses. It was Olive, the Nantwiches' deranged daughter. Her head had appeared over the fence, and she was screaming and pointing at something. What she pointed at was my semi-erect penis; half-erect from Tania's brutal stimulation; half-flaccid from terror at her ferocious strength.

Olive continued to point and shriek. Then she was joined at the fence by Mrs Nantwich. 'Filthy buggers,' said the old woman. 'Get on with yer! Filthy buggers!'

A third head appeared. Red-faced Mr Nantwich. He was just laughing. 'Look at that!' he shouted. 'Look at that.'

Tania wasn't laughing. She looked at me with disgust. 'Bastard,' she spat, climbing quickly back into her clothes. 'Bastard.'

I ran after her. 'You can't make anyone do what they don't want to,' I tried. She shrugged me off tearfully. I let her go.

'Filthy buggers!' Mrs Nantwich muttered.

'You can't make anyone!' I screamed at her.

'Look at that!' laughed Joe Nantwich.

Olive was still shrieking. The power lines were still throbbing. Clive was trying to tell me something, but I wasn't listening. 'It wasn't you,' he was saying. He was pointing up at the pylon. 'It were that.'

I never spoke another word to Tania, and she never came near the pylon again. I was terrified the story would get back to my folks. I didn't see why exactly, but I had the feeling I'd reap all the blame. But a few days later something happened which overshadowed the entire incident.

And it happened to Clive.

One afternoon he and I had been sharing a bottle of Woodpecker. He'd been listening again.

'Old man Astley's found out.'

'Eh? How do you know?'

He looked up at the overhead wires. 'She's been on the phone to the Dog and Trumpet.'

He was always reporting what he'd 'heard' on the wires. We all knew he was completely cracked, but it was best to ignore him. I changed the subject. I started regaling him with some nonsense I'd heard about a burglar's fingers bitten clean off by an Alsatian, when Clive took it into his head to start climbing the pylon. I didn't think it was a sensible thing to do but it was pointless saying anything.

'Not a good idea, that.'

'Why?'

Climbing the pylon wasn't easy. The inspection ladder didn't start until a height of nine feet — obviously with schoolboys in mind — but that didn't stop Clive. He lifted the door we used as a bench and leaned it against the struts of one of the pylon's legs. Climbing on the struts, he pulled himself to the top of the door, and standing on its top edge he was able to haul himself up to the inspection ladder. He ascended a few rungs and seemed happy to hang there for a while. I got bored watching him.

It was late afternoon, and the sky had gone a dark, a cobalt shade of blue. I finished off the cider, unzipped my trousers, and stuck my dick outside the curtains to empty my bladder. A kind of spasm shot through me before I'd finished, stronger even than those

I'd felt before. I ignored it. 'So the burglar,' I was telling Clive, 'knew the key was on a string inside the letter box. So when the owners came home they got into the hallway and found.' I finished pissing, zipped up, and turned to complete the story. But my words tailed off, 'two fingers still holding the string....'

I looked up the inspection ladder to the top of the pylon. I looked at the grey metal struts. I looked everywhere. Clive had vanished.

'Clive?'

I checked all around. Then I went outside. I thought he might have jumped down, or fallen. He wasn't there. I went back inside. Then I went outside again.

Spots of rain started to appear. I looked up at the wires, and they seemed to hum contentedly. I waited for a while until the rain came more heavily, and then I went home.

That night while I lay in bed, I heard the telephone ring. I knew what time it was because I could hear the television signature blaring from the lounge. It was the end of the late night news. Then my mother came upstairs. Had I seen Clive? His mother had phoned. She was worried.

The next day I was interviewed by a policewoman. I explained we were playing under the pylon. I turned my back and he'd disappeared. She made a note and left.

A few days later the police were out like blackberries in September. Half the neighbourhood joined in the fine-toothcomb search of the waste ground and the nearby fields. They found nothing. Not a hair from his head.

While the searches went on, I started to have a recurring nightmare. I'd be back under the pylon, pissing and happily talking away to Clive. Only it wasn't urine coming out, it was painful fat blue-and-white sparks of electricity. I'd turn to Clive in surprise, who would be descending the inspection ladder wearing fluorescent blue overalls, his face out of view. And his entire body would be rippling with eels of electricity, gold sparks arcing wildly. Then slowly his head would begin to rotate towards me, and I'd start screaming; but before I ever got to see his awful face I'd wake up.

We stopped playing under the pylon after that. No one had to say anything, we just stopped going there. I did go back once, to satisfy my own curiosity. The screens had been ripped away in the failed search, but the nettles bashed down by the police were already springing up again.

I looked up into the tower of the pylon, and although there was nothing to see, I felt a terrible sense of dread. Then a face appeared over the Nantwiches' fence. It was Olive. She'd seen me looking.

'Gone,' she said. It was the only word I ever heard her say. 'Gone.'

Summer came to an end, and we went off to our respective schools. I saw Tania once or twice in her straw boater, but she passed me with her nose in the air. Eventually she married a Tory MP. I often wonder if she's happy.

Inevitably Kev and I stopped hanging around together, but not before there was a murder in the district. The landlord of the Dog and Trumpet was stabbed to death. They never found who did it. Joy moved out of the area when her parents split up. She went to live with her mother.

Joy went on to become a rock and roll singer. A star. Well, not a star exactly, but I did once see her on Top of the Pops. She had a kind of trade mark, turning her back on the cameras to wiggle her bottom. I felt pleased for her that she'd managed to put the habit to good use.

Just occasionally I bump into Kev in this pub or that, but we never really know what to say to each other. After a while Kev always says, 'Do you remember the time you hypnotised Tania Brown and....' and I always say 'Yes' before he gets to the end of the story. Then we look at the floor for a while until one of us says, 'Anyway, good to see you, all the best.' It's that anyway that gets me.

Clive Mann is never mentioned.

Occasionally I make myself walk past the old place. A new group of kids has started playing there, including Kev Duffy's oldest girl. Yesterday as I passed by that way there were no children around because an Electricity Board operative was servicing the pylon. He was halfway up the inspection ladder, and he wore blue overalls exactly like Clive in my dream. It stopped me with a jolt. I had to stare, even though I could sense the man's irritation at being watched.

Then came that singular, familiar thrum of energy. The maintenance man let his arm drop and turned to face me, challenging me to go away. But I was transfixed. Because it was Clive's face I saw in that man's body. He smiled at me, but tiny white sparks of electricity were leaking from his eyes like tears. Then he made to speak, but all I heard or saw was a fizz of electricity arcing across the metal brace on his teeth. Then he was the maintenance man again, meeting my desolate gaze with an expression of contempt.

I left hurriedly, and I resolved, after all, not to pass by the pylon again.

Glenn Chadbourne

A GUY WALKS INTO A BAR

By Matthew Costello

Let me tell you. I was there. Saw the whole thing, heard the whole fucking thing. So, as they say, you can't bullshit a bullshitter, right? And what I'm telling you here is no bullshit.

Got that straight?

Good. Shows you got ears. Damn useful things, two leafy chunks of flesh that pick up sound. Pretty fucking neat design— except some people don't seem to know how to use them.

Okay. So what was my deal, on that night? On a Tuesday night, heading down to Two Jays?

Well, I bet you can just guess. Girlfriend on the warpath. And it wasn't even a red-flag day. Just another one of those times that the bitch-meter kicked in big time. Only this night—dunno what happened at work with her—but she was all over me about everything. Starting with how crappy the apartment is, and how we never have any goddam money, and whenever the hell will we be able to afford to buy a place.

Buy a place?

What the hell is she smoking?

(Actually nothing. That's one of the areas we cut back on. That, plus she got in her head that a nightly doobie was sapping me of my ambition. *Riiiight….*)

So she wouldn't let it go. Just kept it up.

Until, like a beacon of sanity, I pictured the warm confines of the

Two Jays. Some quiet drinks, maybe a game on the tube. Wasn't sure there was any Tuesday night football. Not that I really give a damn about football. But anything would be better than her screeching, working herself up, *way* up.

Not for the first time did I think...maybe it was time to bail. Time to cut this one loose.

But we usually made up. She usually apologized, even when it was my fault. I always accepted. Because certain perks came with accepting that apology.

If you catch my drift.

And you look like an intelligent type of guy, so I'm *sure* you do.

So I walk in, get a big hello from Ray, the weeknight bartender. Some old sitcom on his TV. No game on. A few stiffs at the stools, a couple of the younger guys in back shooting pool.

Ray gives me a big "hello" and a "what'll it be."

"Vodka on the rocks," I said. "A double." Ray nods and grabs the Stoli. Like I said, a good guy. Could have poured the Smirnoff and I wouldn't have said a goddam word.

And since he knew my usual was a pint, I didn't even get from him,...*having one of those nights?*

I had discussed my situation with him on previous nights when Mindy was in full throttle. Not tonight, though. Just a big fucking tumbler of vodka with a few rocks.

I put down a ten-dollar bill, and the evening was rolling.

Of course there's only so long you can sit there with your thoughts. Soon you sort of sense your fellow bar mates, and you kinda let yourself drift into their conversation.

You know how it is? Sure you do....

In this case I didn't have to do any drifting at all. Jackie Weeks, at the other end, let out one of those large phlegmy laughs that degenerated into a bone-jarring cough. Christ, I bet the only place you can hear that sound *is* in a bar. A mix of booze and bonhomie camaraderie.

Or some shit—

Anyway, when his cough sputtered to a close, I asked him—

"Jackie, what's so fucking funny?"

And Jackie, like any good barroom stalwart, slid off the stool.

"I was telling Charlie here"—more sputtering laughter and

Jackie walked closer – "what everyone with a dick already knows."

Again, Jackie started his hacking laugh, his face reddening to that burnished glow that one of those days was sure to deliver a nice fat coronary, right here on the crummy floor of the Two Jays.

"And what the hell is that, Jackie?"

Close enough so that he could plant his pudgy hand on my shoulder.

"Why, that a blowjob beats a fuck any goddam day of the week."

I grabbed my tumbler and took a good slug.

"And why is that?"

"Because if you fuck 'em, you have to look them right in the face. But with a blowjob, they're out of sight, and you can get a good view of the tube at the same goddam time!"

Jackie exploded again, his barroom wit absolutely killing him, destroying him.

To be polite I grinned and nodded. Another slug.

"Too true, Jackie, my man. Too true."

"Fucking A," he said.

Anyone who saw his wife would know that in that particular case, option 'A' was definitely the way to go. I for one would have a hard time keeping it up looking at her.

I would even have—whatcha call 'em?—*qualms* about sticking my dick into that mouth. Too fucking—I dunno—*mangy*. Like she might go postal and chomp it right off.

I'd have to ask Jackie sometime if he ever had that particular concern.

Not now though.

Sometime when he was sober.

Which, as far as I could tell, was hardly ever.

"Gonna drain the snake,"

"Thanks for sharing, Jackie."

And the jokemaster general of the evening walked back to the Two Jays' cesspool of a men's room. I mean, I think they clean it once a month whether it needs it or not.

Which was when the door opened.

And, as they say, a guy walked into the bar.

First of all, I gotta tell you I'm not prejudiced.

I mean, I'm not an idiot. I know that the world is changed, that

Brooklyn has changed, and that—well—the way we thought of things when I was growing up in Bay Ridge..., that was just plain *wrong*.

And if you believe that load of bullshit I just dumped on you, then I got a great fucking bridge to sell you.

But seriously, anybody who walks into the Two Jays would get served. Nobody would make any kind of big deal out of it at all. Live and let live. The laughs might get a little lower in volume...and the feeling that it was one great secret club of assholes might disappear. But otherwise no biggie.

So this guy walks in that I never saw before. I noticed Ray clocking him. The guy had dark skin, I guess what they would call a Latino. Half the fucking city's Latino these days, right? But on second glance, maybe he was something else, from somewhere they didn't have the pasty white skin of us micks.

Everyone looked at him for a minute. The guy, standing still for a second, looking at the room, the bar...before walking to a stool.

Oh man, almost forgot. Shit, I'm supposed to try and remember everything, right?

So he had on clean white shirt, like a businessman's shirt. But he was all sweaty like he'd just jogged here from freakin' Eammons Avenue.

He took the stool, and Ray, ever the professional, was right there.

"What'll be?"

I tried not to stare, but something was off with this guy. The sweating, the big wet patches under his arm, like he'd been digging a ditch or something. The guy looked up.

"A beer. Maybe a shot. Something."

Ray nodded. "Seagram's okay?"

"Sure."

No accent for our new guest.

He did look to his left though, and I had to stop staring.

Give the guy some space to enjoy his drink.

Everyone deserves that, don't they? That's what places like this are for.

Enjoy a quiet drink.

Mine, meanwhile, was gone, so I ordered another. Way too early to go home and face Mindy. Wanted her well in bed, snoring her ass off, before I got back, no matter what kind of hangover I cooked up for myself. Wouldn't be a first time I sat at my desk in the Transit Authority building with goddam jackhammers drilling to China via my frontal lobe.

"Another, Ray. And a bag of nuts."

Always good to eat while drinking, they say.

And for a while, the bar was quiet.

* * *

But it's one thing about drinks. Get enough of them out there, and things happen. All sorts of things. Guys talk, they fight, and on weekends when the occasional asshole brings his girl to this dive, they even fuck in the back, tying up the pisser.

So...I'm guessing this was more than a few drinks later.

In bar time, it was one drink after two. Three drinks to four.

In bar time, it was late.

Jackie had shifted topics, to one I would warm up to.

"But what is it with all the bitching? As if I don't work hard. Christ."

"Amen," I said.

"Trouble at home too?" he said to me.

Now I laughed. "Why the hell do you think I'm here...with you freakin' losers?"

I looked right and saw the newcomer, the sweaty patches shrinking, his sleeves all rolled up, looking at me.

"But what's your broad up to?" I asked Jackie.

Broad....thank god there are still places where people use that word. So fuckin' descriptive.

"You know—typical wife bitching. Like we don't have enough money. And we don't do enough goddam vacations. Why can't we fix up the place. And I'm like—what do they call it—a reality check. Like does fucking money grown on a fucking tree?"

Jackie slapped a hand on me.

"Trust me, if I had the bucks I'd gladly spend it all on that crap just to keep her big mouth shut."

And then—

An amazing moment, even in the Two Jays, where there were rules, compadre. Thing you did, and things you didn't do.

The guy down at the end, the new guy with his crisp white shirt and sweaty armpits, laughed.

He freakin' laughed.

Jackie's hand was still on my shoulder, but I could feel the ripple go through him.

You don't spill your guts in the Two Jays, even a little, then have someone laugh. We're brothers in arms against the world and bitchy wives, and it's not one of those times for a chuckle.

And this guy laughs?

Jackie let his hand slip off my shoulder. I spotted Ray, at the other end of the bar polishing his shot glasses, and he looked over, alert. Like I said, as things got late, stuff could happen. Enough talk, enough booze, and things could happen. The regulars knew how to avoid that shit, dodging any confrontational bullets.

But this guy....

Jackie walked past me, down the five or six stools, and stood facing the guy's left side.

Meanwhile—none of us enjoying this—we waited.

And Christ, here's where it got interesting. Real interesting.

And yeah...I know—that word doesn't really fit what happened.

Jackie spoke, the wires in his voice pulled tight.

"Something funny, pal?"

Pal.

Never a good word, that one. I had seen my older brothers crack many a head using that word.

Pal. Pallie.

Mr. White Shirt turned. Like I said, he looked like he might have been a Latino, but after he spoke—well, I'm figuring he's something else. A whole world now filled with people who don't look like they came from County Clare, know what I mean?

The guy looked at Jackie, still a smile on his face, no look of alarm. Nothing to show that this interloper—that's the word, isn't it?—knew that he might be in deep shit here.

"Yes," the guy said. "It was funny, what you said."

Jesus Christ, I thought. We're in goddam Goodfellas here. Pesci asking, *demanding...did I say something funny, something to amuse you?*

We all loved that picture. What's not to love?

And here it was for real.

But Jackie—maybe aware that he was about to replay that scene—simply said:

"Yeah, what was funny? My bitchy wife? The fact I got no money or—"

The guy put up his hands, stopping Jackie. Good, I thought, he's going to end it. Except that smile on his face didn't look scared. Guy looked happy as a clam.

"No. Not that. But when you said…reality check. That was funny. Made me laugh."

The guy picked up his glass and tipped it to Jackie before taking a sip. And as drunk as he was, I saw Jackie begin to ease.

"Yeah. I was her fucking 'reality check' alright." Then, thank god, a laugh from Jackie. "Guess that is a bit funny."

Jackie looked back to me, to Ray—and one of two things—and two things only—were about to happen.

He'd either keep laughing and walk back to his seat.

Or he'd raise a ham fist and send the poor bastard in the white shirt flying backwards like he'd been hit with a sledgehammer.

But instead, sports fans, there was this third thing….

Jackie stood there a moment. He looked at that guy.

"Guess you know, hmm? You got problems at home too, eh mac?"

Mac….

The guy turned and looked at Jackie, and I didn't like the way the guy looked. Something about his grin. Like he had a secret, and maybe—if we were all good—he was about to reveal that secret.

"Problems. Me? Not anymore. My problems…"—he licked up his beer glass and tilted it—"are solved."

Like I said, a freaky smile on his face.

Nobody could like a smile like that. Something was definitively *not* okay with this guy, know what I mean? But Jackie was too bombed to stop talking.

Jackie looked back at us and laughed. "What'd you do—off your old lady? God knows, I've wanted to do that." Another laugh. "What the hell she do anyway, your old lady? Another queen bitch?"

The guy shook his head and then dug into his left rear pocket and pulled out his wallet.

Opened it. Slid something out, and handed it to Jackie.

For a few seconds Jackie did nothing.

A Guy Walks into a Bar

"Shit. I mean sorry, this your wife?"

"I think 'ex' might be the operative prefix."

"No offense, pal, but she's gorgeous. Hey guys, look at this."

Jackie walked back to us. It was interesting to notice that no one else was eager to sidle up to Mr. Strange, gorgeous piece-of-ass wife or not.

But Jackie flashed us a look. We came over warily as he passed the picture.

Even in a little snapshot, she was stunning. Like a freakin' movie star. Absolutely beautiful. If this guy lost her, then he was one stupid son of bitch, no matter what her problems were.

Jackie walked back and handed the guy his picture.

"Too bad. She's some looker."

Again, a smile. More secrets. Then:

"Oh, yes. Beautiful. And she knew it. I thought I was pretty lucky having her." Then slowly, deliberately, he repeated the last words: "pretty...lucky."

"Something happened?"

Jackie, digging in, curious, his words slurred. Opening up a box that I thought, even after all my vodka, was best left shut.

Shit....

"Oh yes. Something happened. She cheated on me. More than once. I think she had a problem. So beautiful and wanting that attention all that time. And the sex. From guys who were blown away by her."

I kept waiting for the jokes. The jokes about "blowing," and her changing riders in the saddle. All that ribbing that we always do to each other in The Two Jays.

But this time—there was none of it.

"So, you kicked her ass out?"

Jackie looked back at us, as if looking for our approval on how the interview was going. I just rolled my eyes, but I think he was too far gone to see that.

"Nope. Didn't do that. After all, I had forgiven her lots of times. So this time...I tried something different."

Quiet—then.

Waiting.

For stupid fat-ass Jackie to ask...*what else?*

But he didn't have to.

Not this time.

* * *

The guy spun around.

"Yup, forgave her beautiful ass so many times. I mean, wouldn't you? Until it was just impossible to do that anymore. Was definitely time to try something else."

I noticed that—standing—the guy was big, kinda built, powerful...you know? The sweat stains under his arms had dried. I had a thought...whatever made him sweat had happened before he put that shirt on.

It was a clean shirt.

A small clue there. A tiny clue.

But about to be overtaken by so much more.

"No, enough with forgiveness. Enough humiliation. It was time for something very old and ancient, I thought."

Another pause. None of us saying shit.

"Punishment. So I gave her a few of her pills ground up in a glass of wine, and when she woke up she was taped and tied to a kitchen chair."

"Christ. Didn't she yell or something?"

The guy's smile broadened.

"Not with the silver tape across her pretty mouth. And then I went to work. Started a little after 7 o'clock. Little cuts mixed in with my talking, remembering each time she fucked someone who wasn't me, reminding her. Just little cuts at first...."

"Christ," one of the guys behind me said.

"Got to tell you. I wasn't sure where I was going with it. Kind of improvised. But it felt damn good when I started. So very...satisfying."

Ray leaned over to me, whispering. "This guy on the level? Some kind of nut? Should I call...?"

The guy saw the move. "Don't worry. It's done now. I'm just, well, sharing what I did." The smile again. "With some of my new friends in the bar."

Ray backed away.

"And the little cuts, led to bigger cuts, until—well she certainly didn't look beautiful anymore. I never knew that there so many places you could slice and *not* kill someone. Though the blood loss…I guess that would have gotten her sooner or later. So—that's when I removed the tape from her lips."

My head pounded.

This was not fucking happening.

I slipped my phone out of my pocket.

I dialed 911 without looking and held it. Thinking: the police must have some kind of GPS crap, don't they? To find the bar, get this nut. And all the time I'm thinking, *do not bullshit a bullshitter.* Is this guy making this all up? A bar story to shock the bums who hung out here?

"I ripped the tape off fast"—and here he made the move with his hand, showing us what that was like. "She tried to scream, but I think something was wrong with her lungs or—wait, yeah, I had cut a hole in her throat, such a sleek throat. One sexy throat. So—not much sound came out. Just this bubbling noise."

"Fucking freak…," Charlie said behind me.

The guy heard that.

"Maybe. But you weren't in my shoes. Least now I could see her mouth open, fish-like, begging for help. That was good. And the tears. Mixing with blood. I was covered in it. Until—well, all good things come to an end. And my cuts didn't do shit anymore. It was over."

Ray went to his phone.

The guy saw him.

"Yeah, guess you better call the cops."

Unless, I thought, it's all some bullshit story.

"They'll find me anyway. But if I take this…they will find me sooner."

He threw down the phone.

"Took a lot of pictures with this. I thought…"—he threw twenty down on the bar—"someone might want to see."

Nobody picked it up at first, as if the cell phone was contaminated. Then Jackie did, looking down, clicking.

"God. Christ. Shit."

About all you could say.

The guy strolled to the door.

"Gotta go. Oh—for the last bit? I took a little video. You can see that too."

I walked over to Jackie. He had found the video file on the camera phone. The video played. The video, the sounds the woman-thing—cause that's what it was—tried to make.

No fucking way to tell it was the same woman from the snapshot. But whoever it was…was in hell.

Hell, the way we always imagined it when Father Gately laid out the whole deal to us in 8th Grade.

The bloody video ended.

Then—the guy stopped at the door. I doubted any of us were about to stop him, I mean, would you really expect that we'd do something crazy like that?

"Great phone, hm? Amazing what they do with technology these days."

With that, he pushed open the door and walked out of The Two Jays.

And all you gotta do—to believe me, or any of us—is take a look at those pictures.

Word of advice though, kemosabe. No bullshit here.

Just make sure you don't look at them after you've eaten…know what I mean?

Why sure you do….

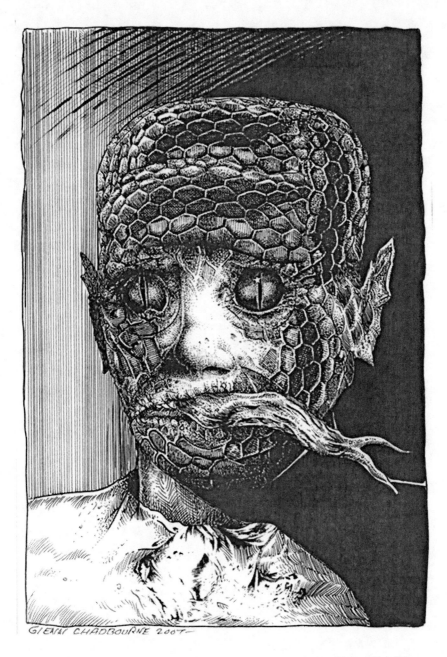

Glenn Chadbourne

HELL HATH ENLARGED HERSELF

By Michael Marshall Smith

I always assumed I was going to get old. That there would come a time when merely getting dressed left me breathless, and I would count a day without a nap as a victory; when I would go to a barber and some young girl would lift the remaining grey stragglers on my pate and look dubious if I asked her for anything more than a trim. I would have tried to be charming, and she might have thought to herself how game the old bird was, while cutting off rather less than I'd asked. I thought all that was going to come, some day, and in a perverse sort of way had even looked forward to it. A diminuendo, a slowing down, an ellipsis to some other place.

But now I know it will not happen, that I will remain unresolved, like a fugue which didn't work out. Or perhaps more like a voice in an unfinished symphony, because I won't be the only one.

I regret that. I'm going to miss having been old.

I left the facility at 6:30 yesterday evening, on the dot, as had been my practice. I took care to do everything as I always had, collating my notes, tidying my desk, and leaving upon it a list of things to do the next day. I hung my white coat on the back of my office door as usual, and said goodbye to Johnny on the gate with a wink. For six months we have been engaged in a game which involves making some joint statement on the weather every time I enter or leave the facility, without either of us making recourse to speech. Yesterday Johnny raised his eyebrows at the dark and heavy clouds, and rolled his eyes—a standard gambit. I turned one corner of my mouth down and shrugged with the opposite shoulder, a more adventurous riposte, in recognition of the fact this was the last time the game would ever be played. For a moment I wanted to do more, to say something, reach out and shake his hand; but that would have been too obvious a goodbye. Perhaps no-one would have stopped me anyway, as it has become abundantly clear that I am as powerless as everyone else—but I didn't want to take the risk.

Then I found my car amongst the diminishing number which still park there and left the compound for good.

The worst part, for me, is that I knew David Ely and understand how it all started. I was sent to work at the facility because I am partly to blame for what has happened. The original work was done together, but I was the one who had always given creed to the paranormal. David had never paid much heed to such things, not until they became an obsession. There may have been some chance remark of mine which made him open to the idea. Just having known me for so long may have been enough. If it was, then I'm sorry. There's not a great deal more I can say.

David and I met at the age of six, our fathers having taken up new positions at the same college—the University of Florida, in Gainesville. My father was in the Geography Faculty, his in Sociology, but at that time—the late Eighties—the departments were drawing closer together and the two men became friends. Our families mingled closely, in countless back-yard barbecues and shared holidays on the coast, and David and I grew up more like brothers than friends. We read the same clever books and hacked the same stupid computers, and even ended up losing our virginity on the same evening. One spring when we were both sixteen, I borrowed my mother's car and the two of us loaded it up with books and a laptop and headed off to Sarasota in search of sun and beer. We found both, in quantity, and also two young English girls on holiday. We spent a week in courting spirals of increasing tightness, playing pool and talking fizzy nonsense over cheap and exotic pizzas, and on the last night two couples walked up the beach in different directions.

Her name was Karen, and for a while I thought I was in love. I wrote a letter to her twice a week, and to this day she's probably received more mail from me than everyone else put together. Each morning I went running down to the mailbox, and ten years later the sight of an English postage stamp could still bring a faint rush of blood to my ears. But we were too far apart and too young. Maybe she had to wait a day too long for a letter once, or perhaps it was me who without realising it came back empty-handed from the mailbox one too many times. Either way the letters started to slacken in frequency after six months, and then, without either of us ever saying anything, they simply stopped altogether.

A little while later I was with David in a bar, and, in between shots, he looked up at me.

'You ever hear from Karen anymore?' he asked.

I shook my head, only at that moment realising that it had finally died. 'Not in a while.'

He nodded, and then took his shot, and missed, and as I lined up for the black I realised that he'd probably been through a similar thing. For the first time in our lives we'd lost something. It didn't break our hearts. It had only lasted a week, after all, and we were old enough to begin to realise that the world was full of girls, and that if we didn't hurry we'd hardly have got through any of them before it was time to get married.

But does anyone ever replace that first person? That first kiss, first fierce hug, hidden in sand dunes and darkness? Sometimes, I guess. I kept the letters from Karen for twenty years. Never read them, just kept them. Last week I threw them all away.

What I'm saying is this. I knew David for a long, long time, and I understood what we were trying to do. He was just trying salve his own pain, and I was trying to help him.

What happened wasn't our fault.

I spent the evening driving slowly down 75, letting the freeway take me down towards the Gulf coast of the panhandle. There were a few patches of rain, but for the most part the clouds just scudded overhead, running to some other place. I didn't see many other cars. Either people have given up fleeing, or all those capable of it have already fled. I got off just after Jocca and headed down minor roads, trying to cut round Tampa and St Petersburg. I managed it, but it wasn't easy, and I ended up getting lost more than a few times. I would have brought a map, but I'd thought I could remember the way. I couldn't. It had been too long.

We'd heard on the radio in the afternoon that things weren't going so hot around Tampa. It was the last thing we heard, just before the signal cut out. The six of us remaining in the facility just sat around for a while, as if we believed the radio would come back on again real soon now. When it didn't we got up one by one and drifted back to work.

As I passed the city I could see it burning in the distance, and I was glad I had taken the back way, no matter how long it took. If you've seen what it's like when a large number of people go together, you'll understand what I mean.

Eventually I found 301 and headed down it towards 41, towards the old Coast Road.

Summer of 2005. For David and me it was time to make a decision. There was no question but that we would go to college—both our families were book-bashers from way back. The money was already in place, some from our parents but most from holiday jobs we'd played at. The question was what we were going to study.

I thought long and hard, but in the end still couldn't come to a decision. I postponed for a year and decided to take off round the world. My parents shrugged, said 'Okay, keep in touch, try not to get killed, and stop by your Aunt Kate's in Sydney.' They were that kind of people. I remember my sister bringing a friend of hers back to the house one time; the girl called herself Yax and her hair had been carefully dyed and sculpted to resemble an orange explosion. My mother just asked her where she had it done and kept looking at it in a thoughtful way. I guess my dad must have talked her out of it.

David went for computers. Systems design. He got a place at Jacksonville's new center for Advanced Computing, which was a coup but no real surprise. David was always a hell of a bright guy. That was part of his problem.

It was strange saying goodbye to each other after so many years in each other's pockets, but I suppose we knew it was going to happen sooner or later. The plan was that he'd come out and hook up with me for a couple of months during the year. It didn't happen, for the reason that pacts between old friends usually get forgotten.

Someone else entered the picture.

I did my grand tour. I saw Europe, started to head through the

Middle East and then thought better of it and flew down to Australia instead. I stopped by and saw Aunt Kate, which earned me big brownie points back home and wasn't in any way arduous. She and her family were a lot of fun, and there was a long drunken evening when she seemed to be taking messages from beyond, which was kind of interesting. My mother's side of the family was always reputed to have a touch of the medium about them, and Aunt Kate certainly did. There was an even more entertaining evening when my cousin Jenny and I probably overstepped the bounds of conventional morality in the back seat of her jeep. After Australia I hacked up through the Far East for a while until time and money ran out, and then I went home.

I came back with a major tan, an empty wallet, and still no real idea of what I was going to do with my life. With a couple months to go before I had to make a decision, I decided to go visit David. I hopped on a bus and made my way up to Jacksonville on a day which was warm and full of promise. Anything could happen, I believed, and everything was there for the taking. Adolescent naïveté perhaps, but I was an adolescent. How was I supposed to know otherwise? I'd led a pretty charmed life up until then, and I didn't see any reason why it shouldn't continue. I sat in the bus and gazed out the window, watching the world and wishing it the very best. It was a good day, and I'm glad it was. Because though I didn't know it then, the new history of the world probably started at the end of it.

I got there late afternoon and asked around for David. Eventually someone pointed me in the right direction, to a house just off campus. I found the building and tramped up the stairs, wondering whether I shouldn't maybe have called ahead.

Eventually I found his door. I knocked, and after a few moments some man I didn't recognize opened it. It took me a couple of long seconds to work out it was David. He'd grown a beard. I decided not to hold it against him just yet, and we hugged like, well, like what we were. Two best friends, seeing each other after what suddenly seemed like far too long.

'*Major* bonding,' drawled a female voice. A head slipped into view from round the door, with wild brown hair and big green eyes. That was the first time I saw Rebecca.

Four hours later we were in a bar somewhere. I'd met Rebecca properly and realised she was special. In fact, it's probably a good thing that they'd met six months before and that she was so evidently in love with David. Had we met her at the same time, she could have been the first thing we'd ever fallen out over. She was beautiful, in a strange and quirky way that always made me think of forests; and she was clever, in that particularly appealing fashion which meant she wasn't always trying to prove it and was happy for other people to be right some of the time. She moved like a cat on a sleepy afternoon, but her eyes were always alive—even when they couldn't co-operate with each other enough to allow her to accurately judge the distance to her glass. She was my best friend's girl, she was a good one, and I was very happy for him.

Rebecca was at the School of Medical Science. Nanotech was just coming off big around then, and it looked like she was going to catch the wave and go with it. In fact, when the two of them talked about their work, it made me wish I hadn't taken the year off. Things were happening for them. They had a direction. All I had was goodwill towards the world and the belief that it loved me too. For the first time I had that terrible sensation that life is leaving you behind and you'll never catch up again; that if you don't match your speed to the train and jump on you'll be forever left standing in the station.

At one AM we were still going strong. David lurched in the general direction of the bar to get us some more beer, navigating the treacherously level floor like a man using stilts for the first time.

'Why don't you come here?' Rebecca said suddenly. I turned to her, and she shrugged. 'David misses you, I don't think you're too much of an asshole, and what else are you going to do?'

I looked down at the table for a moment, thinking it over. Immediately it sounded like a good idea. But on the other hand, what would I do? And could I handle being a third wheel, instead of half a bicycle? I asked the first question first.

'We've got plans,' Rebecca replied. 'Stuff we want to do. You could come in with us. I know David would want you to. He always says you're the cleverest guy he's ever met.'

I glanced across at David, who was conversing affably with the barman. We'd decided that to save energy we should start buying drinks two at a time, and David appeared to be explaining this plan. As I watched, the barman laughed. David was like that. He could get on with absolutely anyone.

'And you're sure I'm not too much of an asshole?'

Deadpan: 'Nothing that I won't be able to kick out of you.'

And that's how I ended up applying for, and getting, a place on Jacksonville's nanotech program. When David got back to the table I wondered aloud whether I should come up to college, and his reaction was big enough to seal the decision there and then. It was him who suggested I go nanotech, and him who explained their plan.

For years people had been trying to crack the nanotech nut. Building tiny biological 'machines', some of them little bigger than large molecules, designed to be introduced into the human body to perform some function or other: promoting the secretion of certain hormones; eroding calcium build-ups in arteries; destroying cells which looked like they were going cancerous. In the way that these things have, it had taken a long time before the first proper results started coming through—but in the last three years it had really been gathering pace. When David had met Rebecca, a couple of weeks into the first semester, they'd talked about their two subjects, and David had immediately realised that sooner or later there would be a second wave, and that they could be the first to understand it.

Lots of independent little machines was one thing. How about lots of little machines which worked together? All designed for particular functions, but co-ordinated by a neural relationship with each other, possessed of a power and intelligence that was greater than the sum of its parts. Imagine what *that* could do.

When I heard the idea I whistled. I tried to, anyway. My lips had gone all rubbery from too much beer, and instead the sound came out as a sort of parping noise. But they understood what I meant.

'And no-one else is working on this?'

'Oh, probably,' David smirked, and I had to smile. We'd always both nurtured plans for world domination. 'But with the three of us together, no-one else stands a chance.'

And so it was decided, and ratified, and discussed, over just about all the beer the bar had left. At the end of the evening we crawled back to David and Rebecca's room on our hands and knees, and I passed out on the sofa. The next day, trembling under the weight of a hangover which passed all understanding, I found a place to stay in town and went to talk someone in the faculty of Medical Science. By the end of the week it was confirmed.

On the day I was officially enrolled in the next year's intake the three of us went out to dinner. We went to a nice restaurant, and we ate and drank, and then at the end of the meal we placed our hands on top of each other's in the center of the table. David's went down first, then Rebecca's, and then mine on top. With our other hands we raised our glasses.

'To us,' I said. It wasn't very original, I know, but it's what I meant. I bet all three of us wished there was a photographer present to immortalise the moment. We drank, and then the three of us clasped each other's hands until our knuckles were white.

Ten years later Rebecca was dead.

The coast road was deserted, as I had expected. The one thing nobody is doing these days is heading off down to the beach to hang out and play volleyball. I passed a few vehicles abandoned by the side of the road but took care not to drive too close. Often people will hide inside or behind and then leap out at anyone who passes, regardless of whether that person is in a moving vehicle or not.

I kept my eyes on the sea for the most part, concentrating on what was the same, rather than what was different. The ocean looked exactly as it always had, though I suppose usually there would have been ships to see, out on the horizon. There probably still are a few, floating aimlessly wherever the tide takes them, their decks echoing and empty. But I didn't see any.

When I reached Sarasota I slowed still further, driving out onto Lido Key until I pulled to a halt in the center of St Armand's Circle. It's not an especially big place, but it has a certain class. Though the stores around the Circle were more than full enough of the usual kind of junk the restaurants were good, and some of the old, small hotels were attractive, in a dated kind of way. Not as flashy as the deco strips on Old Miami Beach, but pleasant enough.

Last night the Circle was littered with burnt-out cars, and the up-scale pizzeria where we used to eat was still smoldering, the embers glowing in the fading light.

We worked through our degrees and out into post-graduate years. At first I had a lot to catch up on. Sometimes Rebecca snuck me into classes, but most of the time I just pored over their notes and books, and we talked long into the night. Catching up wasn't so hard, but keeping up with both of them was a struggle. I never understood the nanotech side as well as Rebecca, or the computing as deeply as

David, but that was probably an advantage. I stood between the two of them, and it was in my mind where the two disciplines most equally met. Without me there, it's probable none of it would ever had come to fruition. So maybe if you come right down to it and it's anyone's fault, it's mine.

David's goal was designing a system which would take the input and imperatives of a number of small component parts and synthesize them into a greater whole—catering to the fact that the concerns of biological organisms are seldom clear cut. The fuzzy logic wasn't difficult—God knows we were familiar enough with it, most noticeably in our ability to reason that we needed another beer when we couldn't even remember where the fridge was. More difficult was designing and implementing the means by which the different machines, or 'beckies', as we elected to call them, interfaced with each other.

Rebecca concentrated on the physical side of the problem, synthesizing beckies with intelligence coded into artificial DNA in a manner which enabled the 'brain' of each type to link up with and transfer information to the others. And remember, when I say 'machines' I'm not talking about large metal objects which sit in the corner of the room making unattractive noises and drinking a lot of oil. I'm talking about strings of molecules hardwired together, invisible to the naked eye.

I helped them both with their specific areas and did most of the development work in the middle, designing the overall system. It was me who came up with the first product to aim for, 'ImmunityWorks'.

The problem of diagnosing malfunction in the human body has always been the number of variables, many of which are difficult to monitor effectively from the outside. If someone sneezes, they could just have a cold. On the other hand, they could have flu, or the bubonic plague—or some dust up their nose. Unless you can test all the relevant parameters, you're not going to know what the real problem is—or the best way of treating it. We were aiming for an integrated set of beckies which could examine all of the pertinent conditions, share their findings, and determine the best way of tackling the problem—all at the molecular level, without human intervention of any kind. The system had to be robust—to withstand interaction with the body's own immune system—and intelligent. We weren't intending to just tackle things which made you sneeze, either: we were never knowingly under-ambitious. Even for ImmunityWorks 1.0 we were aiming for a system which could cope with a wide range of viruses, bacteria and general senescence: a first aid kit which lived in the body, anticipating problems and solving them before they got started. A kind of guardian angel, which would co-exist with the human system and protect it from harm.

We were right on the edge of knowledge, and we knew it. The roots of disease in the human body still weren't properly understood, never mind the best ways to deal with them. An individual trying to do what we were doing would have needed about 300 years and a research grant bigger than God's. But we weren't just one person. We weren't even just three. Like the system we were trying to design, we were a perfect symbiosis, three minds whose joint product was incomparably greater than the sum of its parts. Also, we worked like maniacs. After we'd received our Doctorates we rented an old house together away from the campus and turned the top floor into a private lab. Obviously there were arguments for putting it in the basement—historical 'mad scientist' precedents, for example—but the top floor had a better view, and as that's where we spent most of our time, that kind of thing was an issue. We got up in the mornings, did enough to maintain our tenure at the University, and worked on our own project in secret.

David and Rebecca had each other. I had an intermittent string of short liaisons with fellow lecturers, students or waitresses, each of which felt I was being unfaithful to something or to someone. It wasn't Rebecca I was thinking of. God knows she was beautiful enough, and lovely enough, to pine after, but I didn't. Lusting after Rebecca would have felt like one of our beckies deciding only to work with some, not all, of the others in its system. The whole system would have imploded.

Unfaithful to us, I suppose is what I felt. To the three of us.

It took us four years to fully appreciate what we were getting into and to establish just how much work was involved. The years after that were a process of slow, grinding progress. David and I modeled an artificial body on the computer, creating an environment in which we could test virtual versions of the beckies Rebecca and I were busy trying to synthesize. Occasionally we'd enlist the assistance of someone from the medical faculty, when we needed more of an insight into a particular disease; but this was always done covertly and without letting on what we were doing. This was our project, and we weren't going to share it with anyone.

By July of 2016 the software side of ImmunityWorks was in beta and holding up well. We'd created code equivalents of all of the major viruses and bacteria, and built creeping failures into the code of the virtual body itself—to represent the random processes of physical malfunction. An initial set of 137 different virtual beckies was doing a sterling job of keeping an eye out for problems, then charging in and sorting them out whenever they occurred.

The physical side was proceeding a little more slowly. Creating miniature biomachines is a difficult process, and when they didn't do what they were supposed to you couldn't exactly lift up the hood and poke around inside. The key problem, and the one which took the most time to solve, was that of imparting a sufficient degree of 'consciousness' to the system as a whole—the aptitude for the component parts to work together, exchanging information and determining the most profitable course of action in any given circumstance. We probably built in a lot more intelligence than was necessary, in fact I know we did; but it was simpler than trying to hone down the necessary conditions right away. We could always streamline in ImmunityWorks 1.1, we felt, when the system had proved itself and we had patents nobody could crack. We also gave the beckies the ability to perform simple manipulations of the matter around them. It was an essential part of their role that they be able to take action on affected tissue once they'd determined what the problem was. Otherwise it would only have been a diagnostic tool, and we were aiming higher than that.

By October we were closing in and were ready to run a test on a monkey which we'd infected with a copy of the Marburg strain of the Ebola virus. We'd pumped a whole lot of other shit into it as well, but it was the filovirus we were most interested in. If ImmunityWorks would handle that, we reckoned, we were really getting somewhere.

Yes, *of course* it was a stupid thing to do. We had a monkey jacked full of one of the most communicable virus known to mankind *in our house*. The lab was heavily secured by then, but it was still an insane risk. In retrospect I realise that we were so caught up in what we were doing, in our own joint mind, that normal considerations had ceased to really register. We didn't even need to do the Ebola test. That's the really tragic thing. It was unnecessary. It was pure arrogance, and also wildly illegal. We could have just tested ImmunityWorks on plain vanilla viruses or artificially-induced cancers. If it had worked we could have contacted the media and owned our own Caribbean islands within two years.

But no. We had to go the whole way.

The monkey sat in its cage, looking really very ill, with any number of sensors and electrodes taped and wired on and into its skull and body. Drips connected to bioanalysers gave a second-by-second readout of the muck that was floating around in the poor animal's bloodstream. About two hours before the animal was due to start throwing clots, David threw the switch which would inject a solution of ImmunityWorks 0.9b7 into its body.

The time was 16:23, October 14th, 2016, and for the next 24 hours we watched.

At first the monkey continued to get worse. Arteries started clotting, and the heartbeat grew ragged and fitful. The artificial cancer which we'd induced in the animal's pancreas also appeared to be holding strong. We sat, and smoked, and drank coffee, our hearts sinking. Maybe, we began to think, we weren't so damned clever after all.

Then... that moment.

Even now, as I sit here in an abandoned hotel and listen for sounds of movement outside, I can remember the moment when the read-outs started to turn around.

The clots started to break up. The cancerous cells started to lose vitality. The breed of simian flu which we'd acquired illicitly from the University's labs went into remission.

The monkey started getting better.

And we felt like Gods and stayed that way even when the monkey suddenly died of shock a day later. We knew by then that there was more work to do in buffering the stress effects the beckies had on the body. That wasn't important. It was just a detail. We had screeds of data from the experiment, and David's AI systems were already integrating it into the next version of the ImmunityWorks software. Becky and I made the tweaks to the beckies, stamping the revised software into the biomachines and refining the way they interfaced with the body's own immune system.

We only really came down to earth the next day, when we

realised that Rebecca had contracted Marburg.

Eventually the sight of the St Armand's dying heart palled, and I started the car up again. I drove a little further along the coast to the Lido Beach Inn, which stands just where the strip starts to diffuse into a line of beach motels. I turned into the driveway and cruised slowly up to the entrance arch, peering into the lobby. There was nobody there, or if there was, they were crouching in darkness. I let the car roll down the slope until I was inside the hotel court proper, and then pulled into a space.

I climbed out, pulled my bag from the passenger seat, and locked the car up. Then I went to the trunk and took out the bag of groceries which I'd carefully culled from the stock back at the facility. I stood by the car for a moment, hearing nothing but the sound of waves over the wall at the end, and looked around. I saw no-one, and no signs of violence, and so I headed for the stairs to go up to the second floor and towards room 211. I had an old copy of the key, 'accidentally' not returned many years ago, which was just as well. The hotel lobby was a pool of utter blackness in an evening which was already dark, and I had no intention of going anywhere near it.

For a moment, as I stood outside the door to the room, I thought I heard a girl's laughter, quiet and far away. I stood still for a moment, mouth slightly open to aid hearing, but heard nothing else.

Probably it was nothing no more than a memory.

Rebecca died two days later in an isolation chamber. She bled and crashed out in the small hours of the morning, as David and I watched through glass. My head hurt so much from crying that I thought it was going to split, and David's throat was so hoarse he could barely speak. David wanted to be in there with her, but I dissuaded him. To be frank, I punched him out until he was too groggy to fight any more. There was nothing he could do, and Rebecca didn't want him to die. She told me so through the intercom, and as that was her last comprehensible wish, I decided it would be so.

We knew enough about Marburg that we could almost feel her body cavities filling up with blood, smell the blackness as it coagulated in her. When she started bleeding from her eyes I turned away, but David watched every moment. We talked to her until there was nothing left to speak to, and then watched powerless as she drifted away, retreating into some upper and hidden hall while her body collapsed around her.

Of course we tried ImmunityWorks. Again, it nearly worked. Nearly, but not quite. When Rebecca's vital signs finally stopped, her body was as clean as a whistle. But it was still dead.

David and I stayed in the lab for three days, waiting. Neither of us contracted the disease.

Lucky old us.

We dressed in biohazard suits and sprayed the entire house with a solution of ImmunityWorks, top to bottom. Then we put the remains of Rebecca's body into a sealed casket, drove upstate, and buried it in a forest. She would have liked that. Her parents were dead, and she had no family to miss her, except us.

David left the day after the burial. We had barely spoken in the intervening period. I was sitting numbly in the kitchen on that morning, and he walked in with an overnight bag. He looked at me, nodded, and left. I didn't see him again for two years.

I stayed in the house, and once I'd determined that the lab was clean, I carried on. What else was there to do?

Working on the project by myself was like trying to play chess with two thirds of my mind burned out: the intuitive leaps which had been commonplace when the three of us were together simply didn't come, and were replaced by hours of painstaking, agonizingly slow experiment. On the other hand, I didn't kill anyone.

I worked. I ate. I drove most weekends to the forest where Rebecca lay, and became familiar with the paths and light beneath the trees which sheltered her.

I refined the beckies, eventually understanding the precise nature of the shock reaction which had killed our two subjects. I pumped more and more intelligence into the system, amping the ability of the component parts to interact with each other and make their own decisions. In a year I had the system to a point where it was faultless on common viruses, like flu. Little did the world know it, but while they were out there sniffing and coughing I had stuff sitting in ampoules which could have sorted them out for ever. But that wasn't the point. ImmunityWorks had to work on everything. That had always been our goal, and if I was going to carry on, I was going to do it our way. I was doing it for us, or for the memory of how we'd been. The two best friends I'd ever had were gone, and if the only way I could hang onto some memory of them was through working on the project, that was what I would do.

Then one day one of them reappeared.

I was in the lab, tinkering with the subset of the beckies whose job it was to synthesize new materials out of damaged body cells. The newest strain of biomachines was capable of far, far more than the originals had been. Not only could they fight the organisms and processes which caused disease in the first place, but they could then directly repair essential cells and organs within the body to ensure that it made a healthy recovery.

'Can you do anything about colds yet?' asked a voice, and I turned to see David, standing in the doorway to the lab. He'd lost about two stone in weight and looked exhausted beyond words. There were lines around his eyes that had nothing to do with laughter, and he looked older in other ways too. As I stared at him he coughed raggedly.

'Yes,' I said, struggling to keep my voice calm. David held his arm out and pulled his sleeve up. I found an ampoule of my most recent brew and spiked it with a hypo. 'Where did you pick it up?'

'England.'

'Is that where you've been?' I asked, as I slipped the needle into his arm and sent the beckies scurrying into his system.

'Some of the time.'

'Why?'

'Why not?' he shrugged, and rolled his sleeve back up.

I waited in the kitchen while he showered and changed, sipping a beer and feeling obscurely nervous. Eventually he reappeared, looking better but still very tired. I suggested going out to a bar, and we did, carefully but unspokenly avoiding those we used to go to as a threesome. Neither of us had mentioned Rebecca yet, but she was there between us in everything we said and didn't say. We walked down winter streets to a place I knew had opened recently, and it was almost as if for the first time I felt I was grieving for her properly. While David had been away, it had been as if they'd just gone away somewhere together. Now he was here, I could no longer deny that she was dead.

We didn't say much for a while, and all I learnt was that David had spent much of the last two years in Eastern Europe. I didn't push him, but simply let the conversation take its own course. It had always been David's way that he would get round to things in his own good time.

'I want to come back,' he said eventually.

'David, as far as I'm concerned you never went away.'

'That's not what I mean. I want to start the project up again, but different.'

'Different in what way?'

He told me. It took me a while to understand what he was talking about, and when I did I began to feel tired, and cold, and sad. David didn't want to refine ImmunityWorks. He had lost all interest in the body, except in the ways in which it supported the mind. He had spent his time in Europe visiting people of a certain kind, trying to establish what it was about them that made them different. Had I known, I could have recommended my Aunt Kate to him—not, I felt, that it would have made any difference. I watched him covertly as he talked, as he became more and more animated, and all I could feel was a sense of dread, a realization that for the rest of his life my friend would be lost to me.

He had come to believe that mediums, people who can communicate with the spirits of the dead, do not possess some special spiritual power, but instead a difference in the physical make-up of their brain. He believed that it was some fundamental but minor difference in the wiring of their senses which enabled them to bridge a gap between this world and the next, to hear voices which had stopped speaking, see faces which had faded away. He wanted to determine where this difference lay, pin-point it, and learn to replicate it. He wanted to develop a species of becky which anyone could take, which would rewire their soul and enable them to become a medium.

More specifically, he wanted to take it himself, and I understood why, and when I realised what he was hoping for I felt like crying for the first time in two years.

He wanted to be able to talk with Rebecca again, and I knew both that he was not insane and that there was nothing I could do, except help him.

Room 211 was as I remembered it. Nondescript. A decent-sized room in a low-range motel. I put my bags on one of the twin beds and checked out the bathroom. It was clean and the shower still gave a thin trickle of lukewarm water. I washed and changed into one of the two sets of casual clothes I had brought with me, and then I made a sandwich out of cold cuts and processed cheese, storing the remainder in the small fridge in the corner by the television. I turned the latter on briefly and got snow across the board, though I heard the occasional half-word which suggested that someone was still trying somewhere.

I propped the door to the room open with a bible and dragged a chair out onto the walkway, and then I sat and ate my food and drank a beer looking down across the court. The pool was half full, and a deck chair floated in one end of it.

Our approach was very simple. Using some savings of mine we flew to Australia, where I talked Aunt Kate into letting us take minute samples of tissue from different areas of her brain, using a battery of lymph-based beckies. We didn't tell her what the samples were for, simply that we were researching genetic traits. Jenny was now married to an accountant, it transpired, and they, Aunt Kate, and David and I sat out that night on the porch and watched the sun turn red.

The next day we flew home and went straight on to Gainesville, where I had a much harder time persuading my mother to let us do the same thing. In the end she relented, and despite claiming that the beckies had 'tickled', had to admit it hadn't hurt. She seemed fit and well, as did my father when he returned from work. I saw them once again, briefly, about two months ago. I've tried calling them since, but the line is dead.

Back at Jacksonville David and I did the same thing with our own brains, and then the real work began. If, we reasoned, there really was some kind of physiological basis to the phenomena we were searching for, then it ought to show up to varying degrees in my family line, and less so—or not at all—in David. We had no idea whether it would be down to some chemical balance, a difference in synaptic function, or a virtual 'sixth sense' which some sub-section of the brain was sensitive to—and so in the beginning we just used part of the samples to find out exactly what we'd got to work with. Of course we didn't have a wide enough sample to make any findings stand up to scrutiny: but then we weren't ever going to tell anyone what we were doing, so that hardly mattered.

We drew the blinds and stayed inside, and worked 18 hours a day. David said little and for much of the time seemed only half the person he used to be. I realised that until we succeeded in letting him talk with his love again, I would not see the friend I knew.

We both had our reasons for doing what we did.

It took a little longer than we'd hoped, but we threw a lot of computing power at it and in the end began to see results. They were complex, and far from conclusive, but appeared to suggest that all three possibilities were partly true. My Aunt showed a minute difference in synaptic function in certain areas of her brain, which I shared, but not the fractional chemical imbalances which were present in both my mother and me. On the other hand, there was evidence of a loose meta-structure of apparently unrelated areas of her brain which was only present in trace degrees in my mother and not at all in me. We took these results and correlated them against the findings from the samples of David's brain and finally came to a tentative conclusion.

The ability, if it truly was related to physiological morphology, seemed most directly related to an apparently insignificant variation in general synaptic function which created an almost intangible additional structure within certain areas of the brain.

Not, perhaps, one of the most memorable slogans of scientific discovery, but that night David and I went out and got more drunk than we had in five years. We clasped hands on the table once more, and this time we believed that the hand that should have been between ours was nearly within reach. The next day we split into two overlapping teams, dividing our time and minds as always between the software and the beckies. The beckies needed redesigning to cope with the new environment, and the software required yet another quantum leap to deal with the complexity of the tasks of synaptic manipulation. As we worked we joked that if the beckies got much more intelligent we'd have to give them the vote. It seemed funny back then.

September 12th, 2019 ought to have a significant place in the history of science, despite everything that happened afterwards. It was the day on which we tested MindWorks 1.0, a combination of computer and corporeal which was probably more subtle than anything man has ever produced. David insisted on being the first subject, despite the fact that he had another cold, and in the early afternoon of that day I injected him with a tiny dose of the beckies. Then, in a flash of solidarity, I injected myself. Together till the end, we said.

We sat there for five minutes and then got on with some work. We knew that the effects, if there were any, wouldn't be immediate. To be absolutely honest, we weren't expecting much at all from the first batch. As everyone knows, anything with the version number '1' will have teething problems, and if it has a '.0' after it then it's going to crash and burn. We sat and tinkered with the plans for a 1.1 version, which was only different in that some of the algorithms were more elegant, but couldn't seem to concentrate. Excitement, we assumed.

Then late afternoon David staggered, and dropped a flask of the solution he was working on. It was full of MindWorks, but that didn't matter—we had a whole vat of it in storage. I made David sit down and ran a series of tests on him. Physically he was okay, and protested that he felt fine. We shrugged and went back to work. I printed out ten copies of the code and becky specifications, and posted them to ten different places around the world. Of course the computers already laid automated and encrypted email backups all over the place, but old habits die hard. If this worked it was going to be ours, and no-one else was taking credit for it. Such considerations were actually less important to us by then, because there was only one thing we wanted from the experiment—but old habits die hard. Ten minutes later I had a dizzy spell myself, but apart from that nothing seemed to be happening at all.

We only realised that we might have succeeded when I woke to hear David screaming in the night.

I ran into his room and found him crouched up against the wall, eyes wide, teeth chattering uncontrollably. He was staring at the opposite corner of the room. He didn't seem to be able to hear anything I said to him. As I stood there numbly, wondering what to do, I heard a voice from behind me—a voice I half-thought I recognised. I turned, but there was no-one there. Suddenly David looked at me, his eyes wide and terrified.

'Fuck,' he said. 'I think it's working.'

We spent the rest of the night in the kitchen, sitting round the table and drinking coffee in harsh light. David didn't seem to be able to remember exactly what it was he'd seen, and I couldn't recapture the sound of the voice I'd heard, or what it might have said. Clearly we'd achieved something, but it wasn't clear what it might be. When nothing further happened by daybreak, we decided to get out of the house for a while. We were both too keyed up to sit around any longer or try to work, but felt we should stay together. Something was happening, we knew: we could both feel it. We walked around campus for the morning, had lunch in the cafeteria, then spent the afternoon downtown. The streets seemed a little crowded, but nothing else weird happened.

In the evening we went out. We had been invited to a dinner party at the house of a couple on the medical staff and thought we might as well attend. David and I were a little distracted at first, but once everyone had enough wine inside them we started to have a good time. The hosts got out their stock of dope, doubtless supplied by an accommodating member of the student body, and by midnight we were all a little high, comfortably sprawled around the living room.

And of course, eventually, David started talking about the work we'd been doing. At first people just laughed, and that made me realise belatedly just how far outside the scope of normal scientific endeavor we had moved. It also made me determined that we should be taken seriously, and so I started to back David up. It was stupid, and we should never have mentioned it. It was one of the people at that party who eventually gave our names to the police.

'So prove it,' this man said at one stage. 'Hey, is there a Ouija board in the house?'

The general laughter which greeted this sally was enough to tip the balance. David rose unsteadily to his feet and stood in the center of the room. He sneezed twice, to general amusement, but then his head seemed to clear. Though he was swaying gently, the seriousness of his face was enough to quiet most people, although there was a certain amount of giggling. He looked gaunt, and tired, and everybody stopped talking, and the room went very quiet as they watched him.

'Hello?' he said quietly. He didn't use a name, for obvious reasons, but I knew who he was asking for. 'Are you there?'

'And if so, did you bring any grass?' the hostess added, getting a big laugh. I shook my head, partly at how foolish we were seeming, partly because there seemed to be a faint glow in one corner of the room, as if some of the receptors in my eyes were firing strangely. I made a note to check the beckies when we got back, to make sure none of them could have had an effect on the optic nerve.

I was about to say something, to help David out of an embarrassing position, when he suddenly turned to the hostess.

'Jackie, how many people did you invite tonight?'

'Eight,' she said. 'We always have eight. We've only got eight complete sets of table ware.'

David looked at me. 'How many people do you see?' he asked.

I looked round the room, counting.

'Eleven,' I said.

One of the guests laughed nervously. I counted them again. There were eleven people in the room. In addition to the eight of us who were slouched over the settees and floor, three people stood round the walls.

A tall man, with long and not especially clean brown hair. A woman in her forties, with blank eyes. A young girl, maybe eight years old.

Mouth hanging open, I stood up to join David. We looked from each of the extra figures to the other. They looked entirely real, as if they'd been there all along.

They stared back at us, silently.

'Come on guys,' the host said, nervously. 'Okay, great gag—you had us fooled for a moment there. Now let's have another smoke.'

David ignored him, turning to the man with the long hair.

'What's your name?' he asked him. There was a long pause, as if the man was having difficulty remembering. When he spoke, his voice sounded dry and cold.

'Nat,' he said. 'Nat Simon.'

'David,' I said. 'Be careful.'

David ignored me, and turned back to face the real guests. 'Does the name "Nat Simon" mean anything to anyone here?' he asked.

For a moment I thought it hadn't, and then we noticed the hostess. The smile had slipped from her face and her skin had gone white, and she was staring at David. With a sudden, ragged beat of my heart I knew we had succeeded.

'Who was he?' I asked quickly. I wish I hadn't. In a room that was now utterly silent she told us.

Nat Simon had been a friend of one of her uncles. One summer, when she was nine years old, he had raped her just about every day of the two weeks she'd spent on vacation with her relatives. He was killed in a car accident when she was fourteen, and since then she'd thought she'd been free.

'Tell Jackie I've come back to see her,' Nat said proudly, 'And I'm all fired up and ready to go.' He had taken his penis out of his trousers and was stroking it towards erection.

'Go away,' I said. 'Fuck off back where you came from.'

Nat just smiled. 'Ain't ever been anywhere else,' he said. 'Like to stay as close to little Jackie as I can.'

David quickly asked the other two figures who they were. I tried to stop him, but the other guests encouraged him, at least until they heard the answers. Then the party ended abruptly. Voyeurism becomes a lot less amusing when it's you that people are staring at.

The blank-eyed woman was the first wife of the man who had joked about Ouija boards. After discovering his affair with one of his students she had committed suicide in their living room. He'd told everyone she'd suffered from depression and that she drank in secret.

The little girl was the host's sister. She died in childhood, hit by a car while running across the road as part of a dare devised by her brother.

By the time David and I ran out of the house, two of the other guests had already started being able to see for themselves, and the number of people at the party had risen to fifteen.

After four beers my mind was a little fuzzy, and for a while I was almost able to forget. Then I heard a soft splashing sound from below and looked to see a young boy climbing out of the stagnant water in the pool. He didn't look up but just walked over the flagstones to the gate and then padded out through the entrance to the motel. I could still hear the soft sound of his wet feet long after he'd disappeared into the darkness. The brother who'd held his head under a moment too long; the father who'd been too busy watching someone else's wife putting lotion on her thighs; or the mother who'd fallen asleep. Someone would be having a visitor tonight.

When we got back to the house after the party, and tried to get back into the lab, we found that we couldn't open the door. The lock had fused. Something had attacked the metal of the tumblers, turning the mechanism into a solid lump of metal. We stared at each other, by now feeling very sober, and then turned to look through the glass upper portion of the door. Everything inside looked the way it always had, but I now believe that even early, before we knew what was happening, everything had already been set in motion. The beckies work in strange and invisible ways.

David got the axe from the garage, and we broke through the door to the laboratory. We found the vat of MindWorks empty. A small hole had appeared in the bottom of the glass, and there was a faint trail where the contents had flowed across the floor, making small holes at several points. It had doubled back on itself, and in a couple of places it had also flowed against gravity. It ended in a larger hole which, it transpired, dripped through into a pipe. A pipe which went out back into the municipal water system.

The first reports were on CNN at seven o'clock the next morning. Eight murders in downtown Jacksonville, and three on the University campus. David's cold. Reports of people suddenly going crazy, screaming at people who weren't there, running in terror from voices in their head and acting on impulses that they claimed weren't theirs. By lunchtime the problem wasn't just confined to people we might have come into contact with: it had started to spread on its own.

I don't know why it happened like this. Maybe we just made a mistake somewhere. Perhaps it was something as small and simple as a chiral isomer, some chemical which the beckies created in a mirror image of the way it should be. That's what happened with Thalidomide, and that's what we created. A Thalidomide of the soul.

Or maybe there was no mistake. Perhaps that's just the way it is. Maybe the only spirits who stick around are the ones you don't want to see. The ones who can turn people into psychotics who riot, murder, or end their lives, through the hatred or guilt they bring with them. These people have always been here, all the time, staying close to the people who remember them. Only now they are no longer invisible. Or silent.

A day later there were reports in European cities, at first just the ones where I'd sent my letters, then spreading rapidly across the entire land mass. By the time my letters reached their recipients, the beckies I'd breathed over them had multiplied a thousandfold, breaking the paper down and reconstituting the molecules to create more of themselves. They were so clever, our children, and they shared the ambitions of their creators. If they'd needed to, they could probably have formed themselves into new letters, and lay around until someone posted them all over the world. But they didn't, because coughing, or sneezing, or just breathing is enough to spread the infection. By the following week a state of emergency was in force in every country in the world.

A mob killed David before the police got to him. He never got to see Rebecca. I don't know why. She just didn't come. I was placed under house arrest and then taken to the facility to help with the feverish attempts to come up with a cure. There is none, and there never will be. The beckies are too smart, too aggressive, and too powerful. They just take any antidote, break it down, and use it to make more of themselves.

They don't need the vote. They're already in control.

The moon is out over the ocean, casting glints over the tides as they rustle back and forth with a sound like someone slowly running their finger across a piece of paper. A little while ago I heard a siren in the far distance. Apart from that all is quiet.

I think it's unlikely I shall riot, or go on a killing spree. In the end, I will simply go.

The times when Karen comes to see me are bad. She didn't stop writing to me because she lost interest, it turns out. She stopped writing because she had been pregnant by me and didn't want me involved and died through some nightmare of childbirth without ever telling her mother my name. I hadn't brought any contraception. I think we both figured life would let you get away with things like that. When David and I talked about Karen over that game of pool she was already dead. She will come again tonight, as she always does, and maybe tonight will be the night when I decide I cannot bear it any longer. Perhaps seeing her here, at the motel where David and I stayed that summer, will be enough to make me do what I have to do.

If it isn't her who gives me the strength, then someone else will, because I've started seeing other people now too. It's quite surprising how many—or maybe it isn't, when you consider that all of this is partly my fault. So many people have died, and will die, all of them with something to say to me. Every night there are more, as the world slowly winds down. There are two of them here now, standing in the court and looking up at me. Perhaps in the end I shall be the last one alive, surrounded by silent figures in ranks that reach out to the horizon.

Or maybe, as I hope, some night David and Rebecca will come for me, and I will go with them.

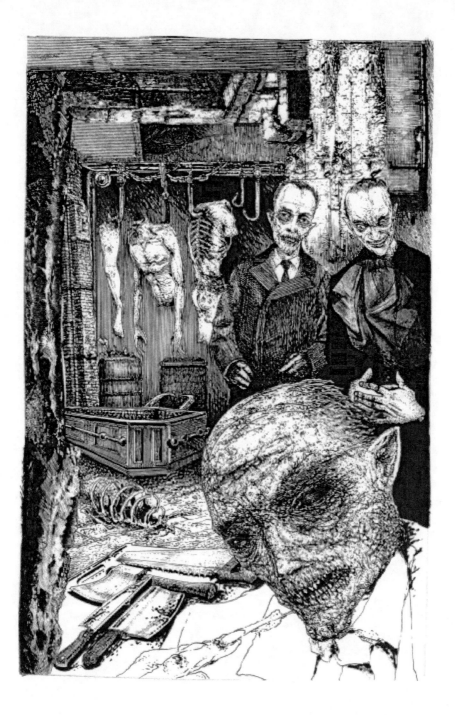

Glenn Chadbourne

FIGURES IN RAIN

By Chet Williamson

There were only two other people waiting in the reception area of the King's Arms Tavern when we arrived. It was 9:30, the last seating time, and when Caitlin and I entered the dimly lit room we spent several seconds folding the umbrella and shaking the droplets from our coats. It was raining furiously, drenching the stones of Williamsburg, plunging the already dark streets into even greater darkness.

The weather did little to improve either our mood or the looks of the town. Colonial Williamsburg was far less picturesque in late February than in the seasons in which we had previously visited it. Caitlin and I had both come here as children, dutifully brought by our parents, and we had done the same with Robert, making the Williamsburg/Jamestown/Monticello circuit the summer when he was between sixth and seventh grades. Too old to wear a tricorn and carry a wooden gun, and too young to appreciate the painstaking care with which the colonial community had been recreated, he found little enjoyment in the two days we spent there. Caitlin and I, however, had been taken with the totality of the experience—the crafts, the buildings, the food, and the people who recreated so vividly what it must have been like to live in English America.

We had found ourselves guiltily wishing that we had been there alone, and had returned to the place one long Easter weekend when Robert was in college. We found that Williamsburg in spring was even more exquisite than in summer. The gardens were a brilliantly hued profusion of lilies, daffodils, and tulips, and the trees were either blossoming or newly greening. It was a glorious time to be there, and there was the further benefit that Caitlin and I were rediscovering, after eighteen years of parenthood, what it was like to be lovers once more. With no duties to Robert beyond the financial and distantly (in space, at least) supportive, we had more time for each other. The empty nest proved, at first, to be as great a blessing for us as independence proved to be for Robert.

Then other concerns replaced those we had had for our son. A series of financial setbacks in my business required my spending more time at my office, and a restructuring of the staff which Caitlin oversaw meant that she brought home far more work than before. We were both at least a decade away from retirement and every day were being made more aware of the necessity of storing up nuts against the long winter. A series of annoying if non-life threatening health problems did little to ease our commercial burdens, and the deaths of my mother and father further increased my depression. Dad went only a few months after my mother died of cancer. They loved each other deeply, and each had depended on the other. I think he willed himself into death when she died, and when it came he welcomed it.

I honestly believe that we went to Williamsburg in late February in desperation. We had grown apart, but not from choice. Both Caitlin and I knew that at this time in our lives more than any other we needed the other's strength and love to help buttress ourselves against the unpredictability of the world and of our own flesh.

Let's get away, we said to each other. We would leave everything behind, go somewhere we loved, and just be together. Our batteries were dead, and maybe several days alone together would give us a jump start. Maybe the world could become remarkable again.

Even before we arrived, it felt wrong. We had overslept and had to pack in haste, not even taking the time to remove from the trunk several boxes of my parents' personal things that I had finally been clearing out of their house. The sky was overcast, and it started raining by mid-afternoon when we crossed the Virginia border.

We arrived at the Williamsburg Visitors' Center just before it closed, and bought multi-day passes, then made reservations at Christiana Campbell's Tavern the following evening and King's

Arms Tavern the next. We had seafood that evening at a restaurant in Merchants' Square, a collection of shops outside the colonial area, and then walked down Duke of Gloucester Street in a light, cold rain that grew heavier as we went. We gave it up, turned around, and went back to the car and drove to our motel. Although we were both tired from the drive, we felt duty-bound to make love. It was done without much passion, as are most deeds inspired by duty.

There followed two more days of intermittent cold rain, during which we spent most of our time indoors. Exteriors offered little: the gardens were brown and yellow, and the trees glistened only with the rainwater on their bark. The streets were dotted with puddles, and the vast, grassy areas were sodden.

The rain and the gray season brought out few tourists, and those who braved the elements seemed more sternly determined to see what they had to see than enchanted with the near-perfect recreation of the past. The costumed re-enactors at each occupied site maintained their good spirits, and energetically tried to brighten the fatally dull day by their interaction with the sparse crowds, but succeeded only fitfully.

Caitlin and I found none of the magic we had sought and so needed. The days were flat and gray. We took little joy in them or in each other's company. The sole pleasure of the first day was the meal at Campbell's Tavern. Though there were a few empty tables, there was still a sense of warmth and conviviality in the candlelit rooms. We were seated away from any windows, so the weather was of no concern, and the food was hearty and abundant.

Still, as soon as we stepped outside into the rain, the gray mood returned. Back at the motel, Caitlin soaked in the tub with a novel, while I, in spite of my promise to myself to do no work, cheated slightly. I brought up a small box of my parents' photo albums and scrapbooks from the trunk of the car, planning to see if there was anything my surviving aunts and uncles might want as a keepsake.

Caitlin gave me a *you promised* look when she came out of the bathroom and saw what I was doing. I closed the books and took a shower. She was sleeping when I climbed into bed.

The second and last full day held more of the same. We spent several hours in the well-lit Rockefeller Folk Art Center, but the proliferation of flat, two-dimensional primitive work did little to assuage our hunger for the deep and rich and unexpected. The shock that our systems required was not to be found there.

It was highly unlikely that we would experience it that night either. The King's Arms Tavern was slightly more formal—and more expensive—than Christiana Campbell's. We checked our wet coats, gave our name to the hostess in colonial dress, and sat down to wait on a bench against the wall. Fiddle and fife music sounded from somewhere within.

I smiled at the young man sitting next to me, and he smiled back. Unlike most tourists, he was wearing a suit, dress shirt and necktie, and his black wingtips were polished to a high gloss. His hair was meticulously combed in the retro style that so many his age are adopting. He was one of those people who look instantly familiar, like someone you might have seen on television in a supporting role for years but to whom you had never attached a name.

"Lousy night," he said without a trace of true complaint. He might rather have been observing that the evening was beautifully clear and balmy.

I agreed, and Caitlin smiled empathetically. "Warm and dry in here, though," I added.

"Yeah. You ever eat here?"

"Oh yes," I said. "It's very good."

"Try the peanut soup," Caitlin advised.

Both the man and his wife gave little laughs of discomfort. The wife was wearing a flowered print dress and low white shoes unseasonable both in terms of weather and style. She was slim everywhere but her abdomen, a rounded mass that told eloquently of her pregnancy.

"How long now?" asked Caitlin with a warm concern that expressed her motherly (or grandmotherly) instincts. They were, I reminded myself sourly, young enough to be our children.

"Two more months," the girl said, her voice as vaguely familiar as her husband's face. I was trying to figure out where I might have seen them before, and was about to ask where they were from, when the hostess came into the room and said that our table was ready.

"Enjoy your meal," I told them as we followed the woman, who led us to the second floor and seated us at one of the two windows in the room that faced the street. Rain still pattered against the glass, and Caitlin and I could just make out the occasional passersby hurrying through the downpour, dimly seen in the tavern's pale, evocative front porch lights, and the residual beams of candlelight that fell onto the street from the windows where we diners sat.

We had ordered our meals, and when I looked up from the Sally Lunn bread I was buttering, I saw that the young couple from downstairs had been seated at the other window table, so that the man and I were facing each other. I smiled and nodded, and he raised his hand in a shy wave.

Throughout the meal, I found myself looking out the windows, focusing not on the kaleidoscopic surface of the glass, where raindrops struck, exploded, and made uneven rivulets as they ran toward the bottom sill, but past and through and around them, out onto the dark street, made darker by the extinguishing of the front lights. No one moved on the street below. The tourists who on previous visits had wandered the ancient streets until quite late, soaking in the ambience that darkness sealed upon the town, had been discouraged by the rain and cold. No one would walk the lanes of Williamsburg tonight out of pleasure.

Still I looked, as did Caitlin. Our attention meandered from the plates before us to the darkness on the other side of the panes, and was claimed at times by the coming and going of our server and the fiddler who drifted through the rooms, playing, I assumed, colonial airs.

Though I hadn't noticed the young couple being served, my attention fixed as it was on the windows, my plate, and the silence that lay between Caitlin and me, their courses kept pace with ours, despite our earlier seating. I occasionally glanced over, and a smile passed between the young man and me signaling a shared appreciation of the food. When I continued to watch, I observed his solicitousness toward his wife, whose back was to me. He spoke quietly to her, frequently took her hand, and on occasion fed her from his own fork when he thought himself unobserved.

As Caitlin and I sat together over our coffee, her expression was sadder than I had ever seen it. Her hand was resting on the tablecloth inches from mine, and I moved until our fingers were just touching. She smiled, just a small flower in the grim winter landscape of her face, and took my fingers in her own, then shook her head and said quietly, "What's wrong with us?"

What indeed? I still loved Caitlin and had no doubt that she loved me. I had no answer and only turned and looked out the window once more.

At first I thought that what I saw was a trick of the light, a car's beams whispering across the dark street, or a soft reflection in the glass from inside the room. I then realized that I was seeing a person walking across Duke of Gloucester Street, a person who was gleaming in the rain and the night as though lit from within. I pressed my face against the glass, cupping my eyes with my hands like blinders to close out the light from within the room.

The tension of my movement alarmed Caitlin, and she leaned toward me, but when I whispered, *"Look,"* she turned her gaze to the pane. From her hissed intake of breath I was sure that she too saw it.

The Raleigh Tavern, open only during the day as an historical site, was across the street, and the figure was moving past it, toward a wooden gate to the right of the building. It was a man, as far as I could tell, wearing a three-cornered hat, a shirt, a vest, and knee breeches. I could make out no colors other than various shades of gray. The figure moved slowly, but with a sense of purpose. It was as though he were walking briskly, but in slow-motion, as though time had slowed for him. We could not see his face, but he carried himself as though he felt no rain. His head was high, his arms swung loosely at his sides.

The monochromatic glow from him illuminated the descending curtain of rain, the wet surface of the street, and, as he drew near to it, the gate, which he did not pause to open but instead passed through. In another few heartbeats he was out of sight.

Caitlin and I slowly drew back from the window, and over her shoulder, behind her pale, shocked face, I saw the young man with the same expression of surprise and disbelief that Caitlin (and certainly I) wore. He was staring at his wife, and they both turned and looked out the window for another moment. Then the young man saw me, and his wife turned, as did Caitlin, both with trepidation, the two women wondering what their husbands were looking at now.

Understanding shot through us. He knew that we had seen it, and I knew the same was true of them. When I looked back at Caitlin, her pale, startled look had been replaced with a pink sheen of excitement. Her posture was erect, and her hands hovered over the table as though she would spring up at any second. Her head jerked toward the window. "Let's go," she said.

I yanked out my money clip, glanced at the bill, and tossed down enough twenties on the tray to cover it and a generous tip. Then, with a conspiratorial grin at the young man, I raced down the stairs, Caitlin behind me. We retrieved our coats, threw them on, and went outside, opening the umbrella as we scurried down the porch steps. Caitlin's arm was wrapped around mine, and I saw the puffs of her excited breath in the cold, damp air.

We paused at the edge of the street, thinking about our next step. The silence between us now was electric and communicative, not sad and awkward as it had been upstairs. We had both seen something unexpected and wanted to see more. Across the street was the Raleigh Tavern, and between it and the building on its right was the small wooden gate through which the ghost, for as such I had naturally come to think of it, had passed.

I looked at Caitlin and gave a small nod, and she nodded back. We had just stepped into the street when a voice behind us called, "Hey...," just loud enough for us to hear over the attack of rain on our umbrella. We both turned and saw the young man and his wife a few steps behind us, huddled under their own umbrella.

Caitlin and I knew what they wanted, to come with us in search of whatever we had seen. I felt disappointed, yet also relieved that we would not be alone, and voiced my sole concern. "Will you be all right?" I asked, looking at the young woman, whose pregnancy was all too obvious beneath her raincoat.

"Oh yes," she said, clutching her husband's arm as tightly as Caitlin did mine.

I gave a shrug of acquiescence, turned, and headed for the gate. It was locked but low, and we were able to climb over, giving extra help to the future mother, who got stuck halfway across. "Oh Tommy...," she said, more in frustration than pain, as her husband and I bodily lifted her over the obstacle.

I recalled that this gate led back to a bake shop that we had visited earlier that day, and also assumed that we were now trespassing on private property, off limits after hours. *We were after a ghost*, I was certain, would not prove an effective motive were we to be apprehended.

The bake shop was on our left as we walked back the path. It was dark, as were the other buildings around us. Ahead of us lay an open space, with a broader area to our right, between Duke of

Gloucester and Nicholson Streets. We stood, uncertain of how to proceed. It was so dark that I could see the young man and woman beside us as only blacker figures against the black night.

Then, to my right, I saw a glimmer of light moving slowly in the direction of the old public gaol across Nicholson Street. "Come on," I whispered, and went toward it. With a thrill I saw that it was the male figure we had seen earlier, and I glanced back at the young couple to share my delight. They were scarcely a yard behind us, and I saw a tense alertness in the way they moved.

I had no sooner turned back to look at the figure, which by now had reached Nicholson Street, than it seemed to flicker and fade, and then wink out entirely. I gave a moan of disappointment and stopped, then turned to Caitlin, who was gripping my arm so hard that I winced. Her attention, however, was not focused on the disappearance ahead, but on the one behind us.

I followed her gaze and saw too that the couple who had been only a matter of feet away from us were now gone. Though we stood in an open area twenty yards from the nearest buildings, all of which were locked and dark, the pair was nowhere in sight.

I stood there slack-jawed. It was obvious that they simply could not have run away without our being aware of it, yet they had vanished as quickly and completely as the glowing figure we had seen and followed.

Before this, I would have said that the most dreadful, disconcerting, and alarming feeling in life would be to suddenly be thrust face to face with the inexplicable, a phenomenon that had no logical first cause. Now I know that is not true.

On the contrary, as Caitlin and I stood there in that sopping, muddy lot, the cold rain still pounding down on us as though it would never stop, I don't believe we had ever felt more thrilled and vital and alive. We held onto each other like children on a roller coaster and felt, perhaps for the same reason, that if we were to let go, we would be yanked away, over the edge of the little conveyance in which we passed through life, and down—or *out*—into some great abyss.

I put my face close enough to hers so that, even in the dark, I could imagine that I saw her expression. She gave a laugh that held a shudder, the kind of laugh you give when, to use another amusement park allusion, you've come out of the house of horrors frightened but unscathed. I laughed too, not because the situation was funny, but because *she* had laughed and because we were alive.

I felt her lips on mine, and though they were cold, she kept them there long enough for them to grow warm. We held each other, the umbrella listing to the side and finally falling, so that the raindrops drenched our hair and faces, and gently bonded our cheeks together.

Then we began to shiver, and that made us laugh more. We didn't understand what had happened, but it didn't matter just then. "We'd better get out of here," I said, "before we get arrested."

We found a path that led back to Duke of Gloucester Street, and followed it, our umbrella back up, arms around each other's waists. I was still frightened, yet revived, and I knew Caitlin felt the same, for she told me later. I didn't want to see another ghost—or ghosts, as I now suspected. Three were enough.

Still, the coda was necessary, the confirmation required, as it is in all these types of stories. We returned to the King's Arms. Its interior lights were still on, and the front door was unlocked. I created the pretext that the couple who sat next to us were acquaintances, and that the woman thought she had left her glasses case at the table and we had said we would check for her, as we had to pass the tavern anyway.

We were not disappointed by the response. The hostess fetched our waiter, who looked slightly puzzled, but led us upstairs. The tables at which we and the other couple had been sitting had been cleaned and cleared, and the waiter crouched down and looked at the darkness of the floor under our table.

"No no," I said, "not us—the couple at *this* table," and I crouched, pretending to look under it.

The waiter seemed hesitant to speak. "Sir," he said at last, "what couple would that have been?"

"The young couple," I said, and I could feel my heart beating in my chest, "who were sitting right here. The woman was pregnant. They ate at the same time we did."

He raised his eyebrows and shook his head. "Sir, I'm sorry, but there's been no one at this table since around eight o'clock."

"Really?" I said, and looked at Caitlin. Her eyes were wide, and she was smiling so that I could see her teeth. "Well," I said, and again, "Well."

We sat in our car for a long time, holding each other's hand on the arm rest. The rain still fell heavily on the roof of the car. I felt Caitlin's hand leave mine, and then felt her fingers passing through my wet hair. I kissed her, long and deeply, and we drove back to our room, frequently glancing out the window, but seeing nothing out of place. Still, it had once more become a remarkable world.

In our room, Caitlin luxuriated in her bath, using the full contents of the complimentary bottle of bubble bath. I took off my wet things, slipped on a bathrobe and waited to succeed her. Sitting at the round table that seems to be a fixture in every motel room, I idly continued to flip through the photo albums that I had brought in from the trunk the previous day. The album I chose was an older one, filled with black and white photos I did not remember ever having seen. When I turned over the second page, I stopped.

Few of my generation really know what our parents looked like when they were young. Our visual knowledge is usually limited to a sepia wedding picture and an early portrait or two that hung on the walls of our childhood homes for so long that they became iconic and unique, always presented, never noticed. So I suppose it's not unheard of that that I hadn't recognized them, those old images made young flesh, moving, speaking, smiling.

Oh Tommy, she had said. She had always called him just Tom for as long as I could remember, or Thomas when she pretended to be peeved.

There they were, held to the page by photo mounts in each corner, looking shyly at the camera, standing holding hands in front of the Governor's Palace, wearing what Caitlin and I had seen them wear tonight at the King's Arms Tavern. My mother's belly was full with what would prove to be her only child.

Wmburg 1947 read the hand-inked caption beneath the small photo, and I looked at it for a long time, until I felt Caitlin's hand on my shoulder, her fingers pressing tighter as she saw too.

I can't explain it, but to note that good parents never stop loving their children or wanting to help them, far beyond the point at which they're capable of doing so. Or maybe what we experienced says that there is no such point.

I won't pretend that the feelings over what we saw that night will be permanent in Caitlin and me, but they certainly provide an emotional base on which to rebuild. What we expect will always come, so every day we look for a trace of the *un*expected, and if we don't find it, we create it, for ourselves and for each other.

Glenn Chadbourne

AS YOU HAVE MADE US

By Elizabeth Massie

Their chapel is a gutted service station at the edge of the blistering city, situated between an abandoned warehouse and a lot choked with briars and detritus. They only come to pray at midnight, for that is when no one is there to stare at them or shoot them for sport.

There is nothing left to the station but four walls, a sagging roof, a restroom in the back that requires a key that has been long since lost, and a counter with a shattered glass case that once held candy, quarts of oil, and colorfully illustrated maps to places far away. The floor is covered with leaves blown in on countless winds and bits of glass or metal or cloth the worshippers leave behind as offerings. Sometimes they cut off tiny pieces of themselves, too, pieces decayed and dead, and leave those, but the vermin that scour the small building in the wee morning hours find them and clean them away, carrying the bits home as treats to their nested families.

There are teens and children, men and women, none so old as most of their kind die before they are forty. They come from the darkest, most hidden places in the city. They are the hated ones, the abandoned ones, those looked upon by the Ordinaries as less than human. They are the Discards—distorted and twisted, deformed and ravaged. Born to destitute mothers who have drugged themselves so badly that nothing whole could grow in their wombs, dumped out with the trash. Rescued by their own, one generation to the next, squirreled away and fed and kept warm as best as can be done, clothed with cast-offs, sheltered wherever shelter might be found.

Their pastor is Ryan. He is like them in many ways, thirty-four, dark-haired, jobless, homeless. His is missing an eye and one of his ears is melted down his neck. His left arm ends at the elbow at three nubbed fingers that flex poorly. He limps violently, for his right leg is twisted. Ryan sleeps on the damp earth in the cellar of an empty garage. The Discards love to hear him preach, though his sermons are short. Most of the services are dedicated to prayer and songs.

Each night, they shamble to the chapel. Ryan locks the door behind them, lights the candles. Those who have knees kneel to pray. Hands, where there are hands, rise toward the heavens. Eyes, where there are eyes, close in humble respect and penitence. Tongues, where there are tongues, recite the prayer of acceptance:

"We are as You have made us. We ask nothing but nourishment for our bellies, covering for our bodies, and darkness in which to hide. We ask that the Ordinaries find other means of entertainment than us, and that when it is our time to die, that You remember us well."

Ryan always brings food for the service. Half-rolls, cooked potatoes and chicken scraps, lumps of cheese, mangled pastries. The Discards never ask where it comes from, the tasty and plentiful offerings, wanting to believe in at least one miracle. He would tell them he found them in bins behind diners if they asked but they don't. They pray, listen, sing, eat, and then wander off through the shit-black shadows.

It is a cool, late September night when the new Discard comes, inching along in a wheelchair that looks like scrap from the early 20th century—scarred wood, caned backing ripped and rotting, two large wheels with one small, wobbling one in the back. He is no worse off than the others, thin, dead legs, hands twisted and skeletal, and a big hole where his right cheek should be. The bones and teeth that are visible through the hole are blackened, and his breath smells like a fire-pit that has been doused in urine. No one makes a fuss over him. They merely nod and offer him weary looks that accept him into the fold.

He rolls toward the counter where Ryan is shrugging out of his tattered coat and tells Ryan that his name is Ben. Ryan looks at him, says, "Bless you, Ben," and then inclines his head toward an open space beside one of the benches where those who are able to sit, sit.

Ben maneuvers his chair to the assigned spot, thumping into some of the others as he goes. A woman drops down onto the bench beside him. Her head is oddly shaped, as if someone has crushed it in a vice. Her skin is scaled like that of a shedding snake. She looks at Ben and tries a smile. It is the ugliest thing Ben has ever seen, outside the Master when he is enraged.

Ben watches as the rest of the Discards find their places. He breathes in and out through the hole in his cheek as his nose is clogged. He hates this place. This station, this city, this fucking world. He grinds his stubbed molars together, recalling how much the Master wants Ryan, how much he drooled over the prospect of such a tasty morsel sucking his dick then being roasted and served on a skewer for dinner. Ben hates the Master yet must please him. To please him is to suffer less. To not please him is to suffer profoundly. Ben shivers, as much from fear as from cold. He is always cold.

And now, added to the cold, a damned headache. It started the moment he got inside the station, hurting like someone digging at his brain with a nail. He's not sure if it's the Master's doing. It might just be the shitty air inside this shitty place, unfiltered through the shitty hole in his face, the fucked-up face of the fucked-up body the Master gave him for this task.

A one-legged devil walks into a bar, lookin' for a good, stiff whiskey....

The Master never appreciates Ben's jokes. He has no sense of humor at all. Yet Ben can't help it. He was always a joker before, always quick and witty in hopes of a laugh, and can't help himself now. He offers puns or wisecracks or stupid stories, hoping someday to make the Master like him more. Hate him less. Whatever.

Ben crosses his arms, hard. The chair creaks beneath him.

The prayers begin, then the songs. There is nothing melodic about the wailings of the twisted creatures, and it's all Ben can do to keep from putting his hands over his ears. It makes his head hurt worse. He pretends to sing and pray, as well, moving his jaw, waggling the stubby tongue the Master gave him.

The service lasts several excruciating hours. At some time during Ryan's speech about earthy temporals and eternal peace, some of the Discards begin to scrape at themselves and drop pieces of flesh on the floor. Ben knew they did this, had been told by the Master, but seeing it makes his gorge rise. Ryan says nothing, as if he doesn't notice, doesn't mind, or has some strange understanding of the acts.

Some of the Discards wriggle in place, working out sounds and smells that cause Ben to tuck his nose under his elbow. The place grows hot and thick with the stink of blood, diarrhea, and resignation.

What do you get when you cross the devil, an angel, and a politician...?

Another joke that fell flat.

Ba-dump-bum.

At long last Ryan raises his good hand and offers the final benediction. The Discards who are down push themselves up. Those who are up push themselves forward, and, silently, they eat the food Ryan has spread out on the countertop. No one speaks, but they nod their thanks then wander away. Several hold hands as if they are lovers, or friends, or are just afraid they might tip and fall over. The rest keep their distance from each other. Out of fear or respect, Ben can't quite tell.

Not that they matter.

It's Ryan who matters to the Master. It is Ryan who has the Master's tongue and loins tingling in delicious anticipation. If Ben can't please the Master with humor, he'll please him with obedience.

The last Discard, a child who looks more simian than human, blows out the candles in the windowsill by the door.

Then there are only Ben and Ryan in the shadowed station.

Ben sits in silence, rubbing his temple, trying to press out the pain in his head. Ryan stands at the counter, gathering the plastic trays, wiping off the crumbs. For all his hideous deformity, Ryan moves with a certain grace that pisses Ben off. It's all for show, though. Certainly Ryan knows Ben is sitting there, watching him. And so Ryan has to play his part as long as there are eyes...or eye...to see. When he leaves this place, he tries to get himself drunk with left over puddles of beer found in bottles on the side of the road, and then he jacks off into the empty bottles, breaks the bottles, and proceeds to cut his legs with the shards. He hates himself more than any person has ever hated himself, so says the Master. And the Master should know. He watches. He sees. He hears. He tastes the fear and the angst within the human race, and he savors it all.

"So...," begins Ben.

Ryan looks up from the trash bag where he's secured the plastic trays, ready to drag them back home to use again tomorrow night.

"How can I help you, Ben?"

"Actually, I was just wondering how I could help you." Ben replies. The words sound hissy without a cheek to help hold in the air and fashion the sound. Couldn't the Master have given him a body that wasn't quite so pathetic? One that at least had an intact face? "Seems nobody else is willing to hang around long enough to ask."

"Yeah, well."

Ryan slings the bag over his shoulder and limps from behind the counter. He looks like Santa in a child's worst nightmare.

Santa, Ben thinks suddenly. *Poor little Julie was scared of Santa, even a smiling Santa in his white beard and red suit. I tried to tease her, to make her laugh so she wouldn't be scared. It didn't work too good but I tried....*

He shakes his pained head and clenches his jaws. The last things he needs are memories of Julie. "Master, don't make me think of her, not now," he whispers.

"What'd you say?" asks Ryan.

"Nothin," says Ben. "I'll get the door."

The night air is a bit fresher than that inside the station, scented with wet leaves and exhaust. Ben struggles with the chair; why he had to be this crippled to do the job is beyond him. His head continues to pound. The wheels snag in deep gravel, and Ryan reaches over to take the chair handles to wriggle Ben free. Ben is caught immediately by the heat roiling off Ryan, pouring from his body in waves. Clearly, the man has some kind of sickness. Ben holds his breath until Ryan steps away; a knee-jerk reaction, left over from the days when he was alive and catching someone else's disease was a thing to avoid.

Ryan then says, "See ya, Ben," and turns north to head into the deeper bowels of the city. His strides are lopsided and wretched, though he picks up a good speed. Ben stares after, then calls, "Hey!" He shoves the heels of his hands against the wheels and, with great effort, chases after Ryan. It's harder steering the thing than he would have imagined. When he reaches Ryan, he is panting.

"What do you want?" Ryan doesn't seem angry, just tired, distracted.

Ben makes sure he stays at least five feet from the preacher. The man's body heat is still detectable. "Listen. I got a couple bucks in my pocket. How about a beer?"

"Beer?"

"Yeah, you know. Bud. Miller. Corona. A beer?"

"I know what a beer is."

"Well?"

One of Ryan's brows furrows; the one over the bad eye looks paralyzed. Then he says, "If it's on you, okay. I'm flat broke. But you sure you want to be seen in public? The rest prefer their privacy. This is a dangerous city, especially for us. Ordinaries have little patience with Discards."

Ben cringed at the name. He was no more a Discard than he was God. He was what he was, a dead, joke-cracking fuck-up who'd gone to hell for living a miserable life he'd pretty much forgotten after seventeen years. Now he spends all his time just trying to humor and please the Master, trying to keep him off his back, trying to keep hell's tortures to a minimum. "I'll be all right. Where's the nearest store?"

The nearest store is up a couple blocks past empty tenements, some closed junk shops, and several bars with blacked-out windows. The store is half the width of a typical shop, with only enough room to squeeze down the narrow aisle between the counter and the single row of shelves. Unable to fit inside, Ben watches from the street as Ryan limps in with the wad of bills Ben has given him and selects a six-pack. The guy at the counter—old, white hair, sneers—growls, "Didn' I tell you damned freaks to stay out of my shop?" until he sees the money in Ryan's hand. Then he shuts up.

A freak preacher walks into a store to buy some beer.... Ben can't think of a punch line for this one. Later, maybe.

Ryan comes out with the six-pack, stands holding it in the pus-yellow light that leaks from the shop's door. Just looking at Ryan makes Ben's head hurt all the more. That damned ear and screwed up eye. The arm that looks like it should belong to some freaky doll. He tries not to let his discomfort show.

"So, where you live?" asks Ben, though he knows. The Master has shown him all he needs to know, told him all he needs to hear. In won't take long to toss out the hook and reel this one in.

Ryan says, "Not too far." The way he says it lets Ben know that Ryan's ability to keep up the kindly minister act is waning fast. He's tired. He's starting to sound irritated.

The devil was sitting on a tombstone one afternoon, waiting for the next soul to come along.... Wait, you've heard this one? Shit....

The empty garage is a dung-hole, that's certain, situated at the back of a small, ruptured parking lot. The faded sign, "Martin's Auto Repairs," has long been down off the top of the building and is propped up against the front wall. Ryan hobbles on, over the potholes and briars, the beer case thwapping against his leg. He glances both ways before pushing through the door of the garage. Ben follows with effort, grimacing, his brain rattling in his skull.

The place still smells of the work that had been done here years earlier. Sweat and oil and gasoline and cold metal. Yet it is as hollow and forlorn as the service station where the Discards go to pray.

Ryan opens a small door near the back and descends the narrow steps. Without looking back he says, "Shut the door behind you and flick the lock."

Ben sits in his chair at the top of the stairs and glares down. He shivers hard, so cold not only in this forsaken place but cold beneath his flesh. "How the hell...," he begins, but Ryan calls up, "Just crawl down. It's not that far."

Fuckedy-fuck! Ben thinks. He has to keep with his charge, but now he'll be even more gimped. Again, the Master is having him on, somewhere out there in the darkness, enjoying Ben's misery.

What do you get when you cross a hole-faced, sluggish mutant with a set of cellar steps? One big splat at the bottom, that's what.

Rim shot....

He shivers hard inside his skin.

Thump-thump-thump-thump. The rough wood of the steps scrapes the palms of his hands, leaving countless, needle-sharp splinters. His ass bounces heavily, his dead legs trailing at odd angles. He works hard not to lose himself and become the splat, the butt of his own stupid joke.

No candles in the cellar, only two battery-powered camping lanterns. It's hard to see at first, and Ben's eyes adjust only partly. There is a cot in a corner. A pile of blankets on the floor. Windows up near the ceiling, covered in wire mesh.

As he slops off the bottom step, he is hit in the face with the stuffy heat in the room. It's like someone has turned a radiator way up. It's Ryan's sickness, whatever it is.

Shit on it all.

Ryan sits on the cot and rubs his knees with his good hand. Then he snatches a beer bottle from the carton on the floor and twists off the top with his teeth. Ben finds this mildly impressive.

"Your place sucks," says Ben.

"You shut and lock the door?"

"No, I couldn't. You know I couldn't."

"Yeah, I know," said Ryan. His voice is softer now, drained, weakened. *He's almost ready for my offer. This shouldn't take long. Good!*

"Hey, Ryan," says Ben. The pain in his head flares again. He grunts through his teeth.

"What?"

Ben drags his sorry body across the concrete floor toward the cot, over a damp drain hole in the center, through several dried and flattened mouse carcasses. "How long you been livin' here?"

"A while."

"You always been like....that? All messed up?"

Ryan shrugs. "Why?"

"Born that way?" Ben cocks his head, and the jaunty motion, meant to display cocky confidence, only makes the pain worse. He pretends it doesn't. "How do you say it in that prayer? 'We are as you have made us?'"

"Why do you want to know, Ben?"

"All that shit you talk about to the other...Discards. Telling them to accept how they are. Are you fucking *kidding* me? Are you fucking *brain damaged*? I know you hate the way you are, the way they are, hell, the way I am right now. Look at me. A bag of human garbage on your floor! Could it get any worse?"

Ryan takes another swig of the beer. "Could it?"

Ben arranges his legs beneath him and pulls a beer from the carton. It's so very hot near Ryan, like being too close to a bonfire. He fumbles with the bottle but his hands are sweaty and he can't get a grip on it; Ryan takes it, opens it, gives it back.

Ben scoots away from Ryan and the man's body heat, clutching the bottle. He takes a draw; some goes down his throat but the rest trickles out through his cheek-hole. The brew is wet and cool, but doesn't taste as good as he remembers from his living days. Or maybe the Master has decided his crappy tongue should have crappy taste buds. He drinks the rest hard and fast, tilting his head to get it down, draining the bottle in just moments.

"Why'd you follow me home, Ben?" Ryan has finished his beer

and he drops the bottle onto the floor. It falls over and rolls toward the drain hole, clack-clack-clack, past Ben and through the dead mice.

"You don't believe the crap you tell those monsters," says Ben. "I know you don't. You only do what you do because there is nothing else for you to do. Pretend it's not so bad. Pretend you…they…are as they are because of some kind of fucking divine intention? Do you ever *look* at yourself? Do you ever *listen* to yourself? It's like watching a bad comedian on the stage, dying with every joke. You're pathetic! Well, my friend, I'm here to turn your sorry life around."

Ryan reaches for another beer bottle but what Ben has said makes him pause. His good eye blinks. He paws at his melted ear with his stubbed fingers. It looks as if he is now trembling, ever so slightly.

Good. This is good. I've got him now.

Ben tries to sit up as straight and tall as he can for a man on the floor with bum legs. He needs to appear confident, in charge. Pain continues to pulse back and forth beneath his skull. The sooner he gets this done, the sooner he can get out of here. The Master will have his hands otherwise full with others he is tormenting and will leave Ben alone for a while.

"It can be different, you know," says Ben. He glances about, sees a floor-length mirror nailed to one of the damp walls. It is covered for the most part with a ratty, mildewed bath towel. He drags himself over to it, panting, catches his breath, then gestures. "If I pull down this towel, you'll see what I see. You'll see what the world sees. You'll see something no one in her or his right mind could care for. You'll see why people in the city take potshots at you when they get to feelin' feisty. You'll see why nobody would ever come close to you, let alone touch you, Ryan. As He made you? You mean God? He made you a piece of shit, a cosmic joke, that's what."

"I don't need to look."

"Yeah, you really do." Ben starts feeling a bit better, now that he's into the job and through with the small talk. He yanks the towel away and watches as Ryan considers himself in the mirror. He can't quite read the expression, but it certainly isn't one of joy.

"When was the last time you got it on?" Ben asks.

Ryan coughs, doesn't answer. He reaches for another beer, cracks off the top, swigs, burps, takes another drink. He gazes again at the mirror.

"Did you ever get it on with something other than your hand, Ryan? Ever get some real juicy pussy? Pussy with a smile? Free, willing pussy? Not one you had to be buyin', Ryan?"

Ryan says nothing.

"You know, you could be a good-looking guy, if you wanted to be. Time to step up and take your golden ticket, boy. Time to claim what you deserve. And I've got it for you."

Ryan looks away, up toward one wire-covered window. "Cover the mirror, Ben."

"No, no, look again, Ryan. See what you are, and let me show you what you can be."

"I don't want to." The voice is very soft now. The one eye appears sad. Ben's spiel is working.

"Seriously, look again." Ben pats the mirror. "Do you see yourself as you can be? I see it. So can you. Look, right there in the mirror! Tall, straight, whole man, handsome, confident! This could be you. Women will want you, fucking throw themselves in your direction! You'll be sought after to work for companies who want an enigmatic, entrancing front man with just that right look. You'll make money. You'll be rich. You'll be more powerful than you could have ever imagined. You'll never have to live like this again; hell, you'll never have to think about this part of your life again."

Ryan struggles up from the cot and limps toward the mirror. As he gets closer, a wave of heat rockets off the man and catches Ben in the face like a slap. Ben wobbles, feels himself losing his balance even as he is sitting on the floor. What is wrong with Ryan? Why is he so goddamned *hot*?

But Ben keeps talking. He has to. No choice. Get it done. *Get it done!* "Just say the word, Ryan. Just say your soul isn't worth that much to you, anyway. Offer it up. An easy trade. Crappy soul for a perfect, flawless, incredible life."

Ryan is closer now, glancing back and forth between the mirror and Ben. The heat from the man is blistering. The hair on Ben's head crisps. His skin reddens. He scoots away. Sweat pours down his check, neck, arms, and buttocks in slick, salty waves. His heart pounds.

"Just say the words, Ryan!" Ben manages, his tongue baked dry. "Just say, 'I want to be handsome, I want to be rich, I want to be out of this body. I give my worthless soul for such a treasure!' Say it,

Ryan! And I promise you, you'll start living your new life!"

Ryan stops a few feet from the mirror. Then he looks at Ben and smiles for the first time. The smile is unexpected.

Relaxed.

Peaceful.

Ben is pissed and scared. "What are you smiling about? Are you taking the deal or not?" He can barely breathe now; the heat burns his eyes and nose and the hole in his face. "Shit, what is *wrong* with you? Do you know who I am?"

"Tell me. Who are you, Ben?" asks Ryan. The voice is different now. It isn't tired. It isn't drunk. It's calm, steady. Terrifying. Commanding.

"I'm a representative of the Master! Don't fuck with me!"

"What Master?"

Ben blinks, swallows a gulp of stagnant air. "*The* Master! The Dark One! The Lord of Eternal Torment."

Ryan chuckles softly. "There's no such thing, Ben."

"Of course there is!" Ben scoots back even farther, slamming up against the cinderblock wall. "Wait! No, no, oh shit, wait! Are you him? Are you him, disguising yourself to screw with me because you can? I was trying to do what you wanted me to do! Don't hurt me anymore! Please!"

"I'm not going to hurt you, Ben."

"You've said that before! You lie! You're the Master of Lies!"

"You're mistaken," says Ryan. "Now I ask you again. Who are you?"

Ben drives the heels of his hands against the floor, as if he could get away by sliding up the wall. The heat continues to stream off Ryan. Ben is certain it will soon melt his skin away.

"Who are you, Ben?" Ryan repeats kindly.

"I'm dead, I'm one of the dead! One of the cursed! You know that!"

"Why do you think you're cursed?"

"Fuck you, Ryan!"

"Why, Ben?"

"I killed my daughter, okay? She was twelve. I was drunk, drove my new convertible into a tree. I...I...." Ben closes his eyes. He does not want to think of it, to remember it.

"Tell me, Ben," says Ryan.

"You know but you just want me to relive it, don't you? Okay, fuck you, but sure! My little girl smashed into the windshield. Split her head wide open. And I left her there to die! I blamed everybody but myself! The guy who sold me the car. The man who sold me the goddamned beers. I blamed Julie, for God's sake, for begging me to let her have a ride! Fuck me, right? Three days later I killed myself, still blaming everyone else. So I went to hell. Now I do whatever the Master tells me to do. I'm one of his groveling, obedient minions. He torments us. He torments me! Sometimes I get out to claim a soul, and if I'm successful he gives me a little break. But then he's back to the tortures. But you know all that! You're *him*!"

"I'm not him."

"Of course you are! I can feel it! You're hot like the eternal flames they told us about when we were kids. Hot like the lake of fire!"

"You say you're in hell?"

"Hell yeah, I'm in hell!"

"And you mentioned eternal flames? The lake of fire?"

"Yeah! All that Biblical crap!"

"Then why do you feel so cold all the time?"

"I...what?"

"If hell is fire, why are you cold all the time?"

"Shit, why'd the chicken cross the road? Why'd the angel buy an umbrella? Why'd the devil rob the barbershop? I don't know! Who really knows anything?"

Ryan nods gently. "Think about this, Ben. When those who are frozen come close to something that is warm, they hurt. They feel the warmth as painful, as if it were fire."

"Shut the fuck up, Ryan! My head aches! I'm burning up! Leave me alone!"

"Look at yourself in the mirror, Ben."

"No...! Why?"

"Just look."

The voice is so certain, so authoritative, Ben finds himself reluctantly dragging his body back across the floor to the mirror.

"What do you see, Ben?"

Ben stares into the reflective glass. He sees himself as he was when he was alive. Ruddy-skinned, healthy, whole. Not handsome but not the worst looking of mankind, either.

"What do you see?"

"Fuck you."

"What do you see?"

"Me. As I was. You know that, though, don't you?"

As Ben stares at his reflection in the glass, something stirs from behind it. It rises deep and dark, a silhouette of ominous shape. No clear features but a perfect and terrifying darkness, stretching out with arms that end in clawed fingers, a head huge with nubs that lengthen upward into pointed horns. Then, punctuating the darkness, two coal-red eyes and white, razor-sharp teeth.

"There!" shrieks Ben. "There! See him? He's there! He's coming for me! I didn't do my job! Can't you just let me have your stupid soul?" He spins about on his ass to face Ryan.

Ryan continues to smile, patiently, kindly.

"He's there!" Ben cries. "In the mirror! Look!"

"You want him to be there, so he is. Just a reflection of what you think should be there."

"What the hell are you talking about?"

"Who are you, Ben?"

"I already told you!"

"You don't really know. You haven't figured it out."

"Figured out *what*?"

"You are Ben. You are as I have made you. Free to do harmful things, free to do good things. I have to admit, though, you've tangled yourself up pretty bad. You couldn't wrap yourself around the terrible thing you did, figured you could never be forgiven, so what the hell, you up and put yourself *in* hell. Peopled with all the crap you believed, even hoped, would be there. The Master. The tortures. The demands. The horrors you've faced. The pathetic chores, trying to steal souls. This twisted body you gave yourself for this, your latest, unnecessary venture. But Ben, there is no such thing as hell."

"Of course there is! It all *is* real!"

"You wanted it to be real, all those horrors. It's been your death-dream. It's all been your imagination."

"Shut up!"

"And you never stole a soul from anyone."

"I did too!"

"Did not."

"Did too!"

Ryan chuckles. He crosses his arms. His nubbed fingers grip his elbow. "Time to get warm again, Ben. We can take it slow, if you want. It won't hurt so much that way."

Ben recoils. "Hold it! Listen to me. Just shut up and hear me out! The Master told me all about you, Ryan. He told me where you preached, and there you were! He told me where you lived, and here you are! It wasn't just lucky guesses!"

"I made those suggestions to you. I let you know about me, where I preached and where I lived. You assumed it was your Master talking. You were so into the hell game with all those self-imposed rules and expectations. But you've played at it long enough. It was time you and I had a little talk. Face to face."

"Who are you?" Ryan wails. Then he stops.

He shakes his head. He stares.

"Oh, Christ."

Ryan laughs lightly. "Some think so. But right now just Ryan."

"Impossible."

"Why?"

"Fuck...just *look* at you!"

"I know. A bit dramatic."

"So you aren't a preacher?"

Ryan just smiles.

Ben licks his cracked lips. "Who are all those others? The Discards?"

"Some are angels in human form to help me out. Others, they're truly as they are. As I have made them. Good people. Perfect. Innocent."

"You preached to them as a person, what, for months already? And what about them now? You'll go off and leave them alone?"

"Don't worry. I've got it covered. One of the angels'll take over. And I'll be watching and listening, of course."

Ben's fists, which were clenched, begin to loosen. He swallows against dryness, runs his tongue along the hole in his cheek. "You put on this whole scenario just for me?"

"Why not?"

"I don't know."

"Don't you think you've put yourself in hell long enough?"

"I...." Ben mind crashes back to the wreck, his drunken stupor, how he'd crawled out of the car and ran away, thinking if he didn't see his daughter dying then she surely couldn't *be* dying. But she was. And she did. Thinking he could not have done what he did. But he had. Julie, the little girl scared of clowns, things in her closet, and spiders. The older girl who loved every stray dog that ever came along. The almost-a-teen, excited because her father had just bought a brand new yellow convertible. The kid who knew nothing of drunks and idiocy and irresponsibility. Reduced by his pathetic defenses and denials that he took his own life to escape. Ben begins to weep.

"You okay, Ben?"

"I'm…. I'm sorry. I'm so fucking sorry for what I did. I'm so goddamned fucking sorry! What I did was horrible! The worst!"

"I know."

"I'm sorry! I'm so sorry!"

Ryan nods.

Ben clenches his skeletal fists. "Oh, God, Julie, forgive me! Please forgive me!"

"That's all we wanted to hear. Now come here."

"No! I can't! You're too hot!"

"You're warming up already."

"I can't!"

"Come here. It'll be fine."

Ben wipes tears and snot from his face, and slowly, hesitantly, scoots over to Ryan, his hands palming the uneven flooring, his twisted legs scraping out behind him like thin, fleshy contrails. He feels Ryan's intense heat licking his skin, but as he gets closer and bears into it, it eases. When he reaches Ryan's feet, there is only warmth.

"See?" asks Ryan.

"Yeah. Wow."

"You ready to shed that skin of yours? It's really just an illusion, anyway."

"I guess."

Ben looks down at the floor. He sighs. All this, all he's been through, his imagination. His spirit wrangling itself, punishing itself.

He looks up.

There, hovering over him, standing where Ryan had stood, is the Master. Dark, cold, red-eyed and claw-handed, snarling and stinking of ash and sulfur. Ben shrieks and covers his face and wails.

"Ben, I'm kidding with you!"

Ben looks up again. Ryan is there once more, a sheepish smile on his distorted face. "I'm sorry, I couldn't help myself. Not funny?"

"Damn! No, not funny!"

"Okay, okay. I apologize. But dealing with sin and death and life and eternity, sometimes you need a sense of humor. You know that. You're pretty funny yourself. You crack me up sometimes. All those jokes."

"Yeah?"

"Yeah. I like that."

Ben feels the corners of his mouth tug into a small smile.

"Hold still now," said Ryan. He reaches out and touches Ben's forehead, and in that instant Ben finds himself standing straight and steady. His headache is gone. He is warm. And Ryan is no longer in the Ryan body, but is transformed into Light.

"Just don't tease me like that anymore, okay?" Ben asks.

"I won't. I promise," says God. He reaches for Ben's hand. Ben's fears fall away. "I love you. And I never break my promises. Oh, and did you hear the one about the one-legged devil who went into the car wash, looking for a whiskey?"

"Yeah. I made that one up."

"Oh, that's right. That was good…really good! Got a big chuckle out of that. Glad to have you back, Ben. Glad to have you back."

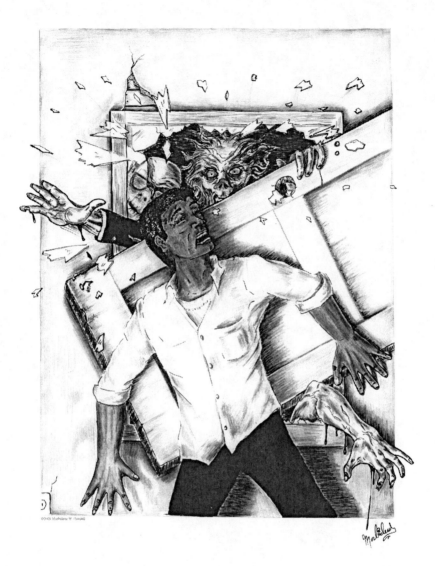

Morbideus W. Goodell

THOUGHTFUL BREATHS

By Peter Crowther

And now I see with eye serene
The very pulse of the machine;
A being breathing thoughtful breath;
A traveller betwixt life and death.
> William Wordsworth,
> "She was a Phantom of Delight"(1807)

IN FOREST PLAINS, just the way it is in many thousands of communities the length and breadth of these United States (and, for that matter, all around the world), the quality of life centers on the relationships formed by people with other people. Small towns, campuses, apartment buildings and office blocks all thrive with the buzz of connecting.

There is an indefinable magic in the way we react with others, whether those relationships are business-orientated contacts, simple platonic friendships, schoolyard liaisons, tempestuous love affairs or the gentle settling together of two people committed to the long-haul. But it's just one of these—the last one—that we're concerned with here.

Boswell Raymond Mendholsson met Irma Jayne Petschek ("–and that's Jayne with a 'Y'", Irma would always say, her voice Katherine Hepburn-ballsy, hand on hip and chin thrust out) when Boz worked the summer at the water purification plant over on the Interstate about 16 miles out of the Plains. It was 1947, the war over two years and Boz looking to find some stability with a regular job, toying with the idea of the GI Bill and trying to forget Iwo Jima. He was 23 years old, the look of a young Robert Taylor—complete with widow's peak and steely-eyed stare—his face gradually smoothing over the tell-tale craters of acne and his feet once more finding their spring.

Irma was the third-stringer from a six-sister family of semi-strict Presbyterian stock come down from Providence in the 1930s when jobs were hard everywhere, not just in the Dust Bowl that that Guthrie feller sang about. She had a wide mouth, full lips, a front tooth—the left one as you faced her—that curled over its partner slightly, legs fit to make Betty Grable throw in her hose, and a laugh that sounded like water running across wind chimes.

Boz thought Irma was the cat's peejays and when Irma caught sight of Boz—no matter how far away he was—her knees buckled fit to snap right in two, like they were made of modeling clay that old Miss Timberlake gave out to her first- and second-graders over to the schoolhouse.

When a job came up at the real estate office down in Forest Plains, Boz applied. He didn't know diddly about selling houses, but he had an air to him that seemed to calm people right down. Folks trusted him and that counts for a lot in real estate selling just as it counts for a lot in life.

Those were the days when fellows took candy and flowers around to their dates' houses, promised to have them home by a reasonable hour and took them maybe to the soda shoppe on Main Street or out to the 'Wi-i-i-ide Screen' drive-in over on the canal road. There was no fooling around permitted by the Screen's head honcho, the matriarchal Josepha Hjortsburg who, ever since the death of her beloved Gabby out in the Pacific, wouldn't show war movies and so made things difficult for herself and her clientele with a string of romances and comedies which tended to make the kids more amorous than when they'd been waiting in line to buy tickets. But, through making constant rounds, the flashlight-laden Josepha made sure all the canoodling stayed right up there on the screen and not out in the parked cars.

On those dates when Boz and Irma made it out to the Screen, Boz liked the newsreels the most. He may have had it with war—which, like most folks in those magical far-off days of the late 1940s, he surely had—but the lure of far-off places burned inside of him like a furnace. Boz maintained that joining the fighting forces was the best way to see the world and he figured there was no way he was ever likely to make it over to ride a trolley car in 'Frisco never mind climb the age-worn steps of the Pyramids or sail the canals of waterlogged Venice. But Irma would squeeze his hand tight when he sounded kind of down-in-the-mouth and she'd tell him that it was good to have a dream. "A person should always have something to aim for in life," the twenty-year-old Irma would proclaim sagely, nodding at the words as though she was underlining them a mite. "One day," she'd finish off, letting the words trail away all by themselves. And Boz would squeeze her right back and consider leaning over to give her a kiss on the cheek, risking the flashlight treatment from Josepha.

The 'one day' that Irma had long dreamed of—even from before she knew Boswell Raymond Mendholsson existed—came on a drizzly fall day in 1949, with the bottle-green leaves of summer turning russet-red and muddy brown. That was the day that Irma, resplendent in a wedding gown (specially made by Boz's Auntie Mildred), walked slowly down the aisle of the Forest Plains Presbyterian Church on Canal Street, her arm in her father Ted's and him looking like the cat that got the cream while his wife, Annie, sitting in the front pew on the left, looked at the two of them with tears rolling down her cheeks onto an angel's smile, and Boz himself glanced over his shoulder, first a little nervously and then all the nerves fading away like ice in a glass of summertime lemonade.

Married life passed without a hitch—so long as you don't count the little problems we all get from time to time—but money was never something the Mendholssons had in abundance. Truth to tell, things started off tight and just got tighter. But they doted on each other right from when the two of them said, breathlessly, "I do," their hearts skipping more beats than Joe Morello. They meant it then and they never had cause to go back on it in all the days and weeks and months and years that were to follow . . . happy times indeed.

Life for the Mendholssons seemed like a summer meadow—beautiful, fragrant and set to go on forever. They were rich in ways that had nothing at all to do with money . . . mainly through just their own company. Irma kind of drifted away from her family and even her friends—excepting Jeannie Gustavson and her husband, Ray—and Boz pretty much followed suit. He did, however, stay in close contact with Phil Defantino. A childhood friend and Boz's Best Man,

Phil had landed a job with ICI Industries down in Philadelphia and he rose quickly through the ranks at a time of great expansion for the company. Within less than two years, Phil was spending a lot of time away from home . . . initially travelling the US and then moving on to worldwide travel to cities that Boz had only ever read about, advising small businesses on how to maximize their profits.

Whenever Phil was home for any length of time, he and Jackie would come out to Forest Plains, the old hometown, to spend time with Boz and Irma. At first, they stayed at the house, giving Boz more time to quiz Phil about his latest trips, but when the house got a little more 'crowded' with the so-called 'patter of tiny feet,' they stayed at the Holiday Inn over on the Interstate. "I reckon I know more about Holiday Inns than the folks who work in them!" Phil said on more than one occasion.

Truth to tell, Irma was a little embarrassed about having houseguests who stayed in the local hotel, but Phil always made sure he let her know the plain and simple truth: that bringing up a family needs all your attention, and that, according to Phil, meant *you need folks getting under your feet like Custer needed more Injuns!* Phil and Jackie never had children and neither Boz nor Irma ever felt comfortable in asking them why. They had their suspicions of course, but they believed that if Phil and Jackie had ever wanted to discuss it then they would have.

The first product of the Mendholssons' union came into the world kicking and squawking just a couple of days before Thanksgiving, 1950, and Irma and Boz had a lot to be thankful for when the Thursday arrived. Sitting alongside Irma's hospital bed, with little James cradled in his wife's arms, Boz told her that he loved her more than anything else in the world, the tears in his eye-corners underlining that a few times.

While the arrival of Baby James served to erode still further the already shaky Mendholsson fortunes, the tough financial situation served only to deepen Boz's determination to provide for his new family. Thus he took an additional job in the kitchens of the Forest Plains Bar 'n' Grill—Irma having nixed other ideas of additional income by virtue of the fact that it wouldn't do for folks to see the guy who was trying to interest them in property also serving drinks at Max's Bar over on the Canal Road or mowing lawns on Saturdays and Sundays. But at night, after chores were done, Boz would disappear into his den, a lavishly mysterious title for a small room which he'd decked out with shelving, where he sat and perused travel books and city guides and the occasional foreign language tome.

It was in here that, after a visit from Phil and Jackie to see the new baby, Boz discovered that Phil had left his billfold—he remembered Phil taking it out of his pants pocket because it was giving him a numb backside. But when he'd called his friend to give him the good news, Phil had said blankly, "Not my billfold, Boz. Must be yours." Boz had laughed at that. He'd flipped it open while he was talking on the phone and there were five $20 bills in there. "Well," Phil had said—and was that just a touch of a smile Boz heard in his friend's voice?—"why'n't you check if there's a name in there." Boz did just that and discovered a handwritten card—handwritten in the unmistakable scrawl of Phil Defantino—proclaiming THIS BILLFOLD AND ALL THAT IT CONTAINS IS THE SOLE PROPERTY OF BOSWELL MENDHOLSSON. "Oh, Phil . . ." was all that Boz could think of to say.

Then, in 1952, the day before Independence, along came Nicola, a gloriously raven-haired companion for young James and whose cherubic face and open, trusting smile filled Boz and Irma with levels of love that even they had not dreamed possible. As the summer was already showing signs of turning to fall, Boz discovered another 'lost' billfold.

Evenings and weekends, the Mendholssons walked their charges along the park paths and the sidewalks, passing the time of day with anyone they happened to meet along the way. These were the magical days of America, a time of peace and plenty, when everything was possible. A time when the picket fences of Rockwell's *Post* covers could still be found in pretty much any small town up and down and left and right across the country. A time when guys still presented their dates with candies and flowers. A time when the human spirit still retained some dignity.

Dignity, the Mendholssons had in abundance. Money—with the exception of the miraculous billfolds which continued to show up in Boz's inner sanctum of travel tomes—they had not. But Irma and Boz never allowed their restricted finances to affect their home life, and their house over on Cedar Avenue rang constantly with the sound of happiness . . . a sound that was a tinkle of baby chuckles for a while, then pre-school mirth, then youthful laughter until at last, in the closing days of the sixties—a troubled decade, in Boz's eyes, when the magical and exotic landscapes on the other side of the world took on a sinister cloak of danger and threat—just a couple of weeks after Man set foot on the moon, the quartet was reduced to a trio with the departure of James Mendholsson to Boston U.

They were all happy for him, of course—after all, what had they strived for so hard all of their life except to improve their children's lot?—but on the day he drove their son out of Forest Plains, the air in Boz's old Pontiac was so thick you'd have needed a knife to cut it.

Now 46 years old, with the big five-oh straddling the horizon like a gunfighter who had called Boz out onto Main Street for a showdown that Boz knew he couldn't win, Boswell Mendholsson retreated into the Den still more, leafing through books on Paris and Provence, the waterways of Venice, the jungles of Peru, and wistful train journeys through China and mainland Europe. In the pages of these books—repeatedly- and often-read pages that Boz would occasionally hold up to his face as he breathed in the imagined aroma of the far-off lands the words described—Boz's life was different. It wasn't that he didn't love or want Irma—the truth of the matter was that he loved and wanted her more than he had ever done—but rather that he felt, if only a tad, unfulfilled. Even the occasional visits from Phil and his tales of airport lounges and cab rides in alien cities (plus the inevitable Grand Den Discovery, which, in line with inflation, had increased in value over the years) did little to assuage Boz's feeling of despondency. To put it plain and simple, he was getting older. Old, even.

The specter of the mortality gunslinger darkened a little more when, one sunny morning in April, 1973, Nicola announced that she and Bobby Eads were planning to marry. Irma shrieked with happiness like a drunken banshee, her arms lifting and lowering as though she were about to take off and soar right up into the sky. Boz meanwhile adopted a fixed smile that made him look like he'd suddenly discovered a worm in that last bite of apple. He had known, of course, that Nicola and Bobby were getting kind of serious but 'kind of serious' in Boz's book was a mighty long way from actual marriage. But as he watched his wife and suddenly-not-so-baby-any-more baby daughter dancing around the worn work surfaces in Irma's kitchen, Boz couldn't hold back the out-and-out

Cheshire cat grin, and he leapt into his women's midst, took their proffered hands as they all danced around like witches around a cauldron on All Hallows.

But later that night, in the Den, Boz's stomach was knotted like a pretzel and it was all he could do to hold back the tears. The door opened slowly alongside him, Boz sitting in the old rocker he'd inherited from his mother while he read John Hillaby's *Journey Around Britain*, and Irma's face peered in at him.

"You okay, honey?"

Boz looked up and gave her a half-smile, intending to tell her *sure I'm okay* and *why shouldn't I be?* but just that question and Irma's face and the fact that their little girl was going to be leaving home . . . all those things just gathered together like street-corner hoodlums and ganged up on him. And the tears came.

"Oh, Boz," Irma said, her voice soft and loving, as she came fully into the room and, hunkering down beside him, threw her arms around her husband. "You big silly," she said.

"I know," Boz said, agreeing in a self-deprecating wish-I-was-different kind of way.

"What am I going to do with you?"

"I dunno," Boz snivelled.

"She's not going far away, you know."

"I know." And he did. Nicola's and Bobby's plan was to buy an apartment across town, so's Bobby could carry on working at the bookstore on Main Street. But it wasn't so much Nicola's actually moving that so tore at Boz's heart as what it represented: and what it represented was an end to the feast. What once had been a sumptuous spread that looked set to last forever now, in Boz's eyes, more resembled picked-over carcasses and emptied bowls and plates.

"We'll be okay," Irma whispered into Boz's ear, and then she kissed him on the cheek.

He nodded. "I guess we will," he said, looking down at a photo of John Hillaby standing on England's south west coastline staring out to sea. *It's almost as though he's looking right at* you, *Boz*, a small voice seemed to whisper in Boz's ear. "We'll be fine," Boz reiterated.

And so they were. For a good long time.

James graduated with a good degree from Boston and took up a job with a small design and communications firm running their business from North Square, just a few yards from Paul Revere's house. He married Angie, the girl he'd met while at university, and the couple bought a nice apartment overlooking the Common. Three children arrived in rapid succession: Anthony Boswell Mendholsson in the spring of '74, Jennifer Jayne (with a 'Y') Mendholsson in the fall of '75, and Maria Spring Mendholsson in November, '77. Viewing Maria Spring on a freezing cold December day just six weeks after her initial appearance, Boswell agreed she was a beauty . . . and then said to his very obviously delighted son (and a mock-disgusted wife), "So, number three is here fit and well. You figured out what's causing it yet or is this likely to be an annual event?"

But while things were going well for one Mendholsson offspring, they weren't so good with the other. Nicola and Bobby split up when Nicola found out that her husband had been looking into more than old books with the store's new and shapely assistant. That was in 1976, Bi-centennial year, and, just like the country itself, the Mendholssons' daughter had regained her independence. But nothing lasts forever, and by 1980 she had met and married an insurance services manager from the bank where she worked—Jim was his name—and both Boz and Irma agreed they liked him a whole lot more than the philandering Bobby.

Nicola's first child miscarried and, for a while, the unspoken feeling was that, of all the Mendholssons, she was leading a tainted life. "I know just how you feel, honey," Jackie Defantino told the gaunt-faced Nicola. "Believe me when I tell you just how much." She and Phil had headed over as soon as they'd received the news from Irma and when Boz and Irma heard what Jackie had to say to Nicola they both looked at each other with a mixture of revelation and understanding. Turning around from where he was sitting, at Nicola's hospital bedside, Phil caught the exchange and he gave a weak smile. Boz reached out and ruffled his friend's hair the way he'd always done when they were both first-graders at Forest Plains Elementary, and when Phil got up his eyes were brimming with tears. "I know," Boz told him wrapping his huge bear arms around the more diminutive Phil: it would seem to outsiders a strange thing to say to a friend under the circumstances but it felt just right to everyone present.

Jim was hugely supportive and, in 1985, when Nicola was 33, Margaret-Jayne (again with a 'Y'—seemed nobody much cared for the name 'Irma' any more) Boswell Henfrey let the world know she had arrived in no uncertain terms. "I reckon she's going to be an opera singer," the increasingly tired-looking Boz announced, and everyone laughed.

Phil and Jackie came right out once again, Phil having retired from ICI and seeming to be enjoying spending time at home. The word was that they were planning to move back to the Plains but it would be in a different area to the one where Boz and Irma resided. It was the summertime. Boz was 61 years old and having trouble peeing.

"You need to go see Doctor Fredricks," Irma told her husband. "I will, I will," he told her. And the sad fact was that it was going to have to be true. By now, with the leaves turning red on the trees, Boz was reduced to sitting on the toilet bowl while he pee'd to avoid getting dead legs from standing there waiting for the drip-drip trickle to empty his bladder. Even Phil was leaning heavily on him. And so Boz bit the bullet, made the call, and went into the MDs office out on Jefferson Place.

Jack Fredricks couldn't make much of a diagnosis without getting inside for, as he put it, 'a look-see' and so he arranged for Boz to come back in the next day for an endoscopy. This entailed a tiny seeing-eye tube being inserted into Boz's penis and shoved up inside so's the doctor could take a look around. Boz wasn't sure which hurt the most, the tube going in or the so-called lubricant (which felt like having toxic jelly squirted into your dick) that preceded it. But the simple physical pain was soon overshadowed by what the seeing-eye saw.

"Prostate," Jack Fredricks announced with a sigh when the investigation was finished. He sat down on the gurney next to Boz while Boz nursed his crotch and fastened his pants.

"Is that bad, Jack?" Boz asked, hardly hearing the words over the thumping of his heart.

"Not going to know until we do a biopsy."

"Biopsy?"

"Got to take a slice off and send it for analysis," he explained, complementing the words with a sawing motion with his hands. "Won't hurt," he said, patting Boz on the shoulder. "But it will mean an overnight stay in hospital."

Boz nodded, zipping up his flies. "So, he said as he slid off the gurney into his waiting shoes. "What's your gut feeling?"

Jack looked at Boz for a few seconds and then looked down at his knees. "I'd say it looks bad," he said. "But let's wait for the –"

"How long?"

"Boz, I said –"

"Jack, you've been down enough guys' dicks to know what you're seeing in there. Let's go for the worst case scenario—I take it we're talking prostate cancer here, yes?"

"Looks that way to me . . . God but I wish it didn't."

"Okay, so, worst case scenario, it's prostate cancer. From what you've seen, how long?"

Jack sighed and looked up at Boz. "I think you'll see Christmas but not Easter."

When Boz spoke again, his voice was shaking. "You *think* I'll see Christmas? Christ, Jack it's already September and I feel as fit as a horse . . . just having a little difficulty peeing is all."

"I know," was all Jack Fredricks could think of to say. "That's the way it goes, though. You'll feel fit right the way until –" He let his voice trail off.

"Until I don't, huh?"

Fredricks nodded.

Boz felt a great pressure behind his eyes, like there was something inside his head that wanted out, like rats on a sinking ship; and it—this thing, whatever it was—had decided that the easiest and fastest way out was through his eye sockets. His breath felt short and his chest hurt. And his legs felt like jelly. "Jesus, Jack," Boz said.

Fredricks nodded again. "I'll give you some pills that may slow the growth down a little—they're actually designed for high blood pressure but they have this side-effect, you know?—but the tumor looks pretty big."

Watching Fredricks, Boz was reminded of when he and Irma had bought a rabbit for James. James named the rabbit Shadow and kept him out in the yard where he even built a special run for it out of wood-ends that Boz had left over after extending some shelving in the den. One day, when Phil and Jackie Defantino had come out to the house, James had excitedly shown off his pet and, still excited and maybe just a little careless, he'd dropped the heavy run onto Shadow's neck. A hysterical James had appeared in the house while Boz and Irma were handing out coffees and slices of cake, the deceased and almost decapitated Shadow lying limply in his outstretched hands. *Daddy, daddy . . . make him better*, five- or six-year-old James had pleaded. But one look at the rabbit and the single eyeball hanging out of one of its sockets on an uncoiled spring showed there was absolutely no hope. Boz reckoned that Fredricks now felt a lot like the way he himself had felt all those years ago: helpless. Like a parent, he was looked up to by his patients as some kind of God, able to dispense life and healing whenever he fancied. Boz didn't feel anyone should feel so wretched.

"Okay, he said, "so give me the pills already. We'll get this thing started right away and maybe we can make medical history."

"Right," Jack Fredricks said, emphasizing their determination with a clap of his hands, but Boz knew just from watching the MD's back that this was going to be one trip that nothing could prevent him from taking.

The results of the biopsy confirmed it. It was an aggressive tumor, big as a baseball (though, when he looked in a mirror, Boz couldn't figure out where the damn thing was hiding itself) and there were signs of secondaries. And while he couldn't figure out whether it was his actual condition or a psychological thing, he was starting to feel sick.

On the day they flipped over the calendar to October, Boz and Irma went in to see Jack Fredricks for the lowdown. It wasn't good. There was no point in trying to operate because there was a 75-80% chance he'd die under the anaesthetic. And even if he didn't, it would only extend his time maybe over Christmas, and all of the extra gain would be spent in a hospital bed. Boz decided that, if he was going to go then it was best not to drag it out unnecessarily, and he preferred the idea of being around somewhere he knew with people he cared about and who cared about him without being paid for doing it. No, he would soldier on until he got too tired, at which point he would take to his bed and wait to start The Great Adventure. Jack Fredricks said it wouldn't take long at that point. Maybe three, four days.

To say there were tears would be an understatement.

Neither Boz nor Irma could imagine life without their partner, and this whole thing had happened so quickly that it took a couple of days for the realization to set in. After that, they decided to tell the children. More tears followed.

The atmosphere in the Mendholssons' home grew dark and

somber. Even Boz's Den failed to provide the relief and respite from the everyday world that he'd grown used to over the years. When he was sitting in there, it seemed as though the books were whispering behind his back . . . asking what was to become of them when he'd — He didn't like even to think about it. But the thing that worried him the most was how Irma would survive without him.

Then, with Hallowe'en approaching, Boz hit on an idea.

* * *

"Honey, Phil's coming around."

"Oh, fine. Did he call? I didn't hear the –"

"No, I called him a few days ago—last week, if I recall. I just remembered about a half-hour ago." Boz stretched to his full height in the kitchen doorway and breathed in the smell of baking. "Smells good."

"Jackie coming too?"

"No, just Phil."

"Any particular reason?"

Boz shook his head. "Just fancied shooting the breeze. Now that they're back in town I figured I'd spend as much –" He paused and re-phrased. "Spend a little more time with him. You know."

"I know, honey. I'll set out the table in the front room and-"

"That's okay, sweetie, we'll have coffee in the den."

"But it's so cramped in there, honey."

He walked over and gave her a kiss on the cheek. Then he licked a finger and rubbed at a patch of flour on her forehead. His heart ached when she allowed her eyes to close and moved her head against his hand like a cat wanting to be stroked. "Don't worry about me, okay? I'm fine."

The truth, however, was that Boz was actually far from fine. He was now starting to feel weak, and the pills designed to keep his prostate growth down to a minimum seemed to be less successful than they'd been at first. But he kept this information to himself.

"Nicola said she'd maybe call you."

"Well, if she does, just tell her I'll call her back. I don't really want to be interrupted when Phil's here."

Irma looked at him, a slight frown on her face, but it passed quickly, like a cloud across the moon, when Boz smiled at her. "I'm sure looking forward to cake," he said, "and the coffee'll help me pee."

She shook her head and waved him away. "Oh, you," she said.

The doorbell rang and Boz said, "That'll be Phil," as he disappeared out into the hall. Irma heard their voices and she stepped out to say hey.

"Hey, Irma," Phil said, his voice wreathed in smiles and consolations. "How're things?"

Irma did a little jig with her head, side to side, and then nodded. "We're doing okay, I think. Aren't we, honey?"

"We're doing fine," Boz agreed. Then, to Phil, "Well, come on into the den. Irma's been cooking all morning so I think fresh cake is heading our way."

Irma smiled bravely at Phil and saw him give her the slightest of nods that would have been all but imperceptible to a casual onlooker. When she dropped her gaze from his eyes, Irma noticed that Phil Defantino was holding a briefcase in his hand. When she looked up at Phil again, about to ask why he'd brought a briefcase, Phil shuffled the case into his other hand and said to Boz, "Okay, show me to a chair—I'm pooped." And the two of them turned around and moved down the hallway to Boz's den.

"You go on in and make yourself comfortable," Boz said as he ushered Phil over the threshold to his book collection. "I'll get the coffee."

"I can bring it in for you, honey," Irma said.

But Boz was already making his way back to the kitchen. "I don't want you waiting on me, sweetie," he said. "And anyway," he added, "I want to have a nice long talk with Phil without any interruptions. It's not you, baby," Boz said when Irma frowned at being labelled as an interrupter, "but you know how Phil can gabble on."

Irma watched Boz open cupboard doors and place mugs on the breakfast counter. She watched the whole process of her husband preparing a tray—milk from the refrigerator, sugar bowl, two plates, two pieces of cake—and all the while she tried to think back to a time when Phil Defantino had gabbled on. For the life of her, she couldn't come up with a single one.

Phil stayed with Boz in the den for over two hours, the pair of them speaking in hushed tones in there. It wasn't that Irma was eavesdropping but just that whenever she went past the den door all she could hear was a dim and distant drone of voices. When Phil emerged, Boz hurried him out of the door while he explained loudly that Irma would be preparing lunch. She took that as a hint and went straight back into the kitchen to make them a couple of omelettes. As she switched on the Mister Coffee, she heard Boz shout "Okay, same time tomorrow," and then close the door.

"He's coming back tomorrow?" Irma asked when Boz appeared at the kitchen door.

"Yeah," he said. "He sure is a sucker for punishment."

"What was in the case?"

"Huh?"

"The briefcase. Phil had a briefcase with him?"

"Oh, yeah," Boz said as he leaned over the frying pan and sniffed in the smell of eggs cooking. "He wanted to show me some stuff he'd picked up on his travels. Books and stuff."

"More books!" Irma said, smiling, and she shook her head. She wondered how she was going to get rid of all those books when the day came but just as quickly as the thought presented itself to her, she dispelled it. And so the moment passed, and as it passed she never gave a thought to the fact that Phil's briefcase looked just as full as it had done when he had arrived.

* * *

"More books?" Irma said when she answered the door the following day and saw Phil standing there in the rain, his arms wrapped around his briefcase.

"Excuse me?" Phil said, stepping past Irma into the house.

"It's okay, Phil. I told her."

Irma turned around to see her husband walking along the hallway, a big *aw shucks* smile etched on his face.

"You told her?" Phil said, smiling, glancing from one to the other.

"Yeah," said Boz taking Phil's coat from him, Phil moving the case from one hand to the other during the process. "She knows you're smuggling books into the house." He shrugged. "I think maybe she's worried I'm going to spread to the other rooms."

Irma smiled, cocking her head on one side as she watched Boz.

Was it her imagination or did he seem to be losing a little weight? Maybe she needed to fatten him up a little. "Coffee and cake?" she asked.

"Irma, you are a beacon of sustenance in a wasteland of famine."

"I'll take that as a yes. Honey? Would you like cake or maybe a sandwich to set you on until lunch?"

"Cake will be fine, sweetie," he said and he kissed her on the cheek. Irma threw her arms around him and, just for a second, wanted desperately to absorb him into her, the way those vampire-type creatures did on that *Outer Limits* episode, but the moment passed and she relaxed her hold.

"Hey, careful there," Boz said with a grin. "Don't you know I'm a sick man?"

"You've always been a sick man," Phil chided, "and it hasn't done you any harm far as I can make out."

They all laughed, though perhaps a little dutifully—just three normal people making polite banter—and then Boz said, "Come on into the den." Turning to Irma, he said, "I'll come get the coffee and cake, sweetie. I'll just get Phil settled in."

Jiminy, Irma thought to herself in the kitchen, *it sounds like he's about to send him into orbit.*

* * *

The following day, Boz came into the kitchen and turned on the Mister Coffee. "You got any more of that cake left?" he asked as he rummaged in different cupboards. "Phil just can't get enough of it."

"He coming around *again*?"

Boz shrugged. "I guess," he said. "I think he's bored. Since he retired, I mean."

"Well, he could at least bring Jackie along. Be nice to have someone to talk to while you two are in the den."

She opened the one cupboard that Phil seemed to have missed and produced the plate containing the cake, wrapped in tinfoil.

"What is it that you talk about in there anyways?"

"Oh, this and that," Boz said. "This and that."

When Phil came around the entire process was repeated: the slightly awkward look on his face as he shuffled the briefcase around, the somewhat contrived pleasantries, the ushering of the guest by her husband into the den, and the profuse declaration that he, Boz, would save her the trouble of bringing cake and coffee in by taking it himself.

On this occasion, however, Irma noticed that Boz's hands were shaking a little. She watched the hands intently as he loaded cake onto the top plate and straightened the mugs so that the handles were accessible. She thought about how those hands had travelled her body and her face over the years, pleasuring her and making her feel safe, and she wondered, just for a few seconds, where those years had gone and how they had gone there so quickly.

When the hands stopped and stayed exactly where they were, Irma looked up and saw Boz watching her. There was a profound sadness in his eyes, a sadness borne of love and a long relationship that could now be measured in weeks . . . and possibly even days, though neither Boz nor Irma would acknowledge that possibility. But that very morning, it had taken Irma some time to get Boz out of bed and into the shower. In fact, she had been considering asking Chris Hendricks, the family odd-job man these past 20 years or more, to come around and investigate putting up a handrail—she just didn't trust Boz's balance any more.

"I'm okay," Boz said, "before you ask."

"I know, honey," she said, lifting a hand and tracing a line with a finger-nail along the back of Boz's left wrist. "I do so love you," she said.

Boz nodded. And as pale and exhausted as he looked—even a little jaundiced around the eyes—there was a twinkle of mischief in those eyes that made Irma frown and narrow her own eyes.

"You up to something, Boswell Mendholsson?"

"Just taking some cake and coffee through is all, sweetie" he said. And with that, he backed out of the kitchen and into the den, closing the door firmly behind him.

And so it went on for several weeks, almost daily visits from Phil Defantino with each stay restricted to the den, usually for between one and two hours. The visits were in the mornings mostly, which was also when the children called around whenever they could— children! what a ridiculous thing to call them, Irma thought to herself on more than one occasion: they were both in their thirties now but, of course, they would always be a little boy and a little girl. And they did so love their father. When they left—they rarely brought their other halves or the children—they would hug Irma tightly, asking if she was okay and managing to keep things under control. Each time she would tell them emphatically that she was fine. And she was.

Irma believed you got an almost spiritual strength from someplace in these situations. She had heard of that before. And while she did not dare to consider what life would be without her husband, she managed to cope with his steadily deteriorating condition with determination, patience and even good humor.

Boz himself seemed to wind down around lunchtime or early afternoon, retiring to the couch where he would watch game shows or, occasionally, the Cartoon Network. Sometimes he would simply call it a day and go straight to bed. Irma would take him a sandwich and a bag of potato chips around five or six o'clock and then Boz would drift in and out of sleep until Irma came to bed herself at around 10.30.

As the November winds buffeted the house and Thanksgiving approached, there were increasingly clear signs that Boz's downhill slide was gaining acceleration. It was just the little things that they both noticed—the swollen ankles from the steroids, the drowsiness from the pain killers, the sickness from the tumor itself—any of which by itself could maybe have slipped beneath the radar but taken all together, things were starting to look a little bleak. And now Boz was starting to wheeze like an old steam train. "It's got into his lungs," Jack Fredricks told Irma one late afternoon as he was leaving the house, the setting sun framing him there on the porch as he buttoned up his overcoat.

Then, one day, Boz cried out in pain as Irma was trying to get him out of his bed. "It's no good, sweetie," he said, his words coming out like knife-stabs, in breathless staccato. "Let me be . . . just let me be." And with that, he slumped down onto the pillow and fell immediately back to sleep, his mouth wide open, stealing as much air from the room as it could manage.

"Hey, Irma," Phil Defantino said when Irma opened the door. They looked at each other in silence, neither one of them making a move, and then Phil said, "Boz not so good?"

She shook her head and wiped at her eyes. She knew that Phil could see she had been crying.

Phil nodded. "Well," he said, drawing the word out and hunching his shoulders against the wind, "maybe it would be better if I called around another time."

"Yes," Irma said, trying to keep from glancing down at Phil's briefcase, "maybe it would at that. I'll get him to give you a call when he's feeling a little better."

When Phil said "Sure," his voice sounded hoarse and broken. He nodded once and turned around, head hung down, and made for the street along the path through the Mendholssons' front yard. He never looked back. And he never saw Boz alive again.

*   *   *

Irma spoke in whispers to Nicola on the telephone.

"Hey honey," she said.

"Hey, Mom. Everything okay? Is it Dad?"

She glanced around to make sure the bedroom door was still closed. "He's not too good, honey."

"Not too good?"

"No, not too good at all. Doctor Fredricks says . . . he says . . . ."

"Mom?"

"He says your daddy will be leaving us soon."

"Oh, Mom."

"I know, honey, I know." A single tear dropped from Irma's cheek onto the telephone cradle and she wiped it away with one finger, rubbing the spot back and forth until there was no trace of it at all. "I called your brother. He's coming home tomorrow. Catching the redeye out of Boston—should be here by mid-morning."

"Will that . . . will that be –"

"Oh, I hope so, honey. I surely do hope so but he's not so good."

"I'll be there."

Irma replaced the telephone and listened to the resulting silence, absolute at first and then, slowly, giving way to house sounds, boards settling, the wind outside, the occasional clank of the heating system. It was all familiar and yet, with the absence of her husband's movements around the place, it was completely alien.

She went back down the hallway and gently eased open the door to the bedroom she had shared with Boz these past 36 years or so. He was still there—*where would he have gone for goodness' sakes?*—but only just, a mere shape beneath the bedclothes, made eerie by the dim nightlight on the bedside table, his chest rising and falling very slowly and with apparent difficulty. She moved silently across the room and sat down on the bed beside him, took one of Boz's thin hands between hers and watched his face.

"Irma?" he croaked without opening his eyes.

"I'm here, honey. I'm right here."

"Irma . . . I feel pretty rough."

"I know, honey. You must rest, save your energy."

Boz opened his eyes and looked straight ahead, past Irma, at the covered shelving and rails that contained all their sweaters and coats, pants and shirts, a lifetime of clothing and shoes. *Half of that will have to go,* Irma thought, following Boz's line of vision. *Oh, dear Lord, give me the stren –*

He turned towards her and, when she saw his milky, watery eyes, Irma let out a small gasp.

"Irma . . ."

"I'm here, dear," she said.

"Irma, you have . . . you have to be strong."

"I know, honey. I will be. You be strong, too."

Was that a laugh he gave or just a cough? Irma couldn't tell any more.

"Irma, I'm going to be going soon and –"

"Hush, please hush saying those –"

Boz shook his head. "Shhh," he said. "Let me finish. I always wanted to go travelling," he said, his voice soft like unfurling parchment, "and now I'm going to get the chance. After all these years . . . ." He coughed again and Irma wiped his mouth with a paper tissue.

"After all these years I'm going to visit all those places we wanted to visit together. Think of me there," he said.

"I will," Irma promised. "I'll think of you."

"Just pret –" He closed his eyes and gave another little shake of his head. "Just *think,*" he continued, "that I'm away from home, seeing wonderful sights and . . . and missing you." He turned to her. "I *will* miss you, sweetie," he said.

"And I'll miss you, too," she said.

He nodded and closed his eyes. After one long, wheezy breath, Boz's chest was still.

"Honey?" Irma said, even though she knew, deep down, that her husband was now too far away to hear her. Even so, she said it again.

And then once more. After a while, she just sat with him, holding his hand, reminding him of all their times together and telling him how much she loved him.

* * *

The funeral was held on a rainy Wednesday in November.

James held onto his mother's arm tightly all through the service, with Nicola standing on her other side, watching Irma carefully throughout the hymns and the sermon. At the end, to the strains of a Glenn Miller tune, they trooped out into the graveyard for the internment.

Irma hadn't realized how well thought of her husband truly was. They had kept themselves pretty much to themselves all through their married life, and yet here were lots of people—people Irma wasn't entirely sure she had ever met—standing out in the driving drizzle to celebrate her husband's life and to mourn, with her, his passing.

"Who *are* all these folks, Mom?" Nicola whispered.

Irma shook her head, her eyes locked onto just one figure standing almost directly across from her, above the open grave beneath Boz's coffin: Phil Defantino. She had not mentioned Phil's stream of visits to either of the children and now, seeing his acknowledge her with the faintest nod of his head, she wondered why.

James's hand grasped her arm, and she turned her head just as the coffin began lowering.

On the way back to the car, Irma stopped and talked to many of the mourners. Everyone said pretty much the same thing, which wasn't much at all. But what could you say? He was gone and that was it. Phil Defantino was different, though. Phil took Irma in his arms and hugged her close to him. "Anything you ever want, Irma, no matter what it is, you only have to call me. Okay?"

She nodded. "Thanks, Phil." They stood looking at each other for a few seconds before James helped his mother into the waiting car. She kept her eyes closed all the way home, praying to her heart to stop beating. But it didn't. Nothing was that easy.

Having made arrangements for Angie and Jim to look after their respective children, James and Nicola had decided to stay on at the house though the first day after the funeral, Thanksgiving, was a baptism of fire. "If I can make it through today," Irma said when Nicola brought her a cup of Earl Gray tea in bed, her voice tired and her eyes bagged from crying all night, "then I can make it through any day."

Nicola made a wonderful turkey dinner with all the trimmings, and the three of them spent the day looking through old photo albums, listening music and crying like babies. When Irma finally made it into bed, she was so completely exhausted that she even refused one of the sleeping tablets prescribed by Jack Fredricks.

As soon as she closed her eyes she dreamed of Boz, and when she woke up the following morning, with shafts of watery sunlight angling through the gap between the curtains, it was like losing him all over again.

"Okay," James announced as he plopped onto the side of his mother's bed, "we need to have a plan."

"James *always* had to plan things, Mom," Nicola observed from where she was standing, leaning against the door frame. "He won't be happy unless he has a list so you might just as well let him get on with it."

Irma forced a brave smile and nodded.

"So, first, Dad's clothes," James said, writing *clothes* in his notebook.

"I don't think I can –" Irma began before being startled by a thud out in the hallway. She looked up and, just for a moment, there was a girlish excitement in her eyes. But the excitement evaporated just as quickly as it had appeared when she realized it was "the mailman!"

"I'll get it," Nicola said and she backed out of the room.

"Okay, Mom, I know how you must feel but –"

"James, you truly have absolutely no idea at all how I feel. Those are your father's clothes . . . his shirts, his pants, his favorite shoes, his –"

She stopped when Nicola reappeared at the door clutching a bundle of envelopes. Her eyes were wide and her mouth seemed to have been chiselled into an 'O' shape.

"Nick? What is it?"

Irma frowned at her daughter. "Nicola?"

Nicola walked across the room and lifted one of the letters from the small bundle, handed it across. Irma accepted it and saw that it was not a letter at all: it was a postcard. From Venice. The picture showed the Bridge of Sighs and a gondolier guiding his craft between high, stone buildings, backdropped by a sun that appeared to be sinking into the canal behind him.

Her heart beating, Irma turned the card over and gasped: the message was written by Boz—she knew his handwriting anywhere.

"Dearest Irma," it began

"Mom?" James said, hardly daring to move.

"Well, here I am in Venice. The trip was less traumatic than I expected. I wish you could see this place—I'll have to bring you when we meet up again. The sound of the gondoliers calling to each other—and singing! my, but they have wonderful voices. The smell is a little strong—kind of fishy—in places but the canals and the buildings—such wonderful buildings—more than makes up for it. Anyway, must go. We're on a tight schedule. I'll write again soon.

"All my love as always,

"Boz"

"Mom, you okay? What is it?"

"It's a postcard," Irma said, her voice reverently hushed.

"A postcard?" Nicola moved over alongside Irma but only managed "Who's it –" before she saw the handwriting. "That's from Dad!"

"A postcard from Dad?" James was half-tempted to add something along the lines of it must have needed one hell of a stamp but decided against it.

"From Venice," Irma added, checking the front of the card again before turning it over and re-reading the words.

"I don't understand," Nicola said.

"It's some kind of sick joke," James said as he reached for the card.

Irma shook her head. "No, it's not a joke. It's a very clever ruse on your dad's part to make me feel better. "

And she went on to tell Nicola and James about the daily visits from Phil Defantion, mentioning the mystical briefcase, the secluded sessions in Boz's den, the fact that Phil had spent his entire life travelling distant countries so he must have built up quite a database of contacts . . . people who, as a favor to Phil—and for such a good reason—would probably not be averse to sending a pre-written card across from their home city to Irma here in the US.

After studying for a while, Irma said, "I'll bet this is the way it works.

"Phil organizes the card from Venice, gets it across here and brings it around for your dad to write. Then Phil takes it away and sends it back to Venice and that same person then sticks a stamp on it and pops it into a box."

"But the timing is so perfect," Nicola said.

"Well, maybe Phil held onto the card until –" She paused and shrugged. "Then he sends the card and tells whoever that it's fine to send it right back."

"'I'll write again soon'? What's that mean?"

"Exactly what it says, I guess, James," Irma said.

"You mean . . . you mean there'll be other cards?"

Irma smiled at Nicola and nodded. "I guess so. I don't know just how many but . . . they were in there a long time every time Phil came around. And Phil came around pretty much every day until your dad got too weak."

James watched his mother turn back to the card and read it again. "How do you feel about it, Mom?"

"I think it's pretty weird," said Nicola, and she gave a little shudder. "It's like dad speaking from beyond the grave."

"That's exactly what it is," ventured Irma, "but it certainly doesn't bother me. After all, that's what a Will is, isn't it? The deceased speaking to his loved ones from beyond the grave . . . with all the statements and clauses in that Will written when the deceased was still alive. This is really no different than that and, of course, it's a delightful idea."

"Still pretty weird if you ask me," Nicola concluded.

But Irma was smiling. "I think it's sweet. And I think I'm ready for a cup of coffee." She went into the TV room and placed the card on top of the television, standing it up against a bowl containing nuts and dates.

"Pride of place, huh?" James said.

Irma nodded without taking her eyes from the card. "Pride of place."

* * *

When Phil Defantino called around James answered the door.

"Hey, James," he said, nodding awkwardly. It had started to snow outside—just a fine powder now but everyone knew that as soon as it warmed up a degree or so they'd get it knee deep—and Phil was wearing a peaked cap like hunters wore, complete with earmuffs, a thick scarf and mitten that made him look like he was hiding freak hands of enormous size. He was a shopping mall dummy on which some over-zealous window-dresser had decided to drop every piece of winter clothing in the store, and James had to smile. Phil frowned at the smile and then said, "I thought I'd call around to see how your mom's doing."

"Oh, she's fine. Thanks to that –"

"Hello, Phil," Irma said. She moved quickly along the hallway and reached around her son to pull Phil into the house.

"I was just going to say to Mr. Defant –"

"Hey, James . . . it's Phil. You're not a kid any more."

James laughed. "Okay, yeah, Phil." He turned to Irma. "I was just going to say how well –"

Irma flashed a wide eyed stare at him and gave a single slight shake of her head. "Why don't you go make us some coffee, honey?" Then, to Phil, "You going stay for a few minutes, yes?"

Phil nodded enthusiastically and started to pull clothing off, depositing it in a heap on the floor just inside the door.

Phil and Irma sat in the TV room for almost an hour, drinking coffee and eating cookies and generally just shooting the breeze. Phil checked to see if Irma was okay and made sure that she didn't need any money or anything, and Irma said she was fine on both counts, with Irma telling him that one of his magical lost billfolds was not required. She had forgotten all about the postcard and she saw Phil notice it there on the television but he didn't say anything so she didn't say anything either. When the snow started to fall heavily outside the window, Phil decided it was time for him to hit the homeward trail. He gave Irma a kiss on the cheek and a big bear hug—God, how she missed her man's strong arms around her!—and then, once more suitably attired, he ventured out into the elements. Irma watched him trudging along the path to his 4x4, watched the lights come on as Phil got in, and then watched the car move off. She waved energetically at the little toot on Phil's horn and closed the door. When she turned around, James was leaning against the stair-banister watching her.

"Why didn't you want me to say anything? About the card, I mean."

"Wasn't anything to do with him."

Irma walked past James heading for the kitchen.

"Wasn't anything to do with Phil? Didn't you tell us that –"

"James," Irma snapped, spinning around at the kitchen door. "However or whyever this thing happened and no matter whose help was used, that card is to me from my husband. My *dead* husband. Writing to me from one of the most wonderful cities on Earth." She shrugged and her stern expression mellowed. "Sure, I could maybe track down the whys and wherefores of it—talk to Phil, ask him to come clean and so on—and where would that leave me? What benefit would I gain from that?"

James could feel the color draining back out of his cheeks.

"You think of religion, right? All those folks traipsing to chapels and churches, synagogues and mosques . . . and all of them doing it, week in and week out, on the back of a fairy story? Oh, it's a pretty widely held and widely believed fairy story but it's still a fairy story. There's no proof. It's like the old saying goes: if you had proof then you wouldn't need faith. And right now, when I thought my life was pretty well over, I get a postcard from the one person in this planet that means more to me than anything else in the world . . . a postcard from Venice, for crissakes—excuse my French—and yes, sure, there's a part of me, maybe just a tiny itsy-bitsy part, that thinks well, maybe he is *in* Venice! And maybe I will get to go there with him one of these days. And until that happens, he's just going to stay in touch with me, writing little messages to me. It doesn't hurt, does it? To believe that, I mean? But you want me to seek out the proof that he just sat in his den day after day, concocting silly meaningless little notes using his travel books so's he could send me postcards from exotic locations for me to read while his body—the body I loved and cherished more than anything else, and that I miss so very very much—just decayed to mulch in the –" Irma slid down the wall sobbing.

James went across to her and crouched down beside her, his own tears rolling down his face. "Oh, mom . . . I'm so sorry. So very very sorr –"

Irma patted his arm and rubbed her eyes with her sleeve. "No, you haven't done anything, honey. It's me should be sorry."

"No, you –"

"Shh. Let me finish. You just wanted me to rationalize everything so's I wouldn't fool myself . . . so's I would face the fact that your dad is dead and gone and I'm alone now. You didn't want me to allow myself to become dependent on . . . on a fantasy. Is that about right?"

James nodded. "That's about right, yes."

"Well, honey, let me reassure you that I'm absolutely fine. I do know the score. Maybe your dad and me . . . maybe we'll meet up again"—Irma waved her hand and shrugged, eyebrows raised as though challenging her son to disagree with her—"someplace else . . . be it Heaven or wherever. And then again," she said with a shrug of resignation, "maybe we won't. But the possibility—no, the *faith* that I have—that I *will* see him again is all that's going to keep me going. And that postcard and maybe others just like it, is a part of that faith.

"Even though, deep down, I know—and I *do* know—that your dad wrote those cards when he was still alive, there's just this wonderful *what if?* element about it . . . like when you see a squirrel gathering nuts and you imagine it going home to a tree-hole where its partner is cooking dinner for it, or on Hallowe'en when you look out of the window and you wonder whether, just maybe, the ghouls and the ghosts are gathering down at the Cemetery gates just waiting for some shmuck to wander by . . . or Christmas Eve, looking out of that same window into the snow and trying real hard, no matter how old you've become, to hear sleigh bells.

"The whole thing about the *very idea* of the cards and that he even thought of doing it and that Phil got so involved—God only knows how much effort *he* had to put into this . . . and maybe is *still* putting into it—well, how could anyone *want* not to believe? It comes right down to this: my man is dead and I have to go on without him. I can make that portion of my time on Earth *very* hard or I can make it just hard—it could never be easy. The postcard helped, God forgive me that I needed such help but I guess I did. And I still do. And if I speak with Phil about it then I break the spell. So all those people he's had lined up and all those visits to the house when your dad was so sick . . . all of that would have been in vain."

The sudden sound of water draining from the bath upstairs broke the silence and Irma smiled, running a hand through her gray hair and sweeping it back from her forehead.

"You're right, Mom," James said, and he threw his arms around her once again. Breathing in the smell of her—her soap or perfume or whatever it was—suddenly made him realize that he wouldn't be smelling his father's unique smell ever again. "I miss him too," he whispered into his mother's ear.

"I know, honey," she said. And then because such a revelation and the enormity of its implications needed to be acknowledged more than once, "I know."

They made a pact that night, Irma and James and Nicola, to keep the postcard—they hardly dared speak of it in plural, not yet at least—a secret amongst themselves. They had a small celebration to mark their decision, a late-night feast of port and cheese and crackers, raising their glasses to the continued success of Boz Mendholsson's travels and adventures. When James went to stand outside in the wind and snow for a cigarette, he looked at the surrounding houses and listened to the snow-muted sounds of the neighborhood and the sussurant hum of the traffic on the Interstate, and he steeled himself to face a world that was now minus one of the half-dozen people who mattered most to him. It was easier than he had imagined.

* * *

The second card—the one from Paris—arrived the following week, wedged between a credit card statement and a letter from Suzanne, Irma's eldest sister. The statement and the letter were ignored until much later in the day, but the other item was devoured voraciously by Irma right there on the doorstep, the wind blowing her hair around her face. Casual passers-by who knew of Irma's loss may have been surprised and possibly even dismayed by the huge grin on her face. "And *au revoir* to you too, honey," Irma whispered when she reached the end.

From then on, the cards arrived with dependable regularity— always one per week and very often two. It seemed that Boz was on a whirlwind tour of the entire world, jetting across continents and time-zones with casual disregard for jet lag or budgetary constraints. Berlin, Amsterdam, Vienna, Austin, Rekjavik, Milan, Rome . . . and every card cross-referenced and referring to ones that came before it. It was a veritable *where's where* of cities, countries and cultures, each card bringing her up to date on how Boz was and providing snapshots of local cuisine and landmarks, the smells, sights and sounds or the world delivered every few days into the Mendholssons' mailbox.

James and Nicola fell into a routine of telephoning Irma purely to get the lowdown on their dad's latest adventures, and whenever they visited the house they relished holding the postcards and reading them for themselves, marveling still, way down inside of them, at the ingenuity and sheer meticulous dedication being employed in this scam of scams. But as the days and weeks rolled into months and seasons, that attitude was eroded and, even in spite of themselves, the cards became the reality of their situation . . . their father off on a prolonged world trip with a brief communication coming from every stop along the way.

By the time Irma flipped the calendar over into 1987, Boz had sent her 71 cards. The one she received on January 7th was from Moscow—or St. Petersburg, as Boz informed her in his note—where he had spent New Year's Eve celebrating in Red Square. In a nice touch at the end he said it was a good thing he didn't feel the cold because it was 10 degrees below.

Irma kept the cards in a special rosewood box by the side of her bed, the cards all filed in date order. There had been a couple of screw-ups in the summer when cards arrived in the wrong order but now she had marked each one with a number and there was a complementary sheet with all the numbers and the dates the cards arrived. At night, before she went to sleep, Irma would sit in bed, with the wind whistling around the streets of Forest Plains, picturing Boz in all these exotic locations. He hit his one-hundredth card in late June—the card even emblazoned with a hand-drawn rosette in red ink proclaiming Boz's literary century.

Irma was glad of the warmer weather. The winter—her second as a widow—had been cold and long, and it had taken its toll on her stamina and her constitution. Nicola insisted that she go to see Doctor Fredricks and, though she refused at first, James was quick to remind her of what she would have said to his dad in a similar situation.

Jack Fredricks said that Irma's blood pressure was up a little but it wasn't anything to worry about. He gave her some pills and congratulated her on dealing with her loss so magnanimously. "You're an inspiration to us all," he told her as he showed her out of the surgery.

"Well," Irma said, "I've had a lot of help." And then she was on her way.

Phil and Jackie Defantino had stayed in close contact over the twenty months since Boz's death, and though Phil was often tempted to mention something to Irma about his special project with Boz, he refrained. He had quickly recognized the danger of stealing the magic from what Boz had conceived and so he never said a thing . . . not even a knowing smile. And Irma, in what Phil considered to be remarkable forbearance, never let her own face slip when Phil would ask her how things were.

But when James and Nicola were shown the one-hundredth postcard they saw something that must have been happening for a while but which they had missed. They didn't say anything as such but James had to ask his mother to clarify some of the message as the words appeared to have been smudged. "Probably dropped in a puddle someplace," was all Irma could say as she took the card and read aloud the whole message. While she read, James looked across at his sister and saw the same concerns in her eyes as he felt sure were present in his own: Boz's handwriting was deteriorating.

The following day, James called around to take his mom to the mall but she wasn't ready. He shouted into the bathroom and asked if it was okay for him to flip through Boz's postcards. "Go ahead," Irma shouted over the noise of the shower. "They're in the box beside my bed."

Sitting on the bed flicking through the cards, James saw that it was worse than he had first thought. Boz's penmanship had become uncontrolled, the words slanting into each other and littered with misspellings and grammatical errors, inconsistencies and duplications. He wondered just when, in his father's illness, these cards had been written.

But, as it was to turn out, James's concerns were overtaken by events.

* * *

The following Monday, James took the day off from work and drove up to Forest Plains to see Nicola. They met up at the coffee shop on Main Street, the plan being to discuss what they were going to do when the cards dried up. It was something they had never really considered, having been swept away on Irma Mendholsson's floodtide of optimism and wonder. Maybe, for just a while there, they too had signed into the belief that their father truly was enjoying a long vacation, writing home every few days to keep them aware of where he was.

"She's going to crash," James said, shaking his head in desperation. "Crash and burn."

"Oh, I don't know that –"

"Nick, she has never mentioned the whole thing ever since that first couple of cards came. Not once. And neither have we. She actually believes now that he's simply out of the country."

Nicola nodded thoughtfully.

"And when the cards finally stop, it's all going to come back to her. It'll be like he's died all over again."

"So what'll we do?"

"I think the time has come to have a long talk with Mom."

With great reluctance, Nicola agreed.

They realized that something was wrong as soon as they saw the folded-up Sunday newspaper lying on the porch.

"Oh, God, Nick," James said as he fumbled for his key.

"Stay cool, it might not mean anything," Nicola said. "Let me try the doorbell." She reached past her brother and pressed the bell. The distant sound of *bing bong* from inside the house only seemed to exacerbate their feeling of impending doom.

Inserting the key in the lock, James turned the handle and opened the door. "Mom?"

They both stood on the porch for a couple of seconds, each of them convincing themselves that they simply didn't want to frighten their mother. But it was more than that. It was something both profound and sublime. So long as they remained outside the house then anything that might have happened in there stayed in the future as a mere possibility. Once they went in and confronted what they now believed to be inevitable, there was no turning back . . . no alternative but to accept.

"Maybe she's sick," Nicola said, taking the first step.

"Slept late?" James offered.

"James, it's two o'clock in the afternoon."

"We should have called," he said moving along the hallway.

"Mom?" Nicola shouted. "It's Nicola and James."

Irma was in the TV room sitting in Boz's chair. She could just have been asleep but they knew immediately that she wasn't.

"Oh, Mom," was all James could think of to say.

Nicola remembered what Frank Garnett had said about when he found his father dead in bed. *You know,* Frank had said, a look of something approaching wonderment on his face, *he just wasn't there any longer. It was his body but it was completely empty. Like a drawing of my dad rather than the actual article.*

And that was exactly how Irma Mendholsson looked, one foot tucked up beneath her leg and her head slumped over to one side.

James knelt down by the chair and felt her forehead. It was ice cold.

"James!" Nicola snapped, her voice barely above a whisper. "Look."

James followed his sister's pointing finger and saw, clamped in his mother's clasped hands resting in her lap, the edge of what appeared to be a piece of paper.

James prised her hands apart and there was another of his father's postcards, this one featuring a picture of Syney Opera House. He tugged at the card –

"She doesn't want to let go of it," Nicola said softly.

– and, through the tears, he read out the message on the back:

"Hey swetie

"Im in Astraylia. It's veryy hot. God, im so tired. i'm missing you like mad. i don't think i can carry on much lonegr. It is very hot here. i love you more than I can say. all my love

"Boz"

"Doesn't sound too good does he?"

"It's worse than that," James said. "The spelling and punctuation is adrift as well." He handed the card over to his sister and thrust his hands into his pockets. "Oh, Mom," he whispered.

* * *

This time the funeral was a quieter affair. Neither James nor his sister wanted a lot of people, so the only others in attendance were Jim and Angie, with Anthony, Jennifer and Maria, and baby Margaret-Jayne, plus, of course, Jackie and Phil Defantino.

At the end of the service and the internment, while Jim and Angie took the children back to their respective cars, James and Nicola stayed back to speak with Phil and Jackie. When they had exchanged the customary commiserations, Phil asked Jackie to wait for him in the car. She looked a little puzzled but did as she was asked.

The three of them watched her walk away, and then Phil turned to James and Nicola and, with a deep sigh, reached into his inside coat pocket and produced a brown paper bag that was about the shape and size of paperback novel. He handed it to James.

"What is it?" Nicola asked.

"I think I know," James said as he opened the bag. Without removing the contents he peered into the bag. For a few seconds it did indeed look like a paperback book, viewed from the page edges rather than from the spine. He folded the bag over again and handed it back to Phil. "There's nothing there that we want, Phil," he said. "Just some cards."

"James –"

"Nicola, remember what I told you Mom had said about destroying the magic?"

Nicola nodded.

James turned back to Phil. What were they like, those last dozen or so postcards? How much did he deteriorate by the time the end came? Suddenly, James felt thankful that his mother had died when she had. He couldn't imagine the heartbreak she would have gone through having to read them right up to the end and then for the cards to stop completely. He said, "Just get rid of them."

"You sure?"

"We're sure."

Nicola nodded and turned away.

"Will you be needing any help? With the house, I mean. Boz's books and magazines . . . all that stuff."

James shook his head and breathed in deeply. The intake of breath made him appear bigger and stronger than he felt. "We're going to get a dealer in, sell the lot. We could do it ourselves, advertising them, but it'd take too long. And we'd sooner see it happen in one hit."

"I understand," Phil said. "Well, if you need any help with anything at all, just give me a call."

"Will do. Nick and I are staying at the house for a few days to sort out all the furniture and, as you say, all of the books. Dad's old firm is doing the realty."

"He'd like that."

"That's what we figured. Anyway, by the end of next week, it'll just be a shell with a *For Sale* board in the yard."

Phil sighed and looked around. Jackie was standing by Phil's 4x4—she waved when she saw him looking and he nodded before turning back to James and Nicola. "Well, I guess that's it." He shook James's hand and gave Nicola a kiss on the cheek. "Keep in touch, huh?"

"You bet," James said.

Watching him walk away from them, they saw him remove a handkerchief from his pocket. In the stillness of the cemetery, the nose-blow— when it came—sounded like a clarion call or *Last Post*. Neither James nor Nicola could decide which.

* * *

The weekend wasn't as traumatic as they had feared it would be. And though they had both expected to be wracked with nostalgia, going through their mother's clothing and furniture proved to be relatively easy, with most of the stuff being either thrown away in a collection of garden refuse bags or stacked in neat piles for the thrift and charity stores off Main Street. In addition, they had a guy calling around early the following Tuesday to take all the furniture they didn't want or need—as it turned out, they didn't need anything and kept back only a couple of items that had earned a place in their memory.

The man from the realtors' office—a guy called Dane—came around on the Sunday and prepared a notice on the property. When he left, after less than an hour, James and Nicola stood watching the *For Sale* board long after his car had disappeared.

Monday morning dawned and with it came a sense of closure. The sun was shining, the house was pretty well cleared, and they were both looking forward to getting back to their own homes. The grieving process had started but, as James said—and had said repeatedly over the weekend—things could have panned out a lot worse than they had done.

By mid-morning, Nicola had wiped down all the paintwork and vacuumed the house from top to bottom. Now it was just a house: all the evidence of its life as the Mendholssons' home was now stored as memories in the cerebral databanks of James's and Nicola's heads to be accessed whenever they were required.

The one thing they hadn't thought of doing occurred to James as he watched the mailman walking along the sidewalk.

"Hey, we need to get in touch with the Post Office to have Mom's mail forwarded on to one of us." He got up from his seat on the floor against the side wall when he saw the mailman turn into Irma's yard. "You want to do it to me?"

"I guess me," she shouted after him, "because I'm here in town and I'm home with Margaret-Jayne most days."

James opened the door. "Makes sense to me," he shouted. Then, to the mailman, "Hey, how are you today?"

"I'm fine, but tired. Seems like I work harder at home on weekends than I do during the week." They both laughed. The mailman handed a small bundle of envelopes to James and expressed his sympathy for his loss. "How you doing anyways? It's a sad time for you."

James nodded as he flicked through the letters. "Yes it is, but I think –"

He stopped when he saw the postcard. He recognized the picture immediately—Venice . . . the Bridge of Sighs, the gondolier, the stone buildings: everything was there, just as it had been on the very first card that Irma had received from Boz.

James turned over the card. The first thing that he noticed was that this card was not addressed to his mother: it was addressed, in his father's hand—a strong hand once again—to him and Nicola care of his mother's address:

"Dearest James and Nicola," the message began. "Well, this is going to be the last card, I'm afraid."

"Is everything okay?" the mailman asked.

"Your mom arrived here yesterday morning—I can't tell you how good it was to see her again. Adventuring all by yourself is such a lonely business."

"James?" Nicola called from the room, her voice echoing in the empty house.

"She wants me to show her everything else and while we've got a mighty long time together now, there's *such* a lot to see!!! Look after each other and your wonderful families.

"Love as always. Dad"

And there was a *ps* at the bottom.

Nicola appeared alongside him just as James was finishing reading and the mailman was walking back down the path, shrugging repeatedly to himself.

Somewhere off on the Interstate a truck horn sounded, dopplering from soft to loud and then back to soft again, like some kind of animal.

"I don't believe it," James said, shaking his head.

He handed the postcard to Nicola and put his hands up to his face.

Nicola read.

"My God," she said. "His handwriting is back to normal and he sounds lucid again. But all this stuff about Mom, how could he have –" She stopped, looked up at her brother and then back down at the card.

"PS," she read. "I'm sure the past few days have been difficult for you both but I'm absolutely fine. Couldn't be happier. Have a wonderful life, both of you. We'll be following your progress— whenever our busy schedule permits it!

"Much love,

"Mom."

"How-"

James interrupted her. "I'll tell you one thing," he said, "about that card, and the one that came before—the first one."

Nicola, wide-eyed, simply nodded her head for him to continue.

"I think we were wrong . . . about the sun setting, I mean."

Nicola turned it over and looked at the photograph closely.

"I'm betting that's a sun*rise!*" He turned and smiled at her. "The start of a brand new day."

> The undiscovered country from whose bourn
> No traveller returns.
> > William Shakespeare, *Hamlet* (1601)

Glenn Chadbourne

NEVER BACK AGAIN

By Mattie Hautala

The young boy sat in the backyard of his house, whittling away at a long oak branch. His father was napping on the deck after another night shift at the hospital, and the boy had managed to slip the scalpel from his dad's white lab coat between snores. The boy's eyes focused hard now on each movement of the scalpel—he watched the blade cut hard around the broken edges of the wood, showing a smoother, cleaner surface underneath.

The boy held the tall oak branch up to the sky and inspected its fine curves and twists against the blue of midday. His gaze remained fixed and focused. He was enjoying himself, but the enjoyment was not that of an eight-year-old boy playing—this was the completion of a task.

He brought the branch back down to his lap to make some final corrections. With each passing second a small piece of wood would scrape off onto the grass and the boy would bring the scalpel back down to the base of the branch to whittle away another second, another piece of the whole.

"One two three, branches come from trees." He sang a little improvised song as his eyes focused intently on the stick—"... four five six, leaves grow on sticks." The young boy continued humming in the same rhythm until his voice lost interest in being heard. He looked over to the empty seat next to him on the bench and thought about how excited he had been when Mommy had told him he was going to have a new brother. He stared at the empty space next to him, hand steady, and he smiled, knowing that Mommy wouldn't ever lie to him.

The sun was sinking fast, heavy with the thought of night. The boy glanced up at the sky and knew he only had an hour left, if that.

* * *

The young boy's mother stood at the kitchen sink, scrubbing away vacantly at the mountain of dishes and pans left there from yesterday. She had used the frying pan the night before and would've left it another day or two, but now she had to wash it to make some stir fry for dinner. Having her husband home for dinner meant cooking "real food" as opposed to the usual hot dogs or American chop suey. To her all the flavors just blended together, but she knew it meant a lot to him.

She had a similar look in her eyes as the young boy did when he practiced his whittling—it was as if her son had inherited both her eye color and the weight of her years. She had been through a lot— two divorces, one miscarriage, and more career changes than she cared to count. She gazed off into the soapy ocean of the sink and spent the next five minutes washing the same plate.

She wondered if anyone—even she—knew what she was thinking or feeling.

* * *

The young boy ran into the kitchen with his freshly carved oak branch tucked under his sweatshirt. He darted past his mother standing sentry at the sink and made for the back door. Just as his small hand pushed open the screen door, his mother dropped the sponge and spoke with a cutting tone that pulled him back inside.

"I hope you're not planning to go over to that pond! I don't like it when you play out there alone. It's too far away and it's starting to get dark. No one could hear you if you needed help." The mother's love and concern for her son were apparent in her words, but her gaze was still fixed on that same plate, her hand running soapy circles, over and over.

She looked up from the sink and shot him a sharp look. The young boy took a second to control himself, to not get mad—he knew if he yelled back at her he wouldn't be allowed to go outside at all, and then he couldn't finish the game he had started at the pond. He took a quick breath and calmly responded, "Alright, Mom, I won't go there... but how many times do I have to tell you that when I'm out there, I'm not alone?"

The moment those last words left his mouth he realized his mistake—she hated talking about his little brother. The boy gripped the stick tightly beneath his sweatshirt.

His mother tensed up her neck then let out a sigh. "Cut it out sweetie! You know you don't have a brother. We... we lost him son. He's gone, and that's hard for Mommy and Daddy, too. But I surely don't intend on losing you, too! Only you, your father, and I live in this house, it's just us." Her voice shook with anger.

The boy looked up at his mother's pinched face. He knew she was angry, and that it was changing her, but he couldn't figure out *why* she was so mad. He was too young to really understand it but he noticed small differences; she would fall asleep watching T.V on the couch instead of reading to him in bed, she had burned the apple pie for dessert last night, she asked him less and less about how school was going. She had even forgotten to cut the crust off his sandwich for lunch. Things were different, and he just wished he could do something to help her feel better.

They hadn't read *The Hobbit* before bed in weeks but he figured that Gandalf was still her favorite character, and he hoped that she would like the wizard staff he had been carving for her. The boy twisted his hand underneath his sweatshirt - he wished that the oak branch was a real wizard staff so he could use its magic right now to help his mom feel better. The gift wasn't quite perfect yet, so he decided it was best to keep it hidden and wait until the time was just right.

His mother was still looking and him, and he realized she was waiting for a response.

"All right, Mom. I'll be safe. I promise. I'm just going to the other side of the road." As he walked out the kitchen door and into the backyard he whispered under his breath, "...and he isn't lost, he's just waiting."

The cold scalpel in his pocket knocked heavily against the boy's body as he ran towards the pond, eager to finish the game.

* * *

The young boy ran through the woods, and a soft breeze followed closely behind him. He tripped hard over a root while running uphill but caught himself and smiled brightly as the dark water came into view.

* * *

He arrived at the pond and ran to the edge of the embankment. He kicked up clumps of dirt as he ran down the hill towards the silent shore of the pond. Half of the surface was covered in slime and lily pads, and the parts of the water that managed to peek through were blacker than oil. The young boy looked anxiously at the glossy face of a lonely lily pad and said, "Hey, Brother, I've come back for you. I'm here."

He felt an excited tremor in his left leg and a tingling sensation ran up his spine and neck, leaving a slight buzz in his ears. The sun was setting quickly; he only had fifteen minutes or so to finish the game. The lily pad shook a little bit, and the young boy continued, "I brought what you asked for, but I want you to tell me what's going to happen.... I know it'll be funner if we're together, but I can't figure this all out alone. Help me, tell me."

A small breeze pushed the lily pad further away from the shore and the glossy leaf started to shake from side to side. The young boy heard the familiar voice whisper, "Does Mommy ever ask about me?" He knew the answer, but he didn't want to upset his little brother so he stood still, waiting. "Does she know I'm trapped here? That I'm stuck underwater, that I can't breathe? I need you, big brother. I need your air."

The young boy thought back to earlier that same day when he and his brother had been swimming in the pond together for hours, having fun and laughing. He wondered why his little brother wasn't laughing now like he was before. The playful, joyous tone was gone. Instead, the voice had a newfound urgency.

Tears came to the boys' eyes, and he said, "Mom just keeps saying we lost you. She never listens to me when I try to tell her that I found you. I just don't.... I want to have a little brother, that's all; someone to read to at night and walk to school with in the morning. It's no fair that I can only play with you out here at the pond. I want you to come home with me."

The voice answered, "I can't go home with you. You need to come home with *me*."

The surface of the water vibrated with a hum, and the lily pad started shaking. The boy looked down at his left leg and noticed a large gash where the scalpel had dug into his thigh during the run to the pond, but he felt no pain, and this comforted him.

The voice from the pond continued, "We'll be able to play together and you'll have a little brother. We'll be together, I promise. I know Mommy keeps saying she lost me, but it's not that simple. She thinks that time is like a tunnel with no way back but there is a way.... I'm waiting for you to come back for me."

The young boy stared at his reflection in the water. The still surface of the pond looked like a clear glass window and it reminded the boy of something. He remembered the dream he'd had the night before of a bird smashing over and over against the clear window in their living room, blood spilling down the cracks in the glass. But the bird wouldn't die. It was so real to him that he had run crying to his mother's room but she had just told him to forget about it, that it wasn't real. *Just a dream.* But didn't she also say that his brother wasn't real?

The boy was confused; he thought hard. The only thing he knew for sure was that the voice hadn't lied to him like Mommy had. The voice spoke simply and softly, always comforting him with words he already knew, and the voice liked playing games, too.

He wiped the tears from his eyes and sucked in a deep breath, air enough to respond; "I can see you," said the boy. "You're right there, sitting with me on the bench in the backyard. It feels like you're trapped underwater, waiting for a friend, just like me." The boy paused and looked down at the oak branch on the ground. "How do I go back for you?"

There was a cold silence as he thought hard. The boy looked up at the tired sun and remembered the time limit, the game. He slipped his hand into his left pocket and thought about what he'd brought for his brother. He took out the heavy scalpel and looked at the lily pad; "Why did you tell me to bring this?"

A strong gust of wind shook the water again and the voice answered back, "To cut me free. To cut away the thick skin that's leaving me trapped and drowned here. You need to cut the surface of the water so that I can breathe, so that *we* can breathe. You know how to find me, right?"

The weight of the question hung heavily above the cold, dead water. The young boy's heart raced and he shook with terror and confusion. What if he *didn't* know how to find his brother?

A sudden pain shot up his left leg and rested right behind his eyes. His vision blurred and the edge of the shore blended seamlessly into the dark water. The voice from underneath continued, "Trust in me; trust in yourself. Once you come in you'll be here with me, and we'll be together. Forever. No more loneliness, that's how you win. Slice me open and release me."

The boy's concentration was broken by the loud splash of a frog jumping into the water next to the lily pad. The distraction gave him a moment to think, and it became clear to the boy what he needed to do.

The ripples from the splash faded away and the boy's mind refocused on the task at hand. He had finally figured out why he brought his dad's knife to the pond—he knew how to win the game. He shouted out the answer, "You breathe water and I breathe air, so we have to switch places! I have to go underwater and give you my lungs, like a fish, right? That way we can keep playing all night and all day and Mommy won't be there to tell us to stop. Mommy won't be able to keep us apart anymore... this way we can both win the game!"

The young boy smiled and made a tight fist around the cold, grey handle and buried the scalpel into his neck, first one side and then the other, over and over, creating gills. The numbing pain of the blade's smooth slices cleared the boy's mind as the knife dug deeper and deeper into his throat. He breathed in warm bubbles of his own blood and a tired smile appeared on his face. He could breathe again.

His heart filled with joy; he was a kid, a kid with a real brother. He had never felt his heartbeat before now but he was suddenly aware of the pounding drumbeat that pushed blood out of his neck. He stumbled hard to the left and his vision steadied slightly as his lungs filled with liquid. His eyes focused proudly on the lily pad as his body fell into the pond, breaking the peaceful glass of the water's surface. The bloody ripples swallowed the young boy's body and his clouded eyes stared numbly at a rock on the floor of the pond. The boy pictured the rock as a baby, growing bigger as he sank closer and closer to it. *You're almost there.*

* * *

The boy's mother stood at the sink looking out at the darkening sky and wondered whether or not she should go looking for her son in the woods. Dinner was almost ready but he still had about ten minutes to get home. She dried her hands hurriedly and felt relieved when she heard two voices coming from the woods, playing and laughing.

She focused in on the second voice– *who is he with? There's no one else out there with him!* "What the f…."

She ran out the kitchen door towards the woods and as she ran the laughter grew louder and louder. What felt like a warm breath swept across her neck and her eyes suddenly flashed shut; her world went silent. She knew this feeling. He was here.

* * *

When she stopped at the shore of the pond, she saw the body of her son resting in the shallow, rusty water. "No, no…," she whispered. Her eyes locked onto a broken lily stem that was laced between the ragged gill slits in her son's neck. She lifted her son up by the shoulder and looked into his eyes: wide open, staring. He had a slight smile on his face, like a boy who had just found something he had been looking for forever, something special. As sad as it was, she thought he looked happy.

She was unable to cry or scream, silenced by the blinding fact that she had lost her second son. She choked for air and imagined a warm umbilical cord wrap around her neck; *this is what it must've felt like,* she thought. *This is what it felt like when you were being born and my body choked the life out of you. What it felt like when you breathed blood.*

The boy's mother brought her hands down from her throat and felt a chilly breeze cool the back of her hand. As she knelt next to the shore her fingertips broke the calm surface of the water. She held her son's hand and saw the scalpel he held tightly in his palm. She wasn't sure if she envied him more for his faith or his innocence. She wasn't sure if there was a difference.

Glenn Chadbourne

A GIRL SITTING

By Mark Morris

The screech of pneumatic drills. Men shouting. Scaffolding. Rubble. Mud.

"It might look like the Somme now," Dunbar said, "but in three months it'll be paradise."

"What's the Somme?" asked Diane, jiggling one-month-old Abigail on her hip.

Matt sighed and preceded his wife and Dunbar into the house.

If Diane had her way—and she usually did—then this would become their first proper family home. For the past three years Matt and Diane had rented a poky flat above the chippy on Dean Street in the city centre. Now she wanted to relocate to this new development in the suburbs, put a deposit down, and move in before the magnolia-white emulsion had barely had chance to dry on the walls. Matt would have preferred something older, something with character, something that wasn't a clone of its neighbours—but he also wanted a quiet life, and he knew the only way to get one was to accede to Diane's requests.

Once inside, he didn't bother waiting for Diane and the estate agent to catch him up. He wasn't interested in Dunbar's 'ideal homes' spiel or in adopting the role of nodding dog in the wake of his wife's squeally enthusiasm. The house as it stood, half-finished and empty, was currently little more than a box divided into a series of echoey spaces, and therefore, in his estimation, nothing to get excited about.

The rooms were of a regular shape and size, there were no cubbyholes, no quirky nooks and crannies, no surprises whatsoever. The place felt cold and smelled of fresh paint and damp plaster. His footsteps echoed hollowly off the walls.

By the time Diane, encouraged by Dunbar, was getting all orgasmic over the waste-disposal unit in the gleaming new kitchen, Matt had drifted upstairs. He stuck his head around the bathroom door, noting its white sink and bath, its corner shower unit—all nice and neutral. The first of three bedrooms overlooked what would eventually be the back garden but for now was a churned-up battlefield. Matt gave it a cursory glance and stepped back on to the landing. As he heard Diane and Dunbar clumping upstairs, he ducked quickly into bedroom number two to avoid Dunbar's banal patter.

There was a girl sitting on a chair against the far wall.

Matt jumped, not because the girl evoked fear, but simply because her presence was so unexpected. She was sitting silently, and perfectly motionless, her hands on her knees, a distracted expression on her face. She was eleven or twelve, clothed in an anonymous brownish dress with white collar and cuffs. Her mousy hair was braided into plaits which brushed her shoulders.

"Hello," Matt said.

She didn't answer, didn't even acknowledge his presence. Her eyes remained fixed on a point somewhere to his left.

"Are you supposed to be here?" Matt asked. And then: "What's your name?"

The girl stayed silent.

Matt felt a little uneasy, which in turn made him feel foolish. He walked slowly towards the girl, his feet clumping on bare floorboards.

"Are you all right?" he asked. "Because –"

He was less than two metres from the girl when she disappeared.

Matt blinked, sucking in air so quickly that it felt fishbone-sharp in his throat. For a moment he wasn't sure what had happened. It was almost as if his attention had been diverted for a split-second, during which the girl had taken the opportunity to slip away. He gaped at the spot where she had been sitting and even stepped forward to waft his hand through the space. He felt tingly, hot and cold at the same time, and his heart raced. Had she been a ghost? Had he just had an honest-to-god supernatural experience?

Mouth dry, he took a few stumbling steps back into the centre of the room—and the girl reappeared, hands on her knees just as before, silent and motionless on her wooden chair. Matt began to shake, but before he could decide what to do the door opened and Dunbar led Diane into the room.

"And this is the second bedroom," the estate agent said, waving his hand extravagantly as though scattering seeds.

"Oh, this is *mint*," said Diane. "This is definitely going to be the nursery. What do you reckon, Matt?"

Matt couldn't reply. His throat felt as if it had narrowed to the circumference of a pencil.

Diane frowned. "What's-a matter with you? You look like a retard."

Matt still couldn't speak. He could only point at the girl.

Diane and Dunbar followed the direction of his finger. As if speaking to a slow-witted child, Diane said, "Yes. We call it a *wall*." Glancing at Dunbar, she raised her eyebrows. "Sorry about this. My husband's not usually such a mong."

Matt's eyes widened. Could they not *see* what he was seeing? Evidently not—which could only mean that he was either psychic or hallucinating.

I see dead people, he thought, and felt a sudden urge to laugh like an idiot. With an effort he swallowed the urge, which released his voice.

"Sorry," he said. "Massive spider. It's gone now."

Three months later they moved in. Matt didn't go into the second bedroom until the removal men had left and Diane was installed on the settee in front of *Loose Women*, Abigail sucking greedily on her nipple.

The upstairs landing was quiet. Quieter than it had been three months ago, now that the carpets were down. Diane had chosen the carpets, blue downstairs, pink up here. Matt had hated the pink, but she had insisted. Just as she had insisted on the mini glass chandelier in the front room. Just as she had insisted on the new flat-screen TV which Matt had spent the last hour installing and tuning in so that she wouldn't miss her soaps.

And just as she had insisted on moving here in the first place, despite his protestations.

Matt had tried everything to change her mind. He had told her that the house was too small; that the building firm had a reputation for shoddy workmanship; that all the decent schools were outside their catchment area; that there was a high-crime estate not more than a mile away.

But his words had fallen on stony ground. Not only had Diane refused to listen, but as usual she had shouted him down, ridiculed and reviled him. *If it hadn't been for Abigail*, he sometimes thought....

But no. He had made his bed and it was his duty to lie in it. Hadn't his parents drummed into him the importance of always making the best of things?

So here he was, once again standing outside the door of bedroom number two—the room that Diane *insisted* was going to be the nursery.

He listened. Aside from the blur of chatter from the TV downstairs, he could hear nothing. The lack of noise reminded him that they were the first to move into the estate, that the houses surrounding them were silent and empty. Bracing himself, he pushed the door open and stepped inside.

The girl in the brown dress was sitting on her chair against the wall.

Matt's heartbeat quickened. His mouth went dry. The girl was just as she had been three months earlier—silent and motionless, gazing abstractedly at a spot just beyond his left shoulder.

He took a deep breath, and then stepped directly into her eye line. Her gaze didn't flicker. She was looking at him, but not looking at him. He moved closer. Closer.

She disappeared.

Later, in bed, he said, "I think we should turn the back bedroom into the nursery."

He sensed Diane's body stiffen. "Why?"

"Because it's a nicer room. It looks out over the back garden, which means it'll be quieter, too. Plus it's next to the bathroom, which'll be more convenient."

She grunted like an exasperated warthog. "We've already decided where Abi's going."

"*You've* decided, you mean? But it's not set in stone, is it? We can change our minds."

"I want Abi next door to us. Where we can hear her."

"We'll be able to hear her wherever she is. It's not exactly the biggest house in the world."

"What's that supposed to mean?"

"Nothing. I'm just saying...."

"Well, don't."

Matt sighed inwardly. After a moment he said, "It's just that that room next door... it's got a funny atmosphere."

She twisted round so quickly that he thought she was going to slap him. "What?"

He felt the familiar sinking feeling he got whenever he was losing an argument. "It's just... something about it doesn't feel right. It gives me the creeps."

It was dark, but he sensed Diane staring at him, her expression scornful. "You're pathetic," she said eventually—and at that moment Abigail, in the cot at the end of their bed, began to cry. "Now see what you've done."

The following week, at Diane's insistence, Matt decorated the nursery. The whole time he was in there, putting up yellow wallpaper with teddy bears on it, the girl sat silently on her chair, staring into space.

Whenever he was forced to turn his back on her, Matt got an itch between his shoulder blades. He kept imagining her rising slowly to her feet, crossing the room towards him in short, jerky strides. And even if he was half-way up a ladder, he would twist his head, convinced that the girl would be standing right behind him.

But she never was. On each occasion she was still sitting on her chair, as motionless as ever. Her manner was innocuous, there was even something forlorn about her, and yet her presence filled him with such dread that sometimes he could barely breathe.

He spoke to her frequently, sometimes calmly, sometimes with a hissing vehemence born of fear. Again and again he would ask her who she was, why she was here, what she wanted. He would plead with her to go away and leave them alone, or simply snarl at her to fuck off. Sometimes he would say, "If you do anything to hurt my family...," before spluttering impotently into silence.

After a while the simple knowledge that she was there, in the house with them, began to wear him down. At night he wouldn't sleep; he would listen for the slightest scrape of movement through the wall. And whatever room he was in, he would always be aware of her presence. She was like a darkness, a tumour, embedded in the body of the house.

Matt lost his appetite. Became thinner. Grew twitchy and nervous. Preoccupied with Abigail, and with befriending their new neighbours, Diane didn't even notice.

After a month or so, Abi moved out of their room and into her new nursery. She slept in her cot against one wall and the girl sat on her chair against the other. Matt would spend as much time as he could, without arousing Diane's suspicions, in the room with his daughter. He would slump against the wall by her cot and stare balefully across the room at the girl, keeping guard.

But he couldn't be there all the time, and when Abi and the girl were alone together, Matt would feel anxiety gnawing at him. He would obsessively watch the baby monitor, jump up at the slightest sound or the merest flicker from the row of green lights beneath the little speaker. He would pretend he needed a pee just so that he could run upstairs and check on his daughter.

And each time the girl would be sitting on her chair, hands on knees, staring.

Matt tried to find out who she was. He thought that if he could do that, then maybe he could exorcise her, lay her to rest. He went to the local library, scoured the internet, but found nothing. There had never been a house or a church or a school on this site. Never been an accident or a murder. For hundreds of years this had been farmland, and before that, forest. The girl was an anomaly. She shouldn't be here. He told her so.

"You've got no right to be in my house," he said. "Why don't you just go away?"

No response. She just sat and stared.

Six weeks after they'd moved in, Diane announced, "I'm going out with Sandra and the girls,"

It was a Wednesday night. Matt was hunched forward on the settee, eyes flickering between the TV and the baby monitor on the sideboard. He had no idea what he was watching. Sleeplessness and stress had turned his brain to cement. He looked up, blinking.

"What?"

Diane rolled her eyes. "Why don't you get a grip? I said I'm going out with Sandra."

"Who's Sandra?"

"Oh, for fuck's sake. She lives at number 12. Her husband's the golfer."

She said this as though he ought to know. Matt let it slide. "What about Abigail?"

"She'll be fine. Milk's in the fridge. You'll just have to warm her bottle. Not too hot though. See you later."

Then she was gone, in a whirlwind of flowery perfume.

As soon as the front door slammed, Matt scuttled upstairs. He entered the dimly-lit nursery and slumped down against the wall beside the cot. Abi was sleeping peacefully. The girl was in her usual position. Matt drew up his knees and stared at the girl. Time passed. The silence was dense, heavy, like the air before a thunderstorm.

He didn't realise he'd fallen asleep until Abi started grizzling. His eyes snapped open in sudden panic, but the girl was still there, unmoving. Wearily Matt rose to his feet, picked up his daughter and tried to calm her. But she was restless, pushing her tiny fists into her mouth.

"All right," he said, putting her carefully back into her cot and glancing across the room at the girl. "I'll get your bottle."

He ran downstairs, heart pounding, hating the thought of leaving Abi alone with the girl. It wasn't until he had plonked the bottle in a pan of hot water in the kitchen and was moving from foot to foot, waiting for it to warm through, that it occurred to him to wonder why he hadn't just brought Abi down with him. Was he unable to think straight because he was exhausted or because the girl was exerting some kind of malign influence over him? Snatching the bottle from the pan, he ran into the hallway.

Above his head a floorboard creaked.

"No!" he shouted, scrambling up the stairs. Reaching the top he leaped across the landing, into the nursery. His eyes darted to where the girl was sitting—except that she wasn't there. Her chair was empty.

And then he detected movement on the other side of the cot. His head twisted so sharply that pain burst in his skull like a firework. Through a cluster of falling stars he saw the girl bent over the cot, both arms reaching inside.

"No!" Matt shouted again, and for the first time the girl seemed to hear him.

She looked up, and on her face was an expression of terrible regret.

"Sorry, Daddy," she whispered.

"Get away from her!" Matt screamed, and plunged towards her, hands outstretched.

As ever, when he got to within a metre of the girl, she smeared out of existence. Falling against the side of the cot, Matt looked down. Abi was lying on her back, arms up beside her head. She was very still and her face was already turning blue. Matt lifted her up and cradled her, smothering her with his warmth.

"Wake up," he whispered, "wake up, wake up, wake up." He repeated the words, over and over, for the next hour. Finally he raised his head, which felt heavy as a boulder, and looked across the room.

The girl was back in her usual place, on her chair against the wall. Matt knew she would always be there for him now, no matter where he went.

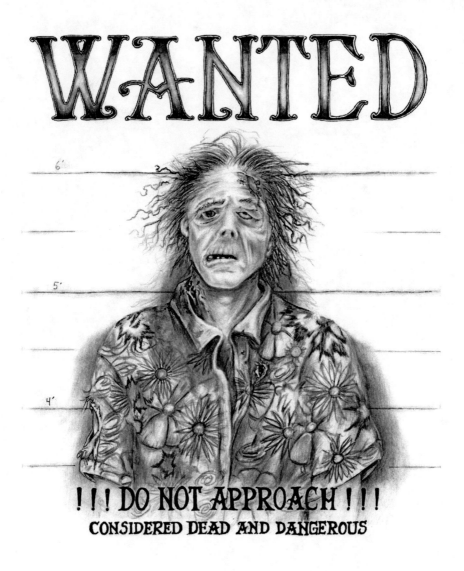

!!! DO NOT APPROACH !!!
CONSIDERED DEAD AND DANGEROUS

Morbideus W. Goodell

BLOOD BROTHERS

By Richard Chizmar

ONE

I grabbed the phone on the second ring and cleared my throat, but before I could wake up my mouth enough to speak, there came a man's voice: *"Hank?"*

"Uh, huh."

"It's me...Bill."

The words hit me like a punch to the gut. I jerked upright in the bed, head dizzy, feet kicking at a tangle of blankets.

"Jesus, Billy, I didn't recog—"

"I know, I know...it's been a long time."

We both knew the harsh truth of that simple statement and we let the next thirty seconds pass in silence. Finally I took a deep breath and said, "So I guess you're out, huh? They let you out early."

I listened as he took a deep breath of his own. Then another. When he finally spoke, he sounded scared: *"Hank, listen...I'm in some trouble. I need you to—"*

"Jesus H. Christ, Billy! You busted out, didn't you? You fucking-a busted out!"

My voice was louder now, almost hysterical, and Sarah lifted her head from the pillow and mumbled, "What's wrong? Who is it, honey?"

I moved the phone away from my face and whispered, "It's no one, sweetheart. Go back to sleep. I'll tell you in the morning."

She sighed in the darkness and rested her head back on the

pillow.

"*Hey, you still there? Dammit, Hank, don't hang up!*"

"Yeah, yeah, I'm here," I said.

"*I really need your help, big brother. You know I never woulda called if—*"

"Where are you?"

"*Close…real close.*"

"Jesus."

"*Can you come?*"

"Jesus, Billy. What am I gonna tell Sarah?"

"*Tell her it's work. Tell her it's an old friend. Hell, I don't know, tell her whatever you have to.*"

"Where?"

"*The old wooden bridge at Hanson Creek.*"

"When?"

"*As soon as you can get there.*"

I looked at the glowing red numbers on the alarm clock, 5:37.

"I can be there by six-fifteen."

The line went dead.

TWO

I slipped the phone back onto its cradle and just sat there for a couple of minutes, rubbing my temple with the palm of my hand. It was a habit I'd picked up from my father, and it was a good thing Sarah was still sleeping; she hated when I did it, said it made me look like a tired old man.

She was like that, always telling me to stay positive, to keep my chin up, not to let life beat me down so much. She was one in a million, that's for damn sure. A hundred smiles a day and not one of them halfway or phony.

Sitting there in the darkness, thinking of her in that way, I surprised myself and managed something that almost resembled a smile.

But the thought went away and I closed my eyes and it seemed like a very long time was passing, me just sitting there in the bed like a child afraid of the dark or the boogeyman hiding in the bottom of the closet. Suddenly—and after all this time—there I was thinking so many of the same old thoughts. Anger, frustration, guilt, fear—all of it rushing back at me in a tornado of red-hot emotion....

So I just sat there and hugged myself and felt miserable and lost and lonely and it seemed like a very long time, but when I opened my eyes and looked up at the clock, I saw that not even five minutes had passed.

I dressed quietly in the cold darkness. Back in the far corner of the bedroom. I didn't dare risk opening the dresser drawers and waking Sarah, so I slipped on a pair of wrinkled jeans and a long sleeve t-shirt from the dirty laundry hamper. The shirt smelled faintly of gasoline and sweat.

After checking on Sarah, I tiptoed down the hallway and poked my head into the girls' room for a quick peek, then went downstairs. I washed my face in the guest bathroom and did my business but didn't flush. For just a second, I thought about coffee—something to help clear my head—but decided against it. Too much trouble. Not enough time.

After several minutes of breathless searching, I found the car keys on the kitchen counter. I slipped on a jacket and headed for the garage.

Upstairs, in the bedroom, Sarah rolled over and began lightly snoring. The alarm clock read 5:49.

THREE

He saved my life once. A long time ago, back when we were kids.

It was a hot July afternoon—ninety-six in the shade and not a breeze in sight. It happened no more than thirty yards downstream from the old Hanson Bridge, just past the cluster of big weeping willow trees. One minute I was splashing and laughing and fooling around, and the next I was clawing at the muddy creek bottom six, seven feet below the surface. It was the mother of all stomach cramps; the kind your parents always warned you about but you never really believe existed. Hell, when you're a kid, the old "stomach cramp warning" falls into the same dubious category as "never fool around with a rusty nail" and "don't play outside in the rain." To adults, these matters make perfect sense, but to a kid...well, you know what I'm talking about.

Anyway, by the time Billy pulled me to the surface and dragged me ashore, my ears had started to ring something awful, and the hell with seeing stars, I was seeing entire solar systems. So Billy put me over his shoulder and carried me a half-mile into town and Dad had to leave the plant three hours early on a Monday just to pick me up at the Emergency Room.

I survived the day, more embarrassed than anything, and Billy was a reluctant hero, not only in our family but all throughout the neighborhood. Old Widow Fletcher across the street even baked a chocolate cake to celebrate the occasion with Billy's name written out in bright pink icing.

I was thirteen, Billy twelve, when all this happened.

Like I said, it was a long time ago, but the whole thing makes for a pretty good story, and I've told it at least a couple hundred times. In fact, it's the one thing I always tell people when the inevitable moment finally arrives and they say, "Jeez, Hank, I didn't know you had a brother."

I hear those words and I just smile and shrug my shoulders as if to say "Oh, well, sorry I never mentioned it" and then I slip right into the story.

This usually happens at social gatherings—holiday work parties, neighborhood cook-outs, that sort of thing. Someone from the old neighborhood shows up and mentions Billy's name, asks what he's been up to, and another person overhears the conversation. And then the questions:

"What's your brother's name? Does he live around here? What's he do for a living? Why haven't you mentioned him before, Hank?"

Happens two, three times a year. And when it does I just grin my stupid grin and tell the drowning story one more time...and then I make my escape before they can ask any more questions. "Excuse me, folks, I have to use the restroom." Or "Hey, isn't that Fred Matthews over there by the pool? Fred, wait up. I've been meaning to ask you...."

It works every time.

* * *

Billy was just a year behind me, but you never would've guessed it growing up. He looked much younger; two, maybe even three years. He was short for his age and thin. Real thin. Dad always used to say—and at the time we could never figure out just *what the hell* he was talking about—that Billy looked like a boy made out of wire. Little guy is tough as wire, he'd always say, and give Billy a proud smile and a punch on the shoulder.

Despite his physical size, Billy was fast and strong and agile and much more athletic than me. His total lack of fear and dogged determination made him a star; my lack of coordination made me a second-stringer. But we both had fun, and we stuck together for the three years we shared in high school. We played all the same sports—football in the fall, basketball in the winter, baseball in the spring.

Baseball. Now, that's where Billy really shined. All-County second-base as a sophomore. All-County and All-State as a junior and again as a senior.

A true-blue hometown hero by the time he was old enough to drive a car.

After graduation, I stayed in town and took business classes over at the junior college. Summer before sophomore year, I found an apartment a few miles away from home. Got a part-time job at a local video store. Played a little softball on Thursday nights, some intramural flag football on the weekends. Stopped by and saw the folks two, three times a week. Ran around with a few girlfriends, but nothing serious or lasting. For me, not too much had changed.

Then Billy graduated and went upstate to college on a baseball scholarship and *everything* seemed to change.

First, there was the suspension. Billy and three other teammates got caught cheating on a mid-term English exam and were placed on academic probation and suspended from the team.

Then, a few months later, in the spring, he was arrested at a local rock concert for possession of marijuana. It shouldn't have been that big a deal, but at the time, he'd been carrying enough weed to warrant a charge for Intent to Distribute. Then, at the court trial, we discovered that this was his second offense, and the university kindly asked him to clear out his dorm room and leave campus immediately. His scholarship was revoked.

He was lucky enough to receive a suspended sentence from the judge but instead of moving back home and finding a job—which is what Mom and Dad hoped he would do—Billy decided to stay close to campus and continue working at a local restaurant. He claimed he wanted to make amends with his baseball coach and try to re-enroll after the next semester if the university would allow him. So he moved in with some friends, and for a time it appeared as though he'd cleaned up his act. He kept out of trouble—at least as far as we (and his probation officer) could tell—and he stopped by on a regular basis to see Mom and Dad, and he even came by my place once or twice a month (although usually only when he needed to borrow a couple of bucks).

So anyway things went well for a while....

Until the rainy Sunday midnight the police called and told Mom and Dad they needed to come down to Fallston General right away. Billy had been driven to the Emergency Room by one of his roommates; just an hour earlier he'd been dumped in the street in front of his apartment—a bloody mess. Both hands broken. A couple of ribs. Nose mashed. Left ear shredded. He was lucky to be alive.

We found out the whole story then: it seemed that my baby brother had a problem with gambling. The main problem being that he wasn't very good at it. He owed some very dangerous people some very significant amounts of money. The beating had been a friendly reminder that his last payment had been twelve hours late.

Billy came home from the hospital ten days later. Moved into his old room at home. This time, Mom and Dad got their way without much of an argument. A month or so later, when Billy was feeling up to it. Dad got him a job counting boxes over at the plant. Soon after, he started dating Cindy Lester, a girl from the other side of town. A very sweet girl. And pretty, too. She was just a senior over at the high school—barely eighteen years old—but she seemed to be good for Billy. She wanted to be a lawyer one day, and she spent most of her weeknights studying at the library, her weekends at the movies or the shopping mall with Billy.

One evening, sometime late October, the leaves just beginning to change their colors, Billy stopped by my apartment with a pepperoni pizza and a six-pack of Coors. We popped in an old Clint Eastwood video and stayed up most of the night talking and laughing. There was no mention of gambling or drugs or Emergency Room visits. Instead, Billy talked about settling down, making a future with Cindy. He talked about finding a better job, maybe taking some classes over at the junior college. Accounting and business courses, just like his big brother. Jesus, it was like a dream come true. I could hardly wait until morning to call the folks and tell them all about it.

To this very day, I can remember saying my prayers that night, thanking God for giving my baby brother another chance.

That night was more than eight years ago.

I haven't seen him since.

FOUR

I drove slowly across the narrow wooden bridge. Clicked on the high-beams.

There were no other cars in sight.

Just empty road. Dense forest. And a cold December wind.

My foot tapped the brake pedal and I thought to myself: *Hank Foster, you've lost your mind. This is crazy. Absolutely crazy.*

I reached the far side of the bridge and pulled over to the dirt shoulder. I sat there shivering for a long couple of minutes. Looking up at the rearview mirror. Staring out at the frozen darkness.

I turned the heater up a notch.

Turned off the headlights.

It was 6:17.

* * *

I looked at my watch for the tenth time. 6:21.

Jesus, this really *was* crazy. Waiting in the middle of nowhere for God knows what to happen. Hell, it was more than crazy, it was dangerous. Billy had sounded scared on the phone, maybe even desperate, and he'd said he was in trouble. Those had been his exact words: *I'm in some trouble.* Even after all this time, I knew the kind of trouble my brother was capable of. So what in the hell was I doing out here? I had Sarah and the girls to think about now, a business to consider....

Or maybe, just maybe, he had changed. Maybe he had left the old Billy behind those iron bars and a better man had emerged. Maybe he had actually learned a thing or two—

—yeah, and maybe Elvis was still alive and catching rays down on some Mexican beach and the Cubs were gonna win the goddamn

Word Series.

Nice to imagine, one and all, but not real likely, huh?

I was starting to sweat now. *Really* sweat. I felt it on my neck. My face. My hands. And I felt it snaking down from my armpits, dribbling across my ribcage. Sticky. Cold and hot at the same time.

I leaned down and turned off the heat. Cracked the window. Inhaled long and deep. The sharp sting of fresh air caught me by surprise, made me dizzy for a moment, and I realized right then and there what was going on: I was scared. Probably more scared than I had ever been in my entire life.

With the window open, I could hear the wind rattling the trees and the creek moving swiftly in the darkness behind me. In the dry months of summer, Hanson Creek was slow-moving and relatively shallow, maybe eight feet at its deepest point. But in the winter, with all the snow run-off, the creek turned fast and mean and unforgiving. Sometimes, after a storm, the water rose so quickly, the police were forced to close down the bridge and detour traffic up north to Route 24. One winter, years ago, it stayed closed for the entire month of January.

The old house where we grew up—where Mom and Dad still live today—was just a short distance north from here. No more than a five-minute drive. Back when we were kids, Billy and I walked down here most every morning during the summer. All the neighborhood kids came here. We brought bag lunches and bottles of pop and hid them in the bushes so no one would steal them. Then we swam all day long and held diving contests down at the rope swing. When the weather was too cool to swim, we played war in the woods and built forts made out of rocks and mud and tree branches. Other times, we fished for catfish and carp and the occasional bass or yellow perch. On *real* lucky days, when it rained hard enough to wear away the soil, we searched for (and usually found) Indian arrowheads wedged in with the tree roots that grew along the creek's steep banks. We called those rainy days *treasure hunts*, and took turns acting as "expedition leader." The creek was a pretty wonderful place.

I thought about all this and wondered if that was the reason Billy had chosen the bridge as our meeting place. Was he feeling sentimental? A little nostalgic maybe? Probably not; as usual, I was probably giving the bastard too much credit....

* * *

Like I told you, I haven't seen him in more than eight years. Not since that long ago autumn night we spent together talking at my apartment. One week later, Billy just up and disappeared. No note, no message, nothing. Just an empty closet, a missing suitcase, and eighty dollars gone from Mom's purse.

And to make matters worse, Mr. Lester called the house later that evening and told us that Cindy hadn't been to school that day, was she with Billy by any chance?

The next morning, Dad called Billy's probation officer. He wasn't much help. He told us to sit tight, that maybe Billy would come to his senses. Other than that, there was really nothing we could do but wait.

And so for two weeks, we waited and heard nothing.

Then, on a Sunday afternoon, Mom and Dad sitting out on the front porch reading the newspaper, still dressed in their church clothes, there was a phone call: *I know I know it was a stupid thing to do but you see Cindy's pregnant and scared to death of her father he's a mean sonofabitch real mean and California is the place to be these days heck we already have jobs and a place to stay and there's lots of great people out here we've got some really nice friends already c'mon please don't cry Mom please don't yell Dad we're doing just fine really we are we're so much in love and we're doing just fine....*

Six months later, Cindy Lester came home. Alone. While walking back from work one night, she had been raped and beaten in a Los Angeles alley. She'd spent three days in the hospital with severe cuts and bruises. She'd lost her baby during the first night. Cindy told us that she'd begged him over and over again, but Billy had refused to come home with her. So she'd left him.

Over the next three years, there were exactly seven more phone calls (two begging for money) and three short handwritten letters. The envelopes were postmarked from California, Arizona, and Oregon.

Then, early in the fourth year, the police called. Billy had been arrested in California for drug trafficking. This time, the heavy stuff: cocaine and heroin. Dad hired Billy a decent lawyer, and both he and Mom flew out to the trial and watched as the judge gave Billy seven years in the state penitentiary.

I never went to see him. Not even once. Not at the trial. Not when Mom and Dad went for their twice-a-year visits. And not when Billy sent the letter asking me to come. I just couldn't do it.

I didn't hate him the way Mom and Dad thought I did. Jesus, he was still my baby brother. But he was locked up back there where he belonged, and I was right here where I belonged. We each had our own lives to live.

So no I didn't hate him. But I couldn't forgive him, either. Not for what he had done to this family—the heartbreak of two wonderful, loving parents; the complete waste of their hard-earned retirement savings; the shame and embarrassment he brought to all of us—

—bare knuckles rapped against the windshield and I jumped so hard I hit my head. I also screamed.

I could hear laughing from outside the car, faint in the howling wind, but clear enough to instantly recognize.

It was him alright.

My baby brother.

Suddenly a face bent down into view. Smiled.

And I just couldn't help it. I smiled right back.

FIVE

We hugged for a long time. Car door open, engine still running. Both of us standing outside in the cold and the wind. Neither of us saying a word.

We hugged until I could no longer stand the smell of him.

Then we stopped and sort of stood back and looked at each other.

"Jesus, Billy, I can't believe it," I said.

"I know, I know." He shook his head and smiled. "Neither can I."

"Now, talk to me. What's this all about? What kind of trouble are—"

He held up his hand. "In a minute, okay? Lemme just look at you a while longer."

For the next couple of minutes, we stood there facing each other, shivering in the cold. The Foster boys, together once again.

He was heavier than the last time I'd seen him; maybe fifteen, twenty pounds. And he was shaved bald, a faint shadow of dark stubble showing through. Other than that, he was still the Billy I remembered. Bright blue eyes. Big stupid smile. That rosy-cheeked baby face of his.

"Hey, you like my hair," he asked, reading my thoughts.

"Yeah," I said, "who's your barber?"

"Big black sonofabitch from Texas. Doing life for first-degree murder. Helluva nice guy, though."

He waited for my response and when I didn't say anything, he laughed. This time, it sounded harsh and a little mean.

"How's the folks?" he asked.

I shrugged my shoulders. "You know, pretty much the same. They're doing okay."

"And Sarah and the girls?"

My heart skipped a beat. An invisible hand reached up from the ground and squeezed my balls.

"Mom and Dad told me all about 'em. Sent me pictures in the mail," he said.

I opened my mouth, but couldn't speak. Couldn't breathe.

"They're twins, right? Let's see...four years old...Kacy and Katie, if I remember right."

I sucked in a deep breath. Let it out.

"I bet you didn't know I carry their picture around in my wallet. The one where they're sitting on the swing set in those fancy little blue dresses—"

"Five," I said, finally finding my voice.

"Huh?"

"The girls," I said. "They just turned five. Back in October."

"Halloween babies, huh? That's kinda neat. Hey, remember how much fun we used to have trick-or-treatin'? 'Member that time we spent the night out back the old Myer's House? Camped out in Dad's old tent. Man, that was a blast."

I nodded my head. I remembered everything. The costumes we used to make. The scary movies we used to watch, huddled together on the sofa, sharing a glass of soda and a bowl of Mom's popcorn. All the creepy stories we used to tell each other before bedtime.

Suddenly I felt sorry for him—standing there in his tattered old clothes, that dumb smile refusing to leave his face, smelling for all the world like a dumpster full of food gone to spoil. I suddenly felt very sorry for him and very guilty for me.

"I didn't break out, you know," he said. "They released me two weeks ago. Early parole."

"Jesus, Billy. That's great news."

"I spent a week back in L.A. seeing some friends. Then I hitched a ride back here. Made it all the way to the state line. I walked in from there."

"I still can't goddamn believe it. Wait until Mom and Dad see you."

"That's one of the things I need to talk to you about, Hank. Why don't we take a walk and talk for a while, okay?"

"Sure, Billy," I said. "Let's do that."

So that's exactly what we did.

SIX

I still miss him.

It's been four months now since that morning at the bridge. And not a word.

I read the newspaper every day. Watch the news every night.

And still there's been nothing.

I think about him all the time now. Much more often than I used to. Once or twice a week, I take a drive down to the old bridge. I stand outside the car and watch the creek rushing by, and I think back to the time when we were kids. Back to a time when things were simple and happy.

God, I miss him.

* * *

He wanted money. Plain and simple, as always.

First, he tried to lie to me. Said it was for his new "family." Said he got married two days after he got out of prison. Needed my help getting back on his feet.

But I didn't fall for it.

So then he told me the truth. Or something close to it anyway. There was this guy, an old friend from up around San Francisco. And Billy owed him some big bucks for an old drug deal gone bad.

Right around thirty grand. If he didn't come up with the cash, this old friend was gonna track him down and slit his throat.

"So how about a little help, big brother?"

Sorry, I told him. No can do. I'd like to help out, but I've got a family now. A mortgage. My own business barely keeping its head above water. Sorry. Can't help you.

So then he started crying. And begging me.

And when that didn't work, he got pissed off.

His eyes went cold and distant; his voice got louder.

He said: "Okay that's fine. I'll just hit up the old man and the old lady. They'll help me out. Damn right they will. And if they don't have enough cash, well, there are always other ways I can *persuade* you to help me, big brother. Yes, sir, I can be mighty *persuasive* when I put my mind to it...

"Let's start by talking about that store of yours, Hank—you're paid up on all your insurance, aren't you? I mean, you got fire coverage and all that stuff, don't you? Jeez, I'd hate to see something bad happen when you're just starting out...And how about Sarah? She still working over at that bank Mom and Dad told me about? That's a pretty dangerous job, ain't it? Working with all that money. Especially for a woman.... And, oh yeah, by the way, what school do the girls go to? Evansville? Or are you busing them over to that private place, what's it called again?"

I stabbed him then.

We were standing near the middle of the bridge. Leaning against the thick wooden railing, looking down at the water.

And when he said those things, I took out the steak knife— which had been sitting on the kitchen counter right next to where I'd found my car keys—I took it out from my coat pocket and I held it in both of my hands and brought it down hard in the back of his neck.

He cried out once—not very loud—and dropped to his knees.

And then there was only the flash of the blade as I stabbed him over and over again...

* * *

Last night, it finally happened. Sarah confronted me.

We were alone in the house. The girls were spending the night at their grandparents'—they do this once a month and absolutely love it.

After dinner, she took me downstairs to the den and closed the door. Sat me down on the sofa and stood right in front of me. She told me I looked a mess. I wasn't sleeping, wasn't eating. Either I tell her right now what was going on or she was leaving.

She was serious, too. I think she thought I was having an affair.

So I told her.

Everything…starting with the phone call and ending with me dumping Billy's body into the creek.

When I was finished, she ran from the room crying. She made it upstairs to the bathroom, where she dropped to her knees in front of the toilet and got sick. When she was done, she asked me very calmly to go back downstairs and leave her alone for a while. I agreed.

An hour or so later, she came down and found me out in the backyard looking up at the moon and the stars. She ran to me and hugged me so tight I could barely breathe, and then she started crying again. We hugged for a long time, until the tears finally stopped, and then she held my face in her hands and told me that she understood how difficult it had been for me, how horrible it must have felt, but that it was all over now and that I had done the right thing. No matter what, that was the important thing to remember, she kept saying—I had done the right thing.

Then we were hugging again and both of us were crying.

When we finally went inside, we called the girls and took turns saying goodnight. Then we went to bed and made love until we both fell asleep.

Later that night, the moon shining silver and bright through the bedroom window, Sarah woke from a nightmare, her skin glistening with sweat, her voice soft and frightened. She played with my hair and asked: "What if someone finds him, Hank? A fisherman? Some kids? What if someone finds him and recognizes him?"

I put a finger to her lips and *ssshed* her. Put my arms around her and held her close to me. I told her everything was going to be okay. No one would find him. And if they did, they would never be able to identify him.

"Are you sure they won't recognize him?" she asked. "Are you sure?"

"Absolutely positive," I said, stroking her neck. "Not after all this time. Not after he's been in the water for this long."

And not after I cut up his face the way I did.

No one could recognize him after all that…not even his own brother.

LITTLE BROTHERS PORTFOLIO

By Stephen R. Bissette

Little Brothers was Rick Hautala's fourth novel, first published by Zebra Books in 1988.

It was my immediate favorite of Rick's novels to date, and between face-to-face blathering over beers at Necon and ongoing phone conversations, I encouraged (well, bullied) Rick to continue writing about the Untcigahunk — the 'little brothers' introduced in the novel — as they seemed to have almost endless story possibilities.

As Rick himself put it in the original publication of the stories:

"The origin of these stories is quite simple: I got a phone call one day from Steve Bissette, a friend of mine, asking if I would be willing to 'expand' on the original concept of *Little Brothers*... which he and Michael Zulli (*The Puma Blues*) would then adapt into comic format for Steve's magazine, *Taboo*.... I liked Steve's suggestion because it sounded like fun; it gave me the impetus to go back to the situation I had created in the book and re-explore it, to look at it from several different angles...." (Rick Hautala, *Night Visions 9*, 1991, Dark Harvest; pp. 175-176)

Actually, there was more to it: I pushed Rick to write the stories because he was in a (justifiable) funk at the time, and had called one afternoon to announce he was giving up writing altogether. I talked him out of it, with the suggestion, then insistence on his following up so we could collaborate on something spinning off from *Little Brothers*.

I'd have done *anything* to get Rick writing again.

Rick indeed did follow up, writing four self-contained but interlocking short stories in remarkably quick order. I loved 'em, and passed these on to Michael, who also enjoyed them.

I powwowed with Rick (including a sunny outdoor picnic in Brattleboro, VT and one trip I took up to Rick's home in Maine) and Michael and I began swapping sketches and drawings back-and-forth. We also deliberated over which of the four stories to begin with, each of us adapting our personal favorite of the quartet.

The three of us settled on proposing a four-issue comics miniseries, adapting each of the four stories into 28-page comic narratives. To that end, Michael and I did full, comprehensive roughs for two of the stories/issues and Michael even completed a gorgeous oil painting cover proposal.

I tell you, it was lovely stuff. We worked on all this for two years, from 1990-1992, then I went looking for a publisher (since *Taboo*, by 1992, was defunct).

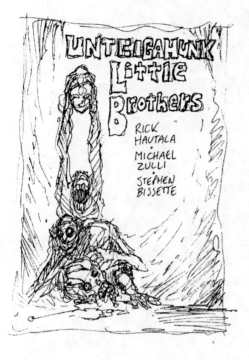

Unfortunately, we never did sell that comics adaptation of the quartet of stories. Damn, I sure tried; we even had a handshake deal with Mike Richardson at Dark Horse Comics in 1992, which (along with two other ventures) quickly proved how little that meant in the comics world. Alas.

I tried again to pitch the project to DC Comics/Vertigo in 1993, only to receive a rejection and kind reply from editor Karen Berger suggesting I seek a home "with the Dark Horse crew or elsewhere."

Rick and Michael and I had a laugh over that. Rick and I later had a beer or two *and* more than a few laughs over that.

Rick dedicated the initial publication of the stories in *Night Visions* to me "with *mucho* thanks *amigo!*" but we never did get it off the ground. I was glad to see later editions of the stories and that Rick was reaching a new generation (and getting further mileage out of them).

The last time we dined together, with Chris Golden and our pals in the Vicious Circle dining "club," Rick asked again if there were any hope for the project to find a new home. Reminding Rick that I'd retired from comics in 1999, I didn't hold out much hope.

Sorry, Rick—I tried, I *really* tried—but I let you down.
But you never held that against me.

Mucho thanks, *amigo*, for the friendship and love.

-    Stephen R. Bissette, June 2013
Mountains of Madness, VT

_____

For more info and artwork, including Rick's sketches and Michael
Zulli's artwork, see my serialized 2009 blog posting on this
project:
http://srbissette.com/?p=3477
http://srbissette.com/?p=3534
http://srbissette.com/?p=3668
http://srbissette.com/?p=3692
http://srbissette.com/?p=3713

TIGHT LITTLE STITCHES

IN A DEAD MAN'S BACK

By Joe R. Lansdale

From the Journal of Paul Marder

(Boom!)

That's a little scientist joke, and the proper way to begin this. As for the purpose of my notebook, I'm uncertain. Perhaps to organize my thoughts and not to go insane.

No. Probably so I can read it and feel as if I'm being spoken to. Maybe neither of those reasons. It doesn't matter. I just want to do it, and that is enough.

What's new?

Well, Mr. Journal, after all these years I've taken up martial arts again—or at least the forms and calisthenics of Tae Kwon Do. There is no one to spar with here in the lighthouse, so the forms have to do.

There is Mary, of course, but she keeps all her sparring verbal. And as of late, there is not even that. I long for her to call me a sonofabitch. Anything. Her hatred of me has cured to 100% perfection, and she no longer finds it necessary to speak. The tight lines around her eyes and mouth, the emotional heat that radiates from her body like a dreadful cold sore looking for a place to lie down is voice enough for her. She lives only for the moment when she (the cold sore) can attach herself to me with her needles, ink and thread. She lives only for the design on my back.

That's all I live for as well. Mary adds to it nightly and I enjoy the pain. The tattoo is of a great, blue mushroom cloud, and in the cloud, etched ghost-like, is the face of our daughter, Rae. Her lips are drawn tight, eyes are closed and there are stitches deeply pulled to simulate the lashes. When I move fast and hard they rip slightly and Rae cries bloody tears.

That's one reason for the martial arts. The hard practice of them helps me to tear the stitches so my daughter can cry. Tears are the only thing I can give her.

Each night I bare my back eagerly to Mary and her needles. She pokes deep and I moan in pain as she moans in ecstasy and hatred. She adds more color to the design, works with brutal precision to bring Rae's face out in sharper relief. After ten minutes she tires and will work no more. She puts the tools away and I go to the full-length mirror on the wall. The lantern on the shelf flickers like a jack-o-lantern in a high wind, but there is enough light for me to look over my shoulder and examine the tattoo. And it is beautiful. Better each night as Rae's face becomes more and more defined.

Rae.

Rae. God, can you forgive me, sweetheart?

But the pain of the needles, wonderful and cleansing as they are, is not enough. So I go sliding, kicking and punching along the walkway around the lighthouse, feeling Rae's red tears running down my spine, gathering in the waistband of my much-stained canvas pants.

Winded, unable to punch and kick anymore, I walk over to the railing and call down into the dark, "Hungry?"

In response to my voice a chorus of moans rises up to greet me.

Later, I lie on my pallet, hands behind my head, examine the ceiling and try to think of something worthy to write in you, Mr. Journal. So seldom is there anything. Nothing seems truly worthwhile.

Bored of this, I roll on my side and look at the great light that once shone out to the ships but is now forever snuffed. Then I turn the other direction and look at my wife sleeping on her bunk, her naked ass turned toward me. I try to remember what it was like to make love to her, but it is difficult. I only remember that I miss it. For a long moment I stare at my wife's ass as if it is a mean mouth about to open and reveal teeth. Then I roll on my back again, stare at the ceiling, and continue this routine until daybreak.

Mornings I greet the flowers, their bright red and yellow blooms bursting from the heads of long-dead bodies that will not rot. The flowers open wide to reveal their little black brains and their feathery feelers, and they lift their blooms upward and moan. I get a wild pleasure out of this. For one crazed moment I feel like a rock singer appearing before his starry-eyed audience.

When I tire of the game I get the binoculars, Mr. Journal, and examine the eastern plains with them, as if I expect a city to materialize there. The most interesting thing I have seen on those plains is a herd of large lizards thundering north. For a moment, I considered calling Mary to see them, but I didn't. The sound of my voice, the sight of my face, upsets her. She loves only the tattoo and is interested in nothing more.

When I finish looking at the plains, I walk to the other side. To the west, where the ocean was, there is now nothing but miles and miles of cracked, black sea bottom. Its only resemblance to a great body of water are the occasional dust storms that blow out of the west like dark tidal waves and wash the windows black at mid-day. And the creatures. Mostly mutated whales. Monstrously large, sluggish things. Abundant now where once they were near extinction. (Perhaps the whales should form some sort of GREENPEACE organization for humans now. What do you think, Mr. Journal? No need to answer. Just another one of those little scientist jokes.)

These whales crawl across the sea bottom near the lighthouse from time to time, and if the mood strikes them, they rise on their tails and push their heads near the tower and examine it. I keep expecting one to flop down on us, crushing us like bugs. But no such luck. For some unknown reason the whales never leave the cracked sea bed to venture onto what we formerly called the shore. It's as if they live in invisible water and are bound by it. A racial memory perhaps. Or maybe there's something in that cracked black soil they need. I don't know.

Besides the whales I suppose I should mention I saw a shark once. It was slithering along at a great distance, and the tip of its fin was winking in the sunlight. I've also seen some strange, legged fish and some things I could not put a name to. I'll just call them whale food since I saw one of the whales dragging his bottom jaw along the ground one day, scooping up the creatures as they tried to beat a hasty retreat.

Exciting, huh? Well, that's how I spend my day, Mr. Journal. Roaming about the tower with my glasses, coming in to write in you, waiting anxiously for Mary to take hold of that kit and give me the signal. The mere thought of it excites me to erection. I suppose you could call that our sex act together.

And what was I doing the day they dropped The Big One?
Glad you asked that, Mr. Journal, really I am.

I was doing the usual. Up at six, did the shit, shower and shave routine. Had breakfast. Got dressed. Tied my tie. I remember doing the latter, and not very well, in front of the bedroom mirror, and noticing that I had shaved poorly. A hunk of dark beard decorated my chin like a bruise.

Rushing to the bathroom to remedy that, I opened the door as Rae, naked as the day of her birth, was stepping from the tub.

Surprised, she turned to look at me. An arm went over her breasts, and a hand, like a dove settling into a fiery bush, covered her pubic area.

Embarrassed, I closed the door with an "excuse me" and went about my business—unshaved. It was an innocent thing. An accident. Nothing sexual. But when I think of her now, more often than not, that is the first image that comes to mind. I guess it was the moment I realized my baby had grown into a beautiful woman.

That was also the day she went off to her first day of college and got to see, ever so briefly, the end of the world.

And it was the day the triangle—Mary, Rae and myself—shattered.

If my first memory of Rae alone is that day, naked in the bathroom, my foremost memory of us as a family is when Rae was six. We used to go to the park and she would ride the merry-go-round, swing, teeter-totter, and finally my back. ("I want to piggy, Daddy.") We would gallop about until my legs were rubber, then we would stop at the bench where Mary sat waiting. I would turn my back to the bench so Mary could take Rae down, but always before she did, she would reach around from behind, caressing Rae, pushing her tight against my back, and Mary's hands would touch my chest.

God, but if I could describe those hands. She still has hands like that, after all these years. I feel them fluttering against my back when she works. They are long and sleek and artistic. Naturally soft, like the belly of a baby rabbit. And when she held Rae and me that way, I felt that no matter what happened in the world, we three could stand against it and conquer.

But now the triangle is broken and the geometry gone away.

So the day Rae went off to college and was fucked into oblivion by the dark, pelvic thrust of the bomb, Mary drove me to work. Me, Paul Marder, big shot with The Crew. One of the finest, brightest young minds in the industry. Always teaching, inventing and improving on our nuclear threat, because, as we'd often joke, "We cared enough to send only the very best."

When we arrived at the guard booth, I had out my pass, but there was no one to take it. Beyond the chain-link gate there was a wild melee of people running, screaming, falling down.

I got out of the car and ran to the gate. I called out to a man I knew as he ran by. When he turned his eyes were wild and his lips were flecked with foam. "The missiles are flying," he said, then he was gone, running madly.

I jumped in the car, pushed Mary aside and stomped the gas. The Buick leaped into the fence, knocking it asunder. The car spun, slammed into the edge of a building and went dead. I grabbed Mary's hand, pulled her from the car and we ran toward the great elevators.

We made one just in time. There were others running for it as the door closed, and the elevator went down. I still remember the echo of their fists on the metal just as it began to drop. It was like the rapid heartbeat of something dying.

And so the elevator took us to the world of Down Under and we locked it off. There we were in a five-mile layered city designed not only as a massive office and laboratory but also as an impenetrable shelter. It was our special reward for creating the poisons of war. There was food, water, medical supplies, films, books, you name it. Enough to last two thousand people for a hundred years. Of the two thousand it was designed for, perhaps eleven hundred made it. The others didn't run fast enough from the parking lot or the other buildings, or they were late for work, or maybe they had called in sick.

Perhaps they were the lucky ones. They might have died in their sleep. Or while they were having a morning quickie with the spouse. Or perhaps as they lingered over that last cup of coffee.

Because you see, Mr. Journal, Down Under was no paradise. Before long suicides were epidemic. I considered it myself from time to time. People slashed their throats, drank acid, took pills. It was not unusual to come out of your cubicle in the morning and find people dangling from pipes and rafters like ripe fruit.

There were also the murders. Most of them performed by a crazed group who lived in the deeper recesses of the unit and called themselves the Shit Faces. From time to time they smeared dung on themselves and ran amok, clubbing men, women, and children born down under, to death. It was rumored they ate human flesh.

We had a police force of sorts, but it didn't do much. It didn't have much sense of authority. Worse, we all viewed ourselves as deserving victims. Except for Mary, we had all helped to blow up the world.

Mary came to hate me. She came to the conclusion I had killed Rae. It was a realization that grew in her like a drip growing and growing until it became a gushing flood of hate. She seldom talked to me. She tacked up a picture of Rae and looked at it most of the time.

Topside she had been an artist, and she took that up again. She rigged a kit of tools and inks and became a tattooist. Everyone came to her for a mark. And though each was different, they all seemed to indicate one thing: I fucked up. I blew up the world. Brand me.

Day in and day out she did her tattoos, having less and less to do with me, pushing herself more and more into this work until she was as skilled with skin and needles as she had been Topside with brush and canvas. And one night, as we lay on our separate pallets, feigning sleep, she said to me, "I just want you to know how much I hate you."

"I know," I said.

"You killed Rae."

"I know."

"You say you killed her, you bastard. Say it."

"I killed her," I said, and meant it.

Next day I asked for my tattoo. I told her of this dream that came to me nightly. There would be darkness, and out of this darkness would come a swirl of glowing clouds, and the clouds would melt into a mushroom shape, and out of that—torpedo-shaped, nose pointing skyward, striding on ridiculous cartoon legs—would step The Bomb.

There was a face painted on The Bomb, and it was my face. And suddenly the dream's point of view would change, and I would be looking out of the eyes of that painted face. Before me was my daughter. Naked. Lying on the ground. Her legs wide apart. Her sex glazed like a wet canyon.

And I/The Bomb would dive into her, pulling those silly feet after me, and she would scream. I could hear it echo as I plunged through her belly, finally driving myself out of the top of her head, then blowing to terminal orgasm. And the dream would end where it began. A mushroom cloud. Darkness.

When I told Mary the dream and asked her to interpret it in her art, she said, "Bare your back," and that's how the design began. An inch of work at a time—a painful inch. She made sure of that.

Never once did I complain. She'd send the needles home as hard and deep as she could, and though I might moan or cry out, I never asked her to stop. I could feel those fine hands touching my back and I loved it. The needles. The hands. The needles. The hands.

And if that was so much fun, you ask, why did I come Topside?

You ask such probing questions, Mr. Journal. Really you do, and I'm glad you asked that. My telling will be like a laxative, I hope. Maybe if I just let the shit flow I'll wake up tomorrow and feel a lot better about myself.

Sure. And it will be the dawning of a new Pepsi generation as well. It will have all been a bad dream. The alarm clock will ring. I'll get up, have my bowl of Rice Krispies and tie my tie.

Okay, Mr. Journal. The answer. Twenty years or so after we went Down Under, a fistful of us decided it couldn't be any worse Topside than it was below. We made plans to go see. Simple as that. Mary and I even talked a little. We both entertained the crazed belief Rae might have survived. She would be thirty-eight. We might have been hiding below like vermin for no reason. It could be a brave new world up there.

I remember thinking these things, Mr. Journal, and half-believing them.

We outfitted two sixty-foot crafts that were used as part of our transportation system Down Under, plugged in the half-remembered codes that opened the elevators, and drove the vehicles inside. The elevator lasers cut through the debris above them and before long we were Topside. The doors opened to sunlight muted by gray-green clouds and a desert-like landscape. Immediately I knew there was no brave new world over the horizon. It had all gone to hell in a fiery handbasket, and all that was left of man's millions of years of development were a few pathetic humans living Down Under like worms, and a few others crawling Topside like the same.

We cruised about a week and finally came to what had once been the Pacific Ocean. Only there wasn't any water now, just that cracked blackness.

We drove along the shore for another week and finally saw life. A whale. Jacobs immediately got the idea to shoot one and taste its meat.

Using a high-powered rifle he killed it, and he and seven others cut slabs off it, brought the meat back to cook. They invited all of us to eat, but the meat looked greenish and there wasn't much blood and we warned him against it. But Jacobs and the others ate it anyway. As Jacobs said, "It's something to do."

A little later on Jacobs threw up blood and his intestines boiled out of his mouth, and not long after those who had shared the meat had the same thing happen to them. They died crawling on their bellies like gutted dogs. There wasn't a thing we could do for them. We couldn't even bury them. The ground was too hard. We stacked them like cordwood along the shoreline and moved camp down a way, tried to remember how remorse felt.

And that night, while we slept as best we could, the roses came.

Now, let me admit, Mr. Journal, I do not actually know how the roses survived, but I have an idea. And since you've agreed to hear my story—and even if you haven't, you're going to anyway—I'm going to put logic and fantasy together and hope to arrive at the truth.

These roses lived in the ocean bed, underground, and at night they came out. Up until then they had survived as parasites of reptiles and animals, but a new food had arrived from Down Under. Humans. Their creators, actually. Looking at it that way, you might say we were the gods who conceived them, and their partaking of our flesh and blood was but a new version of wine and wafer.

I can imagine the pulsating brains pushing up through the sea bottom on thick stalks, extending feathery feelers and tasting the air out there beneath the light of the moon—which through those odd clouds gave the impression of a pus-filled boil—and I can imagine them uprooting and dragging their vines across the ground toward the shore where the corpses lay.

Thick vines sprouted little, thorny vines, and these moved up the bank and touched the corpses. Then, with a lashing motion, the thorns tore into the flesh, and the vines, like snakes, slithered through the wounds and inside. Secreting a dissolving fluid that turned the innards to the consistency of watery oatmeal, they slurped up the mess, and the vines grew and grew at amazing speed, moved and coiled throughout the bodies, replacing nerves and shaping into the symmetry of the muscles they had devoured, and lastly they pushed up through the necks, into the skulls, ate tongues and eyeballs and sucked up the mouse-gray brains like soggy gruel. With an explosion of skull shrapnel, the roses bloomed, their tooth-hard petals expanding into beautiful red and yellow flowers, hunks of human heads dangling from them like shattered watermelon rinds.

In the center of these blooms a fresh, black brain pulsed and feathery feelers once again tasted air for food and breeding grounds. Energy waves from the floral brains shot through the miles and miles of vines that were knotted inside the bodies, and as they had replaced nerves, muscles and vital organs, they made the bodies stand. Then those corpses turned their flowered heads toward the tents where we slept, and the blooming corpses (another little scientist joke there if you're into English idiom, Mr. Journal) walked, eager to add the rest of us to their animated bouquet.

I saw my first rose-head while I was taking a leak.

I had left the tent and gone down by the shore line to relieve myself when I caught sight of it out of the corner of my eye. Because of the bloom I first thought it was Susan Dyers. She wore a thick, woolly Afro that surrounded her head like a lion's mane, and the shape of the thing struck me as her silhouette. But when I zipped and turned, it wasn't an Afro. It was a flower blooming out of Jacobs. I recognized him by his clothes and the hunk of his face that hung off one of the petals like a worn-out hat on a peg.

In the center of the blood-red flower was a pulsating sack, and all around it little wormy things squirmed. Directly below the brain was a thin proboscis. It extended toward me like an erect penis. At its tip, just inside the opening, were a number of large thorns.

A sound like a moan came out of that proboscis, and I stumbled back. Jacobs' body quivered briefly, as if he had been besieged by a sudden chill, and ripping through his flesh and clothes, from neck to foot, was a mass of thorny, wagging vines that shot out to five feet in length.

With an almost invisible motion, they waved from west to east, slashed my clothes, tore my hide, knocked my feet out from beneath me. It was like being hit by a cat-o-nine-tails.

Dazed, I rolled onto my hands and knees, bear-walked away from it. The vines whipped against my back and butt, cut deep.

Every time I got to my feet, they tripped me. The thorns not only cut, they burned like hot ice picks. I finally twisted away from a net of vines, slammed through one last shoot, and made a break for it.

Without realizing it, I was running back to the tent. My body felt as if I had been lying on a bed of nails and razor blades. My forearm hurt something terrible where I had used it to lash the thorns away from me. I glanced down at it as I ran. It was covered in blood. A strand of vine about two feet in length was coiled around it like a garter snake. A thorn had torn a deep wound in my arm, and the vine was sliding an end into the wound.

Screaming, I held my forearm in front of me like I had just discovered it. The flesh, where the vine had entered, rippled and made a bulge that looked like a junkie's favorite vein. The pain was nauseating. I snatched at the vine, ripped it free. The thorns turned against me-like fishhooks.

The pain was so much I fell to my knees, but I had the vine out of me. It squirmed in my hand, and I felt a thorn gouge my palm. I threw the vine into the dark. Then I was up and running for the tent again.

The roses must have been at work for quite some time before I saw Jacobs, because when I broke back into camp yelling, I saw Susan, Ralph, Casey and some others, and already their heads were blooming, skulls cracking away like broken model kits.

Jane Calloway was facing a rose-possessed corpse, and the dead body had its hands on her shoulders, and the vines were jetting out of the corpse, weaving around her like a web, tearing, sliding inside her, breaking off. The proboscis poked into her mouth and extended down her throat, forced her head back. The scream she started came out a gurgle.

I tried to help her, but when I got close, the vines whipped at me and I had to jump back. I looked for something to grab, to hit the damn thing with, but there was nothing. When next I looked at Jane, vines were stabbing out of her eyes and her tongue, now nothing more than lava-thick blood, was dripping out of her mouth onto her breasts, which, like the rest of her body, were riddled with stabbing vines.

I ran away then. There was nothing I could do for Jane. I saw others embraced by corpse hands and tangles of vines, but now my only thought was Mary. Our tent was to the rear of the campsite, and I ran there as fast as I could.

She was lumbering out of our tent when I arrived. The sound of screams had awakened her. When she saw me running she froze. By the time I got to her, two vine-riddled corpses were coming up on the tent from the left side. Grabbing her hand I half-pulled, half-dragged her away from there. I got to one of the vehicles and pushed her inside.

I locked the doors just as Jacobs, Susan, Jane, and others appeared at the windshield, leaning over the rocket-nose hood, the feelers around the brain sacks vibrating like streamers in a high wind. Hands slid greasily down the windshield. Vines flopped and scratched and cracked against it like thin bicycle chains.

I got the vehicle started, stomped the accelerator, and the rose-heads went flying. One of them, Jacobs, bounced over the hood and splattered into a spray of flesh, ichor and petals.

I had never driven the vehicle, so my maneuvering was rusty. But it didn't matter. There wasn't exactly a traffic rush to worry about.

After an hour or so, I turned to look at Mary. She was staring at me, her eyes like the twin barrels of a double-barreled shotgun. They seemed to say, "More of your doing," and in a way she was right. I drove on.

Daybreak we came to the lighthouse. I don't know how it survived. One of those quirks. Even the glass was unbroken. It looked like a great stone finger shooting us the bird.

The vehicle's tank was near empty, so I assumed here was as

good a place to stop as any. At least there was shelter, something we could fortify. Going on until the vehicle was empty of fuel didn't make much sense. There wouldn't be any more fill-ups, and there might not be any more shelter like this.

Mary and I (in our usual silence) unloaded the supplies from the vehicle and put them in the lighthouse. There was enough food, water, chemicals for the chemical toilet, odds and ends, extra clothes, to last us a year. There were also some guns. A Colt .45 revolver, two twelve-gauge shotguns and a .38, and enough shells to fight a small war.

When everything was unloaded, I found some old furniture downstairs and, using tools from the vehicle, tried to barricade the bottom door and the one at the top of the stairs. When I finished, I thought of a line from a story I had once read, a line that always disturbed me. It went something like, "Now we're shut in for the night."

Days. Nights. All the same. Shut in with one another, our memories and the fine tattoo.

A few days later I spotted the roses. It was as if they had smelled us out. And maybe they had. From a distance, through the binoculars, they reminded me of old women in bright sun hats.

It took them the rest of the day to reach the lighthouse, and they immediately surrounded it, and when I appeared at the railing they would lift their heads and moan.

And that, Mr. Journal, brings us up to now.

I thought I had written myself out, Mr. Journal. Told the only part of my life story I would ever tell, but now I'm back. You can't keep a good world-destroyer down.

I saw my daughter last night and she's been dead for years. But I saw her, I did, naked, smiling at me, calling to ride piggyback.

Here's what happened.

It was cold last night. Must be getting along winter. I had rolled off my pallet onto the cold floor. Maybe that's what brought me awake. The cold. Or maybe it was just gut instinct.

It had been a particularly wonderful night with the tattoo. The face had been made so clear it seemed to stand out from my back. It had finally become more defined than the mushroom cloud. The needles went in hard and deep, but I've had them in me so much now I barely feel the pain. After looking in the mirror at the beauty of the design, I went to bed happy, or as happy as I can get.

During the night the eyes ripped open. The stitches came out and I didn't know it until I tried to rise from the cold, stone floor and my back puckered against it where the blood had dried.

I pulled myself free and got up. It was dark, but we had a good moonspill that night and I went to the mirror to look. It was bright enough that I could see Rae's reflection clearly, the color of her face, the color of the cloud. The stitches had fallen away and now the wounds were spread wide, and inside the wounds were eyes. Oh God, Rae's blue eyes. Her mouth smiled at me and her teeth were very white.

Oh, I hear you, Mr. Journal. I hear what you're saying. And I thought of that. My first impression was that I was about six bricks shy a load, gone around the old bend. But I know better now. You see, I lit a candle and held it over my shoulder, and with the candle and the moonlight, I could see even more clearly. It was Rae all right, not just a tattoo.

I looked over at my wife on the bunk, her back to me, as always. She had not moved.

I turned back to the reflection. I could hardly see the outline of myself, just Rae's face smiling out of that cloud.

"Rae," I whispered, "is that you?"

"Come on, Daddy," said the mouth in the mirror, "that's a stupid question. Of course it's me."

"But.... You're... you're...."

"Dead?"

"Yes.... Did... did it hurt much?"

She cackled so loudly the mirror shook. I could feel the hairs on my neck rising. I thought for sure Mary would wake up, but she slept on.

"It was instantaneous, Daddy, and even then, it was the greatest pain imaginable. Let me show you how it hurt."

The candle blew out and I dropped it. I didn't need it anyway. The mirror grew bright and Rae's smile went from ear to ear— literally— and the flesh on her bones seemed like crepe paper before a powerful fan, and that fan blew the hair off her head, the skin off her skull and melted those beautiful, blue eyes and those shiny white teeth of hers to a putrescent goo the color and consistency of fresh bird shit. Then there was only the skull, and it heaved in half and flew backwards into the dark world of the mirror and there was no reflection now, only the hurtling fragments of a life that once was and was now nothing more than swirling cosmic dust.

I closed my eyes and looked away.

"Daddy?"

I opened them, looked over my shoulder into the mirror. There was Rae again, smiling out of my back.

"Darling," I said, "I'm so sorry."

"So are we," she said, and there were faces floating past her in the mirror. Teenagers, children, men and women, babies, little embryos swirling around her head like planets around the sun. I closed my eyes again, but I could not keep them closed. When I opened them the multitudes of swirling dead, and those who had never had a chance to live, were gone. Only Rae was there.

"Come close to the mirror, Daddy."

I backed up to it. I backed until the hot wounds that were Rae's eyes touched the cold glass and the wounds became hotter and hotter and Rae called out, "Ride me piggy, Daddy," and then I felt her weight on my back, not the weight of a six-year-old child or a teenage girl, but a great weight, like the world was on my shoulders and bearing down.

Leaping away from the mirror I went hopping and whooping about the room, same as I used to in the park. Around and around I went, and as I did, I glanced in the mirror. Astride me was Rae, lithe and naked, her red hair fanning around her as I spun. And when I whirled by the mirror again, I saw that she was six years old. Another spin and there was a skeleton with red hair, one hand held high, the jaws open and yelling, "Ride 'em, cowboy."

"How?" I managed, still bucking and leaping, giving Rae the ride of her life. She bent to my ear and I could feel her warm breath. "You want to know how I'm here, Daddy-dear? I'm here because you created me. Once you laid between Mother's legs and thrust me into existence, the two of you, with all the love there was in you. This time you thrust me into existence with your guilt and Mother's hate. Her thrusting needles, your arching back. And now I've come back for one last ride, Daddy-o. Ride, you bastard, ride."

All the while I had been spinning, and now as I glimpsed the mirror I saw wall to wall faces, weaving in, weaving out, like smiling stars, and all those smiles opened wide and words came out in chorus, "Where were you when they dropped The Big One?"

Each time I spun and saw the mirror again, it was a new scene. Great flaming winds scorching across the world, babies turning to fleshy jello, heaps of charred bones, brains boiling out of the heads of men and women like backed-up toilets overflowing, The Almighty, Glory Hallelujah, Ours Is Bigger Than Yours Bomb hurtling forward, the mirror going mushroom white, then clear, and me, spinning, Rae pressed tight against my back, melting like butter on a griddle, evaporating into the eye wounds on my back, and finally me alone, collapsing to the floor beneath the weight of the world.

Mary never awoke.

The vines outsmarted me.

A single strand found a crack downstairs somewhere and wound up the steps and slipped beneath the door that led into the tower. Mary's bunk was not far from the door, and in the night, while I slept and later while I spun in front of the mirror and lay on the floor before it, it made its way to Mary's bunk, up between her legs, and entered her sex effortlessly.

I suppose I should give the vine credit for doing what I had not been able to do in years, Mr. Journal, and that's enter Mary. Oh God, that's a funny one, Mr. Journal. Real funny. Another little scientist joke. Let's make that a mad scientist joke, what say? Who but a madman would play with the lives of human beings by constantly trying to build the bigger and better boom machine?

So what of Rae, you ask?

I'll tell you. She is inside me. My back feels the weight. She twists in my guts like a corkscrew. I went to the mirror a moment ago, and the tattoo no longer looks like it did. The eyes have turned to crusty sores and the entire face looks like a scab. It's as if the bile that made up my soul, the unthinking nearsightedness, the guilt that I am, has festered from inside and spoiled the picture with pustule bumps, knots and scabs.

To put it in layman's terms, Mr. Journal, my back is infected. Infected with what I am. A blind, senseless fool.

The wife?

Ah, the wife. God, how I loved that woman. I have not really touched her in years, merely felt those wonderful hands on my back as she jabbed the needles home, but I never stopped loving her. It was not a love that glowed anymore, but it was there, though hers for me was long gone and wasted.

This morning when I got up from the floor, the weight of Rae and the world on my back, I saw the vine coming up from beneath the door and stretching over to her. I yelled her name. She did not move. I ran to her and saw it was too late. Before I could put a hand on her, I saw her flesh ripple and bump up, like a den of mice were nesting under a quilt. The vines were at work. (Out go the old guts, in go the new vines.)

There was nothing I could do for her.

I made a torch out of a chair leg and old quilt, set fire to it, burned the vine from between her legs, watched it retreat, smoking, under the door. Then I got a board, nailed it along the bottom, hoping it would keep others out for at least a little while. I got one of the twelve-gauges and loaded it. It's on the desk beside me, Mr. Journal, but even I know I'll never use it. It was just something to do, as Jacobs said when he killed and ate the whale. Something to do.

I can hardly write anymore. My back and shoulders hurt so bad. It's the weight of Rae and the world.

I've just come back from the mirror and there is very little left of the tattoo. Some blue and black ink, a touch of red that was Rae's hair. It looks like an abstract painting now. Collapsed design, running colors. It's real swollen. I look like the hunchback of Notre Dame.

What am I going to do, Mr. Journal?

Well, as always, I'm glad you asked that. You see, I've thought this out.

I could throw Mary's body over the railing before it blooms. I could do that. Then I could doctor my back. It might even heal, though I doubt it. Rae wouldn't let that happen, I can tell you now. And I don't blame her. I'm on her side. I'm just a walking dead man and have been for years.

I could put the shotgun under my chin and work the trigger with my toes, or maybe push it with the very pen I'm using to create you, Mr. Journal. Wouldn't that be neat? Blow my brains to the ceiling and sprinkle you with my blood.

But as I said, I loaded the gun because it was something to do.

I'd never use it on myself or Mary.

You see, I want Mary. I want her to hold Rae and me one last time like she used to in the park. And she can. There's a way.

I've drawn all the curtains and made curtains out of blankets for those spots where there aren't any. It'll be sunup soon and I don't want that kind of light in here. I'm writing this by candlelight and it gives the entire room a warm glow. I wish I had wine. I want the atmosphere to be just right.

Over on Mary's bunk she's starting to twitch. Her neck is swollen where the vines have congested and are writhing toward their favorite morsel, the brain. Pretty soon the rose will bloom (I hope she's one of the bright yellow ones, yellow was her favorite color and she wore it well) and Mary will come for me.

When she does, I'll stand with my naked back to her. The vines will whip out and cut me before she reaches me, but I can stand it. I'm used to pain. I'll pretend the thorns are Mary's needles. I'll stand that way until she folds her dead arms around me and her body pushes up against the wound she made in my back, the wound that is our daughter Rae. She'll hold me so the vines and the proboscis can do their work. And while she holds me, I'll grab her fine hands and push them against my chest, and it will be we three again, standing against the world, and I'll close my eyes and delight in her soft, soft hands one last time.

"Tight Little Stitches in a Dead Man's Back" was originally published in the Macklay & Associates anthology *Nukes*. It later appeared in *By Bizarre Hands*, a collection of Lansdale's short stories published by Avon Books; and in *High Cotton: Selected Short Stories of Joe R. Lansdale*, published in 2000 by Golden Gryphon Press. "Tight Little Stitches in a Dead Man's Back" © 1986 Joe R. Lansdale.

Glenn Chadbourne

CRAVING

By Yvonne Navarro

1965.

The girl is very... still.

The knot of kids gathered around her is growing, and Andre lets them prod him forward on the sidewalk, until his foot is almost touching hers. Everything about the girl is small, like him--small hands, small feet, a small, upturned button nose that's leaking a bright, shocking double line of blood down each flushed pink cheek until it disappears into her fine, blonde hair. On her forehead is a blue-black lump the size of a robin's egg, the kiss of the monkey bar's metal when she slipped and fell.

"Move aside—you kids get out of the way right now!"

One of the teachers is finally pushing through the crowd. Andrew doesn't know the teacher's name, just like he doesn't know the little girl's name. He moves back with the others and watches as the man touches a spot on her neck. Another teacher, a woman, has followed into the center of things, and he tells her to call an ambulance, then turns back to the gawking kids and gestures at them angrily. "Go on, now—there's nothing to see here! Take off!"

Most of them obey, but not all.

Not Andre.

He hangs off to the side with one or two other kids, as close as he dares, enduring the aggravated glances of the teachers and the medics. As long as he stays back far enough, they let him alone—

what are they going to do, chase after him? They are far too concerned with the girl, whose face has gone from a fragile, china-white to gray, the color of a concrete sidewalk beneath the hot sun. Andre can feel the surface of his eyes drying out because he's not blinking, he's too afraid he'll miss something. Eventually they lift the girl onto a Gurney and put her in the ambulance, and she disappears into the distance amid a circling of flashing red and white lights and lingering exhaust fumes.

Andre never finds out what happens to her, but he thinks a lot about the little girl over the next couple of days, wondering if she died, if maybe she was dead before they put her into the ambulance. He doesn't think so because on television *they*—that ambiguous, omnipotent group of people who seem to control such things— always put a sheet over dead bodies. Still, that doesn't mean she wasn't dead now; she could have died on the way to the hospital, or afterwards when the doctors' treatment of her injuries failed. It doesn't matter. He will never find out since the girl doesn't go to his school.

* * *

Andre is twenty-four when he meets Rebecca while standing a few feet away from a horrible accident. There aren't many people at the scene—apparently this one is a bit too much for most of the usual gawkers. Andre has been living in this neighborhood for almost three years, since he graduated from college, and there has been a steady stream of accidents at this corner. They usually happen at the intersection where the commuter train crosses the four-lane street and drivers, those who are willing to gamble with their lives in the hopes of getting to work a little faster, lose the game. It is Rebecca who approaches him—Andre is far too engrossed in his study of the man lying on the side of the road a few feet away to pay attention to any of the surrounding crowd.

"Do you think he felt any pain?"

Andre glances to his left and sees the woman who staged-whispered the question, then takes a second look. Like him, she is pale and small-boned, but where he has dirty blonde hair, hers is cut short and so dark it can only be described as gothic. Her dark eyes are wide with curiosity, like pools filled with glistening, black light.

A layer of lip gloss makes her lips glitter as much as her eyes.

It is rare that something that can divert his attention from the scene of an accident or its victim, but this woman does—he has to force his attention to go back to the man lying on the ground only a few feet away. Considering what happened, it's surprising that the police haven't demanded he move back, but they're still too busy talking to the bus driver. The driver is a pudgy, middle-aged black woman whose face has gone gray with shock and guilt as she tries to explain what she doesn't understand. Andre hears her –

"I don't know. I was just driving past. He was standing on the curb and I glanced at the side mirror and saw him jerking all around, and then he just fell over. There was a bump under the back tires, and then... and then...."

She can't continue, but the rest of the story is on the ground at their feet. One of the young man's shoes pokes out from the bottom of a snow-colored sheet; at the other end, the top, the sheet is soaked with scarlet blood and disturbingly flat. It is the best accident scene that Andre has ever been to.

"No," he says to the woman at his side. "He had the seizure, fell in the street in front of the back wheel, and then it was lights out."

"That's what I think, too." She nods, then looks sideways at him. "My name is Rebecca. I think I've... seen you before."

Andre considers this. He doesn't go out much, so if she *has* seen him, it's either on his way to his job or at another time like this one, when he's worked his way closer to the front lines to catch the details of some traffic accident or other incident. It's a long shot, but... is she like him? Secretly studying the damage that can be done to the fragile shell of the human body by so many things? No, of course not—that's impossible.

When she speaks again, her voice is quieter and a little breathless. "I saw you a couple of weeks ago. When that kid on the bicycle...."

She doesn't have to finish—Andre knows what she's talking about and, now that his mind fills with mental photos and revisits that afternoon, he remembers her, too. Her and... yes. That guy over there, about ten feet away. An average man with thick brown hair, glasses, average build; nothing special about him... except for the hunger in his eyes as he stares down at the red Rorschach pattern at the top of the sheet. As Andre looks at him, the guy suddenly lifts his gaze and meets Andre's eyes. Something knowing passes between them, a *kinship*, before the man smiles faintly and returns to his study of the dead man in the street. Andre's forehead creases as his gaze scans the crowd and sees more than a few familiar faces, the same people who, like him, come out when destiny does its worst.

Rebecca moves closer, and Andre jerks a little when she slides her hand against his. Without knowing why, he twines his fingers around hers. Actually, that isn't true. He knows *precisely* why he hangs onto this strange, wraithlike woman—because she *is* like him, and like the man a few yards away, and like the others he has recognized here and there throughout the years. Fascinated by pain, by death, by that rarely seen interval between violence and eternity. It is a captivation that disgusts most people... at least on the surface. Inside, where no one else knows the truth and beneath where so-called normalcy and decorum binds the senses and monitors the behavior, Andre thinks that the majority of mankind is *exactly* like him. But in the meantime....

Where in his life there was once only him, there is now him and Rebecca.

* * *

Theirs is an existence that most do not understand. The apartment in which they live is a monument to disasters and accidents, filled with framed prints showing wrenching scenes from September 11th—the collapsing towers, an unidentified woman falling through the air in an almost absurdly graceful position as she exercises her only escape from the killing black smoke and agonizing flames. Another wall bears photographs from the Oklahoma City bombing, the rubble, the heartbreaking shot of the hopeful fireman carrying the toddler from the ruins; below that are what they call their "fire range": shots of the fireball devouring the compound at Waco, Texas, aerial views of the burned-out homes from a dozen forest fires in Colorado and California.

They have friends, more, perhaps, than most people would expect, a handful of people met in much the same way as Andre met Rebecca but who, like them, would never admit to having a secret, morbid side. Outwardly it all seems so normal, so *acceptable*, and likely it would be... if not for the way that Andre and Rebecca spend all their available free time: visiting one disaster scene after another, collecting touristy little souvenirs and postcards, picking up the rarer items through online auctions and, occasionally, via word-of-mouth, black-market buys. Andre believes they have a great life: he and Rebecca are a joining of two souls whom he would have never thought could find each other in a world so concerned with things constantly politically correct and a *Miss Manners* who dictated everything from whether a person may cross his legs after dinner to how to sign off Instant Messaging. It's all so completely, utterly perfect....

Except for that one, tiny problem.

Rebecca is getting bored.

Andre can feel it—her *blandness*—as surely as he can hear his own heart beat with excitement when they stop at the scene of the latest traffic accident, or get in the car to rush to the latest in a series of lethal house fires that has beset the neighborhood adjoining theirs. It is so unthinkable to him, this sudden disinterest she has towards the things around which their relationship has so thoroughly revolved. Disaster and death has always been the crux of everything for them—when they make love, every time, it is to the flickering backdrop of the television's light as one of their disaster DVDs plays itself out. If her boredom becomes too great, if she actually *leaves* him, where will he find another woman with whom he can truly share the strangeness of his life and himself?

Losing her is incomprehensible.

He will do anything to keep her affection.

He will stop at nothing to regain her attention.

* * *

For a while, a very *short* while, the fires work. There are so many, and they are so close and easy to get to while they still burn. The flames reflect in Rebecca's dark eyes, and Andre can see her exhilaration in the orange lights that dance across her pupils, can feel it in the quickness of her breath as they whisper to each other about the firemen who rush in and out of the building, the ever-increasing number of ambulances and frantic paramedics and burn victims as the elusive arsonist targets larger and larger apartment buildings.

But as to everything, there is an end.

For Andre, it is the danger of being caught that forces him to discontinue his arson spree. Secretly he prides himself on the fact that Rebecca never knew—at least, he doesn't think she did—that it was he who set the fires, he who arranged for innocents to be sacrificed so that her love for him might continue to be fed by her addiction to the sight, sounds and smells of death. He is still a free man, he knows, only because he is not setting the fires because of a love for the flames themselves. He is not a pyromaniac or someone doing a hasty paid job for insurance money. Because of this, he was always able to step back from his actions and plan them much more clinically, much more critically. There is no one breathing down his neck with threats or offered payment and no logic-destroying physical or mental rush to be gained from watching the fire itself. Andre's thrill, his "drug," is watching Rebecca as she watches, so he is meticulous in his methods, infallible in where he procures his materials, untraceable by any evidence. Old high school chemistry books, household materials, planning and prep, utterly random targets and an extreme amount of caution. Detailed, but absurdly easy.

He is never caught, but he also cannot continue.

And Rebecca grows bored again.

She tries to hide it, but Andre can feel it in the way her gaze fails to linger on the victims, the way she shuffles from foot to foot if they stay more than five minutes at any one scene, and most of all, in the way she searches for new ones. Oddly, she begins to spend more time at places where tragedies have already occurred rather than seeking out fresh situations. She starts by bringing flowers to place in the pile in front of a house on the south side where a man went berserk and murdered his girlfriend and her four children before turning the gun on himself, then, incredibly, she flies to the southwest to join the parade of mourners leaving teddy bears and baby toys in front of a storage locker in a nearly nameless dusty town where the mummified remains of three infants were discovered. Andre goes with her, of course, studying Rebecca and the others who stand around these places like silent ghosts and peer through windows and the cracks in locked doors. He tries desperately to understand her sudden desire to revel in the grief that happens *after* some cataclysmic event, to accept the change that has overtaken her. For him there is no joy in this, no excitement, no *need*, yet Rebecca's eyes shine with tears and sorrow, and if wallowing in grief could make a woman more beautiful, then she becomes exquisite. He loves her more than ever.

Back home they go through the motions of cohabitation, but he can see that she finds even less of a thrill in his touch than in the accident scenes that she no longer cares about. Through her, he loses his enthusiasm for the way his life has always been and he, too, stops seeking out the little tragedies that formerly kept him going. His life is as flavorless as dry white toast, and it is all Andre can do not to cry each morning at the sun crests the building and starts another day. He goes to work, he comes home, they grocery shop. He cannot do it himself, but he doesn't understand why, if he has become such a nothing part of her life, Rebecca doesn't simply leave him.

Until that final Saturday morning trip to the store, when it all becomes clear.

Painfully so.

* * *

They are crossing Kimble Avenue a little south of Lawrence, jaywalking, and he is mulling, as he so often does these days, on how or what he can do to salvage his relationship with Rebecca. Her hand, the rounded fingernails coated by pale polish, is nestled in the crook of his elbow—despite their emotional distance, she has never stopped holding onto him in public. They pause in the center of the street to let a large delivery truck pass; it has vegetables painted on the side of it in bright, lifelike colors—a vibrant red tomato, a startlingly green pepper, sun-yellow corn. There's more, an entire assortment of others that Andre does not have time to notice, before Rebecca's hand slips from his elbow, settles into the small of his back –

– and pushes him.

* * *

From where he is wedged beneath the truck, Andre's view is limited to a narrow slice of daylight, the distance between the filthy undercarriage of this Ford truck and the surprisingly chilly concrete beneath his cheek. He can't feel anything else, and he supposes that for this he should consider himself lucky; if he strains his eyes downward in the direction of his torso, he can just glimpse a pool of scarlet, his blood, as it rushes away from the confines of his flesh. There are several dozen pair of feet crisscrossing the horizontal bar of his eyesight, so he must have been unconscious for a bit, long enough to gather a crowd. As he stares, he recognizes a familiar set of sandals; brown leather in a basket pattern with beads woven across the top—he bought them for Rebecca only a week ago.

Andre's vision is going a disturbing gray around the edges, images bleeding into the roadway until everything seems to have melted at the edges like the cheap special effects he's seen in a dozen different science fiction movies, the ones where the camera looks at the trappings of planet Earth from the attacking alien's point of view. The circle in the middle where things are still in focus is growing smaller, but not so much that he doesn't recognize his beloved Rebecca as she kneels next to the truck and peers underneath; crouching with her is a face he also recognizes, even though it has been at least a year. His hair is still thick and dark brown, and the hungry eyes peering from behind stylish glasses haven't changed, either, since May 9, 2004—this is the man who was at the bus accident on the same day that Rebecca introduced herself to him. Even his faint, knowing smile is the same, and somehow Andre isn't surprised when he sees Rebecca slip her hand into the stranger's and hears her ask him, *"Do you think he's feeling any pain?"*

If he could only speak, this time Andre would tell Rebecca that yes, he certainly is.

First appeared in *Outsiders* anthology published by ROC, Oct. 2005

Glenn Chadbourne

Glenn Chadbourne

Glenn Chadbourne

Glenn Chadbourne

IXCHEL'S TEARS

By José R. Nieto

I

Walking steadily over packed snow, frigid water seeping into his inadequate boots, Francisco found that he couldn't stop thinking about the argument. It had started over nothing: an errand forgotten by Elizabeth, his fiancée; a piece of mail undelivered. Annoyed by her calm disposition, he made the mistake of accusing her of not apologizing enough. Elizabeth in turn accused him of always accepting her apologies.

"What am I supposed to do?" Francisco said, incredulously.

"You're supposed to say that it's okay," Elizabeth responded, "that I shouldn't worry about it. You should say that you love me, no matter what I do. When you tell me 'I accept your apology' in that tone of yours—you know, that official voice you put on—it makes me feel awful, like I've done something beyond forgiveness. I mean, does a letter really matter that much to you?" While she spoke Elizabeth squinted her eyes, as if she had trouble focusing.

Francisco shook his head. "It's just cultural," he said to dismiss the issue. Often when they disagreed, when he was tired or horny and did not feel like going at length, he was quick to raise the specter of ethnic difference. It saved the effort of a good argument. Because of their disparate backgrounds—he, the product of a large working-class San Juan family; she, from a privileged Boston suburb—the

~ 233 ~

subject carried the weight and significance of a veiled threat. In normal circumstances the mere mention of culture would serve to stymie the most heated debate, almost as if he had drawn a line on the ground, a fragile border that Elizabeth did not dare cross.

This time, though, maybe because of the holidays, or possibly due to the impending nuptials (still six months away), the two of them went on to rehash the rest of their disagreements: city or country residence, casual wedding or formal reception. Foolishly, Francisco revived an old fight about the language and religion of their future children. That one kept them at it until Elizabeth crossed her arms, glanced down at her shoes and started to cry.

"I don't think we're ready for this," she said. It was those words and that image—Elizabeth closed off, tears flowing in thin rivulets, her face flushed to a pale red—that had sent Francisco out carelessly into the brutal winter, thinly clad. His shoes leaked, the overcoat had small rodent-type holes on the back. Its lining had ripped weeks after he'd bought it at a fancy secondhand store. He wished he'd forgone style and bought sensible winter wear; as a graphic designer he made enough to afford it. As it was, he usually wore the ragged coat with a number of layers, or at least a sweater. Tonight he had on only a T-shirt and cotton sweatpants.

His flight, Francisco now understood, had been propelled by guilt and apprehension. For all their arguments he still cared deeply for Elizabeth. They shared a history, a passage through time. Their relationship (and he thought of it as an individual entity, a growing, living thing) had withstood passion and indifference, conflict and resolution, even a year of separation while Francisco attended art school in Madrid. When he'd first seen her, calmly sipping Grand Marnier from a brandy snifter at a friend's dinner party, he had become convinced that they would end up together. That was three years ago, but he could still picture her perfectly; wrist turned awkwardly, moist lips barely touching the contoured crystal as if she were kissing a relic, bare legs crossed under the kitchen chair, face and glass lit subtly by flickering candlelight. Right then he had fallen in love with her.

The blustering wind sprinkled loose snowflakes on his beard and hair, then swirled around his feet and crawled up his legs to fill his clothes. Even inside the deep pockets his fingers felt stiff and painfully dry. Across Cambridge Street he noticed the colorful lights of a flower shop, gaudily decorated for the holidays. It was then that it hit him: a gift for Elizabeth, that was precisely what he was after. The window display looked like a magic screen, a tempting portal to a lush tropical paradise. Improbable greens mingled with rich reds, purples and yellows, tones made brighter by the dirgeful gray of winter. Most of all, though, the plants promised soothing temperatures. They reminded him of home. Francisco could think of nothing better right now.

Christmas in Puerto Rico: *Noche Buena* up in the mountains, the family gathering as heavy raindrops played a quick rhythm on the tin roof, heavy smell of roasted pork and *gandules* hovering around Francisco like thick cigar smoke. Loud, dissonant conversations over rum and watery beer....

The light changed and Francisco rushed across the street, almost slipping into a pool of dirty slush. When he reached the shop he opened the door so abruptly that the counter person—a short brown man with shiny black hair and inset eyes—jumped from his stool as if startled. The warmth and green scent hit Francisco like a Caribbean wave; for a moment he stood at the entrance and let himself be enveloped. He shook the snow from his face and clothes, then stomped his feet.

"How can I help you?" said the man behind the counter. His words came out with difficulty, twisted by a heavy accent.

"I'm so glad you're still open," Francisco said, "being like it's Christmas Eve and all."

The man didn't respond. His leathery face showed tentativeness that Francisco thought he recognized. He tried again, this time in Spanish. The man smiled and perked up, as if a weight had been removed from his back.

"Last minute we usually do good business," he said, "*plantas y flores*, people don't want to buy them too early. But I was going to close up soon."

"Well, I'm glad you didn't because I am in serious need of something nice for my *prometida*. It's kind of an emergency, really."

"Go ahead, look around. I can wait."

"*Gracias, hermano*," Francisco said, turning toward a majestic display by the left wall. The plants were arranged in shelves, stacked all the way to the ceiling; giant succulent leaves shared space with delicate orchids and spindly lilies. On the floor, plastic buckets held cut flowers: carnations, violets, daffodils, and many others Francisco had never seen before. A whole comer was crowded with red poinsettias — *Flor de Pascuas,* as they called them back home.

The possibilities baffled Francisco. He had no idea what would best serve as a peace offering, what would once again open the channels of communication.

"Is this all you have?" he said.

"No, no, no, we have a refrigerator in the back, you know, with the delicate ones, roses and things."

Roses, that sounded better to Francisco.

"Could I see them? That might be more appropriate."

"Sure, hold on a minute." The man got off the stool and walked to the front door. Immediately Francisco noticed a significant limp; he seemed to drag his right leg rather than step with it. He took a key chain from his stained orange apron and locked the door with some difficulty.

"I'm by myself here," he explained as he fumbled with the lock.

"No problem," Francisco said. The short man turned around and led him to the rear of the store. As they pushed through a little swinging gate behind the counter Francisco wondered if the limp was due to a war wound. The man's accent placed him someplace in Central America, where crippling violence seemed a likely possibility. Francisco considered asking, but thought better of the idea.

"So you're doing the Anglo thing," the man said, "giving Christmas presents, *Santa Clos* and such."

"Yes," Francisco said, then reconsidered. "Well, no, actually. See, I got into a big fight with my *prometida* tonight, that's what happened. Probably holiday stress, I think, combined with the wedding it's making us kind of edgy."

"That's what I've been telling people, why do they go crazy with the gift-giving thing on Christmas? I mean, isn't the Baby Jesus gift enough for everybody? Take it easy, I tell them, wait until the sixth...."

Francisco shrugged. "Well, I'm from Puerto Rico," he said, "and we give presents on both Christmas and Three Kings Day. We kind of play it both ways, I guess."

"Oh," the man said, as if disappointed, "I didn't know they did that in Puerto Rico."

For a moment Francisco expected to become enmeshed in an argument about the Americanization of Puerto Rican culture (Lord knew that he'd heard them before), but as the man limped down the hallway he did not say another word.

They walked past a cluttered supply room—black bags of potting soil, miniature hoes, fertilizer—then through a glass sliding door covered with mist. From inside, the refrigerated case reminded Francisco of a small bodega aisle, if slightly colder. Harsh fluorescent lights illuminated the space, somewhat diminishing the impact of the colorful arrangement. Still, the packed shelves were stunning. Each level displayed hundreds of flowers: roses, cut orchids, tulips. As an artist Francisco was quick to detect subtle permutations of hues and shapes, careful patterns that served to enhance the visual experience; round petals mingled with insect-like blossoms, wiry stigmas hung from bright red poppies and reached lovingly into the adjacent bellflowers.

"Did you do this?" Francisco asked.

"What do you mean?"

"I mean, did you put this room together?"

The man looked around and smiled. "Yes," he said, "that was me. My cousin Eriberto, he owns the store, and he used to keep the place in such a mess, but I straightened it out."

"It's beautiful," Francisco said absently. The man smiled again and nodded, but did not speak.

"Why don't we do this," Francisco said, "why don't you put together an arrangement for me. Put your nicest flowers together in a bouquet, I'll pay whatever it costs."

"We've got catalogues if you want to see them...."

"No, that's fine, I trust you."

"*Bueno*," the man said, then with a quick wave of his arms sent Francisco out to the front of the store.

While he waited for the flowers Francisco paced back and forth, framed by walls of greenery, and in his mind he kept running Elizabeth's words—"I don't think we're ready for this..."—and with every repetition they became more definite, until, after a couple of turns, they had changed to "I know we're not ready for marriage...," and finally "We shouldn't get married." The weight of the imagined statement stopped him in midstep and made him shudder.

A few minutes later the man came forth with the finished bouquet. To his surprise Francisco found it rather disappointing. Not that the arrangement itself was ugly, far from it. The lavender orchids looked sublime nestled within a bunch of yellow chrysanthemums, and the single, central rose, red like a burning torch, conveyed a sense of longing and desire. But as he cradled the flowers in his arms Francisco wondered if such a gift was really suitable. Within days, he realized, the blooms would be nothing but wilted stems and dried petals—not exactly the message he'd wanted to deliver to his fiancée.

Francisco stared at the bouquet for a moment, then glanced quickly at the man. He was smiling, apparently satisfied with his work. Francisco couldn't blame him; he'd really done a good job.

"This is fine," he said as convincingly as possible, "they're beautiful. Now, how much do I owe you?"

The man dropped his smile just as Francisco finished the question. "Make it twenty," he said in a dry voice, "that'll be fine, twenty."

Francisco paid the man, thanked him, then headed for the door. Outside it had started snowing again; thick clumps slid slowly down the tempered glass, leaving watery trails like tears. People walked hurriedly on the frozen sidewalk, wrapped tightly in bright ski jackets and woolen hats. Francisco paused just as he was about to push the door open, right hand stuck to the cold glass. Suddenly he couldn't face the prospect of going back to the apartment, of stepping nakedly into the sharp wind, carrying with him such a slight offering.

"What is it?" the man asked.

Francisco said the first thing that came to mind: "It's the cold, I just can't stand this freezing weather."

After a moment the man said, "Why don't you come out back to the office, I'll make some *café con leche* so we can heat up your insides. It's not like I want to head out there either."

"My name's Agustín Irriñosa," the man began. He held the coffee cup right under his nose and took a deep breath.

"Francisco Arriví."

"You said you're from Puerto Rico, is that right?"

"I live here in Cambridge now, but that's where I'm originally from. I left the island when I was eighteen...."

"I've heard it's nice down there," Agustín said, smiling.

"Well you know," Francisco said, then paused to take a sip. The liquid burned his tongue but felt good going down; he could feel it drip all the way to his belly. "It's home so you don't really think about it much until you're gone."

"Bet you think about it now," Agustín said, "with this weather, I mean."

"Yes, I do," Francisco said plainly.

"I think about home too, Guatemala." Agustín stroked his chin, then leaned back on the chair. Francisco rested his elbows on the crowded desk and sighed.

"Must've been rough," he said. "I've read horrible things about the war."

"The war was one thing," Agustín said, his free hand fluttering, "but there was so much more to life than that. People think it's hell, but we had our share of happiness, me and my family, when the fighting stopped we made *milpe* grow with our hands, we drank *balche* and watched the sun being smothered by the rubber trees. And when the stars came out we told stories to each other, tales of *Cha-Chaac* and *Kukulcan*, but most of all, no matter what the soldiers did to us, we were always warm, and the trees never died, and in the river the water always flowed."

Francisco nodded hesitantly and drank from the steaming cup. At first he did not know how to respond; what Agustín described was so far from his staid urban experience. Instead he stared at a small framed picture of Jesus hanging on the opposite wall. Between his pierced hands he held a realistic-looking heart, like an Azteca sacrifice. *Sagrado Corazón*, Francisco thought.

"What about snow," he said after a moment, "what did you think of it when you first saw it."

Agustín turned away like he'd smelled something awful.

"Bah," he said, "it's just frozen water, that's all it is."

Francisco chuckled, splashing coffee onto the desk. "I was never too hot on it myself," he said as he reached for a napkin to clean the mess. Soon Agustín was laughing as well.

"You hate it here too, huh?" he asked.

While considering the question Francisco ran a hand through his hair and glanced blankly at the paneled ceiling.

Originally he'd come to Boston only for school, fully intending to return to the island. But then his parents divorced and going to

Puerto Rico lost some of its urgency. He got a good job, he made friends in the city, he met Elizabeth. He fell in love.

He remembered the walk to the flower shop, icy gusts running through his flimsy clothes like needles.

"I don't know," he said, "sometimes. I miss a lot of things about Puerto Rico; the language, old San Juan, my family. Adjuntas, up in the mountains where my grandparents lived. I miss the sea, I guess, water warm like from a bathtub. Not like here, *verdad*? Anyway, my fiancée and I talked once about moving down, but you know, Elizabeth has her career, she doesn't speak any Spanish, she's real close to her family –"

Agustín seemed taken aback for a moment. "Elizabeth?" he said like it was a mouthful. "You mean she's a *gringa*?"

"She's Anglo," Francisco said, annoyed by the man's reaction. He'd gotten the same words, the same expression from a number of Latino acquaintances. In his mind Francisco dusted off a long list of arguments to explain his decision.

"I'm sorry," Agustín said, quickly regaining his composure, "I didn't mean to –"

"I understand," Francisco said, and was immediately brought back to his argument with Elizabeth. The thought made something twist uncomfortably in his chest. It was time to go home, he'd been away long enough, almost an hour. Though he wasn't looking forward to facing his fiancée, Francisco realized that gift or not he had little choice. There were, after all, matters left unresolved.

"Listen," he said as he pushed away from the desk, "I really should go back to my *prometida*. Thanks for your hospitality –"

"*Espérese un momentito*," Agustín said quickly, "are you sure that's what you want to take to your fiancée?" He pointed at the bouquet on Francisco's lap. "The way you looked at it," he continued, "you know, when I handed it to you, it was like you didn't care for it at all."

"Well, it's beautiful," Francisco said, gently stroking the rose petals, "but I don't know, maybe I should get her something that's going to last. I thought of getting a plant, but that just wouldn't have the same effect as the flowers. I mean, I already got her a Christmas present, a really nice bracelet in fact, but this, this has to be different...."

Francisco paused, then looked down to the coffee cup. "We really went at it tonight," he said. "Jesus, you should have heard us! And, well, I have a feeling that when I get home tonight, I think there's a chance she's going to tell me that it's over. So you see, what I want, it has to be something special...."

Excited, almost laughing, Agustín stood up and walked to Francisco's side. "I think I have exactly what you need," he said.

With quick steps (considering the man's prominent limp) Agustín led Francisco down a dusty stairwell, past heating ducts and clanking water pipes, then through an iron gate and into the tiny basement. Right across from the entrance, standing slightly askew against the cracked wall, stood a smaller version of the refrigerator upstairs; this one could have actually been a soda dispenser. On the middle shelf there was a delicate ceramic vase decorated with jaguar paws and proud quetzal birds. Within it lay a sole cut orchid, unlike any Francisco had ever seen. Huge silver-colored petals reflected the fluorescent glare like distorted mirrors.

"It's an Ixchel's tear, a moon orchid," Agustín explained, "it came from El Petén, near my home in Guatemala."

"I've never...," Francisco began, but let his voice trail off as he approached the refrigerator door.

"Most people haven't. Only a few of them grow in the entire Yucatán peninsula."

Francisco opened the door and knelt down in front of the flower. From up close the orchid's reddish center seemed to glow, as if it contained a dying ember. Had it not been for the way the petals quivered under his breath, he would have sworn they were made of steel.

"This is," he said, stumbling with the words, "this is unbelievable. Why, I mean, why would you keep it down here, hidden away?"

"Because it's not for sale," Agustín said, looking at the floor. "Eriberto, he doesn't know what to do with it, he doesn't even have a price for it yet."

"If you're not selling it, then why are you showing it to me?"

Agustín paused and stroked his cheek and walked closer to Francisco. He put a heavy hand on his shoulder. "Because I'm giving it to you, that's what I'm doing."

"I don't understand," Francisco said.

"It's Christmas," Agustín said with a forced grin, "and that's what you do for Christmas, right?"

"But won't your boss –"

"What is he going to do, fire me? I'm his cousin and I work for nothing, just room and board. Besides, that orchid didn't cost him a cent. It was me who got it, you see, I brought it with me when I came from Guatemala." For a moment Agustín seemed angry, but at what Francisco could not tell.

The thought of receiving such a gift seemed unreal to Francisco. It was as if a stranger had offered to buy him a house or a car; it just didn't happen. He stepped away from the flower and pursed his lips, then slowly shook his head.

"'Take it," Agustín said with some urgency, "I'm telling you, that's what you want."

"How long will it last?" Francisco asked sheepishly.

"That's the thing," Agustín said, "my Quiché mama, she used to tell me tales of the moon orchid, and what she said to me was that the blossoms, even if they're torn from the plant, they last forever. They never die. This one my mother got years ago, I carried it with me in an ammunition box. I waded across wide rivers and pushed through thick forests, I ran with it across two borders, and now look at it, it's still as beautiful as when she found it."

Perhaps because Agustín seemed to him like a kindred spirit—as much of an artist with flowers as he was with brushes and pens—Francisco found it natural to believe his story about the undying orchid. Aesthetically it made sense; blossoms had always been used to represent feelings of love and affection. Why should they, then, perish?

Reverently, Francisco reached into the refrigerator and took the vase in his hands. To his surprise there was no water inside. He rested it against his chest and felt a strange warmth exuding from the blossom—almost like from an animal—and he thought, Agustín's right: this is exactly what I need. When Elizabeth sees the orchid she will be overwhelmed by its beauty, by the utter perfection of its form, and she will see, actually see, what I truly feel for her. In her slim hands she will hold the full extent of my devotion.

Before, he had told Agustín that he wasn't looking for a Christmas present. He'd been wrong. The moon orchid was the perfect Christmas gift, not just for Elizabeth, but for their relationship; a symbol concretized, like the Baby Jesus, an embodiment of the permanence of love.

"Thank you," he said, "thank you. You don't know how much you've helped us. I think with this you've given us a future."

Agustín opened his mouth but did not say a word. Instead he took Francisco's left hand and shook it vigorously. With visible effort he lifted his fused leg and limped to the cement stairs. Still in awe, Francisco followed.

Once upstairs the man spent a few seconds playing with the lock, then pushed the door open. Immediately, the arctic wind rushed in, tussling the poinsettia leaves and stinging Francisco's face and bare hands.

"*Feliz Navidad,*" he said and stepped into the cold. Through the glass window he saw Agustín mouth the same words.

After tucking the orchid under his coat, he walked to the curb and hailed a cab.

II

From the street the second-floor apartment appeared empty; there were no lights on in the windows, and at eight-thirty Francisco thought it too early for Elizabeth to have gone to bed. Could she have moved out of the house so quickly? He shook his head to dispel the stupid, painful thought; his *prometida* would have never acted so rashly.

As soon as he'd stepped inside Francisco flicked the light switch and yelled "Elizabeth!" but there was no response. Out of habit, he reached behind the couch and plugged in the Christmas tree. The bulbs lit up immediately but took a few minutes to start alternating. This year, because of all the wedding preparations, the smallish fir had ended up sparsely decorated. A single long strand of colored lights clung awkwardly to the abundant needles. Under the tree they kept a wooden manger scene complete with mother, father, baby and animals. The Three Kings—small stubs with golden crowns—stood impassively on the other side of the room. Every night before going to bed Francisco would move them closer to their destination.

He walked with a quick gait to the kitchen and carefully placed the moon orchid on the counter, right by the maple-wood cutting board. Taped to the pantry, Francisco found a hurriedly scrawled note from Elizabeth. In it she explained that she had not felt like being alone tonight, so she'd gone to her sister's, who lived only a few minutes away. At the bottom of the torn sheet she wrote down the phone number (as if he could forget that number) and next to it she inscribed in tall letters CALL ME.

Immediately Francisco reached for the wall-mounted phone and picked up the receiver. He'd already pressed the first digit when he thought, No, no, there you go again, acting, talking without thinking. That's what got you in trouble in the first place, *idiota*!

What was he going to say? He'd placed all his hopes in the orchid, in the meaningful act of giving. How could he have known that he would first have to talk to Elizabeth? Once again he felt the familiar sting of muted panic. It was as if he were standing in front of an empty canvas, pencil tip pressed lightly against the smooth surface, images turning fast inside his head, too fluid to capture in a single frame. The words were all there, but not quite in the right combination.

He sat on the kitchen stool, cracked his knuckles, then shook his arms to loosen up. Obviously he needed a clear mind, and patience. Much patience.

All of a sudden a thought crossed Francisco's mind that he tried hard to ignore; in Spanish he would know exactly what to say to Elizabeth. For all his years in Boston, he still found it easier to communicate emotions in his native language. Even the word *amor* seemed to hold more significance than its English equivalent. In Spanish, after all, he would never say "I love pizza," or "I loved that movie," uses that served to cheapen the expression, making it less meaningful. The phrase *te amo* implied a higher level of passion, a careless ardor that could never be conveyed in English; to Francisco it was almost magical. He'd used it frivolously only once—in an ill-fated attempt to bed a stunning classmate—and he had immediately regretted it.

He closed his eyes for a moment. Rubbing his forehead, he said out loud, "Maybe I should wait for her to call me." Yes, that was the rational thing to do, make sure she has had a chance to cool off. Taking the initiative could only make things worse.

Francisco took a cookie from a porcelain jar in the pantry and began to bite methodically around the sprinkled center. Soon he was staring at the moon orchid. The glittering petals reminded Francisco of his conversation with Agustín, of how easy it'd been to talk to him about his life in the island. When he'd blurted in Spanish that he missed Puerto Rico the man had simply nodded and accepted the statement. If he'd been talking to Elizabeth he would have had to explain so much that in the end he would have given up and said nothing. Sitting as he was on that wobbly stool, staring deep into the fiery heart of Ixchel's tear, Francisco could not deny the attractiveness of cultural symmetry; one person talking in precise, descriptive terms, another listening intently, comprehending fully. How he wished it were that easy with Elizabeth.

He remained still on the stool more than an hour, absorbed by the blossom's delicate curvature. Inside the folds he could see twisted reflections of himself and the kitchen-light particles dancing in swirling, concentric patterns, like water down an open drain. Yes, that was the image; a tiny but powerful maelstrom, its flow drawing the fear and discomfort from him, leaving behind a strange but satisfying emptiness.

He was roused by the persistent ringing of the doorbell. Annoyed by the interruption, he stood up slowly and headed for the downstairs foyer. As he walked through the living room, Francisco discovered that the strand of colored lights had slipped from the Christmas fir. It now lay coiled around the tree's base, blinking arrhythmically.

"Jesus," he said. Before he could take a closer look the doorbell rang again.

He climbed down the stairs as quietly as possible since he didn't want to disturb the Portuguese family on the first floor. The two little girls had to be asleep already. After only eight months in the states they had come to take Santa Claus very seriously.

In the tiny viewer Francisco saw the man from the flower shop. Agustín stood on the porch shivering, even though he was wrapped in a large padded coat that looked like a comforter. Without hesitation, Francisco opened the door.

"Well, this is a surprise," he said. Agustín paid no heed to the pleasantry and pushed past him, then limped fast up the wooden staircase. Hanging from his left hand there was a rusted-green ammunition box. Francisco turned to look at the curious sight but did not move from the foyer.

"Where's the flower, the moon blossom?" the man yelled from upstairs. Francisco reacted like he'd just been shaken from a fond reminiscence. He rushed up the stairs after Agustín. By the time he made it to the kitchen the man had already taken Ixchel's tear from the ceramic vase and was placing it tenderly inside the box.

"Tell me," he said, closing the metal lid, "are you still in love with your fiancée?"

"Of course," Francisco said. As if to convince himself he repeated, "Of course I love her."

Shaking his head, Agustín ran stubby hands over his face and drew closer to him.

"Where's Elizabeth, Francisco?" he said.

"At her sister's, she went to her sister's after our fight this afternoon. Anyway, what does that have to do with my orchid?"

Agustín pulled on a small metal handle to close the latch on the ammunition box. He took off his coat and laid it out on the kitchen stool, then with one smooth motion lifted himself and sat on top of it.

"In the jungle we believe in circles," he began, "for many years my mama tried to explain that to me. Strange that it's in the States where I finally understood."

"Circles?" Francisco asked.

"We Quiché believe that Ixchel's tears are a gift from *la luna*, the sun's consort. So sad is she when she's alone in the sky that she cries, and her tears, when they hit the ground they turn to beautiful things, moon blossoms. So you see, from sadness comes something of beauty.

"But the thing is, it doesn't stop there, because the moon orchids live by sucking the life out of plants around them, they pull *la esencia*, that's why the flowers can live forever. When you find them they're almost always in the middle of an open clearing, surrounded by rotten trees. The Mayas, they used the tears to open up the forest for the *milpe* fields. Better than burning, I'm sure. So you see, death leads to food, to life."

Francisco was reminded of the scene in the living room.

"That's what happened to my Christmas tree," he said, "that's why you kept the flower all by itself in that tiny basement. Well, if that's all, we'll just keep it someplace—"

"Do you realize that Elizabeth is still waiting for you?" Agustín interrupted. The harsh tone made it sound less like a question than an accusation.

Francisco felt like he'd just slipped underwater. All of a sudden he became aware of the stupidity of his thoughts and behavior since he'd arrived at home with the flower. How could he have waited so long to go after his fiancée? Pointing tentatively at the box he said, "Was that, I mean could that have been...?"

Agustín nodded. His eyes were covered with red lines, like cracked marbles.

"But how?" Francisco said.

"After the empire fell apart, *curanderas* like my mama found out that Ixchel's tears could also drain strong feelings from people; hate, anger, jealousy. They can soothe someone who's in pain, or end a fight between brothers." He paused for a second, then said, "They can suck the love from even the most passionate couple...."

Francisco took a step back and glared intently at Agustín. The man lowered his head and began to speak in a low, pleading voice. Throughout his hands remained on his lap, still.

"It was the cold, that's what it was. You walked into the shop and your face was the color of snow and your hands were shaking and you told me how much you hated the cold, how much you wished you were back home, and the thing is, you can go home, you can take a plane tomorrow and you'll be there. Me, I'm stuck here. You see, about a year ago I killed a soldier who'd been trying to burn our fields, and since then my life's been worthless in Guatemala. That's why I ran away, that's why I had to come to this frozen hell to work for my cousin.

"I long for my home as much as you do, but I can't go anywhere, you understand, I don't have a green card, no permits or anything, and if I'm caught they'll send me back to die. But you, all that keeps you here's a woman, a *gringa*...."

"You had no right," Francisco began in anger, but stopped, when he realized that Agustín was quietly weeping.

"I know, I know," he said, "but the thing is, I thought I was helping you, I thought I was giving you the warm beaches and the green mountains, I thought I was giving you back to your family. I mean, what better gift is there than something you wish you could give to yourself?"

Francisco leaned against the counter and put his hands in his pockets. He took a couple of deep breaths, then said calmly, "Why are you here then?"

Agustín looked up. His face glistened with tears.

"Before you left, you said something that stuck in my mind, even after I locked up the store and headed home I just couldn't stop thinking about it. You said that I had given you your future, and I kept thinking about what my *Quiché mama* said to me when she handed me the Ixchel's tear, right before I left. She handed me that ammunition box, and she told me, if you want to feel better, if you miss us too much, open the box and let it clean your mind. I never did though, even when I was starving in refugee camps, even when I broke my knee and spent months in a leper's hospital. You see, she gave me a choice –"

"Which you are now giving me," Francisco interjected. Agustín closed his eyes and nodded quickly.

"The moon orchid can help you," he said, almost whispering. "It can drain the things that make you fight with your *prometida*. But the thing is, it would also let you think, and maybe then you'll decide that it's better to go back home, that you belong in your *islita*. The question is, do you want to take that chance?"

For an instant—perhaps because of his tears and the blue glimmer of the fluorescent lights—Agustín's eyes looked blank, as if he were blind. Francisco was momentarily taken aback by the illusion. Then a curious thought crossed his mind: Agustín's mother, she must have been a wise, wise woman. Right then and there he knew he had the answer.

"Take it away. Please take the flower with you."'

Agustín nodded and jumped down from the stool. He slipped on his coat, took the ammunition box and put it under his arm and walked out of the kitchen. The limp made his body bounce awkwardly, like a needle on a scratched record. A minute later Francisco heard the muffled bang of the outside door being shut and knew that Agustín and Ixchel's tear were gone.

Back to square one, he thought. Guess the man was right about circles.

Elizabeth's note was still where he'd found it, taped to the pantry. The last line—CALL ME—seemed larger than before, as if in the ensuing hours it'd grown in importance. Instinctively Francisco looked at his watch. Five minutes past midnight; maybe it was too late to call.

He picked up the phone anyway. As he dialed his heart beat as if his chest were empty; every palpitation seemed to echo against his ribs and slowly fade away.

"Hello?" The voice took him by surprise; there had barely been a ring. Elizabeth must have been sitting right by the phone. '

"It's me," he said.

"Where have you been?" she said angrily. "I've been waiting here for hours! How could you walk away like –"

Francisco blurted out, "*Te amo*, Elizabeth "

Elizabeth was quiet for a minute. "Francisco," she finally said, and the way she said it—the tenderness in her voice, the music in her inflection—made it clear that she understood.

Morbideus W. Goodell

LIFE DURING DEATH

By Duane Swierczynski

This morning I did something incredibly stupid. And I already had plenty of stupid things to do today, thank you very much.

What happened was this: I stepped out of the shower, toweled myself off as best as possible, removed a clean pair of boxer briefs from my dresser drawer, and accidentally killed myself.

I always thought I'd *know* if death were approaching. I don't deny that it can happen anytime, anywhere, and to anybody—but I figured I'd have a little foreshadowing. But no. I was minding my own business, slipping my underwear over my legs when I lost my balance, pitched forward and slammed my eye socket into the sharp edge of my bedroom dresser. Next thing I knew, I was dead.

This didn't seem fair. I mean, tripping over my own underwear was something I must have done a dozen times before. I'm not exactly the most agile person. Once, my wife even saw it happen. Laughed her ass off. Said it was the funniest thing ever. Was *that* foreshadowing? Anyway, I suppose some vital portion of my brain was punctured when Mr. Dresser met Mr. Eye Socket. I'm no brain surgeon, but something must have clotted up and whammo—cerebral hemorrhage. Perhaps I jammed the part of my brain that regulates breathing.

Next thing I know, there was a woman speaking to me. "Hi, Lewis," she said.

"Hi," I said. I was standing. I didn't remember standing up. She walked closer. Smiling at me. Her face was familiar, but every time I tried to remember, the name slipped away. She reminded me, simultaneously, of every girlfriend I'd ever had. Including my wife. She was wearing clothes, but they were indeterminate as well. Stylish, though.

"Uh," I said, a bit unnerved. "Can I help you?"

"No," she said.

"Are you here to usher me into the afterlife?"

"Not particularly." She looked away from me and down to my lifeless, one-eyed body, which was lying naked on the floor. Then it hit me: *I was in my astral body.* My father always read books about this kind of stuff, and I'd always liked to engage him in conversations about this sort of thing. It fascinated and repulsed me at the same time. I was experiencing the latter sensation at this particular moment.

I looked at the woman. She kept staring at my lifeless nude corpse, gray boxer briefs wrapped around its ankles.

"Is something wrong?" I asked.

"Well...," she said, "to tell you the truth, I'm puzzled. I'm not sure why you're dead."

"I'm no brain surgeon," I said, "but I suppose something vital was punctured...."

"No, no. I comprehend the physical process that led to your death. I just don't know why it's still affecting you."

Now I was irritated. "Could it be because death is *permanent*?" Where were the pearly gates? The white light? My grandmother, welcoming me with open arms and a can of Coke and liverwurst sandwiches?

"You don't understand, Lewis. Death has never affected you before. But I've figured it out. While you were busy thinking angry thoughts..."—and here she paused to give me a sour look—"I scanned the universe and found the culprit: a spectral emanation from a passing meteorite beyond the moon. The trail fell right through your apartment...."

"Whoa," I said. "Slow down, sweetie." I surprised myself. I always call my wife "sweetie." *Foreshadowing?*

The woman smiled at me. "Of course, you don't understand me do you? You know nothing about your gift. The very nature of your gift erases all knowledge of its existence."

"Some gift." I looked down at my naked dead body.

"I suppose you might as well know, now that it's all over. You see, Lewis, you possessed a unique trio of psychic abilities: short-term time travel, telekinesis, and auto-memory erasure. Whenever you accidentally died, you'd simply go back in time a few seconds, steer yourself out of harm's way, then erase all memory of the incident. Your life would continue, as if the accidents never happened."

"*Accidents*, plural? As if to imply this sort of thing happened more than once?"

"It's happened quite a bit," she said. "You're not exactly the most... *agile* person in the world. "

"When have I died? I mean, before?"

"Goodness...when haven't you? Just in the past six months alone...." She breathed heavy. "Okay. Let's see. Okay, two weeks ago you were helping your landlord carry a heavy piece of machinery into his basement."

I remembered that. Damned thing was heavier than an Oldsmobile. And after we were finished dragging it down into the cellar, I'd stepped into a pile of cat shit in the front garden and tracked it through the apartment. Ruined my appetite, but it was nothing life threatening. I told the woman that.

"Wrong. You tripped on the concrete steps and the machinery fell on top of you, crushing your throat."

"Really?" I gulped.

"Yes. But you traveled back ten seconds, changed your foot position, blanked your own memory, and finished the task with no further difficulty."

"Except for the cat shit I stepped in."

"Right."

"Why didn't I use my gift to avoid that?"

The woman sighed and shook her head.

"Okay, what else?"

"Do you really want to me to go on?" she asked.

"Come on. I have to know."

"Okay. Two months ago. You. A subway platform. A speeding subway car, entering the station. A really engrossing magazine. You look up—*pow*. No more Lewis."

"Jesus!"

"Two and a half months ago. You. Playing with one of your cats. Claw swipe. Jugular sliced. Blood jetting ten feet across the room. No more Lewis."

"Which cat?" I demanded. "Buddy? Chickenlips?"

"You see? And I'm just getting started!" the woman cried out, half laughing.

This was a lot to absorb. I'd always been aware of my basic human frailty—I mean, such a complex machine, so many things that could go wrong. But to find out that my life was this incredibly fucking *tenuous*, glued together by unconscious psychic abilities? This was too much. Not to mention that my built-in safeguard didn't even work this time.

"So what happened this time? Why couldn't I save myself?"

"As I was saying, a spectral trail from a passing meteorite seems to have passed through your apartment, negating your psychic abilities. So you actually died this time."

"Great. Just fucking great." The old passing meteorite trick. Gets you every time. I wondered if they were going to mention that in my obituary:

> **ANDRESSON, LEWIS. Unconscious telekinetic time-traveler survived by loving wife, Meghan, and two cats, one of whom accidentally sliced open his throat in an erased incident two and a half months ago. Snuffed out by class-D meteorite passing the Earth's moon.**

The woman looked at me with sad eyes, then turned away. She knelt down beside my dead naked body and touched my chest with her fingers.

I must have stared at her, staring at me, for close to an hour. There was nothing else to do.

Finally, I spoke up. "Isn't there anything I can do?"

The woman looked up. "What do you mean? You're dead."

"I mean, what I am supposed to do? I've been standing here for an hour."

"Time has no meaning here."

"Where is *here*? Look, I know I been a little delinquent in my duties as a Catholic, but I'm sure something can be worked out. I was a church organist for about four years in college, pulling two, sometimes three Masses every Sunday...."

The woman's head jerked up, startling me. "Quiet!" she said.

I was quiet. The moments passed. Finally, I asked: "What?"

Her nostrils flared, as if she were sniffing for evidence of smoke. "Shhh!"

More moments passed. The sun set. Fields of flowers grew and wilted. The Earth shot around the Sun, again and again and again....

Finally, the woman sighed heavily. "There seems to have been a cosmic reprieve," she said. "The meteorite passed out of range before expected. Your psychic abilities will be restored in time, as it turns out."

"You mean… I'm going to live?" I squealed.

"Don't worry," she said, smiling with a touch of sadness in her eyes. She stood up and reached forward to grasp my arm. "You won't remember any of th –"

And suddenly my knee buckled, but my left leg pushed up to support it, and my body righted. I pulled my boxer briefs up over my hips. Snapped the elastic around my waist. Adjusted my crotch.

I looked at the sharp edge of the dresser and thought, *Man would that have been bad if I'd tripped.*

My wife came in from the next room. "You okay?" Her robe was open, revealing the soft curves of her breasts.

"Fine," I said, staring. But in that instant I realized I was lying, because it all came rushing back. The death woman. My astral body. Time travel, telekinesis, auto-memory loss....

Oh no. My grasp on reality was slipping. What mad universe was this where death lurked behind every action and the only escape was unconscious abilities no one believed in? Worse yet, that could be negated by whims of the cosmos? How could I walk through life with this hideous knowledge? How could I ever put underwear on again?

"My God!" I screamed. I was wigging out, big time. "MY GOD DO YOU REALIZE HOW BADLY WE ARE ALL FUCKED!?"

Meghan rushed over to me and grabbed my shoulders. "What are you talking about? What's wrong?"

Goodbye, sanity. Time to wet my pants and start barking like a dog. Ack. Ack. Ninnyferg. I grabbed Meghan's shoulders and shook her soundly. "WE'RE DOOMED! DEATH SURROUNDS US! THE MIND CONTROLS EVVVVERYTHING!"

Meghan gasped, then started to cry.

Instantly, I froze, watching the tears form in her eyes. It killed me.

Which must have done it, because time slid back. The scene with the woman replayed… then erased.

My wife came in from the next room. "You okay?" Her robe was open, revealing the soft curves of her breasts.

"Aside from the fact that I almost killed myself?" I replied. "I'm fine."

I shuffled forward, then yanked my boxer briefs up over my hips. I rubbed my temples. God, my mouth was pasty. I needed a can of Coke, bad. I could tell already, this was going to be one of those days. Felt like I was forgetting something important, but the more I tried to recall it, the more it slipped away. Another item lost.

And I already had a million stupid things to do today, thank you very much.

Glenn Chadbourne

AFTER THE ELEPHANT BALLET

By Gary A. Braunbeck

"Our acts our angels are, or good or ill, Our fatal shadows that walk by us still."
   – John Fletcher (1579-1625) *An Honest Man's Fortune*, Epilogue

The little girl might have been pretty once but flames had taken care of that: burned skin hung about her neck in brownish wattles; one yellowed eye was almost completely hidden underneath the drooping scar tissue of her forehead; her mouth twisted downward on both sides with pockets of dead, greasy-looking flesh at the corners; and her cheeks resembled the globs of congealed wax that form at the base of a candle.

I couldn't stop staring at her or cursing myself for doing it. She passed by the table where I was sitting, giving me a glimpse of her only normal-looking feature: her left eye was a startling bright green, a jade gemstone. Buried as it was in that ruined face, its vibrance seemed a cruel joke.

She took a seat in the back.

Way in the back.

"Mr. Dysart?"

A woman in her mid-thirties held out a copy of my latest storybook. I smiled as I took it, chancing one last glance at the disfigured little girl in the back, then autographed the title page.

I have been writing and illustrating children's books for the last six years, and though I'm far from a household name I do have a Newbery Award proudly displayed on a shelf in my office. One critic, evidently after a few too many Grand Marniers, once wrote: "Dysart's books are a treasure chest of wonders for children and adults alike. He is part Maurice Sendak, part Hans Christian Andersen, and part Madeleine L'engle." (I always thought of my books as being a cross between Buster Keaton and the Brothers Grimm—what does *that* tell you about creative objectivity?)

I handed the book back to the woman as Gina Foster, director of the Cedar Hill Public Library, came up to the table. We had been dating for about two weeks; romance had yet to rear its ugly head, but I was hopeful.

"Well, are we ready?" she asked.

"'We' want to step outside for a cigarette."

"I thought you were trying to quit."

"And failing miserably." I made my way to the special "judge's chair." "How many entries are there?"

"Twenty-five. But don't worry, they can show you only one illustration and the story can't be longer than four minutes. We still on for coffee and dessert afterward?"

"Unless some eight-year-old Casanova steals your heart away."

"Hey, you pays your money, you takes your chances."

"You're an evil woman."

"Famous for it."

"Tell me again: How did you rope me into being the judge for this?"

"When I mentioned that this was National Literacy Month, you assaulted me with a speech about the importance of promoting a love for creativity among children."

"I must've been drunk." I don't drink—that's my mother's department.

Gina looked at her watch, took a deep breath as she gave me a "Here-We-Go" look, then turned to face the room. "Good evening," she said in a sparkling voice that always reminded me of bells. "Welcome to the library's first annual storybook contest." Everyone applauded. I tried slinking my way into the woodwork. Crowds make me nervous. Actually, most things make me nervous.

"I'll just wish all our contestants good luck and introduce our judge, award-winning local children's' book author Andrew Dysart."

She began the applause this time, then mouthed *You're on your own* before gliding to an empty chair.

"Thank you," I said, the words crawling out of my throat as if they were afraid of the light. "I...uh, I'm sure that all of you have been working very hard, and I want you to know that we're going to make copies of all your storybooks, bind them, and put them on the shelves here in the library right next to my own." Unable to add any more dazzle to that stunning speech, I took my seat, consulted the list, and called the first contestant forward.

A chubby boy with round glasses shuffled up as if he were being led in front of a firing squad. He faced the room, gave a terrified grin, then wiped some sweat from his forehead as he held up a pretty good sketch of a cow riding a tractor.

"My name is Jimmy Campbell and my story is called 'The Day The Cows Took Over.'" He held the picture higher. "See there? The cow is riding the tractor and the farmer is out grazing in the field."

"What's the farmer's name?" I asked.

He looked at me and said, "Uh...h-how about Old MacDonald?" He shrugged his shoulders. "I'd give him a better name, but I don't know no farmers."

I laughed along with the rest of the room, forgetting all about the odd, damaged little girl who had caught my attention earlier.

Jimmy did very well—I had to fight to keep my laughter from getting too loud, I didn't want him to think I was making fun of him but the kid was genuinely *funny*; his story had an off-kilter sense of humor that reminded me Ernie Kovacs. I decided to give him the maximum fifty points. I'm a pushover for kids. Sue me.

The next forty minutes went by with nary a tear or panic attack, but after eight stories I could see that several of the children were getting fidgety, so I signaled to Gina that we'd take a break after the next contestant.

I read: "Lucy Simpkins."

There was the soft rustling of movement in the back as the burned girl came forward.

Everyone stared at her. The cumulative anxiety in the room was squatting on her shoulders like a stone gargoyle, yet she wore an unwavering smile.

I returned the smile and gestured for her to begin.

She held up a watercolor painting.

I think my mouth may have dropped open.

The painting was excellent, a deftly-rendered portrait of several people—some very tall, others quite short, still others who were deformed—standing in a semi-circle around a statue which marked a grave. All wore the brightly colored costumes of circus performers. Each face had an expression of profound sadness; the nuances were breathtaking. But the thing that really impressed me was the cloud in the sky; it was shaped like an elephant, but not in any obvious way: it reminded you of summer afternoons when you still had enough imagination and wonder to lie on a hillside and dream that you saw giant shapes in the pillowy white above.

"My name is Lucy Simpkins," she said in a clear, almost musical voice, "and my story is called 'Old Bet's Gone Away.'

"One night in Africa, in the secret elephant graveyard, the angels of all the elephants got together to tell stories. Tonight it was Martin's, the Bull Elephant's, turn. He wandered around until he found his old bones, then he sat on top of them like they were a throne and said, 'I want to tell you the story of Old Bet, the one who never found her way back to us.'

"And he said:

"'In 1824 a man in Somers, New York, bought an elephant named Old Bet from a traveling circus. He gave her the best hay and always fed her peanuts on the weekends. Children would pet her trunk and take rides on her back in a special saddle that the man made.

"'Then one day the Reverend brought his daughter to ride on Old Bet. Old Bet was really tired but she thought the Reverend's little girl looked nice so she gave her a ride and even sang the elephant song, which went like this:

> I go along, thud-thud,
> I go along.
> And I sing my elephant song.
> I stomp in the grass,
> And I roll in the mud,
> And when I go a-walking, I go along THUD!
> It's a happy sound, and this is my happy song
> Won't you sing it with me? It doesn't take long.
> I go along, thud-thud, I go along.

"'Old Bet accidentally tripped over a log and fell, and the Reverend's daughter broke both of her legs and had to go to the hospital.

"'Old Bet was real sorry, but the Reverend yelled at her and smacked her with a horse whip and got her so scared that she ran away into the deep woods.

"'The next day the Reverend got all the people of the town together and told them that Old Bet was the Devil in disguise and should be killed before she could hurt other children. So the men-folk took their shotguns and went into the woods. They found Bet by the river. She was looking at her reflection in the water and singing:

> I ran away, uh-oh, I ran away.
> And I hurt my little friend.
> I didn't mean to fall, but I'm clumsy and old
> I'm big and ugly and the circus didn't want me anymore.
> I wish they hadn't sold me.
> I want to go home.

"'The Reverend wanted to shoot her, but the man who'd bought her from the circus said, "Best I be the one who does the deed. After all, she's mine." But the man wasn't too young either and his aim was a bit off and when he fired the bullet it hit Old Bet in the rear and it hurt and it scared her so much! She tried to run away, to run back to the circus.

"'She didn't mean to kill anyone, but two men got under her and she crushed them and her heart broke because of that. By now the Judge had come around to see what all the trouble was, and he saw the two dead men and decreed right there on the spot that Old Bet was guilty of murder and sentenced her to hang by the neck until she was dead.

"'They took her to the rail yard and strung her up on a railroad crane but she broke it down because she was so heavy. They got a stronger crane and hanged her from that. After three hours, Old Bet finally died while five thousand people watched. She was buried there in Somers and the man who owned her had a statue raised above the grave. Ever since, it has been a shrine for circus people. They travel to her grave and stop to pay their respects and remember that, as long as people laugh at you and smile, they won't kill you. And they say that if you look in the sky on a bright summer's day, you can see Old Bet up there in the clouds, smiling down at everyone and singing the elephant song as she tries to find her way back to Africa and the secret elephant graveyard.'

"Then it was morning, and the sun came up, and the elephants made their way back to a place even more secret than the elephant graveyard. They all dreamed about Old Bet, and wished her well.

"My name is Lucy Simpkins and my story was called 'Old Bet's Gone Away.' Thank you."

The others applauded her, softly at first, as if they were afraid it was the wrong thing to do, but it wasn't long before their clapping grew louder and more ardent. Gina sat forward, applauding to beat the band. She looked at the audience, gave a shrug that was more an inward decision than an outward action, and stood.

Lucy Simpkins managed something like a smile, then handed me her watercolor. "You should have this," she said, and made her way out of the room toward the refreshment table.

As everyone was dispersing, I took Gina's hand and pulled her aside. "My God, did you hear that?"

"I thought it was incredibly moving."

"Moving? Maybe in the same way the last thirty minutes of *The Wild Bunch* or *Straw Dogs* is moving, yes, but if you're talking warm and fuzzy and *It's A Wonderful Life*, you're way the hell off-base!"

Her eyes clouded over. "Jesus, Andy. You're shaking."

"Damn straight I'm shaking. Do you have any idea what that girl has to have been through? Can you imagine the kind of life which would cause a child to tell a story like that?" I took a deep breath, clenching my teeth. "Christ! I don't know which I want more: to wrap her up and take her home with me, or find her parents and break a baseball bat over their skulls!"

"That's a bit...strong, isn't it?"

"No. An imagination that can invent something like that story is not the result of a healthy, loving household."

"Don't be so arrogant. You aren't all-knowing about these things. You don't have any idea what her family life is really like."

"I suppose, Mother Goose, that you're more experienced in this area?" I don't know why I said something like that. Sometimes I'm not a nice person. In fact, sometimes I stink on ice.

Her faced melted into a placid mask, except for a small twitch in the upper left corner of her mouth that threatened to become a sneer.

"My sister had epilepsy," Gina said. "All her life the doctors kept changing her medication as she got older, a stronger dose of what she was already taking, or some new drug altogether. Those periods were murder because her seizures always got worse while her system adjusted. Her seizures were violent as hell but she refused to wear any kind of protective gear. 'I don't wanna look like a goon,' she'd say. So she'd walk around with facial scrapes and cuts and ugly bruises; she sprained her arm a couple of times and once dislocated her shoulder. People in the neighborhood started noticing, but no one said anything to us. Someone finally called the police and Child Welfare. They came down on us like a curse from heaven. They were of course embarrassed when they found out about Lorraine's condition—she'd always insisted that we keep it a secret—but nothing changed the fact that people who were supposedly our friends just *assumed* that her injuries were the result of child abuse. Lorraine had never been so humiliated, and from that day on she saw herself as being handicapped. I think that, as much as the epilepsy, helped to kill her. So don't go jumping to any conclusions about that girl's parents or the life she's had because *you can't know*. And anything you might say or do out of anger could plant an idea in her head that has no business being there."

"What do you suggest?"

"I suggest that you go out there and tell her how much you enjoyed her story. I suggest we try to make her feel special and admired because she deserves to feel that way, if only for tonight."

I squeezed her hand. "It couldn't have been a picnic for you, either, Lorraine's epilepsy."

"She should have lived to be a hundred. And just so you know—this has a tendency to slip out of my mouth from time to time—Lorraine committed suicide. She couldn't live with the knowledge that she was 'a cripple.' I cried for a year."

"I'm sorry for acting like a jerk."

She smiled, then looked at her watch. "Break's almost over. If you want to step outside and smoke six minutes off your life, you'd better do it now. I'll snag some punch and cookies for you."

I couldn't find Lucy; one parent told me she'd gone into the restroom, so I stepped out for my smoke. The rest of the evening went quickly and enjoyably. At the end of the night, I found myself with a tie: Lucy Simpkins (how could I not?) and my junior-league Ernie Kovaks who didn't know no farmers.

Ernie was ecstatic.

Lucy was gone.

* * *

I have only the vaguest memories of my father. When I was four, he was killed in an accident at the steel mill where he worked. He left only a handful of impressions: the smell of machine grease, the rough texture of a calloused hand touching my cheek, the smell of Old Spice. What I know of him I learned from my mother.

His death shattered her. She grew sad and overweight and began drinking. Over the years there have been times of laughter and dieting, but the drinking remained constant, evidenced by the flush on her cheeks and the reddened bulbous nose that I used to think cute when I was a child because it made her look like W.C. Fields; now it only disgusts me.

After my father's death, nothing I did was ever good enough; I fought like hell for her approval and affection but often settled for indifference and courtesy.

Don't misunderstand—I loved her when she was sober.

When she was drunk, I thought her the most repulsive human being on the face of the earth.

I bring this up to help you make sense of everything that happened later, starting with the surprise I found waiting on my doorstep when, after coffee and cheesecake, Gina drove me back to my house.

Someone on the street was having a party so we had to park half a block away and walk. That was fine by me; it gave us time to hold hands and enjoy the night and each other's company. The world was new again, at least for this evening –

– which went right into the toilet when something lurched out of the shadows on my porch.

"...Been waitin' here....a long time...." Her voice was thick and slurred and the stench of too much gin was enough to make me gag.

"Mom? Jesus, what are you –" I cast an embarrassed glance at Gina."—doing here?"

She pointed unsteadily to her watch and gave a soft, wet belch. "...S'after midnight...s'my birthday now...."

She wobbled back and forth for a moment before slipping on the rubber WELCOME mat and falling toward me.

I caught her. "Oh, for chrissakes!" I turned toward Gina. "God, I don't know what—I'm sorry about...."

"Is there anything I can do?"

Mom slipped a little more and mumbled something. I hooked my arms around her torso and said, "My...*dammit!*...my keys are in my left pocket. Would you...?"

Gina took them out, unlocked the front door, and turned on the inside lights. I spun Mom around and shook her until she regained some composure, then led her to the kitchen where I poured her into a chair and started a pot of coffee. Gina remained in the front room, turning on the television and adjusting the volume, her way of letting me know she wouldn't listen to anything that might be said.

The coffee finished brewing, and I poured a large cup for Mom. "How the hell did you get here?"

The shock of having someone other than myself see her in this state forced her to pull herself together; when she spoke again, her voice wasn't as slurred. "I walked. It's a nice...nice night." She took a sip of the coffee, then sat watching the steam curl over the rim of the cup. Her lower lip started to quiver. "I'm...I'm sorry, Andy. I didn't know you were gonna have company." She sighed, then fished a cigarette from the pocket of her blouse and lit it with an unsteady hand.

"Why are you here?"

"I just got to...you know, thinking about your dad and was feeling blue...besides, I wanted to remind you that you're taking me out for my birthday."

My right hand balled into a fist. "Have I *ever* forgotten your birthday?"

"No...."

"Then why would I start now?"

She leaned back in the chair and fixed me with an icy stare, smoke crawling from her nostrils like flames from a dragon's snout. "Maybe you think you've gotten too good for me. Maybe you think because I wasn't a story writer or artist like you, you don't have to bother with me anymore."

Time to go.

"Sit here and drink your coffee. I'm going to walk my friend to her car and then I'll come back and take you home."

"...Didn't get it from me, that's for damn sure...does you no good anyway...drop dead at forty-five and no one will care about your silly books...."

I threw up my hands and started out of the kitchen.

"What's this?" said Mom, pulling Lucy Simpkins's watercolor from my pocket. "Oh, a picture. They used to let us draw pictures when I was in the children's home...did I ever tell you about...?"

She was making me sick.

I stormed out of the kitchen and into the front room in time to see Jimmy Stewart grab Donna Reed and say, "I don't want to get married, understand?"

"Don't worry," said Gina. "They get together in the end." She put her arms around me. I felt like Jason being wrapped in the Golden Fleece.

"I'm so sorry about this," I said. "She's never done this before –"

"Never?"

I looked into her eyes and couldn't make any excuses. "I mean she's never come *here* drunk before."

"How long has she been this way?"

"I can't ever remember a week from my life when she didn't get drunk at least once."

"Have you ever tried to get her some help?"

"Of course I have. She tries it for a while, but she always...always –"

"I understand. It's okay. Don't be embarrassed."

That's easy to say, I thought. What I said was: "I appreciate this, Gina. I really do." I wished that she would just leave so I could get the rest of this over with.

She seemed to sense this and stepped back, saying, "I guess I should, uh, go...."

A loud crash from the kitchen startled both of us.

I ran in and saw Mom on the floor; she'd been trying to pour herself another cup of coffee and had collapsed, taking the coffee pot with her. Shattered sections of sharp glass covered the floor, and she had split open one of her shins. Scurrying on her hands and knees, she looked up and saw me standing there, saw Gina behind me, and pointed at the table.

"W-where did you...did you get *t-that?*"

"Get what?"

"...T-that goddamn...*picture!*"

I moved toward her. She doubled over and began vomiting.

I grabbed her, trying to pull her up to the sink—making it to the bathroom was out of the question—but I slipped and lost my grip –

– Mom gave a wet gurgling sound and puked on my chest--

– Gina came in, grabbed a towel, and helped me get her over the sink –

– and Mom gripped the edge, emptying her stomach down the drain.

The stench was incredible.

Feeling the heat of humiliation cover my face, I looked at Gina and fumbled for something to say, but what *could* I say? We were holding a drunk who was spewing all over –

– what could you say?

Gina returned my gaze. "So, how 'bout them Mets, huh? Fuckin-A!"

That's what you could say.

I didn't feel so dirty.

*　*　*

Gina surprised me the next morning by showing up on my doorstep at eight-thirty with hot coffee and croissants. When I explained to her that I had to take Mom's birthday cake over to her house Gina said, "I'd like to come along, if you don't mind."

I did and told her so.

"Come on," she said, taking my hand and giving me a little kiss on the cheek. "Think about it, if she's hung-over and sees that I'm with you, she might behave herself. If she doesn't behave, then you can use me as an excuse not to stick around."

I argued with her some more; she won. I don't think I've ever won an argument with a woman; they're far too sharp.

Besides an ersatz-apology ("I feel so *silly!*") and a bandage around the gash on her shin, Mom showed no signs that last night had ever happened. Her hair was freshly cleaned, she wore a new dress, and her makeup was, for a change, subtly applied; she looked like your typical healthy matriarch.

We stayed for breakfast. Gina surprised me a second time that morning by reaching into her purse and pulling out a large birthday card that she handed to Mom.

Well, that just made Mom's day. She must have thanked Gina half-a-dozen times and even went so far as to give her a hug, saying, "I'm glad to see he finally found a good one."

"Blind shithouse luck," replied Gina. She and Mom got a tremendous guffaw out of that. I gritted my teeth and smiled at them. Hardy-dee-har-har.

"So," Mom said to Gina. "Will you be coming with us?"

"I don't know," Gina replied, turning to me with a Pollyanna-pitiful look in her eyes. "Am I?"

"You stink at coy," was my answer.

"Good!" said Mom. "The three of us. It'll be a lot of fun."

"Have you decided where you want to go?"

"Yeee-eeessss, I have."

Oh, good, another surprise.

"Where?"

She winked at me and squeezed Gina's hand. "It's a secret. I'll tell you when we're on our way." This was a little game she loved to play—"I-Know-Something-You-Don't-Know"—and it usually got on my nerves.

But not that morning. Somehow Gina's presence made it seem as if everything was going to work out just fine.

Our first stop was Indian Mound Mall, where Gina insisted on buying Mom a copy of the new Stephen King opus and paying for lunch. After we'd eaten, Mom looked at her watch and informed us it was time to go.

"Where are we going? I asked as we got on the highway.

Mom leaned forward from the backseat. "Riverfront Coliseum."

"*Cincinnati?* You want to drive three hours to--"

"It's my birthday."

"But –"

Gina squeezed my leg. "It's her birthday."

I acquiesced. I should have remembered that no good deed goes unpunished.

*   *   *

"A circus!" shouted Gina as we approached the coliseum entrance.

I slowed my step, genuinely surprised. I have been to many circuses in my life, but never with my mother—I always thought she'd have no interest in this sort of thing.

"Surprised?" said Mom, taking my arm.

"Well, yes, but...why?"

Her eyes filled with a curious kind of desperation. "All our lives we've never done anything *fun* together. I've been a real shit to you sometimes and I'll never be able to apologize enough, let alone make up for it. I've never told you how proud I am of you—I've read all your books. Bet you didn't know that, did you?" Her eyes began tearing. "Oh, hon, I ain't been much of a mother to you, what with the...drinking and such, but, if you'll be patient with me, I'd like to...to give it a try, us being friends. If you don't mind."

This part was familiar. I bit down on my tongue, hoping that she wasn't going to launch into a heartfelt promise to get back into AA and stop hitting the bottle and turn her life around, blah-blah-blah.

She didn't.

"Well," she whispered. "We'd best go get our tickets."

"Do we get cotton candy?" asked Gina.

"Of course you do. And hot dogs –"

"– and cherry colas –"

"– and peanuts –"

"– and an ulcer," I said. They both stared at me.

"You never were any fun," said Mom, smiling. I couldn't tell if she was joking or not.

"I never claimed to be."

Gina smacked me on the ass. "Then it's about time you started." It was a blast. Acrobats and lion tamers and trained seals and a big brass band and a sword-swallower, not to mention the fire-eating bear (that was a real trip) and the bald guy who wrestled a crocodile that was roughly the size of your average Mexican chihuahua (A **DEATH-DEFYING BATTLE BETWEEN MAN AND BEAST!** proclaimed the program: "Compared to what?" asked Gina. "Changing a diaper?"). All of it was an absolute joy, right up to the elephants and clowns.

Not that anything happened with the elephants; they did a marvelously funny kick-line to a Scott Joplin tune, but the sight of them triggered memories of Lucy Simpkins's story. I looked at Gina and saw that she was thinking about it as well.

Mom thought the elephants were the most precious things she'd ever seen—and since she used to say the same about my baby pictures, I wondered if my paranoia about my nose being too large was unjustified after all.

At the end of the show, when every performer and animal came marching out for the Grand Finale Parade, the clowns broke away and ran into the audience. After tossing out confetti and lollipops and balloons, one clown ran over to Mom and handed her a small stuffed animal, then, with a last burst of confetti from the large flower in the center of his costume, he honked his horn and dashed back into the parade.

I looked at Mom and saw, just for a moment, the ghost of the vibrant, lovely woman who populated several pages of the family photo albums; in that light, with all the laughter and music swirling around us, I saw her smile and could almost believe that she was going to really change this time. I suspected that it might just be wishful thinking on my part, but sometimes a delusion is the best thing in the world—especially if you *know* it's a delusion.

So, for that moment, Mom was a changed woman who might find some measure of peace and happiness in the remainder of her life, and I was a son who harbored no anger or disgust for her, la-dee-da.

It was kind of nice.

We made our way through the crowd and toward the exit. I don't like crowds, as I've said, and soon felt the first heavy rivulets of sweat rolling down my face.

Gina sensed what was happening and led us to a section near a concession stand where the crowd was much thinner.

As I stood there catching my breath, Gina nudged Mom and asked about the stuffed animal. Mom looked at it then for the first time.

"Oh my. Isn't that...something?" She was smiling, yet she cringed as she touched the tiny fired-clay tusks of the small stuffed elephant in a ballerina pose, wearing a ridiculous pink tutu. Cottony angel's wings jutted from its back.

"That's adorable," laughed Gina.

"Yes...yes, it is," whispered Mom. Her smile faltered for just a moment. I have seen my mother worried before, but this went beyond that; something in her was *afraid* of that stuffed toy.

"Janet Walters!" shouted a voice that sounded like old nails being wrenched from rotted wood.

Mom looked up at me. "Walters" was her maiden name.

"What the...?"

The nun came toward us.

That in itself wasn't all that unusual; it was easy to assume that the nun was herewith some church group. What *was* unusual was the way this nun was dressed; pick your favorite singing sister from *The Sound of Music* and you'll have some idea. Nuns don't have to dress this way anymore, but this one did. The whole outfit was at least fifty years out of date. Her habit was four times too heavy for the weather, and her shoes would have looked right at home in a Frankenstein movie.

Sister Frankenstein barreled right up to Mom and grabbed her arm. "Would you like to hear a story?"

Mom's face drained of all color.

I didn't give a good goddamn if this woman was a nun.

"Excuse me, Sister, but I think you're hurting –"

Sister Frankenstein fixed me with a glare that could have frozen fire, then said to Mom: "He was led across the railroad yards to his private car. It was late at night. No train was scheduled but an express came through. A baby elephant had strayed from the rest of the pack and stood on the tracks in front of the oncoming train, so scared it couldn't move. Jumbo saw it and ran over, shoved the baby aside, and met the locomotive head-on. He was killed instantly and the train was derailed."

My mother began moaning soft and low, gripping the stuffed toy like a life-preserver.

Sister Frankenstein let fly with a series of loud, wracking, painful-sounding coughs and began to stomp away (*I go along, thud-thud!*) then turned back and said, "Only good little girls ever see Africa!"

A crowd of teenagers ran through and the nun vanished behind them.

I was reeling; it had happened so *fast*.

Mom marched over to the only concession stand still open –

– which sold beer.

She took the large plastic cup in her hands and said, "P-please don't start with me, Andy. Just a *beer*, okay? It's just a beer. I need to...to steady...my nerves."

"Who the hell *was* that?"

"Not now." She tipped the cup back and finished the brew in five deep gulps.

Gina took my hand and whispered, "Don't push it."

Right. Psycho Nun On The Rampage and I'm supposed to let it drop.

Gina raised an eyebrow at me.

"Fine," I whispered.

Mom fell asleep the minute we got in the car and didn't wake up until we reached Cedar Hill.

Mom took her mail from the box, then insisted we come in for a slice of cake.

As I was pouring the coffee, Mom opened a large manila envelope that was among the mail.

Her gasp sounded like a strangled cry of a suicide when the rope snaps tight.

I turned. "What is it?"

Gina was leaning over her shoulder, looking at the large piece of heavy white paper that Mom had pulled from the envelope.

"Andy," said Gina in a low, cautious voice. "I think you'd better take a look at this."

It was a watercolor painting of the center ring of a circus where a dozen elephants were all wearing the same kind of absurd pink tutu as the stuffed toy; all had angel's wings unfurling from their shoulders, and all were dancing through a wall of flames. The stands were empty except for one little girl whose face was the saddest I'd ever seen.

There was no doubt in my mind—or Gina's, as I later found out—about who had painted it.

There was no return address on the envelope, nor was there a postmark.

After a tense silence, Mom lit a cigarette and said, "Would you two mind...mind sitting with me for a while? I got something I need to tell you about.

"When I was six years old the county took me and my three brothers away from our parents and put us in the Catholic Children's Home...."

I faded away for a minute or two. I'd heard this countless times before and was embarrassed that Gina would have to listen to it now.

Most of what Mom said early on was directed more toward Gina than me. The Same Old Prologue.

In a nutshell:

Mom's parents were dirt poor and heavy drinkers both. Too many complaints from the school and neighbors resulted in a visit by the authorities. My mother and her brothers remained under the care of the Catholics and the county until they were fifteen; then they were each given five dollars, a new set of clothes, and pushed out the door.

"There wasn't really much to enjoy," Mom continued, "except our Friday art classes with Sister Elizabeth. If we worked hard, she'd make popcorn in the evening and tell us stories before we went to bed, stories that she made up. There was one that was our favorite, all about these dancing elephants and their adventures with the circus. I don't know why I was so surprised to see Sister Elizabeth tonight; she always loved circuses.

"She'd start each story the same way, describing the circus tent and giving the names of all the elephants, then she'd make up a story about one elephant in particular. Each Friday it was a new story about a different elephant. The stories were real funny and we always got a good laugh from them.

"Then she got sick. Turned out to be cancer. She kept getting sadder and angrier all the time so we started to draw pictures of the elephants for her, but it didn't lift her spirits any.

"The stories started getting so...bitter. There was one about an elephant that got hanged that gave some of the girls bad dreams for a week. Then Sister quit telling us stories. We heard that she was gonna go in the hospital, so we bought her flowers and asked her to tell us one last story about the elephants.

"God, she looked so thin. She'd been going to Columbus for cobalt treatments. Her scalp was all moist looking and had only a few strands of wiry hair and her color was awful...but her eyes were the worst. She couldn't hide how scared she was.

"She told us one more story. But this one didn't start with the circus tent. It started in Africa."

I leaned forward. This was new to me.

"I never forgot it," said Mom. "It went like this: The elder of the pack gathered together all of the elephants and told them that he had spoken with God, and God had said the elder elephant was going to die, but first he was to pass on a message.

"God had said there were men on their way to Africa, sailing in great ships, coming to take the elephants away so people could see them. And people would think that the elephants were strange and wonderful and funny. God felt bad about that 'funny' part, and He asked the elder to apologize to the others and tell them that as long as they stayed good of heart and true to themselves they would never be funny in His eyes.

"The elder named Martin the Bull Elephant as the new leader, then lumbered away to the secret elephant graveyard and died.

"The men came in their ships and rounded up the elephants and put them in chains and stuffed them into the ships and took them away. They were sold to the circus where they were made to do tricks and dances for people to laugh at. Then they were trained to dance ballet for one big special show. The elephants worked real hard because they wanted to do well.

"The night of the big show came, and the elephants did their best. They really did. They got all the steps and twirls and dips exactly right and felt very proud. But the people laughed and laughed at them because they were so big and clumsy and looked so silly in the pink tutus they wore. Even though they did their best, they felt ashamed because everyone laughed at them.

"Later that night, after the circus was quiet and the laughing people went home, the elephants were alone. One of them told Martin that all of their hearts were broken. Martin gave a sad nod of his head and said, 'Yes, it's time for us to go back home.' So he reached out with his trunk through the bars of the cage and picked up a dying cigar butt and dropped it in the hay and started a big fire.

"The elephants died in that fire, but when the circus people and firemen looked above the flames they saw smoke clouds dancing across the sky. They were shaped like elephants and they drifted across the continents until they reached the secret elephant graveyard in Africa. And when they touched down the elder was waiting for them, and he smiled as an angel came down and said to all of them,

'Come, the blessed children of my Father, and receive the world prepared for you....'"

She cleared her throat, lit another cigarette, and stared at us.

"That's *horrible*," said Gina.

"I know," whispered Mom. "Sister Elizabeth didn't say anything after she finished the story, she just got up and left. It really bothered all of us, but the Sisters had taught us that we had to comfort each other whenever something happened that upset one or all of us. They even assigned each of us another girl that we could go to if something was wrong and there wasn't any Sisters around. Sister Elizabeth used to say that we were all guardian angels of each other's spirit. It was kinda nice.

"The girl I had, her name was Lucy Simpkins. She'd been really close to Sister, and I think it all made her a little crazy. On the night Sister Elizabeth died, Lucy got to crying and crying until I thought she'd waste away. She kept asking everyone how she could go to Africa and be with Sister Elizabeth and the elephants.

"Everyone just sort of looked at her and didn't say anything because we knew she was upset. She was a strange girl, always singing to herself and drawing....

"She never said anything to me. Not even when I went to her and asked. At least, that's how I remember it.

"You see, sometime during the night she got out of bed and snuck down to the janitor's closet, found some kerosene, and set herself on fire. She was dead before anyone could get the flames out."

Mom rose from the table, crossed to the counter, and looked at her birthday cake. "I never told anyone that before."

She took a knife from the cutlery drawer and cut three slices of cake. We ate in silence.

She went to bed a little while later and Gina came over to my place to spend the night.

At one point she nudged me, and said, "Have you ever read any Ray Bradbury?"

"Of course."

"Don't you envy him? There's so much joy and wonder in his stories. They jump out at you like happy puppies. They make you believe that you can hang on to that joy forever." She kissed me, then snuggled against my chest. "Wouldn't it be nice to pinpoint the exact moment in your childhood when you lost that joy and wonder, then go back and warn yourself as a child? Tell yourself that you mustn't ever let go of that joy and hope. Then you wouldn't have to worry about any...regrets coming back."

"I think it's a little late to go back and warn Mom."

"I know," she whispered. "You really love her, don't you? In spite of everything."

"Yes, I do. Sometimes I've wished that I didn't, it would have made things easier." I tried to imagine what my mother must have been like as a child but couldn't: to me, she was always *old*.

"I can't do this to myself, Gina. I can't start feeling responsible for the way her life has turned out. I've done everything I'm capable of, but it seems as if she doesn't *want* to be happy. Dad's being alive filled some kind of void in her, and when he died something else crawled into his spot and began sucking the life out of her.

"I remember once reading about something called 'The Bridge of the Separator.' In Zoroastrianism it's believed that when you die you meet your conscience on a bridge. I can't help but wonder if...if...."

"If what?"

"I used to look at Mom and think that here was a woman who had died a long time ago but just forgot to drop dead. And maybe that's not so far from the truth. Maybe the really *alive* part of her, the Bradbury part of joy and wonder and hope, died with my father—or maybe it died with Lucy and that nun.

"Whatever the reason, it's dead and there's no bringing it back, so is it so hard to believe that her conscience has gotten tired of waiting at the bridge and has decided to come and get her?"

* * *

I awoke a little after five a.m. and climbed quietly out of bed so as not to wake Gina. I stood in the darkness of the bedroom, inhaling deeply. Something smelled.

I puzzled over it –

– sawdust and hay, the aroma of cigarettes and beer and warm cotton candy and popcorn and countless exotic manures –

– I was smelling the circus.

The curtains over the bedroom window fluttered.

The circus smell grew almost overpowering.

I put on my robe and crossed to the window, pulled back the curtains, and looked out into the field behind my house –

– where Lucy Simpkins stood, her sad, damaged hands petting the trunk of an old elephant whose skin was mottled, gray, and wrinkled. Its tusks were cracked and yellowed with age. When Lucy fed it peanuts, its tail slapped happily against its back legs.

A bit of moonlight bounced off Lucy's green eye and touched my gaze. The old elephant looked at me through eyes that were caked with age and dirt and filled with the errant ghosts of many secrets.

My first impulse was to wake Gina, but something in Lucy's smile told me that they had come to see only me. I went downstairs and out the back door.

I became aware of the damp hay and sawdust under my feet. If I had thought this a dream, a small splinter gouging into my heel put that notion to rest. I cried out more from surprise than pain and shook my head as I saw blood trickle from the wound. Leave it to me to go out in the middle of the night without putting on my slippers.

Lucy smiled and ran to me, throwing her arms around my waist, pressing her face into my chest. I returned her embrace.

She led me to the elephant.

"I thought you might like to meet Old Bet—well, that's what I call her. To Sister Elizabeth, this is Martin."

"And to my mother?"

"This would be Jumbo. Everyone has a different name for it."

The elephant wound the end of its trunk around my wrist: How's it going? Pleased to meet you.

I fed it some peanuts and marveled at its cumbersome grandeur. "Is this my mother's conscience?"

Lucy gave a little-girl shrug. "You could call it that, I guess. Sister Elizabeth calls it 'the carrier of weary souls.' She says that when we grow too old and tired after a lifetime of work, then it will lift us onto its back and carry us over the bridge. It will remind us of all we've forgotten. It knows the history of the whole world, everyone who's lived before us, and everyone who will come after us. It's very wise."

I stroked its trunk. "Have you come to take my mother?"

Lucy shook her head. "No. We're not allowed to take anyone— they have to come to us. We're only here now to remind."

She tapped the elephant, it unwound its trunk from my wrist so she could take both of my hands in hers. I was shocked by their touch, though they looked burned and fused and twisted, they felt healthy and normal—two soft, small, five-fingered hands.

Her voice was the sound of a lullaby sung over a baby's cradle: "There's a place not too far from here, a secret place, where all the greatest moments of our lives are kept. You see, everyone has really good moments their whole life long, but somewhere along the line there is one moment, one great, golden moment, when a person does something so splendid that nothing before or after will ever come close. And they remember these moments. They tuck them away like a precious gem for safekeeping. Because it's from that one grand moment that each guardian angel is born. As the rest of life goes on and a person grows old and starts to regret things, something –" She gave a smile. "– *reminds* them of that golden moment.

"But sometimes there are people who become so beaten-down they forget they ever had such a moment. And they need to be reminded." She turned toward the elephant. "They need to know that when the time comes and Old Bet carries them across the bridge that that moment will be waiting, that it will be given back to them in all its original splendor and make everything all right.   Again. Forever."

"...And Mom has forgotten about her...moment?"

"So have you. You were there. You remember it. You don't think you do, but...."

"I don't –"

"Shh. Watch closely."

The elephant reared back on its hind legs and trumpeted. When it slammed back down, its face was only inches from mine. Its trunk wrapped around my waist and lifted me off the ground until my eyes were level with one of its own –

– which was the same startling jade-green as Lucy's.

I saw myself as clearly in its gaze as any mirror, and I watched my reflection begin to shimmer and change: me at thirty, at twenty-one, then at fourteen and, at last, the six-year-old boy my father never lived to see.

He was sitting in his room—a large pad of drawing paper on his lap, a charcoal pencil clutched in his hand—drawing furiously. His face was tight with concentration.

His mother came into the room. Even then she looked beaten-down and used-up and sadder than any human being should ever be.

She leaned over the boy's shoulder and examined his work.

"Remember now?" whispered Lucy.

"...*Yes*. I'd kept my drawing a secret. After Dad died, Mom didn't spend much time with me because...because she said I looked too much like him. This was the first time in ages that she'd come into my room. It was the first time in ages I'd seen her sober."

The woman put a hand on the little boy's shoulder and said something to him.

My chest hitched.

I didn't want to remember this; it was easier to just stay angry with her.

"What happened?"

"She looked through all the drawings and...she started to cry. I was still mad as hell at her because of the way she'd been treating me, the way she never hugged me or kissed me or said she loved me, the way she spent all her time drinking...but she sat there with my drawings, shaking her head and crying and I felt so embarrassed. I finally asked her what the big deal was and she looked up at me and said –"

"– said that you had a great talent and were going to be famous for it someday. She knew this from looking at those drawings. She knew you were going to grow up to be what you are today. She told you that she was very proud of you and that she wanted you to keep on drawing, and maybe you could even start making up stories to go with the pictures –"

"– because she used to know someone who did that when she was a little girl," I said. "She said that would be nice because...oh, Christ!...it would be nice if I'd do that because it would make her feel like someone else besides her was remembering her childhood."

Old Bet gently lowered me to the ground. My legs gave out and I slammed ass-first into the dirt, shaking. "I remember how much that surprised me, and I just sat there staring at her. She looked so proud. Her smile was one of the greatest things I'd ever seen and I think—no, no, wait—I *know* I smiled back at her. I remember that very clearly."

"And that was it," said Lucy. "That was her moment. Do you

have any idea how much it all meant to her? The drawings and your smile? When you smiled at her she knew for certain that you were going to be just what you are. And for that moment, she felt like it was all because of her. The world was new again." She brushed some hair out of my eyes. "Do you remember what happened next?"

"I went over to give her a hug because it felt like I'd just gotten my mother back, then I smelled the liquor on her breath and got angry and yelled at her and made her leave my room."

"But that doesn't matter, don't you see? What matters is the moment before. That's what's waiting for her. That's what she's forgotten."

"Jesus...."

"You have to remember one thing, Andy. It wasn't your fault. None of it. You were only a child. Promise me that you'll remember that?"

"I'll try."

She smiled. "Good. Everything's all right then."

I rose and embraced her, then patted Old Bet. The elephant reached out and lifted Lucy onto its back.

"Are you going back without Mom?" I asked.

She *tsk*-ed at me and put her hands on her hips, an annoyed little girl. "Dummy! I told you once. We aren't allowed to take people. Only *remind* them. Except this time, we had to ask you to help us."

"Are you...are you her guardian angel?"

She didn't hear me as Old Bet turned around and the two of them lumbered off, eventually vanishing into the layers of mist that rose from the distant edge of the field.

The chill latched onto my bones and sent me jogging back inside for hot coffee.

Gina was already brewing some as I entered the kitchen. She was wearing my extra bathrobe. Her hair was mussed and her cheeks were flushed and I'd never seen such a beautiful sight. She looked at me, saw something in my face, and smiled. "Look at you. Hmm. I must be better than I thought."

I laughed and took her hand, pulling her close, feeling the warmth of her body, the electricity of her touch. The world was new again. At least until the phone rang.

A man identifying himself as Chief something-or-other from the

Cedar Hill Fire Department asked me if I was the same Andrew Dysart whose mother lived at –

– something in the back of my head whispered *Africa.*

Good little girls.

Going home.

* * *

My new book, *After the Elephant Ballet,* was published five weeks ago. The dedication reads: "To my mother and her own private Africa; receive the world prepared for you." Gina has started a scrapbook for the reviews, which have been the best I've ever received.

The other day when Gina and I were cleaning the house ("A new wife has to make sure her husband hasn't got any little black books stashed around," she'd said), I came across an old sketch pad: **MY DrAWiNG TaLlAnt, bY ANdy DySArT, age 6.** It's filled with pictures of rockets and clowns and baseball players and scary monsters and every last one of them is terrible.

There are no drawings of angels.

ANdY DySArT, age 6 didn't believe in them because he'd never seen proof of their existence.

In the back there's a drawing of a woman wearing an apron and washing dishes. She's got a big smile on her face and underneath are the words: **MY mOM, thE nICE lAdy.**

The arson investigators told me it was an accident. She had probably been drinking and fallen asleep in bed with a cigarette still burning. One of them asked if Mom had kept any stuffed animals on her bed. When I asked why, he handed me a pair of small, curved, fired-clay tusks.

On the way to Montreal for our honeymoon, Gina took a long detour. "I have a surprise for you."

We went to Somers, New York.

An elephant named Old Bet actually existed. There really is a shrine there. Circus performers make pilgrimages to visit her grave. We had a picnic at the base of the gorgeous green hill where the grave lies. Afterward I laid back and stared at the clouds and thought about guardian angels and a smiling woman and her smiling little boy who's holding a drawing pad and I wondered what Bradbury

would do with that image.
    Then decided it didn't matter.
    The moment waits. Still.
    I go along, thud-thud.

    In memory (goddammit!) of Rick Hautala, who once told me this was one of his favorite pieces of mine.

Glenn Chadbourne

OVERNIGHT GUEST

By Craig Shaw Gardner

Did he really look like that?

George stared at himself in the bathroom mirror. It was the lighting in these places, always much too bright. It made you look one step away from rigor mortis. "The Curse of the Hotel Bathroom!" He smiled at the thought despite himself. His teeth looked yellow in the glare.

"George, honey? What's taking you so long?"

Julie's voice startled him from his reverie. She was so young, so cheerful, so fresh—so different from his wife.

"Be there in a second, honey." He allowed himself one last masochistic glance. Those bags under his eyes weren't always that dark, were they? Those smile lines on the sides of his mouth were long and well defined, like half-circles chiseled in stone. Remember when he had hair all the way across his head?

"I'm coming!" he called, and turned away. He shouldn't pay any attention to the mirror. What should these little things matter, anyway, now that he had found Julie?

She sat on the edge of the double bed, her pale pink negligee a pleasant contrast to the light blue of the bedspread and the walls. Her dark brown hair framed her pale face, so white it might be made of porcelain. Her eyes, more almond-shaped than oval, gave her features a slight Oriental cast and made her one of the most beautiful women George had ever seen. A perfect picture, he thought as he approached her, my love in pale pastels.

She closed her eyes as he leaned down to kiss her.

"What took you so long?" she whispered when he paused for breath.

"Foolish vanity," he replied after a moment's pause.

"But I can't wait. I need you so much now." She wrapped her arms around him. "Kiss me," she whispered. "Free me."

He did as he was told.

* * *

It was funny, sometimes, how your life could change overnight.

George stared past the red glow of his cigarette, held out against the dark. Shadows fled across the room as cars passed on the road below. A window of light played across the pale wallpaper, flowing by the TV, a dresser with a knob missing, and a picture of the sea. Julie slept beside him. Her soft breathing mixed with the distant voice of crickets. Together they spoke of peace and warmth and love.

George put the cigarette to his lips and breathed deeply. He thought of his wife.

Life with Alice wasn't really so bad. It was just so ordinary. He realized that, now that he had found Julie.

But he hadn't told Alice where he was going or how long he would be gone. Thoughts of Julie made it difficult to talk. He hadn't had time to explain, only to go. How would he explain this weekend to Alice?

Maybe he wouldn't go back.

The thought sliced through him like a cold wind, disturbing and exciting at the same time. How could he leave his wife, his kids? What would the guys say down at the plant when, day after day, he wouldn't show up for work?

If he never showed up for work, what did it matter what the guys said?

He held back a laugh. He mustn't wake Julie. He had heard of this sort of thing before, men who vanished completely and left their entire lives behind. Marriages, mortgages, jobs, obligations: Poof! He'd heard about it, but this was the first time he really thought about the implications.

Right now, the idea rather appealed to him.

Another car rushed by below. He rose from bed with the headlight's glare, drawn by the pale pattern sweeping across the wall. Somehow, thoughts like this required movement.

He found himself standing in front of the dresser, surrounded by the night. He felt a little foolish now, alone in the darkness. He needed to calm down and get some sleep. Maybe a glass of water would help. He stumbled to the bathroom.

The light hurt his eyes. That damn yellow glare again.

It was those two old light bulbs overhead, the kind with clear glass. You could stare right at the filament and blind yourself. He should have found the faucet in the dark somehow. He squinted into the mirror as he poured the water. He really didn't look that bad. He wouldn't call himself old. Distinguished. That was a much better word. It was all a matter of attitude. Having a girl like Julie changed your whole world.

There was a buzzing in his ear as he swallowed the water. It was a low, level sound, something he couldn't even be sure he heard. Insects, maybe. There could be crickets in the walls. He wouldn't be surprised at anything in a place as old as this one.

He set the plastic cup by the sink and walked the three steps to the door. The buzzing was fainter here. There was probably something wrong with the light above the mirror. An old bulb, maybe, or something wrong with the circuit. He thought of insects trapped in that garish, glowing bulb, flying frantically, looking for escape that wasn't there. Serves them right, he thought, for coming to a hotel like this.

The smile stayed on his face all the way back to bed.

* * *

"Good morning, lover!"

George opened his eyes. Julie's eyes stared back at him, less than a foot away. They were beautiful dark eyes, brown with flecks of green, and he would have been content to look at them for hours if her lips hadn't been so close as well.

Her kiss aroused him, and they made love in the early morning light. The sheets beneath them glowed yellow with the sun, and Julie's soft skin seemed to glow as well under his caress. He found himself filled with a vitality he thought he had lost years before. Her touch was magic. He could make love to her a hundred times and never tire. She laughed, bright and warm, when he touched her just so, and her laughter filled him with a joy that could only be contained when they were in each other's arms. If he could not touch her, could not kiss her, if they could not make love, he would surely shatter into a million pieces.

But her kisses were there, and her love was there, and when it was over, he found his tension was gone, and all it left was peace.

"What should we do today?" Julie asked after a while.

He wanted to say "make love," but he suggested breakfast instead.

Julie hummed to herself as she dressed. George went into the bathroom to shave.

The yellow, glaring light was good for this sort of thing. It showed every pockmark and wrinkle, but it showed every chin hair as well. A clean shave every time, you handsome devil, George thought as he pushed on the electric razor. It was no wonder Julie was crazy about him. He was getting better looking every day.

The hum of the razor reminded him of the buzzing he'd heard in here the night before. He flipped the razor off. The buzzing was still there, faint but definite. He could hear it clearly now that he was awake.

Well, he wasn't going to let a little buzzing noise ruin his weekend. His electric razor swallowed the lesser noise again. He and Julie had been lucky to find this place, getting away at the last minute, and in tourist season, too. This was the first time he'd been this far north, but Julie knew the area a little, and she had remembered this place just out of sight of the main highway.

Julie called from the other room. He followed her downstairs and across the courtyard to the motel's coffee shop.

A little bell rang as they opened the door. There didn't seem to be anyone in the place. They walked to a booth with faded green seats. There was a little jukebox over the table, the kind you hardly saw anymore. A hand-written note on the top informed them "Out of order! Don't waste your money!"

A woman with a bright yellow cap appeared in a doorway behind the counter. "With you in a minute!" she chirped, and then she was gone again.

"I want my eggs sunny side up." Julie smiled as she rose from her seat. "Be back in a minute." She grabbed her purse and walked across the room to a door marked "Women."

George stared after her for a moment, then turned his attention to the old jukebox. It was awfully quiet in this place. It was too bad this old thing didn't work.

Look at these songs! Apparently, the jukebox had been out of order for some time. He flipped through the selections row-by-row. There wasn't anything here even close to current. George didn't pay that much attention to the radio, but he couldn't remember hearing any of these songs for years.

There were a couple of titles he recognized—old standards, the kind that got recorded over and over again. He remembered, with sudden clarity, listening to one of the songs in the kitchen of his first home. Alice had sat across the table from him. Jane, their youngest, just a baby then, sat in Alice's lap. It was late afternoon in early autumn, and the sunlight streaming had a golden tinge you only saw at that time of year. It had shone on his wife and child so they looked like they were filled with the sun. It made them more beautiful than anything he had ever seen.

He looked across the table at a neon sign that snapped and buzzed in the window. He wanted to talk to Alice. Maybe there was a phone in here someplace. If he could just hear the sound of Alice's voice….

He could ask the waitress. What was taking her so long, anyway?

Julie stepped out of the ladies' room. Even in the harsh fluorescent glare of the coffee shop, she was beautiful.

The waitress appeared right behind her. They both ordered ham and eggs. George wasn't quite sure when the waitress left. He was too aware of the pressure of Julie's foot against his ankle and the way her fingers played against his open palm.

This would be their day.

* * *

Julie led him into the room, but he hurried her to the bed. He had to have her now. He felt like he hadn't made love in half a year rather than half a day. All afternoon, when they walked along the beach into town, when they poked together through the little shops, while they ate lunch in that overcrowded sandwich place, all he could think about was her touch, her laugh, the way her eyes looked into his.

Now at last they were alone. He laid Julie across the bed. She laughed, a warm, welcoming laugh. He laughed in response, a sound that came from deep inside. He used to laugh like that, long ago. When had he forgotten about laughter?

He laughed again as she pulled him down to join him, a laughter full and warm and young. Julie has given me this, too, he thought as their lips met. And then they were clutched tight in each other's arms, and there was no more breath for laughter.

* * *

The buzzing was far worse in here now. He could hear it clearly, even over the noise of the TV Julie so avidly watched in the other room. Oh, well. For a woman as wonderful as that, he supposed he could forgive a weakness for sitcoms. They couldn't make love all the time, after all.

God, was it noisy here! His ears seemed to become more and more attuned to it every time he turned on the light. At first, he hadn't been sure anything was there. Now he was listening for nuances of sound.

There were three noises, really, in this bathroom. That buzzing sound was only the most prominent. There was a knocking far off, the kind you always heard in old houses. Or old hotels. And he heard another sound, too, an alternate sighing and whistling, surely the wind finding its way through this not-too-well-made structure.

He flushed the toilet and walked over to the sink. Maybe if he hit the old bulb a couple of times it would stop its racket. Looking at the flickering light, he remembered fifth grade. The florescent tubes had never been very good in that classroom. One had flickered worse than this. He and his classmates, who were very much into outer space at the time, decided it was the Martians trying to contact them. Absently, George wondered who was trying to contact him now.

He forgot about the bulb when he looked into the mirror.

He had all his hair. His receding hairline was gone. And his hair was deep, curly brown, not the wispy gray so prevalent the last couple of years.

So it wasn't his imagination. He was getting younger.

"Julie!" he cried as he ran from the bathroom. She looked up from the TV.

"What happened?" he asked.

Her smile turned to a half-frown. "You saw yourself in the mirror."

He nodded.

"Your younger self. It's something that happens here."

He stared at her. The warm, giving woman had suddenly become a stranger. What was she saying? What was happening to him?

"Come." She smiled again and patted the bed beside her. "Sit by me."

He moved to turn off the television, but Julie shook her head vehemently. She waved him forward.

"I haven't told you everything," she said as he sat down beside her. "I've been here before. With other men."

He pulled away from her. Her eyes stared into him—wide open, innocent eyes, eyes maybe a little afraid. What did he expect, anyway, after the way they had met in the park?

She stroked the side of his face. "You're different, though. Stronger than the others. I could leave here with you. With you I could be free of this place."

She kissed him, slowly and tenderly. In a voice just barely a whisper, she said, "Let's leave this place forever."

He kissed her again. "Anything you say." And again. "In a minute."

"One more time, then," she replied. "Then we must go."

* * *

He should have turned off the bathroom light. He could hear it as they made love, even over the television, and in that moment before climax the sound filled his brain, as if small flies nested in his inner ear.

They made love this time all in a rush, and at the end they lay exhausted in each other's arms, the sheet beneath them drenched with sweat.

He freed himself from Julie's embrace with a groan. His head was pounding with the noise of the TV and that constant rustling buzz behind it. He rose from the bed on shaky legs and flipped off the television, then stumbled to the bathroom. If he could get rid of that other noise, maybe his headache would go away.

It was funny how your head could amplify things at a time like this. The noise sounded like a chain saw, as if someone was trying to cut through the walls. The pounding was there, too, slamming against his skull. The sighs of wind sounded like urgent whispers, as if someone had a message that George had to hear.

He looked at himself in the mirror.

He had lost twenty years from his face. All the age had dropped away. The eyes of a man barely out of college stared back at him.

If only this damned noise—oh, who cared about the bulb! He looked the same age as when he had married. He didn't know how it had happened, but it was a gift.

His first years with Alice filled his head. He needed to see his wife again.

How would he explain this change to Alice? What would she think? She'd be happy for him, wouldn't she?

He stepped from the bathroom and saw Julie watching him. She was afraid of this place for some reason. She looked as if she wanted to say something but couldn't. There was a lot here that he didn't understand. He'd get Julie out of here now. He owed her that much. After they were free of this place, he'd figure out what to do about Alice.

"Come on," he said. "We're going."

He hurried into his clothes as Julie gathered hers about her. He grabbed her hand and rushed her from the room. They didn't stop until they reached his car outside.

"Where do we go now?" Julie was smiling.

He paused to catch his breath. ""We'll have to find a place for you to stay." He leaned down and unlocked the door on the passenger side.

Julie looked horror-struck. "Aren't we going to stay together?"

"Sure," he said, walking around the car. "We would, if this were a perfect world. But I don't think we can, not for a little while at least. I don't know, really. I have to go see my wife."

He got into the car beside her. She was crying. He looked at her and sighed. "There are weekends like this, and then there's the rest of life."

He started the car and saw his eyes reflected in the rearview mirror.

His wrinkled eyes, set in a fifty-year-old face, with too little hair on the top of his head. He looked old, older even than he did before.

"Julie?" he whispered.

"I'm sorry," she said. "We left so suddenly. I wasn't ready. There are things you have to do if you want to stay that way."

"I'm old."

"You can look in the mirror again if you want to." She opened her car door.

He followed her up the stairs. There were liver spots on the back of his hand that he had never seen before. How old was he now?

Julie opened the door to the room. They had turned off the bedroom light when they left, but the light in the bathroom still burned, spilling across the room, a pathway to the magic mirror.

George walked forward, surrounded by the noise. The walls groaned as he approached; the wind screamed with a hundred voices, all underscored by that grinding, like stone trying to escape stone, like a hornet's nest behind his eyes.

He looked in the mirror at an adolescent boy. Younger still, then? He reached in wonder to touch his image and saw the liver spots still on his hand.

The mirror was a lie.

He wasn't getting younger. The mirror only told him so. He was old, then, older than he ever imagined. He'd never realized how much age had changed him, until he looked into this mirror.

Anger rose in him. Everything was a lie; the image in the mirror, his weekend of passion, his life with Alice. It made him furious. The sounds filled his head. He thought he heard a hundred voices laughing.

He raised his fist to smash the mirror.

* * *

It was cold and it was dark. As much as he tried, he could not really speak.

He was old, but not as old as the others. There were many of them, hundreds perhaps. There was no way for him to know.

Then there was light, and he could see after a fashion, although not as he was once used to seeing. And a man stood there and looked at all of them, but only saw an image of himself, a false image.

And he who was inside tried to call out, to scream with all his will. And the hundred around him screamed as well, but none of them had voices as they once did, and their cries could be taken for a whisper of wind, a groan of wood, a buzz of wings.

Then the light was gone, and there was nothing but laughter—Julie's laughter, and that of a man, a man who sounded a lot like George, when he was younger.

Glenn Chadbourne

SPRINGFIELD REPEATER

By Jack M. Haringa

The first time I killed my brother I was 12 years old.

We had driven to the top of Mount Tom, or as close to the top as you could get by station wagon, for a Saturday afternoon nuclear family picnic. Turning off right after the Log Cabin restaurant, my father followed a gravel road to a shaded parking lot dotted with rusting hibachis just below the ranger station. I sat in the center of the backseat, peering between my parents' shoulders for the ride up the mountain, a cooler full of food and drinks to my left and a picnic basket of plates and utensils to my right. My brother Bobby slumped in the rear-facing third bench next to the charcoal, sourly frowning at the toes of his high-tops. Whenever I'd glance back at him, he'd covertly flip me the bird.

The Aspen ground to a halt in front of one of the grills, and my mother took the picnic basket to let me out of the back. Bobby kicked open the rear door and slouched over to a picnic table, scuffing at the dirt as he went. My father scowled but didn't say anything, too used to Bobby's moodiness to bother with vain admonishments. He unloaded the car himself and set about firing the charcoal, while my mother laid out the table settings as she bounced to some rhythm in her head. I had always found my mother's high spirits infectious, and immediately nodded along with the unvoiced melody, straightening napkins and laying down the plastic ware in her wake.

Bobby was immune to the beat, but he did find the energy to pick up a stone and fling it at a curious squirrel.

My father squirted lighter fluid over the charcoal and lifted his chin at us. "You guys take a walk for about half an hour. Look around. Dinner will be on the grill when you get back."

Bobby was on his feet immediately, scuffing up the path away from the table, away from us, and into the woods.

"Hey, kiddo," my mother shouted after him. He stopped but didn't look back. "Aren't you forgetting something?"

Bobby's shoulders rose and his wrists sank deeper into the pockets of his jeans, but he turned around slowly and raised an eyebrow. My mother kissed the top of my head and pushed me up the path toward my brother.

"Keep an eye on Kevin," my mother said, and I could see a sneer start at the corner of Bobby's mouth. "Make sure he doesn't get lost."

Lost was the nicest thing my brother wanted to happen to me from the look on his face, but he mumbled an "OK" and slowly pivoted on his heel as I approached. I knew not to get too close to him, especially once we were out of sight of my parents, unless I wanted a rap on the skull with his big knuckles or a stiff forefinger jammed into my ribs. He'd take a shot at me just because I was there, no matter how carefully I tried to avoid his attention, and he'd learned to hit me where I wouldn't visibly bruise.

Thinking about it now I realize Bobby had always resented me, always hated me, and probably with good reason. I was the good kid, you see: neat, polite, obedient, studious, quiet. And I was the miracle baby.

After Bobby was born the doctors told my parents they couldn't have any more kids, so they doted on my brother through his wailing infancy, his truly terrible twos and threes, right into his spoiled, demanding, destructive fours. My dad called Bobby his little hellion, and he said it with a little bit of love and a little bit of fear. Then I showed up and, as Bobby told me whenever my parents were out of earshot, ruined everything. Suddenly I was the center of their world, and Bobby had become an angry shadow in their peripheral vision.

I'm sure he would have smothered me in my sleep if he had ever had the chance. Instead, he satisfied himself with crushing my toys, tearing pages out of my books, doing any kind of damage that he could think of to what my parents gave me. Breaking things of mine was about the only thing Bobby was ever really good at. Funny, then, that in the end I was the one who broke him.

* * *

So I followed Bobby up the path, the sun high and bright through the pines, the scent of baked earth and juniper on the weak breeze. The trail rounded a corner and the woods ended abruptly, the path broadening into a scenic look-out at the edge of a ravine. Below lay a cascade of granite, its lower edge bordered by slender birch leading into young maple. Beyond the trees the new subdivisions of East Hampton, some with front yards of dirt and others freshly covered in bright lines of sod, had been carved into the land on either side of State Route 109. Through the August haze you could make out the big mall in Chicopee and, even farther out, the vague outlines of Springfield's tallest buildings.

It's amazing the kind of details you remember when it comes to the most significant, most traumatic moments of your life, isn't it? I can picture myself perfectly in that instant: brown corduroy cut-off shorts ending just above my bony knees, white gym socks with two parallel red stripes around the tops pulled to the middle of my calves, my feet in bright red Keds. A white tee-shirt with a *Charlie's Angels* iron-on transfer across the front. Gold-rimmed aviator glasses sliding down my nose. You might as well have hung a sign that said "Pussy" around my neck.

Bobby was infinitely cooler in his jeans and black Dead Kennedys tee, his hair two inches longer than what my father thought made him look like a girl. He was cooler still when he dropped to one knee and pulled up his cuff to slip a pack of Camels and a lighter from the top of his sock. He looked up at me as he drew a cigarette from the pack and stuck it between his lips.

"Say anything and you're dead, shit-for-brains." He flicked the lighter for punctuation.

"Dad would kill you first," I said, and instantly regretted it. Bobby stood up fast and poked the end of his lighter hard into my stomach, then leaned over and blew smoke into my face.

"Fuck. You." He raised his fist, let me flinch and cower, and turned around with a snort. "Family fucking picnic."

I edged away from him, keeping my eye on his broad shoulders, waiting for another prod or strike. But he just looked out at the horizon and smoked.

I moved closer to the edge of the precipice, looking down on the sharp granite boulders and the way they seemed to dissolve into smaller and smaller stones as they approached the tree line below. I felt a kind of exhilarating vertigo as I followed the tumble of a pebble that I kicked out into the air. On its second bounce over the closest big stone, I sensed Bobby behind me, saw his shadow eclipse my own, just before his fingertips dug into my ribs.

I don't think he planned to send me over the edge of the cliff, to trace the arc of the pebble I had launched down the rocky face below us. At least, I don't think that now. At the time, though, I panicked, my heart leaping up to thicken my throat, my knees weakening at the prospect of sudden descent. Bobby had pulled his hands back to jab me again, harder, wanting to make me cry as he had so many times before in retribution for my very existence; he threw his elbows out and leaned forward to add force to his stiff driving fingers. And in weakness, I just dropped.

I fell not over the lip of the look-out but only to my heels, crumpling straight down to the ground like a discarded marionette. And Bobby went right over me.

His shins caught on my bowed back and his arms crossed over his chest as his momentum carried him forward over me and beyond the limits of the path into air where he continued to roll, his arms now flailing and his heels lifting above the plane of his head, which in turn seemed aimed toward the smooth unyielding curve of a boulder below. But Bobby twisted as he dropped, striking the stone with his left shoulder instead of his skull, and his right arm flashed out, his hand grappled with lichen and then rock and somehow the tips of those cruel fingers found purchase.

I still rested on my heels, my arms around my knees, my eyes following Bobby's trajectory with a newfound reverence for gravity. When he finally stopped on the rock, one arm hanging useless by his side and the other twisted above him clinging to that slender crack in the granite's face, my brother looked up at me. His eyes narrowed in pain, but his mouth was twisted with anger. I couldn't see any fear on his face at all.

"Help me," he gasped, trying to draw himself up the boulder by his one good hand. He coughed and kicked his heels. "Give me a fucking hand here, Kevin."

I sat in stunned silence, and I could feel a tear leak from the corner of my eye and carve a path down my sunburned face. Then I unfolded myself and stretched prone across the edge of the path, extending my legs along the ground and reaching as far as I could with one arm. I could just touch the knuckles on Bobby's good hand where he clung to the rock.

Bobby didn't seem able to take a deep enough breath to scream. "Go get Dad. Hurry," he said. When I didn't move, he turned his head to look at me again. "Go get someone you stupid shit. For fuck's sake, Kevin, get help. I'm going to beat you…to fucking death…with my one good arm…when I get up there."

"Sorry," I whispered. "I'm sorry." Then I reached out, just under the lip of the path, and picked up a stone no larger than my small fist. Stretching over Bobby again, I brought it down on his knuckles over and over until he couldn't hold on anymore.

*   *   *

It took the rangers and rescue workers the rest of the day to retrieve Bobby's body from the bottom of the ravine. My father cried a little at first, but mostly he was stoical, holding fiercely to my mother and me. My mother was inconsolable. Whatever troubles she had had in raising Bobby, he still had been her first son. She wailed and beat the ground at the look-out while she watched the EMTs strap Bobby's twisted body to a stretcher. Her grief was biblical; I expected gnashing of teeth and rending of garments and shrank from her ferocity.

I don't recall going back and telling them what had happened or how much I said at first. I think that by the time I dragged them up to the look-out, "Bobby fell. There was an accident," had become my mantra. Everything about that day revolved around the path and the rocks.

Except for later when we went home to a house that felt strangely empty considering it was still three-quarters full. There, lying alone in my room, came the first pricks of shamed tears, as I recognized the strongest emotion I felt about Bobby's absence was relief.

* * *

They say the first is the hardest, and the one you remember best. I suppose that's true about me and Bobby to some degree, but in other ways it was the second time that was more important. I mean, you don't ever expect to have to kill the same person twice.

It had been almost two weeks since Bobby had died, a week since the crowded, noisy funeral and the deluge of sympathy that nearly drowned my parents. I spun in its eddies but it never sucked me under, maybe because I wasn't weighted with enough guilt.

We had all lost track of time, and suddenly August had ended. It was the night before school started. I was in bed staring at the ceiling by the dim light of the street lamp coming through the window and wondering what seventh grade was going to be like and how I was going to be treated now that Bobby was gone and why girls were suddenly so much more interesting than they had been last year.

A thick shadow bent across the posters on my wall and the stippled stucco of my room's ceiling. It rolled from side to side and I thought it was too dense and well-formed to be the leaves on the tree that stretched to within inches of the window. I knew I didn't want to look out and see what made that shadow. And I knew that I had to.

Bobby leered at me through the screen. At first he seemed perched on the nearest branch, but then I realized that he was clinging to the window frame by his lichen-encrusted fingers, his toes balanced on the outside sill. His mouth was moving, and even though the window was open I couldn't hear him. I didn't want to.

Still, I got up and cautiously approached him. His whisper could barely be made out over the susurrus of the leaves brushing together. I wondered if the dead always sounded like this, like some dry thing lightly passing through the grass.

"Can't wait for school, can you, you little shit? I'd rather die than go back to school—oh, wait, I am dead. You killed me, didn't you? Little fucking bastard crushed my fingers. Should have been you at the bottom of the rocks, Kevin, you fucker." He just went on and on like that, and as soft as it was I could hear him right through my hands as I pressed them to my ears. My eyes started to burn and my hands quivered when I took them from my head and leaned against the window frame just where Bobby's hands clung to the outside.

"Shut up shut up shut up shut up," I kept muttering as I lifted my leg and kicked through the screen into Bobby's face. He fell out and down onto a wheelbarrow laden with rakes and shovels, and I could see the blade of a hoe sink into the side of his neck. The wheelbarrow went over with the impact, spilling tools and my twice-dead brother onto the lawn. Then I screamed.

* * *

That was the last time I told my parents anything about Bobby and me. When I described his appearance at my window and why the screen had a hole in it and why the garden tools were scattered and broken, I ended up in therapy with my mother. Post-traumatic stress syndrome they were calling it by then, and it got me out of another two weeks of school. Of course they called it that because they couldn't find the body I claimed was there, and how would they when he was already dead and buried.

But I knew he had been there, knew he would be back, and knew I'd keep my mouth shut about it from now on. And I'd still keep killing the son of a bitch.

* * *

When I was sixteen, Bobby showed up behind my dad's Buick just about the time I had convinced Ursula Something-Or-Other to get into the backseat with me. We were parked in a scenic spot overlooking the Connecticut River, and I told her to get comfortable while I got a blanket out of the trunk.

Bobby's neck sported a ragged gash about the length of a hoe blade, and while no blood flowed from it, it puckered and gaped when he spoke. His fingernails had paint from the side of the house mixed with dirt and dry lichen bits beneath them still, and it was hard for me to look away from them to get the keys out of my pocket. He kept whispering details of what he'd like to do to Ursula as I popped the trunk and dug under the blanket to find the tire iron. I worked up a sweat smashing his skull with the lug wrench end and dragging his body down to the water. I hoped the current would drag him all the way to Long Island Sound. I threw the iron as far as I could into the river, then knelt at the bank and washed my hands. Then I strolled back up to the car and got into the backseat.

Ursula was another first, but I remember Bobby better. After high school, I'd never see Ursula again. But Bobby? Bobby would always be with me.

* * *

By my high school graduation, I had started carrying a knife. After I gave my valedictorian speech I found Bobby loitering behind the gym, his head misshapen and his skin pale and puffy from his river excursion. He looked tired but still a sullen sixteen, and I realized I was the bigger brother now. He seemed surprised to see me approach him so boldly, but he started his nasty little whispers the minute he laid eyes on me.

I stabbed him in the stomach and chest until my wrist grew sore, and then I hauled his slight and bloodless corpse over the lip of a dumpster. I wiped the knife and threw my robe and cap in on top of him. I kept the tassel—a drop of red at the end of its gold threads— as a reminder.

Back inside I hugged my parents hard when I found them in the crowd. They threw me the best graduation party I could have imagined. My dad bought me a new car to drive to college—and back home—so my mom wouldn't have to worry so much about her remaining son.

* * *

I didn't see Bobby for three years after that, and I almost started to have a normal life. While my mother never really got over the death of her first-born, she finally stopped looking at me with shadows of regret and accusation in her eyes. My father remained the stiff and stoical cliché. He probably considered himself a rock onto which my mother could cling to keep from being swept away in her years of grief and recriminations, but in truth he presented the same lusterless stare whether he was watching the evening news or me hit a homerun or my mother suddenly break into sobs at the dinner table. There were times I wanted to hit him to gain any sort of reaction at all, and times when I doubted he'd fog a mirror held under his nose.

Despite my parents' failings, I almost started to have a normal life. Based on the stories I heard from my friends, my home life was apparently no more dysfunctional than anyone else's, and at least my parents were still together. And how could I, of all people, hold their faults against them? I went a little wild after graduation, though, just like a lot of college-bound teenagers, and my parents indulged me in that. Maybe they saw a little of Bobby in me when I came home too late or a little buzzed or with a scratch in the fender. And after my freshman year at U. Mass., I wasn't looking over my shoulder all the time, waiting for Bobby to slouch out of the shadows and spoil any moment that might mean something to me. I met a girl or two over the last couple of years, and some of those encounters even skirted the shoals of relationships. Bobby didn't so much as blow me a raspberry when I rented my first off-campus apartment, though I slept with all the lights on for two weeks running in anticipation of his return. He didn't flash a smug leer when I smoked my first joint. He didn't sneer at my joining a frat or winning a scholarship to study abroad my junior year or becoming captain of the shooting team. I started to forget the sound of his whispered insinuations and the cruel curl of his anemic lips. I started to think my life could be normal.

But normal is relative when you've killed your brother a few times, when you hold a secret like that deep down close to your heart the way you cup a match against the bitter winter wind. You become possessive of the way it fires you inside, and you shield it, too, because it would burn you and everyone around you to the ground if you ever shared it. Protecting something like that distances you from the world, though; and no matter how much love or hate someone might throw at me, I could never, ever show them that flame. The outside world is a little dimmer when you're lit from within, and your reactions to it become proportionately muted. Nothing's ever sweet enough or hot enough or bright enough or loud enough. I guess that's sort of a method halfway between poetry and Psych 101 of saying repeatedly killing my brother has colored me all the shades of fucked up and not likely to get a hell of a lot better.

This is why things went the way they did between Tara and me a couple of weeks ago. I'm used to blaming myself for all sorts of things; I'm the living example of when "It's not you, it's me" is the God's honest truth.

I have to give her credit—she lasted a hell of a lot longer than most of them. She might even have made some decent dents in me. God knows there were nights, lying next to her, that I wanted to reveal all, to let that little flame catch us both up in the conflagration of revealed truth. Maybe I'd discover we weren't made of paper and tinder-sticks. But in the end I couldn't take that chance, and I closed my hand tighter around the match. She was important to me, but she couldn't ever know.

As the door closed behind her, I heard Bobby whispering.

I was wiping a tear from my cheek when I heard that dry and hateful sound. I pushed my knuckles into my mouth to keep from screaming while my blurry gaze frantically scanned the room for his desiccated corpse.

But Bobby seemed to have learned something over the last three years. He let me hear him, but he wouldn't let me see him. Just that voice, telling what he would have done with Tara, what he could have done *to* her, again and again. He never had to pause for breath; it was as if a steady wind of foul air streamed through his unquenchable throat, stopped and started only by the clicking of his leathery tongue against his teeth.

I ran that night. Got drunk at a friend's and slept on his couch. And by the next afternoon Bobby's voice had found me. I checked everywhere in the apartment, literally beat the bushes outside my friend's window, but I couldn't find him.

For the last week I've moved from place to place, escaping the whispers sometimes for a day, sometimes only for a few hours at a time. It's been exhausting, but in the process Bobby has gotten careless. I'll catch a glimpse of him out of the corner of my eye, see him stepping through a doorway just as I turned, note him fading behind a tree as I approach a wooded lot. He's gotten quicker and smarter in the last three years, while I became complacent. He wears coats and hats over his faded jeans and ragged punk T-shirt, and he's adept at blending into crowds and lurking at the back of lecture halls.

He can pass for just another student on campus, unless you know what to look for. You have to know the tell-tale signs, the too-pale flesh and the bloodless lips, the flat and too-dark eyes, the filthy fingernails. He hides the gash in his neck under scarves or upturned collars. He's good at hiding in crowds, good at whispering. But I have something he doesn't.

I have a gun.

It's only a .22 gauge bolt-action rifle, but I've gotten very good with it. I wouldn't be captain of the shooting team if I weren't.

Of course, I can't carry it around with me everywhere, and besides, a rifle isn't much good at close quarters. I need a spot with an unobstructed view of the campus, so I can see him coming, scan a wide swath of ground when I hear the whispers start again. This afternoon, from the top of the library. He likes it when I go to the library. So many places he thinks he can hide and whisper to me. I have to be careful, have to watch closely. He could be dressed like anyone. The kid with the Sox cap and the windbreaker, the shaggy one with the wool hat and the vest, the preppy in the blazer and sunglasses. I'll be looking for the sign. Listening for the whispers.

Taking aim.

Glenn Chadbourne

Conjurer

Book I: The Grieve

By Tom Piccirilli

I'd been called before the vampire lords to atone for my crimes. They sent a murder of crows across the city to find me. I sat in an open-air café and watched the black birds arcing high against brownstones, museum edifices, and factory smokestacks pluming into the night. The crows called to me with their squawks and screeches, like men being flayed. They darted among the cabs and carriages on the avenue, eyes blazing, but I was too well-concealed by my spells and hexes. I drank *chocolat chaud*, went back to reading my novel, and thought, To hell with the Grieve.

After that, the royals took a more direct approach. They left veiled messages scrawled with daggers in the corpses of drug-addicted prostitutes. The feds thought a new serial killer was at work and locked down the worst of the flesh-peddling areas of lower downtown. I could imagine the high the Grieve got off the blood, lounging in their silken chambers as queasy and intoxicated as slumming English nobility lying in opium dens a century ago.

When that failed to impress, they attempted to lure me into their courts by sending word on the street that they'd captured my brother, Simon, and were savagely torturing him.

They thought it would bring me rushing into a trap, where I'd kneel before the throne and beg for his life. It proved that even agents of the Grieve could get their information wrong. If they really knew anything about us they'd have realized that my brother and I hated each other.

For three days I heard about the heinous abuse they inflicted on him. Some of it made me smile in grim satisfaction; some of it forced me to grit my teeth. I sat in my apartment paging through family photo albums. The eyes of my parents told me enough was enough. They implored me from their graves to save their firstborn son. I paced for hours, performed a few rituals of protection, and finally grabbed my jacket and crossed the city on foot.

The fortress-like abbey of the Grieve sat nestled on a low bluff to the north of the city, where the river fed *le lac de la foi*, the lake of faith. It had supposed divine healing powers, and the ill, elderly, and dying gathered in the nearby parks and plazas, waiting for their chance to bathe in the therapeutic waters. The priests held services in St. Michael's, and the monks helped the afflicted and the crippled through the abbey to the bathing pools. The brothers would mark the terminal cases with invisible brands, and the Grieve would pluck them from the crowds and bleed them nearly dry before letting them stumble back through the city to die of apparent natural deaths. A place of miracles was the perfect cover for butchery.

It was midnight. The faithful slept in their makeshift lean-tos among the park trees. There wasn't much reason for stealth. The Grieve were expecting me. I was here by invitation. As I approached the great gates a monk moved into my path and said, "I'm sorry, my son, you must wait for morning prayers –"

"I say my prayers in the dark," I told him. I threw my arm around his throat, got him in a headlock, and pulled him into the shadows until his neck snapped with a dull crack. I drew on his robes and cowl and followed my brother's witch's scent through the cloisters. Occasionally a passing priest blessed me. I returned the gesture. I eased silently into the heart of the Grieve courts, eventually finding the royals in their throne room, enjoying their spectacle of agony.

Now I could see the stories weren't half as bad as the truth. They'd strapped Simon to a wooden rack and had been at him with whips, red-hot pincers, thumb-screws, *bootikens* to crush his feet, and the *turcas* to pull out fingernails. His head was bound by and intricate pattern of knotted ropes so they could *thraw* him, jerking his neck violently side to side. Members of the court, so proud of their sophistication and refinement, quivered in their silk robes wanting to taste his witch's blood.

They were going old school on him because that's how the Grieve thought. They were each several hundred years old and trapped in their memories of the plague years and the Renaissance. They oozed European poise and savoir-faire. In their lives they had been Italian artists and from ancient families of French nobility. They dressed like it was still the seventeenth century. A few even wore powdered wigs and rouge.

The belief that vampires cast no reflection was a farce. The chamber was filled with full-length mirrors. I stepped to the nearest one and tapped quietly on the glass. I put my ear to it, focusing past my brother's screams, listening to the great dark depths. There was no response. I moved on to the next mirror and knocked on it. I concentrated. I waited. I stepped to the next mirror.

They had a leather gag tightened in my brother's mouth. They needn't have bothered. He was and is seven shades of stupid. He wouldn't have uttered a sound no matter what they inflicted on him. He'd been tortured before. By coven masters, dirty cops, syndicate hitters, and assassins possessed by the infernal order. Always because they sought leverage against me.

I stepped lightly around the outer rim of the gathered observers, keeping hidden. The Grieve enjoyed their pageantry and forced the monks to bear witness. Chiseled trenches in the stone floor made it difficult to navigate the room silently. The Grieve would usually skin or impale their victims and let the running blood fill the trenches, which led to open-mouthed gargoyle heads and fountains. Servants would fill goblets and chalices for their masters. Only a newly-turned slave would get on its knees and lap at the floor.

Lord D'Outremal's nostrils flared. He was dressed in tight white breeches, a heavily ruffled shirt, and a coat and tails of velvet. The fresh blood of my brother speckled his garments. The vampire lord lifted his chin and let his lips drape into a lazy smile.

"The conjurer is among us."

A collective murmur went up. Black-clad sentries dressed like novitiate priests tried to sniff me out, but it hadn't been the scent of a witch that had alerted their master. The king was more discerning than that. He sensed my will and intent. He could feel the heat of my contempt and defiance.

He turned and hissed, "Thomas? Magician? Will you do tricks for us tonight?"

Sophia stood at the left hand of her father. Her dark eyes gleamed, and her chin was cocked slightly in my direction. She perceived me as well. I felt that same wild surge of excitement I always got when I saw her. Everything about her did it to me. The way her blonde waves fell across the edges of her face. The pink of her lips and even the hint of her fangs. The haunting sorrow of her stance, the thrust of her chest, the sensual manner her cloak draped about her bare legs.

She was one of the youngest of her breed in the room, born of the vampire blood, no more than an adolescent at fifty in their world. She appeared to be no older than eighteen. When we rode in horse-drawn carriages across the park, people stared because we looked so right together. We'd picnic in the moonlight. My love for her was one of the crimes I'd been called to the courts for.

The royals barked orders. A duchess I wasn't familiar with snorted a pinch of snuff and sipped a teacup of my brother's blood. The drone-like guards growled and began clawing their way through the brothers. Shrieking monks retreated in terror, begging for mercy as their wounds spurted and filled the stone channels.

I drummed at the next mirror with the pads of my thumbs. I heard something move sluggishly in the abyss. I undid my robe and let it fall. I stuck my hand in my pocket and pulled out my wallet. I nabbed one of my maxed-out credit cards and used the edge to slice open the tip of my index finger. It was barely a paper cut. But I bled.

I scrawled my name on the glass and wrote out a series of sigils with my bleeding finger and invoked the pale rider. I caught D'Outremal's eyes in the reflection of the glass. He was amused by me. He'd always been amused by me, which is why I was still alive.

"You've hurt yourself," he said. "How careless."

The mirror began to bow out just as the first of the vampire sentries reached me. He was huge and mindless like all the slaves, with only the basest hive intelligence remaining. I still had a lot to prove to the Grieve as both a witch and a man. Sophia watched me intently. To anyone else she would appear expressionless and cold, but I could tell she was on the verge of a scream. The corners of her mouth edged downward, the muscles in the hinges of her jaw had tightened.

I filled my hands with hexes but my attention couldn't be diverted. My focus remained on the mirror. My palms burned with blue flame of power, but it wasn't going to be enough to stop the guards.

I was fast. My spells and talismans made me faster. From the small of my back I drew my *athame*, my witch's blade, used in solemn ceremonies on the holiest of the high days. I had never used it for sacrifice, not even an animal or a newt. I stood my ground. The drone reached out for me, jaws wide, spittle slathering across his fangs and hanging in strings from his chin to his collar.

It had once been a man and was now only posing as one, nothing more than a corrupted system of instincts gone insane with need. In ten or twenty years he would gain enough control of his need to begin forming a personality again. A decade after that he might be able to join in on simple conversations. In a half-century he might be a philosopher or scholar. This is what the Grieve did. They took some terminal bastard so afraid of death that he wanted to believe in miracles, and they ushered him into a whole new world of desire and loss.

I pressed one hand to his eyes and burned his skull out with hexfire. His tongue blackened and curled in his mouth, teeth charring, eyes bulging. Millennia of pagan worship and belief flowed through me. I whispered a quiet incantation of grace and hate. The guard's vestments steamed.

It was hardly enough to slow him down. Another death hardly mattered to a vampire. He reached out for me, lips shriveling away, his hair on fire and wisps of white smoke rising from his nostrils. He snorted at me and the stink made me cough. His fingertips brushed my throat.

D'Outremal had sent the drone to humble and enrage me. It worked. I deserved a little more tact. He'd gone to great lengths to bring me here, and now he made a show of contempt in front of the Grieve. In my own way I had just as much of a dramatic flair as he did.

I dodged right, spun in a tight half-circle, and brought my blade around in a high arcing swing, plunging it into the drone's left ear. It went halfway through his head. The power of the *athame* was enough to stop him. It might even be enough to kill him, eventually.

It didn't matter. He blinked once at me and the nub of his tongue tried to crawl slug-like over what remained of his bottom lip. D'Outremal let out a gleeful cry. Sophia's eyes narrowed. I shifted my weight, took the drone by the wrist, and flipped him over my hip.

He somersaulted through the air directly into the mirror I'd bewitched. The glass didn't shatter. Instead, the bowing silver extended itself and caught him, almost lovingly, in its sweeping currents. The waves swept him under.

I watched as D'Outremal waved off the other guards and peered at me with joy. "A sacrifice was it?" he asked. "To call forth one of your playthings?"

The other royals seemed to perk up at that. A flash of sorrow passed over Sophia's face and was gone in an instant. She knew that her father's boredom would only drive him to more and more dangerous games until someone like me destroyed the lot of them somewhere down the road.

An angel of death appeared and stepped free of the mirror. It was Yazael, a seraph of the seventh legion. He'd been sent to show me I was still in disfavor with the divine and infernal orders. Like all angels he was beautiful, nearly as beautiful as Lucifer himself. Yazael stood in the glass, wings folded, golden curls draped across his shoulders, blue eyes full of love and devotion for heaven, a burning sword in one hand, a rolled parchment in the other. The parchment was for me. I knew what it would say. He thrust it forward, and I had no choice but to take it.

D'Outremal clapped his hands happily like a child. "You summon a demon!"

"You summoned it with my brother's blood," I said.

"Did I?" He appeared genuinely astounded. "How glorious."

I had to admit that I liked his buoyant sense of wonder, which he'd held onto for six centuries, mostly thanks to the suffering of others. Because of their pain, he still found the world vibrant and fascinating.

"You intend to keep all the Grieve at bay with the threat of a single demon?"

"I do."

I didn't. I knew D'Outremal would demand proof. He would sacrifice one or more of his own just to see what an angel of death was capable of against his minions. The parchment would say that I was running out of favors among the infernal order. It would say that Yazael would be allowed to take only one life before its proper time. And only to show the Grieve that their immortality had made enemies in the depths. It would be written in a hellish and lovely script. It would be signed with flourish.

I stood shoulder to shoulder with the angel. He held out his sword and I replaced my knife in the sheath under my jacket. It added more drama to step forward empty-handed.

I met D'Outremal before the rack. My brother's blood hardly flowed anymore. He was as close to death as you could get and still have a pulse.

"We followed the rules of torture set down in the *Malleus Mallificarum*," the lord of the vampires said.

"You needn't have bothered," I told him. "My brother's not a witch."

"But he smells like one. And I prefer the tried and true methods of confession."

"I know you do."

You couldn't help but notice his hands first. They were pale and perfectly manicured, small and rather feminine, and he wore an onyx ring imprinted with the family crest of the Grieve. He placed one cold palm to the side of my face. His touch was full of tenderness. In his own way, he loved me. I kept his life interesting. I impressed him with my skulls. I was *this close* to being his son-in-law and a member of the Grieve myself. But he was condemned to follow the rules he and his brethren had set down centuries ago. He had his own role that he couldn't diverge from even if he wanted to.

"Someday you'll confess to me, Thomas."

"Sure," I said. "At high noon tomorrow, right in the park outside."

He had a pleasant smile, but his laughter was shot through with something like hysteria. It grated on my nerves. I suspected it grated on everybody's nerves, especially the other royals who'd been forced to listen to it for half a millennia. Several of them winced. While we waited for him to quit giggling I made several subtle incantations, my hands at my sides, scrawling against my pants legs, spelling names and marking the royals that I knew.

When D'Outremal finally fell into silence he leaned forward until our noses nearly touched. "So tell me, magician. What will you offer the Grieve in return for your brother's life?"

"Not a damn thing."

The edges of Sophia's mouth hitched the slightest bit, exposing the very point of one of her fangs. She had nipped me with them. The pulse in my neck began to throb.

Thinking of our times together brought the loneliness up in me like a scrabbling animal. It clawed at the underside of my heart. My breathing hitched. D'Outremal recognized my pain and cackled once more. The rest of us all winced again. Yazael moved to me and tapped my arm with the flat of his sword. His wings fluttered nervously, as if he desperately wanted to take flight. Angels were notoriously impatient. He wanted his payment.

Duke Petrovitch, seated in a high-backed chair, his lengthy white beard dappled with red stains, spoke in a wearisome voice tinged with the slightest bit of fear. "My king, we must relent." He had seen angels of death before. "The conjurer has proven he's capable of great feats of power. He is marking us even now."

"Calling on powerful figures to fight in your stead is not a feat of power, my dear Petrovitch."

"You are as strong as your mightiest ally."

"Our magician has no true allies. Only those he has deceived. And deception is only a momentary circumstance."

Yazael's sword began to burn brighter. The Grieve looked at one another and at last began to understand their situation. One of them was going to die tonight. The possibility thrilled them. Sunlight could maim and disfigure them, but it couldn't destroy them. Religious icons held no threat. An ash-wood stake to the heart brought them a little discomfort. Half of them had death wishes without even knowing it. They watched me hopefully. Others lowered their shoulders and bowed almost imperceptibly to me. They still got enjoyment out of their profane existence.

D'Outremal placed one of his pretty hands on my chest, over my heart. "You let him suffer for three days. How will you explain that to your brother?"

"I won't have to. He already knows I hate him."

"Does he? And yet you still came for him."

I nodded. "You were having too much fun."

I stepped over the channels of blood and moved to the rack. D'Outremal tried to reach for me again, and Yazael extended his fiery sword around and placed it firmly under the chin of the lord of vampires. D'Outremal giggled and applauded. The Grieve who wanted to live lost their remaining sense of propriety and rushed for the doorways, hoping to escape into their secret chambers and crypts. It wouldn't help.

Simon couldn't glare at me because he had no eyes. He couldn't haul off and bust my jaw with an uppercut because all the bones from his elbows down had been shattered. The *thrawing* had pulverized most of his neck muscles so that he couldn't hold his head up straight anymore. He couldn't stand on his feet because his toes had been crushed.

I undid the straps. He tumbled from the rack and dropped into my arms with a huff of air. It was going to take me weeks of spellwork to heal him. I picked up his ragged, broken, nearly bloodless body and hefted him over my shoulder.

He was my older brother by two and a half minutes. We were fraternal twins but still looked a hell of a lot alike. I knew if the Grieve ever got me on the rack like this they wouldn't be half as kind.

I turned to Sophia and said, "Will you come with me this time?"

"No," she said. "Nor ever, my love."

I passed Yazael as I headed for the door. "Take any one of them but those I've marked."

His eyes grew hungry. His beautiful face became even more breathtaking as it filled with a celestial joy. He took a step forward. His wings unfurled to their full span and flapped once as he lunged into the center of the gathering. D'Outremal put his hands together as if in prayer. The remaining royals were too composed to scream, but the attendants, retainers, and even the drone guards broke ranks and made a run for it. I was curious as to who Yazael would choose, but I didn't bother to watch. I carried my brother out of the abbey past the stone columns and golden braziers, beyond the shores of the lake of faith where the desperate and the damned would bathe in the morning.

Simon, with only half a tongue, whispered, "It would have been...worth it...if only they'd killed you."

Glenn Chadbourne

THE YEAR THE MUSIC DIED

By F. Paul Wilson

Nantucket in November. Leave it to Bill to make a mockery of security. And of me. The Atlantic looked mean today. I watched its gray, churning surface from behind the relative safety of the double-paned picture windows. I would have liked a few more panes between me and all that water. Would have liked a few *miles* between us, in fact.

Some people are afraid of snakes, some of spiders. With me, it's water. And the more water, the worse it is. I get this feeling it wants to suck me down. Been that way since I was a kid. Bill has known about the phobia for a good twenty years. So why did he do it? Bad enough to set up the meeting on this dinky little island, but to hold it on this narrow spit of land between the head of the harbor and an uneasy ocean with no more than a hundred yards between the two was outright cruel. And a nor'easter coming. If that awful ocean ever reared up....

I shuddered and turned away. But no turning away in this huge barn of a room with all these picture windows facing east, west, and north. Like a goddamn goldfish bowl. Not even curtains I could pull closed. I felt naked and exposed in this open pine-paneled space. Eight hours to go until dark blotted out the ocean. But then I'd still be able to *hear* it.

Why would my own son do something like this to me?

Security, Bill had said.

A last-minute off-season rental of an isolated house on a summer resort island in the chill of November. The Commission members could fly in, attend the meeting, then fly out again with no one ever knowing they were here. What could be more secure?

I'm a stickler for security, too, but this was ludicrous. This was—

Bill walked into the room, carefully not looking in my direction. I studied my son a moment: a good-looking man with dark hair and light blue eyes; just forty-four but looking ten years older. A real athlete until he started letting his weight go to hell. Now he had the beginnings of a hefty spare tire around his waist. I've got two dozen years on him and only half his belly.

Something was wrong with the way he was walking... a little unsteady. And then I realized.

Good Lord, he's drunk.

I started to say something but Bill beat me to it.

"Nelson's here. He just called from the airport. I sent the car out for him. Harold is in the air."

I managed to say, "Fine," without making it sound choked.

My son, half-lit at a Commission meeting, and me surrounded by water—this had a good chance of turning into a personal disaster. All my peers, the heads of all the major industries in the country, were downstairs at the buffet brunch. Rockefeller was on the island, and Vanderbilt was on his way; they would complete the Commission in its present composition. Soon they'd be up here to start the agenda. Only Joe Kennedy would be missing. Again. Too bad. I've always liked Joe. But with a son in the White House, we all had serious doubts about his objectivity. It had been a tough decision, but Joe had gracefully agreed to give up his seat on the Commission for the duration of Jack's Presidency.

Good thing, too. I was glad he wouldn't be here to see how Bill had deteriorated.

His son's going down in history while mine is going down the drain.

What a contrast. And yet, on the surface, I couldn't see a single reason why Bill couldn't be where Jack Kennedy was. Both came from good stock, both had good war records and plenty of money behind them. But Jack had gone for the gold ring and Bill had gone for the bottle.

I wasn't going to begrudge Joe his pride in his son. All of us on the Commission were proud of the job Jack was doing. I remember that inner glow I felt when I heard, "Ask not what your country can do for you; ask what you can do for your country." That's *just* the way I feel. The way everybody on the Commission feels.

I heard ice rattle and turned to see Bill pouring himself a drink at the bar.

"Bill! It's not noon yet, for God's sake!"

Bill raised his glass mockingly. "Happy anniversary, Dad."

I didn't know what to say to that. Today was nobody's anniversary.

"Have you completely pickled your brains?"

Bill's eyebrows rose. "How soon we forget. Six years ago today: November 8, 1957. Doesn't that ring a bell?"

"No." I could feel my jaw clenching as I stepped toward him. "Give me that glass."

"That was the day the Commission decided to 'do something' about rock 'n' roll."

"So what?"

"Which led to February 3, 1959."

That date definitely had a familiar ring.

"You *do* remember February 3, don't you, Dad? An airplane crash. Three singers. All dead."

I took a deep breath. "That again."

"Not again. Still." He raised his glass. *"Salud."* Taking a long pull on his drink, he dropped into a chair.

I stood over him. The island, the drinking...here was what it was all about. I've always known the crash bothered him, but never realized how much until now. What anger he must have been carrying around these past few years. Anger and guilt.

"You mean to tell me you're still blaming yourself for that?" The softness of my voice surprised me.

"Why not? My idea, wasn't it?"

"The plane crash was nobody's idea. How many times do we have to go over this?"

"There never seems to be a time when I *don't* go over it. And now it's November 8, 1963. Exactly six years to the day after I opened my big mouth at the Commission meeting."

"Yes, you did." And how proud I was of him that day. "You came up with a brilliant solution that resolved the entire crisis."

"Hah! Some crisis!"

A sudden burst of rain splattered against the north and east windows. The storm was here.

I sat down with my back to most of the glass and tried to catch Bill's eye.

"And you talk about how soon *I* forget? You had a crisis in your own home—Peter. Remember?"

Bill nodded absently.

I pressed on. Maybe I could break through this funk he was wallowing in, straighten him out before the meeting.

"Peter is growing to be a fine man now and I'm proud to call him my grandson, but back in '57 he was only eleven and already thoroughly immersed in rock and roll—"

"Not 'rock *and* roll,' Dad. You've got to be the only one in the country who pronounces the 'and.' It's 'rock 'n' roll'—like one word."

"It's *three* words and I pronounce all three. But be that as it may, your house was a war zone, and you know it."

That had been a wrenching time for the whole McCready clan, but especially for me. Peter was my only grandson then, and I adored him. But he had taken to listening to those atrocious Little Richard records and combing his hair like Elvis Presley. Bill banned the music from the house but Peter was defying everyone, sneaking records home, listening to it on the radio, plunking his dimes into jukeboxes on the way home from school.

But Bill's house was hardly unique. The same thing was happening in millions of homes all over the country. Everyone but the kids seemed to have declared war on the music. Old-line disc jockeys were calling it junk noise and were having rock and roll record-smashing parties on the air; television networks were refusing to broadcast Presley below the waist; church leaders were calling it the Devil's music, cultural leaders were calling it barbaric, and a lot of otherwise mild-mannered ordinary citizens were calling it nigger music.

They should have guessed what the result of such mass persecution would be: The popularity of rock and roll *soared*.

"But the strife in your home served a useful purpose. It opened my eyes. I say with no little pride that I was probably the only man in the country who saw the true significance of what rock and roll was doing to American society."

"You *thought* you saw significance, and you were very persuasive. But I don't buy it anymore. It was only music."

I leaned back and closed my eyes. *Only music....*

Bill was proving to be a bigger and bigger disappointment with each passing year. I'd had such high hopes for him. I'd even started bringing him to Commission meetings to prepare him to take my seat someday. But now I couldn't see him ever sitting on the Commission. He had no foresight, no vision for the future. He couldn't be trusted to participate in the decisions the Commission had to make. Nor could I see myself leaving my controlling interest in the family business to him.

I have a duty to the McCready newspaper chain: My dad started it with a measly little local weekly in Boston at the turn of the century and built it to a small string. I inherited that and sweated my butt to expand it into a publishing empire that spans the country today. There was no way in good conscience I could leave the McCready Syndicate to Bill. Maybe this was a signal to start paying more attention to Jimmy. He was a full decade younger but showing a *lot* more promise.

Bill had shown promise in '57, though. I'll never forget the fall meeting of the Commission that year when Bill sat in as a non-voting member. I was set to address the group on what I saw as an insidious threat to the country. I knew I was facing a tough audience, especially on the subject of music. I drew on every persuasive skill I had to pound home the fact that rock and roll was more than just music, more than just an untrained nasal voice singing banal lyrics to a clichéd melody backed by a bunch of guitar notes strung together over a drumbeat.

It had become a social force.

Music as a social force—I knew that concept was unheard-of, but the age of mass communication was here and life in America was a new game. I saw that. I had to make the Commission see it. The Commission had to learn the rules of the new game if it wanted to remain a guiding force. In 1957, rock and roll was a pivotal piece in the game.

Irritating as it was, I knew the music itself was unimportant. Its status as a threat had been created by the hysterically negative reaction from the adult sector of society. As a result, untold millions of kids under eighteen came to see it as *their* music. Everyone born before World War II seemed to be trying to take it away from them. So they were closing ranks against all the older generations. That frightened me.

It did not, however, impress the other members of the Commission.

So for weeks before our regular meeting, I hammered away, throwing facts and figures at them, sending newspaper accounts of rock and roll riots, softening them up for my pitch.

And I was good that day. God, was I good. I can still remember my closing words:

> And gentlemen, as you all know, the upcoming generation includes the post-war baby boom, making it the largest single generation in the nation's history. If that generation develops too much self-awareness, if it begins to think of itself as a group outside the mainstream, catastrophe could result.
>
> Consider, gentlemen: In ten years most of them will be able to vote. If the wrong people get their ear, the social and political continuity that this Commission has sworn to safeguard could be permanently disrupted.
>
> The popularity of the music continues to expand, gathering momentum all the time. If we don't act now, next year may be too late. We cannot *silence* this music, because that will only worsen the division. We must find a way to *temper* rock and roll...make it more palatable to the older generations, fuse it to the mainstream. Do that, and the baby boom generation will fall in line! Do nothing and I see only chaos ahead!

But in the ensuing discussion it became quite clear that nobody, including myself, had the foggiest notion of how to change the music.

Then someone—I forget who—made a comment about how it was too bad all these rock and roll singers couldn't give up their guitars and go into the religion business like Little Richard had just done.

Bill had piped up then: "Or the Army. I'd love to see a military barber get a hold of Elvis Presley. Can't we get him drafted?"

The room suddenly fell silent as the Commission members—all of us—shared an epiphany:

Don't go after the music—go after the ones who *make* the music. Get rid of the raucous leaders and replace them with more placid, malleable types.

Brilliant! It might never have occurred to anyone without Bill's remark.

The tinkling of the ice in Bill's glass as he took another sip dragged me back to the present, to Nantucket and the storm. In what I hoped he would take as a friendly gesture, I slapped Bill on the knee.

"Don't you remember the excitement back then after the Commission meeting? You and I became *experts* on rock and roll. We listened to all those awful records, got to know all about the performers, and then we began to zero in on them."

Bill nodded. "But I had no idea where it was going to end."

"No one did. Remember making the list? We sat around for weeks, going through the entertainment papers and picking out the singers most closely associated with the music, the leaders, the trendsetters, the originals."

I still savor the memory of that time of closeness with Bill, working together with him, both of us tingling with the knowledge that we were doing something important.

Elvis was the prime target, of course. More than anyone else, he personified everything that was rock and roll. His sneers, his gyrations, everything he did on stage was a slap in the face to the older generations. And his too-faithful renditions of colored music getting airplay all over the country, the screaming, fainting girls at his concerts, the general hysteria. Elvis had to go first.

And he turned out to be the easiest to yank from sight. With the Commission's vast influence, all we had to do was pass the word. In a matter of weeks, a certain healthy twenty-two-year-old Memphis boy received his draft notice. And on March 24, 1958—a landmark date I'll never forget—Elvis Presley was inducted into the US Army. But *not* to hang around stateside and keep up his public profile. Oh, no. Off to West Germany. Bye-bye, Elvis Pelvis.

Bill seemed to be reading my thoughts. "Too bad we couldn't have taken care of everyone like that."

"I agree, son." Bill seemed to be perking up a little. I kept up the chatter, hoping to bring him out some more. "But someone would have smelled a rat. We had to move slowly, cautiously. That was why I rounded up some of our best reporters and had them start sniffing around. And as you know, it didn't take them long to come up with a few gems."

The singers weren't my only targets. I also wanted to strike at the ones who spread the music through the airwaves. That proved easy. We soon learned that a lot of the big-time rock and roll disc jockeys were getting regular payoffs from record companies to keep their new releases on the air. We made sure that choice bits of information got to congressmen looking to heighten their public profile, and we made sure they knew to go after Alan Freed.

Oh, how I wanted Freed off the air back then. The man had gone from small-time Cleveland d.j. to big-time New York music show impresario. By 1959 he had appeared in a line of low-budget rock and roll movies out of Hollywood and was hosting a nationwide music television show. He had become "Mr. Rock 'n' Roll." His entire career was built on the music and he was its most vocal defender.

Alan Freed had to go. And payola was the key. We set the gears in motion and turned to other targets. And it was in May, only two months after Presley's induction, that the reporters turned up another spicy morsel.

"Remember, Bill? Remember when they told us that Jerry Lee Lewis had secretly married his third cousin in November of '57? Hardly a scandal in and of itself. But the girl was only fourteen. *Fourteen!* Oh, we made sure the McCready papers gave plenty of press to that, didn't we. Within days he was being booed off the stage. Yessir, Mr. Whole Lotta Shakin'/Great Balls of Fire was an instant has-been."

I laughed, and even Bill smiled. But the smile didn't last.

"Don't stop now, Dad. Next comes 1959."

"Bill, I had nothing to do with that plane crash. I swear it."

"You told your operatives to 'get Valens and Holly off the tour.' I heard you myself."

"I don't deny that. But I meant 'off the tour'—not *dead!* We couldn't dig up anything worthwhile on them so I intended to create some sort of scandal. We discussed it, didn't we? We wanted to see them replaced by much safer types, by pseudo-crooners like Frankie Avalon and Fabian. I did *not* order any violence. The plane crash was pure coincidence."

Bill studied the ceiling. "Which just happened to lead to the replacement of Holly, Valens, and that other guy with the silly name— The Big Bopper—by Avalon, Fabian, and Paul Anka. Some coincidence!"

I said nothing. The crash *had* been an accident. The operatives had been instructed to do enough damage to the plane to keep it on the ground, forcing the three to miss their next show. Apparently they didn't do enough and yet did too much. The plane got into the air but never reached its destination. Tragic, unfortunate, but it all worked out for the best. I couldn't let Bill know that, though.

"I can understand why you lost your enthusiasm for the project then."

"But *you* didn't, did you, Dad? You kept right on going."

"I had a job to do. An important one. And when one of our reporters discovered that Chuck Berry had brought that Apache minor across state lines to work in his club, I couldn't let it pass."

Berry was one of the top names on my personal list. Strutting up there on stage, swinging his guitar around, duck-walking across back and forth, shouting out those staccato lyrics as he spread his legs and wiggled his hips, and all those white girls clapping and singing along as they gazed up at him. I tell you it made my hackles rise.

"The Mann Act conviction we got on him has crippled his career. And then later in '59 we finally spiked Alan Freed. When he refused to sign that affidavit saying he had never accepted payola, he was through. Fired from WNEW-TV, WABC-TV, and WABC radio—one right after the other."

What a wonderful year.

"Did you stop there, Dad?"

"Yes." What was he getting at? "Yes, I believe so."

"You had nothing to do with that car crash in sixty—Eddie Cochran killed, Gene Vincent crippled?"

"Absolutely not!" *Damn!* The booze certainly wasn't dulling Bill's memory. That crash had been another unfortunate, unintended mishap caused by an overly enthusiastic operative. "Anyway, it remains a fact that by the middle of 1960, rock and roll was dead."

"Oh, I don't know about that—"

"Dead as a *threat*. What had been a potent, divisive social force is now a tiny historical footnote, a brief, minor cultural aberration. Only two years after we started, Elvis was out of the service but he was certainly not the same wild man who went in. Little Richard was in the ministry, Chuck Berry was up to his ears in legal troubles, Jerry Lee Lewis was in limbo as a performer, Alan Freed was out of a job and appearing before House subcommittees."

Bill tossed off the rest of his drink and glared at me. "You forgot to mention that Buddy Holly, Richie Valens, and Eddie Cochran were dead."

"Unfortunately and coincidentally, yes. But not by my doing. I say again: Rock and roll was dead then, and remains dead. Even Presley gave up on it after his discharge. He got sanitized and Hollywoodized and that's fine with me. More power to him. I bear him no ill will."

"There's still rock 'n' roll," Bill mumbled as he got up and stood by the bar, glass in hand.

"I disagree, son," I said quickly, hoping he wouldn't pour himself another. "I stay current on these things and I know. There's still popular music they *call* rock and roll, but it has none of the abrasive, irritating qualities of the original. Remember how some of those songs used to set your teeth on edge and make your skin crawl? That stuff is extinct."

"Some of it's still pretty bad."

"Not like it used to be. Its punch is gone. Dried up. Dead." I pointed to the radio at the end of the bar. "Turn that thing on and I'll show you."

Bill did. A newscast came on.

"Find some music."

He spun the dial until the sweet blend of a mixed duet singing "Hey, Paula" filled the room.

"Hear that? Big song. I can live with it. Find another so-called rock 'n' roll station." He did and the instrumental "Telstar" came on. "Monotonous, but I can live with that, too. Try one more." As a d.j. announced the number one song in the country, a twelve-string guitar opening led into "Walk Right In."

Bill nodded and turned the radio off. "I concede the point."

"Good. And you must also concede that the wartime and post-war generations are now firmly back in the fold. There are pockets of discontent, naturally, but they are small and isolated. There is no clear-cut dividing line—*that's* what's important. Jack's doing his part in the White House. He's got them all hot for his social programs like the Peace Corps and such where their social impulses can be channeled and directed by the proper agencies. They see themselves as part of the mainstream, *involved* in the social continuum rather than separate from it.

"And we saved them, Bill—you, me, and the Commission."

Bill only stared at me. Finally, he said, "Maybe we did. But I never really understood about Buddy Holly—"

I felt like shouting, but controlled my voice.

"Can't you drop that? I told you—"

"Oh, I don't mean the crash. I mean why he was so high on your list. He always struck me as an innocuous four-eyes who hiccupped his way through songs."

"Perhaps he was. But like Berry and Little Richard and Valens and Cochran, he had the potential to become a serious threat. He and the others originated the qualities that made the music so divisive. They wrote, played, and sang their own songs. That made me extremely uneasy."

Bill shook his head in bafflement. "I don't see...."

"All right: Let's suppose the Commission hadn't acted and had let things run their course. And now, here in sixty-three, the wartime and post-war baby boom generation is aware of itself and a group, psychologically separate and forming its own subculture within ours. A lot of them are voting age now, and next year is an election year. Let's say one of these self-styled rock and roll singers who writes his own material gets it into his head to use his songs to influence the generation that idolizes him. Think of it: a thinly disguised political message being played over and over again, on radios, TVs, in homes, in jukeboxes, hummed, sung in the shower by all those voters. With their numbers, God knows what could happen at the polls."

I paused for breath. It *was* a truly frightening thought.

"But that's all fantasy," I said. "The airwaves are once again full of safe, sane Tin Pan Alley tunes."

Bill smiled.

I asked, "What's so funny?"

"Just thinking. When I was in London last month I noticed that Britain seems to be going through the same kind of thing we did in

'57. Lots of rock and roll bands and fans. There's one quartet of guys who wear their hair in bangs—can't remember the name now—that's selling records like crazy and packing the kids into the old music halls where they're screaming and fainting just like in Elvis Presley's heyday. And I understand they write and play and sing their own music, too."

I heard the windows at my back begin to rattle and jitter as hail mixed with the rain. I did not turn to look.

"Forget Britain. England is already a lost cause."

"But what if their popularity spreads over here and the whole process gets going again?"

I laughed. That was a good one.

"A bunch of Limeys singing rock and roll to American kids? That'll be the day."

But I knew that if such a thing ever came to pass, the Commission would be there to take the necessary measures.

Glenn Chadbourne

PROPERTY CONDEMNED

A STORY of PINE DEEP

By Jonathan Maberry

Author's Note: This story takes place thirty years before the events described in the Pine Deep Trilogy, of which Ghost Road Blues is the first volume. You do not need to have read those books in order to read —and hopefully enjoy— this little tale set in rural Pennsylvania of the early 1970s.

-1-

The house was occupied, but no one lived there.

That's how Malcolm Crow thought about it. Houses like the Croft place were never really empty.

Like most of the kids in Pine Deep, Crow knew that there were ghosts. Even the tourists knew about the ghosts. It was that kind of town.

All of the tourist brochures of the town had pictures of ghosts on them. Happy, smiling Casper sort of ghosts. Every store in town had a rack of books about the ghosts of Pine Deep. Crow had every one of those books. He couldn't braille his way through a basic geometry test or recite the U.S. Presidents in any reliable order, but he knew about shades and crisis apparitions, church grims and banshees, crossroads ghosts and poltergeists. He read every story and historical account; saw every movie he could afford to see. Every once in a while Crow would even risk one of his father's frequent beatings to sneak out of bed and tiptoe down to the basement to watch Double Chiller Theater on the flickering old Emerson. If his dad caught him and took a belt to him, it was okay as long as Crow managed to see at least *one* good spook flick.

Besides, beatings were nothing to Crow. At nine years old he'd had so many that they'd lost a lot of their novelty.

It was the ghosts that mattered. Crow would give a lot—maybe everything he had in this world—to actually *meet* a ghost. That would be…well, Crow didn't know what it would be. Not exactly. 'Fun' didn't seem to be the right word. Maybe what he really wanted was proof. He worried about that. About wanting proof that something existed beyond the world he knew.

He believed that he believed, but he wasn't sure that he was right about it. That he was aware of this inconsistency only tightened the knots. And fueled his need.

His *hunger*.

Ghosts mattered to Malcolm Crow because whatever they were, they clearly outlasted whatever had killed them. Disease, murder, suicide, war, brutality…abuse. The cause of their deaths was over, but they survived. That's why Crow wasn't scared of ghosts. What frightened him—deep down on a level where feelings had no specific structure—was the possibility that they might *not* exist. That this world was all that there was.

And the Croft house? That place was different. Crow had never worked up the nerve to go there. Almost nobody ever went out there. Nobody really talked about it, though everyone knew about it.

Crow made a point of visiting the other well-known haunted spots—the tourist spots—hoping to see a ghost. All he wanted was a glimpse. In one of his favorite books on hauntings, the writer said that a glimpse was what most people usually got. "Ghosts are elusive," he wrote. "You don't form a relationship with one, you're lucky if you catch a glimpse out of the corner of your eye; but if you do, you'll know it for what it is. One glimpse can last you a lifetime."

So far, Crow had not seen or even heard a single ghost. Not one cold spot, not a single whisper of old breath, not a hint of something darting away out of the corner of his eye. Nothing, zilch. Nada.

However, he had never gone into the Croft place.

Until today.

Crow touched the front pocket of his jeans to feel the outline of his lucky stone. Still there. It made him smile.

Maybe now he'd finally get to see a ghost.

-2-

They pedaled through dappled sunlight, sometimes four abreast, sometimes in single file when the trail dwindled down to a crooked deer path. Crow knew the way to the Croft place, and he was always out front, though he liked it best when Val Guthrie rode beside him. As they bumped over hard-packed dirt and whispered through uncut summer grass, Crow cut frequent covert looks at Val.

Val was amazing. Beautiful. She rode straight and alert on her pink Huffy, pumping the pedals with purple sneakers. Hair as glossy black as crow feathers, tied in a bouncing ponytail. Dark blue eyes, and a serious mouth. Crow made it his life work to coax a smile out of her at least once a day. It was hard work, but worth it.

The deer path spilled out onto an old forestry service road that allowed them once more to fan out into a line. Val caught up and fell in beside him on the left, and almost at once Terry and Stick raced each other to be first on the right. Terry and Stick were always racing, always daring each other, always trying to prove who was best, fastest, smartest, strongest. Terry always won the strongest part.

"The Four Horsemen ride!" bellowed Stick, his voice breaking so loudly that they all cracked up. Stick didn't mind his voice cracking. There was a fifty cent bet that he'd have his grown-up voice before Terry. Crow privately agreed. Despite his size, Terry had a high voice that always sounded like his nose was full of snot.

Up ahead the road forked, splitting off toward the ranger station on the right and a weedy path on the left. On the left-hand side, a sign leaned drunkenly toward them.

PRIVATE PROPERTY

NO ADMITTANCE

TRESPASSERS WILL BE

That was all of it. The rest of the sign had been pinged off by bullet holes over the years. It was a thing to do. You shot the sign to the Croft place to show that you weren't afraid. Crow tried to make sense of that, but there wasn't any end to the string of logic.

He turned to Val with a grin. "Almost there."

"Oooo, spooky!" said Stick, lowering the bill of his Phillies ball-cap to cast his face in shadows.

Val nodded. No smile. No flash of panic. Only a nod. Crow wondered if Val was bored, interested, skeptical, or scared. With her you couldn't tell. She had enough Lenape blood to give her that stone face. Her mom was like that, too. Not her dad, though. Mr. Guthrie was always laughing, and Crow suspected that he, too, had a lifelong mission that involved putting smiles on the faces of the Guthrie women.

Crow said, "It won't be too bad."

Val shrugged. "It's *just* a house." She leaned a little heavier on the word 'just' every time she said that, and she'd been doing that ever since Crow suggested they come out here. *Just* a house.

Crow fumbled for a comeback that would chip some of the ice off of those words, but as he so often did, he failed.

It was Terry Wolfe who came to his aide. "Yeah, yeah, yeah, Val, you keep saying that but I'll bet you'll chicken out before we even get onto the porch."

Terry liked Val, too, but he spent a lot of time putting her down and making fun of whatever she said. Though, if any of that actually hurt Val, Crow couldn't see it. Val was like that. She didn't show a thing. Even when that jerk Vic Wingate pushed her and knocked her down in the schoolyard last April, Val hadn't yelled, hadn't cried. All she did was get up, walk over to Vic, and wipe the blood from her scraped palms on his shirt. Then, as Vic started calling her words that Crow had only heard his dad ever use when he was really hammered, Val turned and walked away like it was a normal spring day.

So, Terry's sarcasm didn't make a dent.

Terry and Stick immediately launched into the Addams Family theme-song loud enough to scare the birds from the trees.

"*...They're kooky, mysterious and spooky....*"

A startled doe dashed in blind panic across their path, and Stick tracked it with his index finger and dropped his thumb like a hammer.

"Pow!"

Val gave him a withering look, but she didn't say anything.

"*...So get a witch's shawl on, a broomstick you can crawl on....*"

They rounded the corner and skidded to a stop, one, two, three, four. Dust plumes rose behind them like ghosts and drifted away on a breeze as if fleeing from this place. The rest of the song dwindled to dust on their tongues.

It stood there.

The Croft house.

-3-

The place even *looked* haunted.

Three stories tall, with all sorts of angles jutting out for no particular reason. Gray shingles hung crookedly from their nails. The windows were dark and grimed, some were broken out. Most of the storm shutters were closed, but a few hung open and one lay half-buried in a dead rosebush. Missing slats in the porch railing gave it a gap-toothed grin. Like a jack o' lantern. Like a skull.

On any other house, Crow would have loved that. He would have appreciated the attention to detail.

But his dry lips did not want to smile.

Four massive willows, old and twisted by rot and disease, towered over the place, their long fingers bare of leaves even in the flush of summer. The rest of the forest stood back from the house as if unwilling to draw any nearer. Like people standing around a coffin, Crow thought.

His fingers traced the outline of the lucky stone in his jeans pocket.

"Jeeeez," said Stick softly.

"Holy moly," agreed Terry.

Val said, "It's *just* a house."

Without turning to her, Terry said, "You keep saying that, Val, but I don't see you running up onto the porch."

Val's head swiveled around like a praying mantis's, and she skewered Terry with her blue eyes. "And when *exactly* was the last time you had the guts to even come here, Terrance Henry Wolfe? Oh, what was that? Never? What about you, George Stickler?"

"Crow hasn't been here either," said Stick defensively.

"I know. Apparently three of the four Horsemen of the Apocalypse are sissies."

"Whoa, now!" growled Terry, swinging his leg off his bike. "There's a lot of places we haven't been. *You* haven't been here, either, does that make you a sissy, too?"

"I don't need to come to a crappy old house to try and prove anything," she fired back. "I thought we were out riding bikes."

"Yeah, but we're here now," persisted Terry, "so why don't you show everyone how tough you are and go up on the porch?"

Val sat astride her pink Huffy, feet on the ground, hands on the rubber grips. "You're the one trying to prove something, Terry. Let's see you go first."

Terry's ice-blue eyes slid away from hers. "I never said I wanted to go in."

"Then what *are* you saying?"

"I'm just saying that you're the one who's always saying there's no such thing as haunted houses, but you're still scared to go up there."

"Who said I was scared?" Val snapped.

"You're saying you're not?" asked Terry.

Crow and Stick were watching this exchange like spectators at a tennis match. They both kept all expression off their faces, well aware of how far Val could be pushed. Terry was getting really close to that line.

"*Everyone*'s too scared to go in there," Terry said, "and –"

"And *what*?" she demanded.

"And…I guess nobody should."

"Oh, chicken poop. It's just a stupid old house."

Terry folded his arms. "Yeah, but I still don't see you on that porch."

Val made a face, but didn't reply. They all looked at the house. The old willows looked like withered trolls, bent with age and liable to do something nasty. The Croft house stood, half in shadows and half in sunlight.

Waiting.

It wants us to come in, thought Crow, and he shivered.

"How do you know the place is really haunted?" asked Stick.

Terry punched him on the arm. "*Everybody* knows it's haunted."

"Yeah, okay, but…how?"

"Ask Mr. Halloween," said Val. "He knows everything about this crap."

They all looked at Crow. "It's not crap," he insisted. "C'mon, guys, this is Pine Deep. Everybody knows there are ghosts everywhere here."

"You ever see one?" asked Stick, and for once there was no mockery in his voice. If anything, he looked a little spooked.

"No," admitted Crow, "but a lot of people have. Jim Polk's mom sees one all the time."

They nodded. Mrs. Polk swore that she saw a partially formed figure of a woman in Colonial dress walking through the backyard. A few of the neighbors said they saw it, too.

"And Val's dad said that Gus Bernhardt's uncle Kurt was so scared by a poltergeist in his basement that he took to drinking."

Kurt Bernhardt was a notorious drunk—worse than Crow's father—and he used to be a town deputy until one day he got so drunk that he threw up on a town selectman while trying to write him a parking ticket.

"Dad used to go over to the Bernhardt place a lot," said Val, "but he never saw any ghosts."

"I heard that not everybody sees ghosts," said Terry. He took a plastic comb out of his pocket and ran it through his hair, trying to look cool and casual, like there was no haunted house forty feet away.

"Yeah," agreed Stick, "and I heard that people sometimes see *different* ghosts."

"What do you mean 'different ghosts'?" asked Val.

Stick shrugged. "Something my gran told me. She said that a hundred people can walk through the same haunted place, and most people won't see a ghost because they can't, and those who do will see their own ghost."

"Wait," said Terry, "what?"

Crow nodded. "I heard that, too. It's an old Scottish legend. The people who don't see ghosts are the ones who are afraid to believe in them."

"And the people who *do* see a ghost," Stick continued, "see the ghost of their own future."

"That's stupid," said Val. "How can you see your own ghost if you're alive?"

"Yeah," laughed Terry. "That's stupid, even for you."

"No, really," said Crow. "I read that in my books. Settlers used to believe that."

Stick nodded. "My gran's mom came over from Scotland. She said that there are a lot of ghosts over there, and that sometimes people saw their own. Not themselves as dead people, not like that. Gran said that people saw their own *spirits*. She said that there were places where the walls between the worlds were so thin that past, present and future were like different rooms in a house with no doors. That's how she put it. Sometimes you could stand in one room and see different part of your life in another."

"That would scare the crap out of me," said Terry.

A sudden breeze caused the shutters on one of the windows to bang as loud as a gunshot. They all jumped.

"Jeeeeee-zus!" gasped Stick. "Nearly gave me a heart attack!"

They laughed at their own nerves, but the laughs died away as one by one they turned back to look at the Croft house.

"You really want me to go in there?" asked Val, her words cracking the fragile silence.

Terry said, sliding his comb back into his pocket, "Sure."

"No!" yelped Crow.

Everyone suddenly looked at him. Val in surprise, Stick with a grin forming on his lips, Terry with a frown.

The moment held for three or four awkward seconds, and then Val pushed the kickstand down and got off of her bike.

"Fine then."

She took three decisive steps toward the house. Crow and the others stayed exactly where they were. When Val realized she was alone, she turned and gave them her best ninja death stare. Crow knew this stare all too well; his buttocks clenched and his balls tried to climb up into his chest cavity. Not even that creep Vic Wingate gave her crap when Val had that look in her eyes.

"What I ought to do," she said coldly, "is make you three sissies go in with me."

"No way," laughed Terry, as if it was the most absurd idea anyone had ever said aloud.

"Okay!" blurted Crow.

Terry and Stick looked at him with 'nice going, Judas' looks in their eyes.

Val smiled. Crow wasn't sure if she was smiling at him or smiling in triumph. Either way, he put it in the win category. He was one smile up on the day's average.

Crow's bike had no kickstand so he got off and leaned it against a maple, considered, then picked it up and turned it around so that it pointed the way they'd come. Just in case.

"You coming?" he asked Stick and Terry.

"If I'm going in," said Val acidly, "then we're *all* going in. It's only fair and I don't want to hear any different or so help me God, Terry...."

She left the rest to hang. When she was mad, Val not only spoke like an adult, she sounded like her mother.

Stick winced and punched Terry on the arm. "Come on, numb-nuts."

-4-

The four of them clustered together in the lawn, knee deep in weeds. Bees and blowflies swarmed in the air around them. No one moved for over a minute. Crow could feel the spit in his mouth drying to paste.

I want to do this, he thought, but that lie sounded exactly like what it was.

The house glowered down at him.

The windows, even the shuttered ones, were like eyes. The ones with broken panes were like the empty eye-sockets of old skulls, like the ones in the science class in school. Crow spent hours staring into those dark eye-holes, wondering if there was anything of the original owner's personality in there. Not once did he feel anything. Now, just looking at those black and empty windows, made Crow shudder, because he was getting the itchy feeling that there *was* something looking back.

The shuttered windows somehow bothered him more than the open ones. They seemed...he fished for the word.

Sneaky?

No, that wasn't right. That was too clichéd, and Crow had read every ghost story he could fine. 'Sneaky' wasn't right. He dug through his vocabulary and came up short. The closest thing that seemed to fit—and Crow had no idea *how* it fit—was 'hungry'.

He almost laughed. How could shuttered windows look hungry?

"That's stupid."

It wasn't until Stick turned to him and asked what he was talking about that Crow realized he'd spoke it aloud.

He looked at the others and all of them, even Val, were stiff with apprehension. The Croft house scared them. Really scared them.

Because they believed there was something in there.

They all paused there in the yard, closer to their bikes and the road than they were to that porch.

They believed.

Crow wanted to shout and he wanted to laugh.

"Well," said Val, "let's go."

The Four Horseman, unhorsed, approached the porch.

-5-

The steps creaked.

Of course they did. Crow would have been disappointed if they hadn't. He suppressed a smile. The front door was going to creak, too; those old hinges were going to screech like a cat. It was how it was all supposed to be.

It's real, he told himself. *There's a ghost in there. There's something in there.*

It was the second of those two thoughts that felt correct. Not 'right' exactly—but correct. There was some*thing* in that house. If they went inside, they'd find it.

No, whispered a voice from deeper inside his mind, *if we go inside it will find us.*

"Good," murmured Crow. This time he said it so softly that none of the others heard him.

He wanted it to find them.

Please let it find them.

They crossed the yard in silence. The weeds were high and brown as if they could draw no moisture at all from the hard ground. Crow saw bits of debris there, half-hidden by the weeds. A baseball whose hide had turned a sickly yellow and whose seams had split like torn surgical sutures. Beyond that was a woman's dress shoe; just the one. There was a Triple-A road map of Pennsylvania, but the wind and rain had faded the details so that the whole state appeared to be under a heavy fog. Beyond that was an orange plastic pill-bottle with its label peeled halfway back. Crow picked it up and read the label and was surprised to see that the pharmacy where this prescription had been filled was in Poland. The drug was called *Klozapol*, but Crow had no idea what that was or what it was used for. The bottle was empty but it looked pretty new. Crow let it drop and he touched the lucky stone in his pocket to reassure himself that it was still safe.

Still his.

The yard was filled with junk. An empty wallet, a ring of rusted keys, a soiled diaper, the buckle from a seat beat, a full box of graham crackers that was completely covered with ants. Stuff like that. Disconnected things. Like junk washed up on a beach.

Val knelt and picked up something that flashed silver in the sunlight.

"What's that?" asked Terry.

She held it up. It was an old Morgan silver dollar. Val spit on her thumb and rubbed the dirt away to reveal the profile of Lady Liberty. She squinted to read the date.

"Eighteen-ninety-five," she said.

"Are you kidding me?" demanded Terry, bending close to study it. He was the only one of them who collected coins. "Dang, Val...that's worth a lot of money."

"Really?" asked Val, Crow, and Stick at the same time.

"Yeah. A *lot* of money. I got some books at home we can look it up in. I'll bet it's worth a couple of thousand bucks."

Crow goggled at him. Unlike the other three, Crow's family was dirt poor. Even Stick, whose parents owned a tiny TV repair shop in town, had more money. Crow's mom was dead and his father worked part-time work at Shanahan's Garage. His dad drank most of what he earned. Crow was wearing the same jeans this year that he wore all last season. Same sneakers, too. He and Billy had learned how to sew well enough to keep their clothes from falling apart.

So he stared at the coin that might be worth a few thousand dollars.

Val turned the coin over. The other side had a carving of an eagle with its wings outstretched. The words UNITED STATES OF AMERICA arched over it and ONE DOLLAR looped below it. But above the eagle where IN GOD WE TRUST should have been, someone had gouged deep into the metal, totally obscuring the phrase.

Terry gasped as if he was in actual physical pain.

"Bet it ain't worth as much like that," said Stick with a nasty grin.

Val shrugged and shoved the coin into her jeans pocket. "Whatever. Come on."

It was a high porch, and they climbed four steep steps to the deck, and each step was littered with dried leaves and withered locust husks. Crow wondered where the leaves came from; this was the height of summer. Except for the willows, everything everywhere was alive; and those willows looked like they'd been dead for years. Besides, these were dogwood leaves. He looked around for the source of the leaves, but there were no dogwoods in the yard. None anywhere he could see.

He grunted.

"What?" asked Val, but Crow didn't reply. It wasn't the sort of observation that was going to encourage anyone.

"The door's probably locked," said Terry. "This is a waste of time."

"Don't even," warned Val.

The floorboards creaked, too, each with a different note of agonized wood.

As they passed one of the big shuttered windows, Stick paused and frowned at it. Terry and Val kept walking, but Crow slowed and lingered a few paces away. As he watched, the frown on Stick's mouth melted away and his friend stood there with no expression at all on his face.

"Stick...?"

Stick didn't answer. He didn't even twitch.

"Yo...Stick."

This time Stick jumped as if Crow had pinched him. He whirled and looked at Crow with eyes that were wide but unfocused.

"What did you say?" he asked, his voice a little slurred. Like Dad's when he was starting to tie one on.

"I didn't say anything. I just called your name."

"No," said Stick, shaking his head. "You called me 'Daddy.' What's that supposed to mean?"

Crow laughed. "You're hearing things, man."

Stick whipped his ball-cap off his head and slapped Crow's shoulder. "Hey...I *heard* you."

Terry heard this, and he gave Stick a quizzical smile, waiting for the punch-line. "What's up?"

Stick wiped his mouth on the back of his hand and stared down as if expecting there to be something other than a faint sheen of spit. He touched the corner of his mouth and looked at his fingers. His hands were shaking as he pulled his ball-cap on and snugged it down low.

"What are you doing?" asked Terry, his smile flickering.

Stick froze. "Why? Do I have something on my face?"

"Yeah," said Terry.

Stick's face blanched white and he jabbed at his skin. The look in his eyes was so wild and desperate that it made Crow's heart hurt. He'd seen a look like that once when a rabbit was tangled up in some barbed wire by the Carby place. The little animal was covered in blood and its eyes were huge, filled with so much terror that it couldn't even blink. Even as Crow and Val tried to free it, the rabbit shuddered and died.

Scared to death.

For just a moment, Stick looked like that; and the sight of that expression drove a cold sliver of ice into Crow's stomach. He could feel his scrotum contract into a wrinkled little walnut.

Stick pawed at his face. "What is it?"

"Don't worry," said Terry, "it's just a dose of the uglies, but you had that when you woke up this morning."

Terry laughed like a donkey.

No one else did.

Stick glared at him and his nervous fingers tightened into fists. Crow was sure that he was going to smash Terry in the mouth. But then Val joined them.

"What's going on?" she demanded.

Her stern tone broke the spell of the moment.

"Nothing," said Stick as he abruptly pushed past Terry and stalked across the porch, his balled fists at his sides. The others gaped at him.

"What –?" began Terry, but he had nowhere to go with it. After a moment he followed Stick.

Val and Crow lingered for a moment.

"Did they have a fight or something?" Val asked quietly.

"I don't know what that was," admitted Crow. He told her exactly what happened. Val snorted.

"Boys," she said, leaving it there. She walked across the porch and stood in front of the door.

Crow lingered for a moment, trying to understand what just happened. Part of him wanted to believe that Stick just saw a ghost. He wanted that very badly. The rest of him—*most* of him—suddenly wanted to turn around, jump on the bike that was nicely positioned for a quick escape, and never come back here. The look in Stick's eyes had torn all the fun out of this.

"Let's get this over with," said Val, and that trapped all of them into the moment. The three boys looked at her, but none of them looked at each other. Not for a whole handful of brittle seconds. Val, however, studied each of them. "Boys," she said again.

Under the lash of her scorn, they followed her.

The doors were shut, but even before Val touched the handle, Crow knew that these doors wouldn't be locked.

It wants us to come in.

Terry licked his lips and said, "What do you suppose is in there?"

Val shook her head, and Crow noted that she was no longer saying that this was *just* a house.

Terry nudged Crow with his elbow. "You ever talk to anybody's been in here?"

"No."

"You ever know anyone who knows anyone who's been in here?"

Crow thought about it. "Not really."

"Then how do you know it's even haunted?" asked Val.

"I don't."

It was a lie and Crow knew that everyone read it that way. No one called him on it, though. Maybe they would have when they were still in the yard, but not now. There was a line somewhere and Crow knew—they all knew—they'd crossed it.

Maybe it was when Stick looked at the shuttered windows and freaked out.

Maybe it was when they came up on the porch.

Maybe, maybe….

Val took a breath, set her jaw, gripped the rusted and pitted brass knob, and turned it.

The lock clicked open.

A soft sound. Not at all threatening.

It wants us to come in, Crow thought again, knowing this to be true.

Then there was another sound, and Crow was sure only he heard it. Not the lock, not the hinges; it was like the small intake of breath you hear around the dinner table when the knife is poised to make the first cut into a Thanksgiving turkey. The blade gleams, the turkey steams, mouths water, and each of the ravenous diners takes in a small hiss of breath as the naked reality of hunger is undisguised.

Val gave the door a little push and let go of the knob.

The hinges creaked like they were supposed to. It was a real creak, too. Not another hungry hiss. If the other sound had been one of expectation then the creak was the plunge of the knife.

Crow knew this even if he wasn't old enough yet to form the thoughts as cogently as he would in later years. Right now those impressions floated in his brain, more like colors or smells than structured thoughts. Even so, he understood them on a visceral level.

As the door swung open, Crow understood something else, too.

Two things, really.

The first was that after today he would never again need proof of anything in the unseen world.

And the second was that going into the Croft house was a mistake.

-6-

They went in anyway.

-7-

The door opened into a vestibule that was paneled in rotting oak. The globe broken light fixture on the ceiling above them was filled with dead bugs. There were no cobwebs, though, and no rat droppings on the floor.

In the back of Crow's mind he knew that he should have been

worried about that. By the time the thought came to the front of his mind, it was too late.

The air inside was curiously moist, and it stank. It wasn't the smell of dust, or the stench of rotting meat. That's what Crow had expected; but this was different. It was a stale, acidic smell that reminded him more of his father's breath after he came home from the bar. Crow knew that smell from all of the times his father bent over him, shouting at him while he whipped his belt up and down, up and down. The words his father shouted seldom made any sense. The stink of his breath was what Crow remembered. It was what he forced his mind to concentrate on so that he didn't feel the burning slap of the belt. Crow had gotten good at that over the years. He still felt the pain—in the moment and in the days following each beating—but he was able to pull his mind out of his body with greater ease each time as long as he focused on something else. How or why that distraction had become his father's pickled breath was something Crow never understood.

And now, as they moved from the vestibule into the living room, Crow felt as if the house itself was breathing at him with that same stink.

Crow never told his friends about the beatings. They all knew – Crow was almost always bruised somewhere—but this was small town Pennsylvania in 1974, and nobody ever talked about stuff like that. Not even his teachers. Just as Stick never talked about the fact that both of his sisters had haunted looks in their eyes and never—*ever*—let themselves be alone with their father. Not if they could avoid it. Janie and Kim had run away a couple of times each, but they never said why. You just didn't talk about some things. Nobody did.

Nobody.

Certainly not Crow.

So he had no point of reference for discussing the stink of this house. To mention it to his friends would require that he explain what else it smelled like. That was impossible. He'd rather die.

The house wanted us to come in, he thought, *and now we're in.*

Crow looked at the others. Stick hung back, almost crouching inside the vestibule, and the wild look was back on his face. Terry stood with his hands in his pockets, but from the knuckly lumps under the denim Crow knew that he had his fists balled tight. Val had her arms wrapped around her chest as if she stood in a cold wind. No one was looking at him.

No one was looking at each other. Except for Crow.

Now we're inside.

Crow knew what would happen. He'd seen every movie about haunted houses, even read every book. He had all the Warren *Eerie* and *Creepy* comics. He even had some of the old E.C. comics. He knew.

The house is going to fool us. It'll separate us. It'll kill us, one by one.

That's the way it always was. The ghost—or ghosts—would pull them apart, lead them into darkened cellars or hidden passages. They'd be left alone, and alone each one of them would die. Knives in the dark, missing stairs in a lightless hall, trapdoors, hands reaching out of shadows. They'd all die in here. Apart and alone. That was the way it always happened.

Except....

Except that it did not happen that way.

Crow saw something out of the corner of his eye. He turned to see a big mirror mounted on the wall. Dusty, cracked, the glass fogged.

He saw himself in the mirror.

Himself and not himself.

Crow stepped closer.

The reflection stepped closer, too.

Crow and Crow stared at each other. The boy with bruises, and a man who looked like his father. But it wasn't his father. It was Crow's own face, grown up, grown older. Pale, haggard, the jaws shadowy with a week's worth of unshaved whiskers; vomit stains drying on the shirt. A uniform shirt. A police uniform. Wrinkled and stained, like Kurt Bernhardt's. Even though it was a reflection, Crow could smell the vomit. The piss. The rank stink of exhaled booze and unbrushed teeth.

"Fuck you, you little shit," he said. At first Crow thought the cop was growling at him, but then Crow turned and saw Val and Terry. Only they were different. Everything was different, and even though the mirror was still there, nothing else was the same. This was outside, at night, in town. And the Val and Terry the cop was cursing quietly at were all grown up. They weren't reflections; they were real, they were here. Wherever and *whenever* here was.

Val was tall and beautiful, with long black hair and eyes that were filled with laughter. And she *was* laughing—laughing at something Terry said. There were even laugh lines around her mouth. They walked arm-in-arm past the shop windows on Corn Hill. She wore a dress and Terry was in a suit. Terry was huge, massive and muscular, but the suit he wore was expensive and perfectly tailored. He whispered to Val, and she laughed again. Then at the corner of Corn Hill and Baker Lane, they stopped to kiss. Val had to fight her laughs in order to kiss, and even then the kiss disintegrated into more laughs. Terry cracked up, too, and then they turned and continued walking along the street. They strolled comfortably. Like people who were walking home.

Home. Not home as kids on bikes, but to some place where they lived together as adults. Maybe as husband and wife.

Val and Terry.

Crow turned back to the mirror, which stood beside the cop— the only part of the Croft house that still existed in this world. The cop—the older Crow—stood in the shadows under an elm tree and watched Val and Terry. Tears ran like lines of mercury down his cheeks. Snot glistened on his upper lip. He sank down against the trunk of the tree, toppling the last few inches as his balance collapsed. He didn't even try to stop his fall, but instead lay with his cheek against the dirt. Some loose coins and a small stone fell out of the man's pocket.

Crow patted his own pocket. The lucky stone was there.

Still there.

Still his.

The moment stretched into a minute and then longer as Crow watched the drunken man weep in wretched silence. He wanted to turn away, but he couldn't. Not because the image was so compelling, but when Crow actually tried to turn...he simply could not make his body move. He was frozen into that scene.

Locked.

Trapped.

The cop kept crying.

"Stop it," said Crow. He meant to say it kindly, but the words banged out of him, as harsh as a pair of slaps.

The cop froze, lifting his head as if he'd heard the words.

His expression was alert but filled with panic, like a deer that had just heard the crunch of a heavy footfall in the woods. It didn't last, though. The drunken glaze stole over it and the tense lips grew rubbery and slack. The cop hauled himself to a sitting position with his back to the tree, and the effort winded him so that he sat panting like a dog, his face greasy with sweat. Behind the alcohol haze, something dark and ugly and lost moved in his eyes.

Crow recognized it. The same shapeless thing moved behind his own eyes every time he looked in the mirror. Especially after a beating. But the shape in his own eyes was smaller than this, less sharply defined. There was usually more panic in his eyes, and there was none at all here. Panic, he would later understand, was a quality of hope, even of wounded hope. In the cop's eyes, there was only fear. Not fear of death--Crow was experienced enough with fear to understand that much. No, this was the fear that, as terrible as this was, life was as good as it would ever be again. All that was left was the slide downhill.

"No...," murmured Crow, because he knew what was going to happen.

The cop's fingers twitched like worms waiting for the hook. They crawled along his thigh, over his hip bone. They found the leather holster and the gnarled handle of the Smith and Wesson.

Crow could not bear to watch. He needed not to see this. A scream tried to break from him, and he *wanted* it to break. A scream could break chains. A scream could push the boogeyman away. A scream could shatter this mirror.

But Crow could not scream.

Instead he watched as those white, trembling fingers curled around the handle of the gun and pulled it slowly from the holster.

He still could not turn...but his hands could move. A little and with a terrible sluggishness, but they moved. His own fingers crawled along his thigh, felt for his pocket, wormed their way inside.

The click of the hammer being pulled back was impossibly loud.

Crow's fingers curled around the stone. It was cold and hard and so...*real.*

He watched the cylinder of the pistol rotate as the cop's thumb pulled the hammer all the way back.

Tears burned like acid in Crow's eyes and he summoned every ounce of will to pull the stone from his pocket. It came so slowly. It took a thousand years.

But it came out.

The cop lifted the barrel of the pistol and put it under his chin. His eyes were squeezed shut.

Crow raised his fist, and the harder he squeezed the stone the more power he had in his arm.

"I'm sorry...," Crow said, mumbling the two words through lips bubbling with spit.

The cop's finger slipped inside the curled trigger guard.

"I'm so sorry...."

Crow threw the stone at the same moment the cop pulled the trigger.

The stone struck the mirror a microsecond before the firing pin punched a hole in the world.

There was a sound. It wasn't the smash of mirror glass and it wasn't the bang of a pistol. It was something vast and black and impossible, and it was the loudest sound Crow would ever hear. It was so monstrously loud that it broke the world.

Shards of mirror glass razored through the air around Crow, slashing him, digging deep into his flesh, gouging burning wounds in his mind. As each one cut him, the world shifted around Crow, buffeting him into different places, into different lives.

He saw Terry. The adult Terry, but now he was even older than the one who had been laughing with Val. It was crazy weird, but somehow Crow knew that this was as real as anything in his world.

Terry's face was lined with pain, his body crisscrossed with tiny cuts. Pieces of a broken mirror lay scattered around him. Each separate piece reflected Terry, but none of them were the Terry who stood in the midst of the debris. Each reflection was a distortion, a funhouse twist of Terry's face. Some were laughing—harsh and loud and fractured. Some were weeping. Some were glazed and catatonic. And one, a single large piece, showed a face that was more monster than man. Lupine and snarling and so completely *wrong*. The Terry who stood above the broken pieces screamed, and if there was any sanity left in his mind it did not shine out through his blue eyes. Crow saw a version of his best friend who was completely and irretrievably *lost*.

Terry screamed and screamed, and then he spun around, ran straight across the room and threw himself headfirst out of the window. Crow fell with him. Together they screamed all the way down to the garden flagstones.

The impact shoved Crow into another place.

He was there with Val. They were in the cornfields behind Val's house. A black rain hammered down, the sky veined with red lightning. Val was older...maybe forty years old. She ran through the corn, skidding, slipping in the mud. Running toward a figure that lay sprawled on the ground.

"Dad!" screamed Val.

Mr. Guthrie lay on his stomach, his face pressed into the muck. In the brightness of the lightning, Crow could see a neat round bullet hole between his shoulder blades, the cloth washed clean of blood by the downpour.

"NO!" shrieked Val. She dropped to her knees and clawed her father into her arms. His big old body resisted her, fighting her with limpness and weight and sopping clothes, but eventually Val found the strength to turn him onto his back.

"Daddy...Daddy...?"

His face was totally slack, streaked with mud that clumped on his mustache and caught in his bushy eyebrows.

Val wiped the mud off his face and shook him very gently.

"Daddy...*please*...."

The lightning never stopped, and the thunder bellowed insanely. A freak eddy of wind brought sounds from the highway. The high, lonely wail of a police siren, but Crow knew that the cops would be too late. They were already too late.

Crow spun out of that moment and into another moment. There were police sirens here, too, and the flashing red and blue lights, but no rain. This was a different place, a different moment. A different horror.

He was there.

He was a cop.

He was sober. Was he younger or older? He prayed that this was him as an older man, just as Val and Terry had been older.

Older. Sober.

Alive.

However the moment was not offering any mercies.

Stick was there. He was on his knees, and Crow was bent over him, forcing handcuffs onto his friend's wrists. They were both speaking, saying the same things over and over again.

"What did you do? Christ, Stick, what did you *do*?"

"I'm sorry," Stick said. "I'm sorry."

On the porch of the house a female cop and an EMT were supporting a ten-year-old girl toward a waiting ambulance. The girl looked a lot like Janie and Kim, Stick's sisters, but Crow knew that she wasn't. He knew that this girl was Stick's daughter. Her face was bruised. Her clothes were torn. There was blood on her thighs.

"What did you do, Stick, what did you *do*?"

"I'm sorry," wept Stick. His mouth bled from where Crow had punched him. "I'm sorry."

Crow saw other images.

People he did not know. Some dressed in clothes from long ago, some dressed like everyone else. He stepped into sick rooms and cells, he crawled through the shattered windows of wrecked cars and staggered coughing through the smoke of burning houses.

Crow squeezed his eyes shut and clapped his hands over his ears. He screamed and screamed.

The house exhaled its liquor stink of breath at him.

-8-

Crow heard Val yell. Not the woman, but the girl.

He opened his eyes and saw the Morgan silver dollar leave her outstretched hand. It flew past him and he turned to see it strike the mirror. The same mirror he'd shattered with his lucky stone.

For just a moment he caught that same image of her kneeling in the rain, but then the glass detonated.

Then he was running.

He wasn't conscious of when he was able to run. When he was *allowed* to run.

But he was running.

They were all running.

As Crow scrambled for the door he cast a single desperate look back to see that the mirror was undamaged by either stone or coin. All of the restraints that had earlier held his limbs were gone, as if the house, glutted on his pain, ejected the table scraps.

And so they ran.

Terry shoved Stick so hard that it knocked his ball-cap off of his head. No one stooped to pick it up. They crowded into the vestibule and burst out onto the porch and ran for their bikes. They were all screaming.

They screamed as they ran and they screamed as they got on their bikes.

Their screams dwindled as the house faded behind its screen of withered trees.

The four of them tore down the dirt road and burst onto the access road and turned toward town, pumping as hard as they could. They raced as hard and as fast as they could.

Only when they reached the edge of the pumpkin patch on the far side of the Guthrie farm did they slow and finally stop.

Panting, bathed in sweat, trembling, they huddled over their bikes, looking down at the frames, at their sneakered feet, at the dirt.

Not at each other.

Crow did not know if the others had seen the same things he'd seen. Or, just their own horrors.

Beside him, Terry seemed to be the first to recover. He reached into his pocket for his comb, but it wasn't there. He took a deep breath and let it out, then dragged trembling fingers through his hair.

"It must be dinner time," he said, and he turned his bike toward town and pedaled off. Terry did not look back.

Stick dragged his forearm across his face and looked at the smear, just as he had done before. Was he looking for tears? Or for the blood that had leaked from the corners of his mouth when the older Crow had punched him? A single sob broke in his chest, and he shook his head. Crow thought he saw Stick mouth those same two terrible words. *I'm sorry.*

Stick rode away.

That was the last time he went anywhere with Crow, Val or Terry. During the rest of that summer and well into the fall, Stick went deep inside of himself. Eight years later, Crow read in the papers that George Stickler had swallowed an entire bottle of sleeping pills. Stick was not yet as old as he had been in the vision. Crow was heartbroken but he was not surprised, and he wondered what the line was between the cowardice of suicide and an act of bravery.

For five long minutes Crow and Val sat on their bikes, one foot each braced on the ground. Val looked at the cornfields in the distance and Crow looked at her. Then, without saying a word, Val got off her bike and walked it down the lane toward home. Crow sat there for almost half an hour before he could work up the courage to go home.

None of them ever spoke about that day. They never mentioned the Croft house. They never asked what the others had seen.

Not once.

The only thing that ever came up was the Morgan silver dollar. One evening Crow and Terry looked it up in a coin collector's book. In mint condition it was valued at forty-eight thousand dollars. In poor condition it was still worth twenty thousand.

That coin probably still lay on the living room floor.

Crow and Terry looked at each other for a long time. Crow knew that they were both thinking about that coin. Twenty thousand dollars, just lying there. Right there.

It might as well have been on the dark side of the moon.

Terry closed his coin book and set it aside. As far as Crow knew, Terry never collected coins after that summer. He also knew that neither of them would ever go back for that coin. Not for ten thousand dollars. Not for ten million. Like everything else they'd seen there–the wallet, the pill bottle, the diaper, all of it—the coin belonged to the house. Like Terry's pocket comb. Like Stick's ballcap. And Crow's lucky stone.

And what belonged to the house would stay there.

The house kept its trophies.

Crow went to the library and looked through the back issues of newspapers, through obituaries, but try as he might he found no records at all of anyone ever having died there.

Somehow it didn't surprise him.

There weren't ghosts in the Croft house. It wasn't that kind of thing.

He remembered what he'd thought when he first saw the house. *The house is hungry.*

-9-

Later, after Crow came home from Terry's house, he sat in his room long into the night, watching the moon and stars rise from behind the trees and carve their scars across the sky. He sat with his window open, arms wrapped around his shins, shivering despite a hot breeze.

It was ten days since they'd gone running from the house.

Ten days and ten nights. Crow was exhausted. He'd barely slept, and when he did there were nightmares. Never—not once in any of those dreams—was there a monster or a ghoul chasing him. They weren't those kinds of dreams. Instead he saw the image that he'd seen in the mirror. The older him.

The drunk.

The fool.

Crow wept for that man.

For the man he knew that he was going to become.

He wept and he did not sleep. He tried, but even though his eyes burned with fatigue, sleep simply would not come. Crow knew that it wouldn't come. Not tonight, and maybe not any night. Not as long as he could remember that house.

And he knew he could never forget the house.

Around three in the morning, when his father's snores banged off the walls and rattled his bedroom door, Crow got up and, silent as a ghost, went into the hall and downstairs. Down to the kitchen, to the cupboard. The bottles stood in a row. Canadian Club. Mogen-David 20-20. Thunderbird. And a bottle of vodka without a label. Cheap stuff, but a lot of it.

Crow stood staring at the bottles for a long time. Maybe half an hour.

"No," he told himself.

No, agreed his inner voice.

No, screamed the drunken man in his memory.

No.

Crow reached up and took down the vodka bottle. He poured some into a Dixie cup.

"No," he said.

And drank it.

Glenn Chadbourne

PLAYING THE HUDDYS

By John M. McIlveen

The young man loped up to the chain-link fence, retrieved the softball, and deftly rifled it from left field to second base. Bib overalls, and little if nothing else from the look of it, hung loosely on his sharp shoulders from frayed denim straps. Dark grime caked the visible edges of his bare feet like dried mustard. His toenails were cracked and had a similar tint of yellow. His unruly, yet matted hair clearly hadn't crossed paths with shampoo in ages.

He watched idly as his throw single-hopped to the second baseman, who barehanded it. The batter slid into second beneath the extended hand, raising a plume of dry defiance to an empty blue sky.

"Daif!" yelled the outfielder. He turned dull eyes our way, pinning us where we stood outside the leftfield fence. "Him daif," he repeated, clearly seeking an affirmation.

"Nice toss, Champ," I said. "Almost nailed him."

An epic smile split his face revealing horsey, gapped teeth. Semi-dried mucus and filth caked his meager moustache, which had me initially believing it was much fuller.

"Nee gud na duhmbel," he said to us and galloped back into position.

"What the fuck he say?" Rich Berlander asked.

Rich's voice always reminded me of two bricks rubbing together, dry and ragged; a perfect companion to his surly, deeply grooved face. Despite the rasp, Rich enunciated rattlesnake words that gave the impression that he was eternally pissed off. He had me convinced.

"Got me," Marcus Spracher offered. "Something about a dumbbell,"

"He said he got a double," I offered.

"You speak his language?" Rich asked me, an eyebrow cocked dubiously.

I ignored the remark. I'd known Berlander for nearly eight years. A battle of words with him was like trying to climb a waterfall.

We, the sixteen members of Prime Circuit Technology's softball team, watched the men on the field with a mixture of amusement, irritation, and disgust.

"What are they doing here?" Rich asked me. "I thought you reserved the field."

"They appear to be playing ball," I answered, somewhat piqued by Rich's apparent assumption that being the coach empowered me to answer such questions. "And I *did* reserve the field. Do they look like they live by any schedule or rules?"

We redirected our attention to the spectacle on the ball field almost in unison. The third baseman, a tall blonde fellow, was shirtless and shoeless, as were most of the ballplayers on the field. He wore filthy, thick-ribbed corduroy pants that were probably last in fashion before he was born, and rocked incessantly from foot to foot. He jammed an index finger forcefully into his left nostril and drilled as if he were trying to tunnel to his eardrums, occasionally removing it to tuck the findings into his mouth.

Another male of undetermined age stood on deck, wearing a self-absorbed smile that displayed an absence of teeth. He held a wooden bat in one grubby hand while the other writhed down the front of his khaki shorts. He was either scratching himself with the passion of a flea-ridden rabbit, or, the other likelihood I preferred not to ponder.

A loud crack heralded a solidly hit ball. Our friend in left field backpedaled, crouched low as if awaiting a good moment to flee, and at the last moment, stabbed his gloved hand up and plucked the ball out of the air. He peered into the glove to assure that the prize was indeed his and barked a laugh that sounded like it preferred to stay inside of him. *Gnaa-hunh!*

He granted us that childish grin and said, "Him out!"

Rich Berlander huffed. "That was almost coherent," he said.

The players all watched their outfielder as if awaiting the words of a great oracle. He raised his arm proudly and they swarmed off of and onto the field, changing sides.

They, more specifically, were the Huddys. Hedging on legendary, the Huddy family had earned an extraordinary level of notoriety for being unabashedly incestuous. Three generations of their highly-concentrated blue-blooded cocktail had stranded the majority of them on the lower rungs of the intellectual ladder, yet a few inexplicably had managed to persevere and exhibit an almost respectable level of astuteness. Sadly, even for them, the incestuous calling was just too strong.

Numerous tales floated about Taylor Falls, and a fair share of neighboring towns, about the Huddys and the peculiar occurrences that involved them. Whether true or not was anyone's call, but a few moments of observation would convince anyone that with the Huddys, anything was not only possible, but more likely probable.

Years earlier the town of Taylor's Falls, through charities and certain agencies, managed to fund a new home for the Huddys, hoping that it would instill some pride, honor, and maybe even some decency in the family and initiate a miraculous turn-around. It also gave license to tear down the horrid plywood structure that served as the Huddy's home, standing for years on the border to the town dump. Though the donated home was pleasant and worthy of any middle-class community, those involved had the wisdom and enough wherewithal to set it off in a remote corner of town. I never knew or cared where.

Regardless, within a year the house was said to be worthy of condemning.

It was also said that so many Huddys lived in the house that the flow of bodies churned through the doors and windows like a waterwheel, day and night. Stories of dogs, cats, goats, chickens, and occasional pigs, that ranged freely both inside and outside the home, scattering waste wherever they went, like walking gumball machines. I had heard of a family dog that lay dead under the kitchen table for two weeks before the authorities, Department of Health or whoever, removed it. Hard to envision, but who knows?

"You gonna tell *them* to get off?" Billy Sanford asked me, sounding more challenging than inquisitive.

He spit over the fence, took a pull from a bottle of Rolling Rock, and then spit over the fence again. There was a mischievous gleam in Billy's dark eyes, but then, there usually was. A tall and rugged guy with an intimidating posture, he always looked ready to kick someone's ass. In truth, he was a big-hearted soft-touch, usually neck deep in charity work. He had an affinity for children, and they for him, which was fortunate since he and his wife Debbie had eight or so of their own. Watching the Sanford family was akin to seeing two rowboats bobbing unperturbed on the waters of a mosquito-infested pond.

As for the Huddys, there were probably twenty-five or thirty of *them* on and off the field. They were relatively harmless, but they did what they wanted, where and when they wanted. Few people had the nerve or desire to request anything of them, so the Huddys trumped on that advantage. Trying to get them to leave, if they didn't want to, would be like squeezing cider from marble.

Bob Huddy, known to most as "Buddy" Huddy, was the most approachable of the family. He was the person I needed to talk to if there were any hopes of getting the field for practice.

I scanned the diamond and found Buddy standing near the far dugout with his arms folded like Cochise. Being more verbally adept and quite possibly the most intelligent, he was the one who dealt with the public when necessary. He was also rumored to have the singular honor of getting his sister, daughter, and granddaughter pregnant within months of each other.

"Be right back," I said to my surprised teammates and started around the field. I felt curious eyes follow me from both sides of the fence.

A few of the Huddy women sat, or variable forms of the verb, on the home team bleachers. They were an intriguing lot, most of them with similar faces that ranged from plain to downright repellent. Evidence of their ancestral plight was exhibited well in their features, through broad foreheads, weak beady eyes, and large gapped teeth with prominent gums. Of all the Huddy women, the most conspicuous were Simone, Jenny, and Linny, who sat side-by-side-by-side. Possibly mother and daughters, maybe sisters, but a common assumption was that they were equal portions of both.

Simone, believed to be the matriarch of the clan, looked to be around fifty-five and tipped the scales in the region of three hundred pounds. Her muumuu-clad bulk spread liberally over a healthy portion of the twelve-foot by five-tier structure. The great doughy folds of her arms and legs escaped from various points of her dress, exaggerating each of her movements with reverberated jiggles. The billowing meat of her butt draped loosely over two levels of seating. Close-cropped black hair exposed the severity of her face, which constantly displayed an aura of barely bridled lunacy. She was said to have the temperament of an infected Pit bull and was always ready to pounce. There was a facial similarity as well.

Jenny appeared on track to twin the older woman, easily two-fifty, yet youthfully clad in a seam-splitting tank top and a pair of stretch pants that didn't have an iota of stretch left. I foolishly imagined the cellulite adorning those two bodies resembling giant, clear baggies filled with five-hundred pounds of wet oatmeal. My stomach lurched and I almost had to reverse direction, but I instead focused on Linny.

Linny was the genetic freak of the family. Firm, trim, pretty, and as sexy as the day was long. She sat sprawled like everybody's favorite centerfold with her long, supple legs spread and resting on the bench in front of her. High cut denim shorts barely concealed what her pose outwardly ached to display. A blue plaid button-down shirt—held in check by her shorts for no buttons were fastened—only just concealed bountiful breasts that were unhindered by anything so binding as a bra. Her shoulder-length hair may or may not have been dirty, but the unkempt look of her chestnut mane only added to her feral sexuality. Linny was well worthy of admiration... until she opened her mouth.

Shifting to offer a generous view of very nice cleavage, she greeted me with a nasal, "Hi minsder," eliciting an anomalous symphony of chortles from her kin. Her forced, almost hypnotic sensuality, when combined with her simpleton voice, was disturbing. It didn't belong there. It was like the cat that went "moo."

I veered wide of the bleachers. It was a good decision, since Simone was known to award those not to her liking with a huge wad of well-aimed phlegm. Fortunately, I was out of range.

Filthy Huddy children of assorted ages and various stages of undress swarmed the visitors' bleachers, from a dwarfish little girl wrapped in a winter jacket, to another little girl of about three, buck naked and squatting under the bleachers. The children were perpetual motion, weaving ferret-like through the metal and wood, twisting and threading and emitting a cacophony of shouts and incoherent words.

An English sheepdog trotted by with two children in close pursuit. "Pooka, Pooka!" they call to it.

One child noticed me, pointed a dirty little finger, and in a froggy little voice asked loudly, "Who him?"

In a fury of motion the children retreated under the bleachers, their minimal eyes following my passage.

"Who you!" the same voice inquired.

"Me?" I said. "Lew."

"Mee-loo," the child copied, and then all the voices were saying it. "Meeloo—meeloo—meeloo."

I grinned and held the smile as I approached Buddy Huddy. Arms still folded, the man watched me with wary eyes. Many of his kinfolk halted play on the field, which made me a little uneasy. He was probably fifty, give-or-take a few years, though he physically looked much younger. His body was well formed and muscular, but his face was a ruddy display of filth and parchment, deeply weathered by the elements. His hair was a tousled graying confusion of twists and spikes. He remained silent as I walk up to him. A few of the men on the field approached, loyal disciples to the overlord of their twisted empire.

"Uh, hi Buddy," I stammered, feeling like Livingston greeting the cannibals. I figured it was unlikely that anything communicable could be transmitted through a handshake, but why risk it? I refrained from offering. "I'm Lewis Larabee."

Buddy leveled a cagey gaze at me but said nothing.

"That's my team over there," I explained, pointing to the men mulling about outside the leftfield fence. "We reserved this field last week with the recreation department...so we could practice."

"Why you here today?" Buddy's suspicion seemed to elevate.

"Pardon?"

"You reserved the field last week. Why you here today?" Buddy asked. His expression unchanging, though I had a notion that I was being toyed with.

"What I mean is, we reserved...."

"We're here today," Buddy continued through my words. "We play, and you play, too."

"I don't think…," I started to say, picturing an intolerant few on my team trying to share the field with the Huddys. It was not pretty.

"You play us," Buddy expounded. Many of the Huddy boys, their mouths slack, agape, and by Christ, some even drooling, nodded in agreement.

"You want my team to play your… uh… team?" Stunned, I was about to dispute, but quickly contemplated it. I had heard, more than a few times, that the Huddys were very good softball players. Maybe there was a worthwhile scrimmage here.

"Let me ask the guys," I said and then retraced my steps back to my team.

My proposition to take the Huddys up on their challenge was not exactly met with favor.

"Are you fucking nuts?" Rich Berlander asked. He looked at me as if I had suggested circumcision with a weed-whacker.

Billy Sanford smiled. "You can't be serious." He pointed to the gathering of men who were watching us expectantly. "You *do* realize who they are, right?"

"Yeah, they're the fuckin' Rockefellers," I said sarcastically. "Of course I know who they are, and I've also heard that they are great softball players."

"Yeah mon, so are we," Jamaal Wilner said in his rich Rastafarian accent. "But we not contagious!" He scratched at his mane of dreadlocks as if suddenly infested.

"I'm not asking you to screw them, just to play ball," I said.

It took nearly ten minutes to convince my team that playing softball with the Huddys would not promote gaseous gangrene, typhoid, or a penchant to sodomize their own sisters.

Finally conceding, we made our way to the visitors' team dugout, walking as if we were in an alien world. We paced a wide swath around the mountainous matron Simone, yet stole eyefuls of the accommodating Linny. The bleacher full of children was motionless as they watched us pass, save for one child whom Pooka had firmly mounted and was enthusiastically trying to hump.

"Bad Pooka," the little girl said, struggling to squirm from beneath the large dog.

"Well, at least they stick to their own species," someone muttered. Others chuckled.

I nodded assent to Buddy who returned the nod and moved the encouraged Huddy tribe en masse to the home team side of the field. As if on cue the lot of children ran to the opposing bleachers and resumed their sinuous navigations there.

Most of my team looked a little dumbfounded by the visual overload as they moved dreamily around the dugout, going through the motions while stealing flitting, shocked glances at the Huddys.

Linny had skillfully repositioned herself to a forty-five degree angle with the dugout. Leaning with her left elbow on her left knee she presented us a clear view of one succulent globe. So obvious were her intentions, yet not a single Huddy seemed to either notice or care.

Jamaal and Richie, a slight and lean kid who hit harder than anyone his size had a right to, watched Linny in action.

"Dat so unfair, mon," Jamaal complained. "What cosmic glitch make someone so sexy as her in dat family?"

"Careful, Jamma. Your pervert is showing," Carl Steinman said.

Billy Sanford rummaged through the bat bag looking for a decent ball to toss around. He said, "Hey, Jamma, she could probably straighten your hair," he motioned a nod to the clan of Huddy men across the field. "Think of all the experience she has."

"Ah, god!" Richie cried. "Thanks for the visual, Sandman."

I chuckled and dramatically cleared my throat when I saw Buddy walking towards us. "We bat," Buddy said and turned back.

On the bleachers, Simone Huddy tilted to her left and farted enormously, forcing a tympanic rattle from the metal seating. Again, not a single Huddy seemed to notice.

"Are you fucking kidding me?" Berlander barked with pure disgust. He walked out of the dugout looking like he'd just ingested a shit sandwich.

We warmed up on the field until the Huddys were ready to bat. Only four came up to bat that first inning, one hit and then three outs. When we got up to bat we managed three hits and a run before the Huddy boys retired us.

Though we were winning, the Huddy's bats had connected solidly. I figured it would be close, judging by the first inning. *Might be a good game,* I thought.

And then, all hell broke loose.

I had heard most of the axioms; they took us to the cleaners, wiped us out, swabbed the deck with us, cleaned house, pummeled, trounced, crushed, knocked our dicks in the dirt, and annihilated us. None of those fully described what happened in the next five innings.

The Huddys were like a hitting machine, directing the balls with maddening precision, placing them exactly where we were not, and sending a healthy supply over the fence. And they were even better in the field.

I stopped keeping score when it was twenty-six to three; that was in the fourth inning. The thought came to me that maybe the only reason we got up to bat again was because the Huddys got tired of belting the ball around.

By the end of the sixth inning, our team (one of the top four in New Hampshire's men's league the previous year) conceded to the Huddys. Stunned and humiliated we shuffled our sorry selves off of the field.

"Goo gayum boyaz," Linny Huddy yelled to us and then literally brayed laughter like a donkey. Looks were exchanged and eyebrows were raised, but we were otherwise silent until we reached the parking lot. We gathered around my Dodge pickup.

Ed Winston swung the bat bag into the bed of the truck, looked at us one by one, and asked, "What the hell just happened?"

"Seems we just got our balls served to us on a platter," Berlander answered.

I leaned back on the truck's fender, interested to see how the team reacted to such a sound beating.

"Yeah?" said Marcus Spracher. "Well, they play dirty."

I was about to censure Marcus for being whiny, but I realized in time that it was a joke.

"It's like the fucking *Twilight Zone*," Billy Sanford said. "Or *Deliverance*."

"Wait! I think I can hear them banjos down yonder," said Richie Berlander.

Carl Steinman pulled a flattened pack of Marlboros from his pants pocket, extracted a banana-shaped cigarette from within and lit up. "Ya rekkin?" he asked.

"Yeah mon, I reckon," said Jamaal. "I reckon I be going to Malarkey's, order a big-ass hamburger, a pitcher of Bud, and drink tonight out from my head."

This scenario garnered vast approval and the men started for their vehicles. Marcus Spracher called out to Jamaal, "Hay Jamma, why don't you invite Linny, looks like you could use a friend." Then he brayed like a donkey.

I climbed behind the steering wheel of my truck and watched until the last of my teammates drove out of the parking lot. I started the engine and turned to see Linny Huddy approaching. She was scratching her head vigorously and I felt a quick urge to hightail it out of the lot, but it wasn't in me. I rolled down my window and Linny leaned against the door, all but pushing her d-cups right out of her shirt.

"Daddy wan'da know if it you dhat leave da note in hid car," Linny said.

I looked at her pretty face, surprised that her breath smelled of fresh mint. I tried to puzzle together what she just said. "Your dad wants to know if I left a note in his car?"

"Ya." She cocked her head endearingly, and the realization came to me that underneath it all she was just a kid like any other kid, wanting approval.

"What kind of note?"

"Note sayed come play today."

A set-up? Who? I wondered. *Richie? Jamaal?*

I couldn't help smiling, and then the laughter escaped. Linny's trouble-free gaze held mine, and then she succumbed to braying laughter. She had an unconstrained laugh, unhindered and unabashed like a child's. If only we could all laugh like that.

"Sorry," I said. "Tell your dad it wasn't me, but tell him we did have fun."

"Wa-ever," she smiled. "Dad say thank you for a goo game." She smiled coyly, offered a cute wave and headed back to her family.

I started the truck, gave two quick beeps for the Huddys, and then headed for Malarkey's. That hamburger sounded good.

Glenn Chadbourne

CRASHING DOWN

By Weston Ochse

Sometimes during the night I wake to find my body shivering with frenetic memories of the old me. Cocaine and LSD had been my high-octane energy for over twenty years—happy Janus, psychotropic dreams responsible for my best times, my worst times, two divorces, the loss of eighteen girlfriends, my last nine jobs, and the death of both my wife and my son.

Even though I'd been sober for three years now, my body still remembered. I could never be sure whether my spasming muscles were the result of my body begging for another hit or if chemicals were still racing along the closed loop of my system. Whatever the cause, at 4:02 this morning, I awoke on sweat-soaked sheets and tried not to cry. As always, I stared at the ceiling and tried to imagine who I could have been, what I could have done.

And as always, I failed.

The world was filled with too many reminders. Like the white stucco drips on the ceiling, forever dangling above my head and reminding me of my nose and the way it had drip-dripped after seventy-two hour nights of blurry-faced women, disco lights, and the rugged search for another fix.

I fought, but the memories took hold.

The walls closed in.

The ceiling descended until I was tempted to sniff, ready to strip the very paint from it. Shadows reached out and embraced me, crushing, promising serenity within soft, impossible darkness.

Unable to free myself from the paranoia and need, I threw on a gray sweatshirt and a pair of jeans, grabbed a pair of gym shoes and within minutes was walking the early morning streets, trading the monotony of my steps for the nightmares of my life. Times like these were like a hard crash. A body can only take so much. Once the chemicals outnumber the white-blood cells, life signs take a dive and you crash down. Back when I was still tripping, my cure for the crash was a day in the spa, sweating out my addiction while beefy Russian gals with man hands pounded my bones back into recognizable shapes.

Now, my only cure was to walk.

Walk and try not to think.

I was almost alone, with only a street sweeper, a few early morning commuters, and paper delivery trucks to accompany me in my misery. Even so, the quietness of the city during these moments was the therapy my over-medicated body required. Like a psychic salve, the very lack of humanity stilled jangling nerves that were too much like the frenzied traffic of midday.

Fourteen blocks later, shoulders hunched, eyes down, and hands shoved deep within my pockets, I noticed the man standing upon a stepladder in the middle of an empty sidewalk. I slowed, then shook my head to give the image a chance to dissipate before I actually began believing it, certain I was in the midst of one my thrice-weekly flashbacks.

I closed my eyes, stunned. I counted to fifty, knowing, just knowing that the man and the ladder would be gone. But when I reopened them the man was still there, now reaching into the air with his right hand. His face held a smile of such serenity it made my heart ache. I remembered one of my more lucid moments, when I'd worn that very same smile as I placed my five-year old son upon the top step of the school bus on his first day of school.

Above me on the stepladder, the man's gaze began shifting between joy and sadness, all the while spotting the concrete sidewalk with tears. He mumbled to the air, threw back his head and laughed.

I slowed, curious about a man whose dementia seemed to match my own. My city-raised instinct for tragedy was well-honed and I knew that behind the precariously perched man atop the ladder in the empty city morning there was a story. Still, rather than disturb him, I would have stood there and allowed the man his privacy as I tried to imagine what thing could have driven him to such an end.

Ultimately, he over-balanced and fell hard to the ground. I hurried over and offered my hand but jerked it back as he began first giggling, then laughing, until his uproarious guffaws echoed down the empty street.

Although my empathy was strong, I have to admit that discovering somebody on the higher end of the *Fucked Up Scale* made me feel better. Sandy-haired, blue eyes, slim with a blue pinstriped button-down shirt and blue jeans, he seemed to be just an average Joe.

He could be me.

He could be an accountant.

Just goes to show, I suppose. The domesticated were so terrified of the squeegee men, the homeless and the crack heads. It would rock their world to know that death and insanity preferred not to dress down.

Although I felt guilty staring at this spectacle of a man as he fought with his personal demons, I was unable to move on. I was too curious. So I stood there and empathized, my arms askew and ready, not knowing if in the next instant I would be helping or warding off an impending blow. He saved me from my indecision.

"Have you ever seen what happens to a body after a long fall?"

Before I could answer the strange question, he continued.

"People think that skin is such a weak and tender thing. A husk too fragile to contain the incredible miracle of life. Sure, we all remember the skinned knees and the stitches of our youth, but falling is so much different. God or whatever malicious being created us knew what He was doing. One would think a person would explode, you know?"

He rolled into a kneeling position. His hand caressed a section of the sidewalk as if it were a child's cheek, and he stared at a spot high in the air, seeing something I couldn't. I was uncomfortable, embarrassed, and the humanity in me demanded I walk away. But I couldn't. The voyeur within took charge and held me fast.

"I used to be a father," he sighed. "There's something special about being a father. The perfect love you see in the most casual glance of a child. The knowledge that your every word, every action, has tremendous consequence. Being a father is all about love. It's a *scary love*, you know?"

"Yes," I said before I even realized the word had escaped.

He turned and stared at me as if he was just realizing he had an audience. The pained icy-blue of his eyes pierced me, and we shared an intimacy that sliced far deeper than love. I didn't even breathe.

Why had I spoken?

Why?

It was the *Scary Love* comment, of course—such a perfect description for the terrifying reality of fatherhood. So much could go wrong. You didn't need to be there. A father's influence transcended time, space and reason. *Scary Love* indeed. The tragedy, of course, was that the child didn't know enough to be scared as well.

The man's eyes were now focused firmly upon me as if he was reading my thoughts. He smiled wistfully and nodded, then gazed up at the high windows of the thirty-story building behind us

"You really never know what's going to happen. You can plan. You can sign them up for the best schools. Buy them the finest clothes. Partition them from the vulgarities of life. But after all that, you better be sure to pray that whatever fickle entity is in charge of the universe that day is busy enough to leave you alone."

He leaned over like a Moslem at prayer and placed his forehead against the sidewalk. Softly, he rubbed his cheek against the rough surface and cooed. Anyone else might have laughed. I could not. More than empathy, there was a similarity of pain. I no longer wished to leave. I ignored the muscles of my right calf as they began to twitch in anticipation of a fast run.

"It was one of those days when everything went wrong, you know?"

Didn't I, though. I'd survived a thousand days like that. The day after tripping though the pulsating halls of *Forever Never Land* where I was God and God was me and my spleen was splashed across the sky. Each of those days had been a drop from the glory of divinity into the malicious depravity of humanity.

"Emily, my wife, awoke late for work. So late, she didn't even have time to take Jericho to the sitters. When she left, I was still mostly asleep. Hell, I'd only been home for a few hours. A business trip, you know?"

A giggle escaped the man. Stifling the sound with the back of a hand, he stood. He picked up the fallen stepladder and set it back into place. There were only five steps, but as he ascended each, it looked like he left a small piece of his unsteadiness behind, until with his feet perched upon the next to the top step, he rose to his full height and his face turned beatifically sane.

"I can feel him here. Right here," he said, holding a hand out into the air. "A part of him is in the pavement, but that's only his sad part—the part that felt the pain. It was as if his soul paused while his body bounced. The rest of him is *here*. Sometimes, when I'm standing up here, I can see him. Especially in the mornings, because that's when it happened. Yes, in the mornings when there's nobody else around and all is silent. Sometimes," the word was almost garbled in a sob, "he speaks to me."

The man and the ladder and his son and the story suddenly coalesced, and the reality of it all drove me to my knees. Heaviness filled my heart and moved outwards, locking my body in a breathless grip.

I'd heard enough.

Too much.

I wanted to stand and run. Like a bad trip, however, I was locked within the progression of events.

A door opened in the building and a woman skipped down the stairs, a briefcase in one hand and a newspaper in the other. She sidestepped the ladder, her gaze sailing across our spectacle. My mouth and hands were unable to work so I reached out with my mind and begged her to free me. She paused as if she'd actually heard my pathetic psychic plea, then shook her head and continued on her way, indicating that we were none of her business.

I envied her.

I tried to ignore the man when he started speaking again.

I tried to blot out his existence with happy memories, but I had none.

As he spoke of his dead son, I remembered my own.

"Days like this, I can almost hear him laugh. Jericho had the most wonderful laugh, but then I suppose all sons do."

Yes, I thought. *All of them do. Right up until the point where they discover their father is a beast.*

"I used to be a day trader, watching the computer as if it were a crystal ball. I was good at it, too. Sure, I made some small mistakes, but by the end of each week I was far enough ahead they were forgotten. Sometimes, while feeding Little Jerry and watching the numbers slide by, I'd jab his cheek with a spoonful of food. Instead of being irritated, the fool kid would laugh at me. It was as if he understood my embarrassment. To get me back on track, he'd yell *Crash*."

Every molecule of my body cringed at the word.

Crash.

It was one of the few words in the English language that sounded just like the event it stood for. A split-second impact, the crunch of metal, the shattering of glass, the screams of the dying, all woven together in the incredible static hiss of the word *Crash*.

"We used to play the old landing of the plane game, with me making motor sounds and swooping in with a full spoon. For a while, it was the only way he would eat.

Motor, swoop, land.

Motor, swoop, land.

"When I wasn't paying attention and the spoon missed his mouth, I'd smile and tell him that Daddy crashed. Pretty soon, even that was a game. He'd beg me to do it, yelling *Daddy Crash*."

Oh, God, please let this stop. Of all of the streets in the city, why had I chosen to walk this one?

"I felt so cool when he said that. So in charge."

Didn't I know it? Drugs could make you feel that way. Like an earthbound God, your every movement was an attempt at release, because you know that if you were ever freed, you could become part of existence itself.

"That morning I ignored his cries. I kept telling myself just a few more minutes then I'll get up. Just a little more sleep was all I needed. I remember rolling over and wishing he'd stop making such a racket. Then I heard a real crash." He giggled. "I thought he'd tipped over a glass or something."

I closed my eyes.

"Funny thing. He'd never seemed to notice the windows before. He didn't even realize what a tremendous view we had. I mean, seriously. Four bedrooms and floor-to-ceiling windows are what most couples dream of. My wife loved the view."

As I listened to him, I remember that my own wife had begged me not to drive that day. She told me I was fucked up, and I remember smiling at her, admiring the way the purple and yellow hues swirled just beneath her skin. She was so beautiful with the psycho-paisley addition. I remember reaching out to touch the electric colors, not in fear of her voltage, but looking forward to an electric sting. To this day, I could swear I was using just one hand, but when she screamed and I looked down, I noticed I was using both of them. I remember wondering who was driving the car. The doctors and the police and the judge insisted it'd been me, but I told them, *how could I have been driving when my hands weren't even on the wheel?*

The man continued. "When I heard the third crash from the living room, I finally pulled myself out of bed. Like always, the Little Man was in his walker. He was in the living room and when he saw me, he laughed and screamed, *Crash.* Jericho had gotten to the point where he was almost ready to walk, you know? He'd stand up in the hard plastic walker and boy those little legs could move. He'd propel himself from one side of the house to the other like a little Mario Andretti with a death wish. I was wiping the sleep from my eyes when I noticed the cracks in the living room window. I just couldn't move fast enough, you know? He headed straight for it laughing and screaming *crash* the entire way, you know? This time, he went right through. I ran and fell to my knees and leaned out, watching him fall the last five stories. I watched as he struck the pavement and bounced. It seemed like such a huge bounce. I remember my screams as he hit again. That time his bounce was so small."

His words sent my brain twisting me back to the day everything changed. They said I'd driven our Mazda off the fourth story of the parking garage. They said that my son and I were lucky to be alive. When I rolled my wheel chair into his room that night, I no longer felt lucky. It's a terrible thing to be condemned by a ten-year old, and the glare of blame and hatred he sent my way was too much— probably the reason why I didn't fight when my mother-in-law took me to court for custody.

"And do you know what's really funny?" the man asked, as if he didn't even know I was there.

Life is.

"My first instinct was to spank him. Can you believe that? I was going to spank my dead son!"

The suddenness of reality throws us all off track, I noted.

"Our priest told us that my little boy was in Heaven now. The doctors said that he never felt the bounce...that he was unconscious before he hit the ground. I think the both of them are clueless," he said, an edge shading his tone. "I still remember Jericho's screams...and I remember when they abruptly stopped. And there is no Heaven, either. If there is, then why is my boy's soul still here?"

I jerked my head up and stared.

"What do you mean?" I asked, feeling his answer was somehow important.

"You ever been to a Civil War battlefield? Ever notice how quiet it is, as if the birds and nature itself is somehow subdued. Battlefields are somber places. It's almost as if you can feel a certain heaviness about them. The reason's simple, really. When people die, their souls remain in place. They don't enter a fucking white light. They don't transcend. Hell, nobody even comes back as a silly Hindu cockroach if their karma is all skewed. People die and their soul stays where they die. Simple."

"So then graveyards?"

"Are nothing more than a place for the living. I betcha people all over the world know this, but it'd be crazy as hell if there was a headstone in every place a person died. Imagine that. Why, the interstates would be fucking impassable."

His words had a certain logic. During my peyote days, I remember some of my Navaho friends telling me about their belief in what they termed *A Sense of Place*. I remember driving though Arizona and New Mexico and seeing shrines all along the roads, each one a crazy syncretic mixture of Catholicism and Old Time Religion, each one a place where someone had died.

"So when I die, it means that there will be no great reunion where all of my family greets me at the pearly Gates. Wherever I die, I'll be alone, unless of course some other poor *schmuck* died in the same place. What would your choice be--spending your death with a stranger, alone, or with your family?"

People were beginning to make their way to work. More than a few passers-by gave us strange looks, glances of domesticated reason I hadn't seen since my days of psychedelic roaming. Even more cursed our impediment to their paths. High up on the building the sun was winking off the glassy surfaces of the windows. The man squinted as if he was seeking one window in particular.

"Funny thing about death, something I never in a million years would've guessed. Even if it's your fault, the dead forgive you. Like it's a rule or something, you know? When Jericho speaks with me he never mentions my mistake."

The words speared me.

When Jericho speaks with me....

The man shook his head, as if everything he just said was still so unbelievable, and backed down the stepladder. He folded it, gripped it sideways, and turned toward me, standing as straight as if the burdens of life had been lifted from his shoulders. His face, previously a blend of sad reminiscence and happy insanity, was now stoic with determination.

"Hold this, will you? I'm not going to be needing it any longer."

I stood there, gripping the rough wood as he entered the building. I imagined him almost whistling as he pressed the UP button on the elevator. This stranger had solved the equation I'd spent the better part of my life trying to figure out. This man understood...as my own son understood. No longer would I ask the empty heavens why.

Two years to the date of the accident, I'd received a call from my mother-in -law. For some peculiar reason, I was sober, acid-free, and only experiencing the second day of a cocaine glide—coincidence, really.

"It's all your fault," she'd screamed.

I thought she was talking about her daughter, again. I thought she was going to lay some more blame on me for killing my wife, but it was a terribly different message. Amidst her tears and raw rage I heard the very worst.

My son had committed suicide.

At sixteen, he was dead.

My sweet boy had taken the elevator to the fourth floor of the parking garage that had changed all of our lives and leapt head first to join his mother.

And now I knew why.

"Even if it's your fault, the dead forgive you," the man had said.

I turned, the weight of the ladder awkward against my side. Other pedestrians shuffled out of my way, no doubt wondering why a man was carrying a ladder down the sidewalk. I could see their lack of understanding in their eyes.

I was half a block away when I heard the glass shatter. A second after that, I heard screams and the fleshy impact of a body bouncing. I didn't turn back. I didn't have time. I had an appointment with my family...and if their souls had indeed crashed, I knew a way to be with them.

Forever.

And maybe in death they'll forgive me.

Maybe in death I can forgive myself.

Glenn Chadbourne

About the Authors and Artists

Glenn Chadbourne is a freelance artist specializing in the horror/dark fantasy genres. His artwork has appeared in over fifty books as well as numerous magazines, comics, and computer games. His trademark pen-and-ink illustrations have accompanied the works of today's best-selling horror writers, most notably Stephen King. He created the extensive artwork that appears in both volumes of King's *The Secretary of Dreams*, as well as PS Publishing's edition of *The Colorado Kid*. Chadbourne has a longstanding relationship with Cemetery Dance Publications where a great body of his work can be seen in various books published by the company. He lives in Newcastle, Maine, with his wife, Sheila. For more information, visit his website at *www.glennchadbourne.com*

_____*It's said that you can count your real friends—your true friends, the kind that would search frantically for water if you found yourself afire (up here that's pronounced a-fiya)—on one hand, and I buy that bit of sage wisdom. Rick was that for me, a real true friend. He was the best man at my wedding, and I can't recall a day we didn't talk on the phone. Even now I catch myself picking up the phone to critique some stupid flick or rant about the right wing. In a sense I suppose you could say I'm haunted. But if so, it's a pleasant haunting from a much loved familiar spirit.*

Neil Gaiman has written highly acclaimed books for both children and adults. He has won many major awards, including the Hugo and the Nebula, and his novel *The Graveyard Book* is the only work to ever win both the Newbery (US) and Carnegie (UK) Medals. His books for readers of all ages include the bestselling

Coraline, also an Academy Award-nominated film; *Odd and the Frost Giants*; and *The Wolves in the Walls*. Originally from England, Gaiman now lives in the United States.

Graham Joyce, a winner of the O. Henry Award, the British Fantasy Award, and the World Fantasy Award, lives in Leicester, England, with his family. His books include *The Silent Land*, *Smoking Poppy*, *Indigo* (a *New York Times* Notable Book of 2000), *The Tooth Fairy* (a *Publishers Weekly* Best Book of 1998), and *Requiem*, among others.

Matthew Costello has written and designed dozens of best-selling games including the critically acclaimed *The 7th Guest*, *Doom 3*, *Rage* and *Pirates of the Caribbean*. His novel *Beneath Still Waters* was filmed by Lionsgate. His recent novel, *Vacation*, was a 2011 release from St. Martin's Press, and the sequel, *Home*, was published this past October. Next year brings *Star Road*, co-authored with Rick Hautala.

> _____*"What is it like to be in an anthology that you could never, ever imagine? Mr. October (indeed!) gone? Unbelievable. But at least we have this massive and rich effort thanks to his good friend Chris Golden, a true memorial and honor from peers that —trust me! —old Rick would have just loved...."*

Michael Marshall Smith has published three novels, *Only Forward*, *Spares*, and *One of Us*, and is the only person to win the British Fantasy Award for best short story four times. Writing as Michael Marshall, he is also a *Sunday Times* and *New York Times* bestselling thriller writer. His most recent novel is *We Are Here*.

> _____*Our genre—heck, any genre—shines most brightly through people like Rick, was not just a great writer, but great at making others feel included and welcome.*

Chet Williamson is the author of over two dozen books, most in the field of horror and suspense, and over a hundred short stories which have appeared in numerous anthologies and magazines such as *The New Yorker, Playboy,* and *The Magazine of Fantasy and Science Fiction.* His backlist is available in ebook format through Crossroad Press and Amazon, as are his two newest novels, *Hunters* and *Defenders of the Faith.* An actor, he has narrated dozens of audiobooks for Audible.com, including several of his own, as well as the works of Clive Barker, Jack Ketchum, Michael Moorcock, and others.

_____*I first met Rick at our universally-beloved NECON, and Laurie and I both fell in love with his humorous, self-effacing manner which earned him the sobriquet of "The Eeyore of NECON." And later we fell just as hard for Holly, who made his final years so happy. I picked "Figures in Rain" for this volume because it's a ghost story (and Rick loved ghost stories), and is about not only the survival of life after death, but of love after death. I can't think of any concept that better honors Rick Hautala. His love for people and their love for him will live for a long time. Calm seas and prosperous voyage, my friend....*

Elizabeth Massie is a two-time Bram Stoker Award- and Scribe Award-winning author of novels, short fiction, media tie-ins, and social studies/science educational materials for the global market. She lives in Virginia with illustrator Cortney Skinner, and in her spare time knits, manages Hand to Hand Vision (through Facebook), and tracks down geocaches.

_____*Rick was one of my best friends in the horror field. Funny, self-deprecating, honest, and just plain adorable; a talented nut in a pair of flip flops. It was always more fun with Rick was around, and he never held back a kind word when there was one to share. I absolutely loved Rick Hautala.*

Peter Crowther is the recipient of numerous awards for his writing, his editing, and, as publisher, for the hugely successful PS Publishing (now including the Stanza Press poetry subsidiary and PS Artbooks, a specialist imprint dedicated to the comics field). As well as being widely translated, his stories have been adapted for TV on both sides of the Atlantic and collected in *The Longest Single Note, Lonesome Roads, Songs of Leaving, Cold Comforts, The Spaces Between the Lines, The Land at the End of the Working Day* and the upcoming *Jewels In The Dust*. He is the co-author (with James Lovegrove) of *Escardy Gap* and *The Hand That Feeds*, and author of the *Forever Twilight* SF/horror cycle and *By Wizard Oak*. Pete lives and works (and still reads a lot of comicbooks *and* buys far too many CDs!) with his wife and PS business partner, Nicky on the Yorkshire coast of England. He is currently writing a sequence of novelettes set against a background of alien invasion and the implosion of the multiverse.

_____*Rick and I didn't get to meet up too often—a couple of World Fantasy Conventions maybe, and NeCon (of course)—but he was someone Nicky and I always looked forward to spending time with (particularly at the NeCon dart-throwing Championship). We first 'met up' via Moonbog (thanks to Stephen King's cover-puff—see, never let anyone tell you that blurbs aren't worth a damn) and we corresponded pretty regularly after that, with me ending up chasing him for stories for various anthologies I was doing (plus the wonderful Reunion novella he wrote for PS). When Chris asked for a story I didn't hesitate in picking 'Thoughtful Breaths'. It's pretty much everything I want to say about that dreadful time when friends and lovers have to part. Happy trails, fella!*

Matti Hautala lives in Austin, Texas with his fiancée Aly Dixon and their pup Tengo. Matti is an intake counselor at a mental health clinic in Texas but he's always enjoyed reading and writing in his spare time (must be a genetic thing). Matti's story "Abduction," co-written with his father and his brother Jesse, can be found in Rick Hautala's short-story collection *Occasional Demons*.

_____*The support and love for my father that came from the writing community has been a great lesson in karma. My pops had me convinced he was an introvert, so it's been surprising to see that he kept up regular correspondences with so many students, fans, and new writers. My dad gave 200% of himself to everything he did, whether it was writing, teaching, mentoring, being a father or just fully investing himself in each moment he spent with you. Thank you all for giving 200% back. Whenever Rick talked about death he would say "I think I'll just let the mystery be," quoting an Iris Dement song. It's no mystery to me now how Rick will live on — he lived his life in books and he's still there.*

Mark Morris became a full-time writer in 1988 on the Enterprise Allowance Scheme, and a year later saw the release of his first novel, *Toady*. He has since published a further thirteen novels, among which are *Stitch, The Immaculate, The Secret of Anatomy, Mr Bad Face, Fiddleback* and *Nowhere Near An Angel*. His short stories, novellas, articles, and reviews have appeared in a wide variety of anthologies and magazines, and he is editor of the highly-acclaimed *Cinema Macabre*, a book of fifty horror-movie essays by genre luminaries. Forthcoming work includes a *Hellboy* novel entitled *The All-Seeing Eye* and another book in the immensely popular *Doctor Who* range, published by BBC Books in the UK.

Richard Chizmar is the founder and publisher/editor of Cemetery Dance magazine and the Cemetery Dance Publications book imprint. He has edited more than a dozen anthologies, including *The Best of Cemetery Dance, Night Visions 10, October Dreams,* and the *Shivers* series. Chizmar's fiction has appeared in dozens of publications, including *Ellery Queen's Mystery Magazine* and *The Year's 25 Finest Crime and Mystery Stories.*

_____*I chose "Blood Brothers" because it was always one of Rick's favorites. In fact, he and I had planned to adapt it into a short script at some point. Rick really understood this type of story about dark love and darker choices.*

Stephen R. Bissette, a pioneer graduate of the Joe Kubert School, currently teaches at the Center for Cartoon Studies and is renowned for *Swamp Thing*, *Taboo* (launching *From Hell* and *Lost Girls*), *'1963,'* *Tyrant®*, co-creating John Constantine, and creating the world's second '24-Hour Comic' (invented by Scott McCloud for Bissette). He writes, illustrates, and has co-authored many books; his latest include *Teen Angels & New Mutants* (2011), the short story "Copper" in *The New Dead* (2010), and illustrating *The Vermont Monster Guide* (2009). Bissette is currently completing *S.R. Bissette's How to Make a Monster* (Watson-Guptill/Random House) for 2014 publication.

_____*My contributions, "Inn Cleaning" and the "Little Brothers" sketches, are here because (1) Rick loved ghost stories, and this is my favorite of the few ghost stories I've scribed; (2) Rick always thought my character Cardinal Syn was creepy, and that's Syn cleaning the inns; and (3) the "Little Brothers" is explained in my intro for those sketches.*

Joe R. Lansdale is the author of more than a dozen novels, including *Edge of Dark Water*, the Edgar Award-winning *The Bottoms*, *Sunset and Sawdust*, and *Leather Maiden*. He has received nine Bram Stoker Awards, the American Mystery Award, the British Fantasy Award, the Grinzane Cavour Prize for Literature. He lives with his family in Nacogdoches, Texas.

Yvonne Navarro lives in southern Arizona and works on historic Fort Huachuca. She's had twenty-two novels published so far, including award-winning solo novels and media tie-ins, plus a whole bunch of short stories. Her latest adventure is a quarterly column called "Double X Chromosome" in *Dark Discoveries* magazine. *www.yvonnenavarro.com*

_____I met Rick at the very first NeCon I attended decades ago, and his smile never dimmed in all the years I knew him. Now, from somewhere in the Great Writers' Beyond, Rick's smile sends sunshine down on all of us.

José R. Nieto is the co-author (with Keith DeCandido) of *Spider-Man: Venom's Wrath*. His short stories have been published in David Hartwell's *Christmas Magic*, the *Ultimate Supervillains* anthology, and the literary magazine *Washington Square*. José is also an award-winning graphic designer and is currently senior creative at Argus Communications in Boston.

Duane Swierczynski is the author of several crime thrillers and also writes the X-Men spinoff *Cable* and *Immortal Iron Fist* for Marvel Comics. His latest novels include *Expiration Date*; *Level 26*, co-written with CSI creator Anthony E. Zuicker; and *Severance Package*, which has been optioned by Lionsgate films. He lives in Philadelphia with his wife and children.

Gary A. Braunbeck is the author of the acclaimed Cedar Hill Cycle, which includes the novels *In Silent Graves*, *Coffin County*, and *A Cracked and Broken Path*. His most recent collection, *Rose of Sharon*, was released this fall. Gary's work has been honored with six Bram Stoker Awards. Visit him online at *www.garybraunbeck.com*

Craig Shaw Gardner served as president of HWA at the same time that Rick Hauaula served as V.P., and they never once stopped speaking to each other. Craig has also written bunches of short stories and dozens of novels. You can find out more about them at craigshawgardner.com.

_____*I got the idea for "Overnight Guest" while staying in a very rustic motel on the coast of Maine. When asked to submit a story to this anthology, the creepy story about Maine seemed the proper choice.*

Jack M. Haringa is the co-founder of *Dead Reckonings*, a review journal of horror and the dark fantastic. His stories and essay have been published by Hippocampus Press, Prime, Necro Publications, and St. Martin's. He has been on the board of advisors for the Shirley Jackson Awards since their inception and served as a juror for the 2012 and 2013 awards. When not writing, he teaches English at an independent school in central Massachusetts.

_____*Mention of Rick's work always brings to mind certain tropes at which he excelled: the ambiguity of ghostly encounters; the complex dynamics of domestic life; and the importance of a sense of place, of landscape and locale that informs so many of his novels. I was lucky enough to count Rick as a friend, and I cherish the memories of discussing writing and literature with him at conventions and dinners over the fifteen years that I knew him. His humanity, his humor, and his generosity are reflected in many of his protagonists, but those qualities—along with his determined humility—shone so much brighter in the man himself. I chose "Springfield Repeater" because it attempts to use those elements that I found most powerful in Rick's work, though I know I employed them far less expertly than Rick would have done.*

Tom Piccirilli is the author of *The Last Kind Words, Shadow Season, The Cold Spot, The Coldest Mile, A Choir of Ill Children,* and other titles. He has won two International Thriller Writers Awards and four Bram Stoker Awards, and has been nominated for the Edgar, the World Fantasy Award, the Macavity, and Le Grand Prix de l'Imaginaire. A native of Long Island, New York, he lives in Colorado.

_____*I chose this story "Conjurer" because it was filled with supernatural/occult matters and atmosphere reminiscent of Rick's work.*

F. Paul Wilson is the award-winning, NY *Times* bestselling author of fifty books and many short stories spanning horror, adventure, medical thrillers, science fiction, and virtually everything between. More than nine million copies of his books are in print in the US and his work has been translated into twenty-four foreign languages. He also has written for the stage, screen, and interactive media. *Cold City* and *Dark City* feature his urban mercenary, Repairman Jack. His latest is *The Proteus Cure,* a disturbing medical thriller written with Tracy Carbone. Paul resides at the Jersey Shore.
http://www.repairmanjack.com.

_____*This story was born one day as I was thumbing through the Rolling Stone Rock Almanac and noted all the deaths, injuries, drop-outs, and plain bad luck that had befallen every single major name in rock 'n' roll during a two-year period in the late fifties. They had dropped like the proverbial flies. Most people would say, "Isn't that something," and read on.*

I, of course, saw a hideous conspiracy.

I chose this one for the anthology because Rick and I both loved old rock 'n' roll, and I believe he loved a good conspiracy theory more than I. It seems a perfect match.

Jonathan Maberry is the multiple Bram Stoker Award-winning author of *The King of Plagues*, *The Dragon Factory*, *Ghost Road Blues* and *Rot & Ruin*, among others. He also wrote the novelization of the movie *The Wolfman*. His work for Marvel Comics includes *Captain America*, *Punisher*, *Wolverine*, *DoomWar*, *Marvel Zombie Return* and *Black Panther*. He has been inducted into the International Martial Arts Hall of Fame.

John M. McIlveen is...

_____*I will always remember and —more so —miss Rick's kindness, loyalty, and sense of humor, and how huge a role this humble and kind man played in my life in our nearly thirty years of friendship. I first called Rick in late 1984 when I was a mere 22 years-old. I was fairly new to book collecting and brand new to author stalking– Rick was my first. I had read Rick's first two novels* Moondeath *and* Moonbog, *and loved them. Garnering the nerviness we book addicts have, I looked up Rick's number and called him. I figured, worst-case he'd see me for the stalker I was and hang up, but he was pleasant, funny, very humble, and even suggested we meet for lunch at some point. I agreed, figuring he'd forget me as soon as we hung up, but he called back a couple of weeks later saying he was going to be in southern New Hampshire and that we should get together, which we did. The first time I met Rick in person he was carrying a huge manuscript for his forthcoming novel* Nightstone, *which he inscribed to me. This was Rick. I still have the manuscript... always will.*

I owe a lot to Rick. If not for him I may have never attended a little convention called Necon. Through him I met some of my dearest friends, Christopher Golden, James A. Moore, Bob, Mary, Dan Booth, Sara Calia, Matt Bechtel, Jack Ketchum... the list is quite long. Though he may be gone, Rick will live on in the hearts of so many.

Weston Ochse is the author of *Seal Team 666* and many other novels. He won the Bram Stoker Award for First Novel and has been nominated for a Pushcart Prize for short fiction. He is a retired U.S. Army intelligence officer and is currently an intelligence officer for the Defense Intelligence Agency.

Morbideus W. Goodell is an artist and illustrator living in Maine with his wife and two children. Morbideus and his wife, Dee, also own and run Postmortem Productions of Maine, selling t-shirts, Morbideus's artwork, and Dee's photography.